DARK HIGHWAY
HOME

A POST APOCALYPTIC JOURNEY

BOOK TWO – REACHING HOME

DARK HIGHWAY HOME

A POST APOCALYPTIC JOURNEY
BOOK TWO – REACHING HOME

LARS H. LARSEN

REACHING HOME

Copyright © 2023 by Lars H. Larsen

Cover Design: www.getcovers.com
Editing: Fabled Planet
Book Design and Typesetting: Enchanted Ink Publishing
Publication Assistance: Self-Publishing Services,
selfpublishingservices.com

ISBN: 979-8-9874111-3-1 (E-book)
ISBN: 979-8-9874111-4-8 (Paperback)
ISBN: 979-8-9874111-5-5 (Hardcover)

7th Edition

CONTENTS

BACKSTORY
BOOK ONE

This journey began five days ago in Las Vegas, Nevada.

Jon Kristen, ex-Special Forces, and his five co-workers—Renee, Melissa, Kathy, Monica and Kris—were on an annual corporate get-together when two nuclear-tipped missiles, sent from North Korea, detonated in the upper atmosphere, one over Colorado and the other over Ohio. The resulting electromagnetic pulse, or EMP, took down the entire North American electrical grid. The pulse also rendered anything with a computer chip useless. . . essentially sending the US back to the eighteenth century.

Jon and his team embarked on a hazard-filled journey back to the Pacific Northwest, determined to return to their homes in Seattle. Later, the group made the decision to head directly to Jon's family ranch in Montana, after Kris, frustrated with their slow progress, stole a working vehicle from a ranch in Nevada and left them.

While in Battle Mountain, Nevada, Jon and Melissa had been retrieving ranch hands for their hosts, Sig and Molly Alderson, when they had to put down three men attempting to rob a hospital pharmacy. Susan Foster, a deputy sheriff, wounded in the gun battle during the robbery attempt, was brought into their fold and has joined them on their journey to Montana.

On day five, Jon and his team have caught up with Kris and rescued her from a truck driver, Clint, who had kept Kris bound in his semi-truck's sleeper cab and used her in terrible ways.

They are seven travelers, plus a military working dog, Greta—the sole survivor of an ambush the group stumbled upon—who want nothing more than to get to safety at Jon's parents' ranch in Montana.

We now find them in Burns Junction, Nevada, having just rescued Kris.

DAY SIX

LINENS & MEDS. RENEE'S BIG NEWS.
STUART & IZZY. TRUCKERS. LAVA FIELDS.

ONE

Susan and I stood overwatch while the remaining five women were out searching the abandoned semi-trucks' cabs for bills of lading, shipment packing lists, and other identifying paperwork. Finding paperwork listing the trailer's contents would be a huge timesaver, allowing them to avoid having to open and physically search each trailer.

It was snowing again, much heavier now, with our tire tracks, footprints, and events of the past hour already covered. I glanced toward Clint, and saw he was now just an odd snow-covered shape in an otherwise flat parking lot. I felt a tinge of regret for what had befallen him, but knew in my heart that given the opportunity, he would have gone on and harmed other women.

"It's really piling up. Gonna need a snowplow to clear a path for us," Susan said, concern in her voice. "Like that's going to happen. Not."

She was trying to tighten her black service plate carrier which wasn't quite sitting comfortably yet after it had been cleaned and dried by Molly Alderson at the Alderson's ranch outside Battle Mountain. With her other arm in a sling, she was struggling one-handed with the adjustment straps. I stepped in and took over for her.

And she was right. Even with all three of our vehicles being four-wheel drive, it was still going to be slow going.

I cinched the last strap and stepped back.

"Thanks." She donned Kris's NVs and cycled them up. "Wow," she exclaimed, swiveling her head from right to left as she took in the inky black darkness which had magically turned into day. "These night vision goggles are amazing. Battle Mountain PD never had the funds for these."

"They are amazing. They've allowed us to make it this far." I scanned the road in both directions with the thermal, and all was clear. The thermal's effectiveness waned markedly in the heavy snow but the scope's screen indicated a reliable reading out to a range of just over 400 yards, far less than its optimum range of 1,100 yards, but good enough.

"Maybe we should shelter in the trucks' sleeping compartments for the night," she said, her NVs pointing in the general direction of the dead semi-trucks. "Hide our trucks behind the semi-trailers."

"That's not a bad idea. Though we'd be more exposed than I'd like."

"If we can't drive in this snow, then most likely, no one else can," she countered.

"True. Though if we did head out, chances are we'd have the highway to ourselves. Which is ideal."

The NVs picked up the five women making their way back to where we were waiting behind the Cruiser. Like the professional she was, Greta was hugging Renee's left side. Each of the ladies had put on boonie hats and tucked their hair up underneath. NVs were down over eyes, and with weapons carried in a cradled resting position, they looked like a typical nighttime recon patrol in Afghanistan.

"Find anything?" I asked the group.

"Five of the six cabs are locked," Melissa answered.

"But we found this," Monica said, handing me an official-looking document. "It was in the one open cab. It's a bill of lading and packing list. And you'd be all set if you were building a new housing tract of eighty-two houses and needed HVAC units for each."

"HVAC? As in air conditioning units?"

"Yep. Totally useless now, of course."

"Can't win 'em all," I said. "Listen, ladies. Susan has suggested that maybe we should take shelter in the cabs' sleeping compartments for the night. We can rest up and get going again at first light. Or we can keep going and use the darkness and heavy snowfall to our advantage. What do you think?"

"Keep going," Kathy answered without hesitation. "We can take turns driving. Let's burn up some distance. Besides, as you say, we own the night. Not the day."

"There's snowplow markers along the side of the road," Renee said. "The top six inches or so are coated with some kind of reflective material. If you turn your running lights on, I bet they'll glow like crazy in our night vision and the going will be a whole lot easier."

"Good idea, Renee," Melissa said. "I say we keep on going."

"I'm with you guys. Let's keep moving," Monica said. "I just want to get to Montana and feel safe and secure again. I've had enough of living with constant danger."

"Ditto that," Kris said.

"Susan, resting in the semis' sleeper cabs was a good idea, but I agree with the others. We should keep going. But first, let's search the other cabs and see if we can find anything useful," I said, opening the Cruiser's driver's door and grabbing the crowbar from underneath the driver's seat.

Susan had been standing by, watching the other women being busy with the search. Maybe it would be a good idea to have her chip in.

"Susan, will you provide overwatch for us?" I asked, handing her the thermal.

"You betcha," she replied, walking fifteen yards toward the road and taking up a kneeling firing position. With her arm immobilized in a black sling, she was unable to carry a rifle and only had her Glock for protection.

"No heroics, please. See something, say something."

"Roger that."

I made my way to the first locked truck. The ladies followed and stood back as I stepped up onto the cab's entry steps and, with one good whack of the heavy crowbar, shattered the driver's door window.

I reached into the cab and unlocked the door. I found the bill of lading in the center console under the truck's Qualcomm messaging unit.

I flipped the NVs up and, using one of Burt's headlamps, read through the multi-page document.

"Another bust, ladies—it's a trailer-load of auto parts."

The second locked truck contained twenty-two pallets of bagged landscape mulch destined for a national home-improvement center in Bakersfield, California. The next was full of Yamaha outboard motors—from small four horsepower four-stroke babies up to eight-cylinder, 400 horsepower behemoths. The fourth locked cab was from Vancouver, Canada, carrying a full load of linens and towels destined for a dozen Vegas hotels and resorts. Now that, at least, was of some interest.

I found the trailer's door key in the spare-change cubby. "According to the bills of lading, this trailer was headed to classy Las Vegas resorts with a full load of bed sheets, towels, bathmats, and other linens," I said, making my way to the back of the trailer. "I'm sure my mother and sister would be most appreciative if we were to bring them a lifetime supply of high-end sheets and towels."

I inserted the key, and the lock sprang open. I swung open the trailer's two rear-facing doors, and my headlamp illuminated pallet after pallet of cardboard cartons. Each pallet was tightly shrink-wrapped, but lo and behold, each was clearly labeled with their respective contents. The first pallet, closest to the door and ordered by the Mirage Hotel, held queen and king sheet sets, along with duvets, bath towels, face towels, washcloths, bathmats, and shower curtains.

"Looks as if each pallet is packed with an assortment of linens," Melissa said. "There are probably a couple hundred sets of each size on each pallet."

"We have room in our trailer for a couple of pallets worth of stuff," Renee said.

"Let's keep some free space in the trailer, so one pallet should do," I said. "Melissa, will you move the Humvee over here and park the trailer so it's below the trailer's doors? No sense in lugging these boxes a hundred yards through the snow."

"Will do," she replied, already headed toward the vehicles.

"Monica and Kathy, hop up here and throw down this pallet's cartons," I said, patting the Mirage's pallet, then removing my knife from its vest-mounted sheath, and slicing the shrink wrap from the top of the pallet down to the wood base. "There's nothing breakable, so just toss them down into the back of the trailer once Melissa has brought it over. We'll straighten and stack them later."

"Does this mean we're looters?" Monica asked.

"Hell, no," Kathy answered.

"It means we got to it before anyone else," I said. "Besides, what good does any of this do just sitting here?"

"I get what you're saying. It's just that it feels weird taking something that isn't ours," Monica answered.

I helped the two ladies climb up into the trailer, and then jumped to the ground, joining Renee who was waiting for me below. We made our way over to the last truck, broke the glass, and opened the cab's driver's door. We found several bills of lading listing toys and puzzles, cabinet door pulls and hinges, and six pallets of USPS Approved, roadside mailboxes.

There was one last shipment listed on the master manifest, and I knew we couldn't leave without first loading it into our trailer. Shipped by Kingman Pharmaceutical Distributors of Spokane, Washington, and bound for Sunset Pharmacy in Henderson, Nevada, the bill of lading stated, *Must arrive by Monday December 18th—New store initial stock.* We'd have to find the shipment's packing list to know exactly what the pallet contained.

I found a loaded key ring under the passenger seat, and after several attempts with various keys, found the one that opened the lock for the trailer's two rear-facing swing doors. I heaved them open, and the Kingman Pharmaceutical pallet was right there, sitting pretty, first in line. It was a standard-sized wood pallet, but was loaded high with locked, dark-blue, plastic security totes, towering to within an inch of the trailer's eight-foot ceiling. The packing list was taped to a tote which was held in place behind several layers of tightly wound shrink wrap. I ripped away the wrap until I had the packing list in hand. The list was thirty-eight pages long with forty items on each page. Listed were drugs of every sort, some I recognized, but most of them strange to me. There was page after page of every kind of drug and item a full-fledged drugstore would need to stock behind a pharmacy counter.

"Well?" Renee asked.

"Jackpot, babe," I said, folding the paperwork and stowing it in one of my pants' large cargo pockets. "It's a pallet-load of drugs destined for a new pharmacy opening in Henderson, Nevada. There are even two full totes of insulin. I'm not sure if insulin needs to be kept cool, but it's refrigerator-cold outside, so I bet it's still good. We'll take them regardless."

"Can insulin freeze and still be effective?" she asked. "Anything liquid is going to freeze if left in the trailer."

"Good question... I don't know. But we can clear some space in the Humvee and make sure it doesn't get that cold. I'll transfer a few ammo cans from the Humvee's rear storage area to the trailer."

I keyed the comms and asked Melissa to bring the trailer over to us.

"Roger that," she replied. "Give us two or three minutes and we'll be finished transferring the linens."

"Help me up there, and I'll lend a hand tearing off the rest of the shrink wrap," Renee said, looking up at me from the ground.

She held both hands up and I hefted her up into the trailer. Greta looked up at us in expectation of joining in the fun. "Sorry, honey, you stay and guard," Renee said. Greta thumped her tail and started surveying the area around us.

We made quick work of the pallet's shrink wrap and sat on two of the locked totes to wait for the trailer's arrival.

"I've got something to tell you, Jon," Renee said. "I've been waiting to be sure, but now I'm fairly certain. . . I think I'm pregnant."

I looked her in the eyes, but stayed silent as I digested the news.

"Renee—" I said a minute later.

"I've missed two periods now. I've never missed a period. Ever."

"Renee—" I said again.

"I think it happened when we were in Cabo," she said, eyes locked on Greta down below us.

"Renee, I think—"

"I have to be honest. Besides being in love with you, it's one of the reasons I wanted to come along. If we are pregnant, the child should grow up with both parents. Even if it's in shitty times like this."

Renee brought her eyes up and looked at me in question.

"Can I talk now?" I asked with a wide grin.

"You look happy. Are you?" she asked.

"I am. Very. And excited at the possibility of having our own little human running around the ranch."

I brought her in close and crushed her in a bear hug, whispering, "I love you, Renee. I'll do everything I can to make you and our child safe and happy."

"Let's not say anything to the others until we're sure," she said.

I leaned back, nodded, then asked, "Have you noticed any changes in your body?"

"My boobs are bigger and tons more sensitive. And I've been hornier than usual."

"Bigger, more sensitive boobs. And hornier than usual. It all works for me."

"Yeah, yeah," she said, delivering a light punch to my arm.

The Humvee drove by the trailer's rear door followed by our trailer. Monica and Kathy, and now with Kris, hopped up into our own trailer and, using Burt's headlamps, quickly rearranged and stacked the boxes of sheets and towels. Renee and I carefully handed down the pharmacy totes, and the ladies gently stacked and arranged them in the trailer.

I handed the two insulin totes down, said, "Leave those two there, please. I've got to make sure they haven't already frozen. If not, I'll clear a space for them in the back of the Humvee."

I jimmied both insulin totes open and found the bottles still in a liquid state. With Renee's help, we transferred ten ammo cans from the Humvee's rear storage area to the trailer. We loaded the two insulated insulin totes into the Humvee and returned to help finish transferring the other totes.

"Kris, careful now," I said. "Those Steri-Strips can only handle so much. So don't overdo it."

"I won't. Promise."

Five minutes later, we were finished transferring the totes. We had the cartons and totes leveled off, matching the height of the other boxes and supplies already in the trailer. The tarp was secured, and we were finished. We still had a good four feet of empty space in our trailer, more than that if we were to double stack.

Greta lifted her head and let out a low growl. Renee and I strained to see through the falling snow but saw nothing.

Ten seconds later, the comms came to life. "We have a vehicle approaching from the south," Susan reported. "Four hundred yards and slowing."

———————

"HEADLAMPS OFF, NVS BACK ON, ladies," I said. "And spread out and get prone like we practiced. Safeties on until I tell you otherwise."

"Turn on the red dots?" Renee asked.

"No. Good question, though. But it's too dark for that."

I strained to see the Cruiser and could barely make it out. It was covered by several inches of snow and could easily be mistaken for being abandoned along with the six semi-trucks.

"Susan, can you get over to us without them seeing you?"

"Negative. Going prone."

Kris was prone a yard or two to my left. She lifted her head, looked at me, said, "The ground is really cold."

"Fingers off triggers, ladies," I said. "Kris, get up and hop in the back of the Humvee. You're not armed, and the back seat is the safest place for you."

Headlights lit up the road parallel to our position. Susan was prone fifty feet from where the vehicle would pass, the rest of us a hundred yards.

"Jon?" Susan said, her voice sounding stressed.

"Stay there, Susan. How many occupants?"

"It looks like two, a woman driving with a child in the passenger seat. It's an older-model Bronco and towing a single-axle, open-sided trailer—like ours, but much smaller."

The Bronco slowed to a crawl, turned toward the Cruiser and semis, missing Susan by ten yards. It came to a stop, its headlights going dark, and the engine shut down. Aside from the engine ticking in the chilled early-morning air, all was quiet.

"Jon?" This from Susan again, now in a hushed, strained voice.

"Susan, I've got you covered."

"Roger that."

"Chill, everyone," I said.

"Chill? How about freezing," Renee responded.

"I could have said, stay frosty," I said dryly.

"You're all hilarious," Melissa said.

"Quiet now, everyone. And turn your comms volume down—I can hear someone's off to my left."

The Bronco's driver's door opened, and a woman emerged. She was short, maybe five-two or -three, slender, though it was hard to tell with the knee-length, puffy parka she was wearing. She had a black knit ski hat on with a Snowbird ski resort logo on the front.

The woman reached back inside the cab and came out with a long gun which she attached to a single-point sling. She stood in place and listened for a good sixty seconds. *She's a cautious one*, I thought.

Satisfied, she patted the hood and the passenger emerged, quietly closing the door behind him. Her passenger was a young boy, maybe ten or eleven, and was wearing a puffy jacket and similar ski hat, though logo free. He appeared unarmed.

She took his hand, and they walked side by side toward the Cruiser, stopping at the driver's door.

"I hope there's something to drink or eat inside, Mom."

"Me too, honey. Let's keep an eye and ear out for approaching cars."

"I will. I have good hearing."

"I know you do."

She was reaching for the door handle when I yelled out, "Stop right there, miss."

She immediately let go of the boy's hand and grabbed hold of the rifle.

I quickly closed the distance between us. It was pitch dark, snowing heavily, and I doubted they could see me. "Not a good idea. Let the rifle hang. There are several of us."

"We mean you no harm," Renee shouted, thirty feet to the woman's right.

Hearing a woman's voice must have been reassuring, for the new arrival let the rifle hang as instructed. She took hold of the boy's hand and peered out into the falling snow.

"Please, let us be on our way," she pleaded.

"Release the weapon from the sling, set it at your feet, then step back five paces," Melissa commanded, her voice booming out of the darkness, thirty feet to the woman's left. "We're going to send someone out to search you and the boy. It's for your safety as much as ours. Do you have any other weapons on you or in the Bronco?"

"No, this is our only weapon," she answered, her head swiveling right and left, trying to track the voices. But she released the rifle, placed it on the ground, and stepped back. "Please, let us be on our way. There's trouble following us, and you don't want any part of it."

"Susan, search them please," I said, walking out of the darkness to within ten feet of the two newcomers.

Susan stood and came up behind the woman and child. "Hi there," she said.

Both jumped in surprise at the voice behind them, the sound of Susan's crunchy footsteps evidently having mixed with my own.

"Open your coats and put your hands behind your head," Susan commanded. Using her one good hand, she patted both down.

"She's got night vision, Mom," the boy said. "Are you a member of the military, ma'am?" he asked, directing his question to Susan.

"Deputy sheriff," she answered.

"Cool," he said.

Susan stepped back. "They're clean."

"Check the Bronco and trailer, Susan."

"What are your names?" Monica asked.

"I'm Emily Talbot and this is my son Peter."

"I'm Jon and the young lady behind you is Susan. She is a deputy sheriff from Battle Mountain, Nevada."

"Are you by chance missing your driver-side mirror?" I asked.

"Yes, some asshole driving down the middle of the. . ." was as far as she got. "Uh oh, I'm guessing that was you?" she asked, after several seconds of uncomfortable silence.

"Pretty sure it was," I answered.

"Oh, sorry. We needed to retrieve Peter from my in-laws and my husband was going as fast as he dared. A neighbor of ours was able to get the Bronco working earlier today. We brought the trailer to haul his parents and their food stocks back to our place in Burns, but we stumbled into a bunch of people looting their house."

"No worries. Hardly scratched our fender."

"If you're not going to rob and kill us, can you spare some water and something to eat," she asked, voice filled with a steely resolve. "I haven't had water today and I'm feeling the effects."

I keyed the comms, said, "Monica, can you grab some bottled water and trail bars and bring them on over?"

"Roger that," she answered.

"Bronco and trailer are clear," Susan reported. "Trailer is empty as is the Bronco."

"Susan, pick up her rifle and place it in her trailer. Ma'am, you'll get that back once we part company," I said.

Monica appeared out of the dark with bottled water and a handful of trail bars.

"She has night vision too, Mom," the boy said.

"I can see that."

Monica handed over the water and bars. Mother and son chugged a full bottle of water each, then attacked the trail bars.

Between bites, the mother said, "Thank you. All of you. . . however many of you there are."

Renee walked out of the darkness. "You said your husband was driving. Where is he?" she asked.

Emily Talbot's steel resolve melted away and she started crying, taking huge breaths, chest rising and falling in an attempt to control her emotions.

"Dad was shot and killed at Gramps and Nana's house," the boy answered for her, wrapping his arms around his mom's waist. "They killed my grandparents, too. Gramps told me to hide in the barn's hayloft. I saw them kill him and my grandmother. When I saw the Bronco drive up, I ran and jumped in the back seat."

"I'm so sorry," Kathy said, emerging out of the darkness and coming to a stop in front of the pair. "We're living in bad times, and it's only going to get worse."

"You have a place to go?" Renee asked.

"We do. Our home in Burns. It's well-stocked and very defendable. We have neighbors that have banded together to protect our subdivision."

"What did you mean when you said trouble is following you?" I asked.

"The men that killed my husband and his parents are ten miles or so behind us. Brad killed four of them before they dropped him. Peter and I were in the Bronco waiting for him. He'd made it to the passenger door when he was hit. Peter held them off with the rifle while I checked Brad's vitals—I'm a physician's assistant—but he was gone. We had no choice but to hightail on out of there."

"How many are there?" I asked.

"Ten or fifteen," she answered.

"More like twenty," her son said. Looking up at her, he said, "Sorry for correcting you, Mom. There were a few behind the house that you never saw."

"Not a problem," she said, rubbing her hand across his shoulders.

"Where did this happen?" Susan asked.

"Five miles south of Blue Mountain Pass. A couple miles past where we touched fender and mirror."

"You know for sure they're following you?" I asked.

"They have four working vehicles, three older-model pickup trucks and an old VW Bug," she said. "They were behind us for several miles. I was watching in the rearview mirror when the lead truck must have hit an icy spot and went off the road and into a shallow drainage ditch where it came to a stop and flipped onto its side."

"The rest of them stopped to help try to flip it back up," Peter added. "I lost sight of them when the road dipped. When we came up the next hill, I couldn't see them through the falling snow."

"We wouldn't have stopped here knowing they're behind us, but we really needed to find something to drink. I was starting to have problems concentrating—I know that's a sign of severe dehydration."

"Do you know any of them?" I asked.

"I don't," the mother answered.

"I do," Peter said. "The two that shot and killed Gramps and Nana are workers at the ranch across the highway from their place. One is named Stuart and the other Izzy. Gramps and I went over there a bunch of times before the blackout happened and they were both there."

"Stuart and Izzy. You're sure?" Susan asked.

"Yes," Peter answered firmly. "I'm sure."

"Jon, can we help them?" Renee asked. "Help as far as doing something about the group following them."

"Best to allow us to get on home and you on your way," Emily answered quickly.

"Your tire tracks will be visible for a couple more hours," I pointed out. "Easy enough for them to follow you all the way to your place in Burns."

"Oh," she said, with a tinge of resignation, realization setting in.

"Ours too, if we were to leave now," Melissa added.

I stepped closer, said, "If you want, we could put an end to this right here, right now. Only question is: do you want them all dead or just this Stuart and Izzy."

"You'd do that for us? You don't even know us."

"He wouldn't offer if he wasn't serious," Renee said.

"Well, I guess the two that killed my husband and in-laws."

"We like to be democratic when it comes to situations like this. So, what say you, ladies?"

It was unanimous on helping mother and son.

"Okay. Drive your Bronco and trailer to the road and position it so that both lanes are blocked. Do it now. Then come back here."

Mother and son moved the Bronco, and soon both lanes were blocked with no way to get around either side.

Once they were back, I had both mother and son join Kris in the Humvee's back seat.

"Susan, please go with them."

"Jon, let me at least—"

"No arguments, please," I said, cutting her off. "Just take them. I need someone to watch over them."

"One thing, Mrs. Talbot. You said you're a physician's assistant?"

"Yes. I work under Dr. Candace Brunk in Burns. She's a surgeon specializing in female reproductive and oncological issues."

"Would you mind looking at one of our travel mates? She was taken and suffered knife cuts to her breasts. I cleaned and bandaged them as best I could, but it would be good to have a professional check my work."

"Of course."

"Thank you. She's in the Humvee."

I watched as Susan escorted the mother and son to the Humvee.

"The goal is to stop the vehicles and have a chat with the occupants," I told the women.

"Monica, Kathy, and Melissa, I want you three to position yourselves fifty feet south of the Bronco on the far shoulder. Monica, from there, walk three car lengths south and Kathy, two car lengths. Melissa, stay at the fifty-foot mark. Renee and I will be on this side of the Bronco. All three of you then pace off twenty feet back from the roadway and take a knee. Set your rifles to three-round bursts. Melissa, full auto. The lead vehicle will stop when they spot the Bronco blocking the two lanes. When I tell you, I want the three of you to run toward the four cars—Melissa toward the first car in line, Monica the second and Kathy the third. Point your weapons at them but do not fire. Renee and I will do the same on this side. I'll be on the fourth vehicle. When we're in position, I'm going to fire a sustained burst on full auto as a warning."

"At them?" Melissa asked.

"No, over them. Then I'm going to shout out commands. You cover the windows for any shooters."

All heads nodded.

"What if they fire on us?" Kathy asked.

"Then return fire. Don't even hesitate. We're way beyond trying to be nice. We all good?" I asked.

Again, the women nodded.

"Okay. Good. Go get yourselves five extra magazines, then take your positions. Not sure how long we're going to have to wait, but we'll give it a half hour and then reevaluate. Go."

"What do I do with Greta?" Renee asked, petting the loyal gal behind her ears.

"She stays by your side. She's trained for just this kind of situation. She'll be right beside you until you tell her otherwise.

"Let's ammo up."

FIVE MINUTES LATER, WE WERE in position. And ten minutes after that, it was once again Greta who first alerted us to approaching vehicles.

"I see them. Four vehicles in single file," Melissa reported. "Three pickups and an old VW Bug."

"Okay. It's them. Safeties off."

"Renee, I'm going thirty feet down the road. You watch the passenger side of the first vehicle. I'll handle the other three. Everyone, watch windows for sudden heroes."

Thirty seconds after I was in position, the lead vehicle passed me. It was a mid-1950s pristinely restored Dodge Power Wagon. Sitting on the front bumper was the biggest winch I'd ever seen on a pickup truck. Thirty feet south of the Bronco, it came to a sudden stop.

I keyed the comms. "Approach now," I said, as I ran toward the third and fourth vehicles in line, a VW Bug and an older Chevy pickup. I raised the barrel of my rifle and fired off a full clip over all four vehicles. I dropped the empty mag and inserted a fresh one.

"You, in the vehicles, place your weapons at your feet then put hands on heads. Now!" I shouted. "Do not lower your hands until I tell you. If we find a weapon on you, not only will you die, but the one next to you will die as well. Do as we tell you, and you will not be hurt. Drivers, turn your headlights and engines off. Leave ignition keys in the vehicle."

All was silent until a single three-round burst from Renee took out the passenger-side front window of the second vehicle in line. A shooter had tried to stick his shotgun out the window. He was now howling in pain.

Renee approached the wounded man.

"Back off, Renee," I yelled, as I ran toward her. "Leave him to me."

"He was going to shoot. I had to—"

"I saw. You did good," I said, opening the pickup's passenger door and taking the guy's shotgun. The shooter, an older teenager in dirty mechanic's overalls, slid to the roadway and lay on his back screaming in pain.

I keyed the comms, said, "Ladies, pick a vehicle and approach. Watch the occupants. If any lower their hands, fire on them."

"Renee, you and Greta take up position between the lead truck and the Bronco. I'm going to bring these guys up to you, car by car. Have Greta guard like she did with Clint."

I started with the last car in line—the VW Bug. Four men were inside, and I had them exit after I opened both doors. I frisked each one and, with hands behind heads, walked them past the three trucks. I made them kneel in front of Renee.

While patting down the five men from the truck in front of the VW, one broke from the group and made a run back down the highway. Greta whined and pranced in place. Renee pointed her hand toward the runner, said, "Go."

The runner disappeared into the snowy darkness with Greta fifty feet behind. A human cry soon echoed out of the dark with panicked shouts of, "Stop it. Stop it!"

Greta then herded the runner back toward us, appearing out of the inky darkness, trailing the man who was massaging his left forearm. It wasn't until the man was standing next to his buddies, that Greta gave up her charge and rejoined Renee.

I had the rest of them out of the trucks and kneeling next to the Bronco a few minutes later. I counted twenty-one. I hadn't found any further weapons.

I dragged the one that Renee had wounded to a spot in front of the others. He was clutching his stomach and moaning in pain. He wouldn't last long.

I swung the M4 to my side, took out the Glock, and put a single round through his heart.

I turned and addressed the kneeling men. "I'm sorry I had to do that. But he was suffering and was going to die horribly."

"He aint a fuckin' family pet, dude," the driver of the VW shouted, visibly upset.

"You're responsible for the death of three people earlier today," I said, ignoring the comment. "You probably don't know their names, but they were Mr. and Mrs. Talbot and their son Brad. You point out the ones that did the killing, and I will let the rest of you live. You have my word."

A flurry of hands left heads and pointed to two men in the second row. I walked over and stood over the men.

"Names?" I asked the two.

"Dumb and Dumber," one of the men in the back row answered.

"It probably fits, but give me their real names," I said.

"Izzy and Stuart."

"Thank you."

I pointed the Glock at another man, this one much older than the rest, and asked if that was the truth.

"Yes, sir."

"And it was these two that did the killing?" I asked, pointing to the two men. "No one else?"

"That is correct, sir."

"Which one is Izzy?"

"The one in the red jacket."

"Fuck you, Jared," Izzy screamed. "You fuckin' pussy."

I backed off and stood next to Renee.

"Izzy and Stuart, come up here next to your buddy," I said, pointing to the dead man lying in the snow.

"Fuck that, asshole," the man in the red jacket shouted out. "You're goin' to just—"

A shot rang out and the man known as Izzy slumped over in the snow, blood squirting out of his neck and onto the man kneeling behind him.

Melissa had done it again.

"The man asks you to do something, you do it. Understood?" Melissa shouted at the crowd.

"Yes ma'am," nineteen men shouted out in answer.

"Stuart, get on up there. Now!" Melissa commanded.

Stuart stood and slowly walked up to me.

"Kneel." Which he did. "You shoot those people, Stuart?"

"No."

"Bullshit."

"Liar."

"He done it," were just a few of the many responses from his buddies.

"They're fuckin'—"

I pointed the Glock at Stuart's forehead.

"Please, mister," he pleaded.

"Did you give the Talbot's a pass?" I asked.

"Well, I—" he started to say.

I pulled the trigger, and Stuart slumped onto the dead window guy.

Twelve rounds left.

"The rest of you are going to walk back to that house, and you are going to bury all three Talbots. We'll give you eight hours to get it done. You'll stay there until we show up. We'll be there eight hours from now," I said, looking at my watch. "But first, I want you to throw your wallets up here. That way, we'll know where to locate you if we find that you haven't done what you're told."

Several wallets landed at my feet. The rest of them didn't have wallets, which I understood. *Who needs wallets anymore?*

They then sat in silence. None moved.

"Get going, now!" Melissa shouted, raising her rifle's muzzle and firing a quick burst over their heads.

That did it. They all stood and started running south down the highway, falling and skidding on the slippery roadway. It was almost comical.

"Are we really going to the Talbots'?" Melissa asked, once the group was out of earshot.

"Hell, no," I answered. "But they don't know that. Monica and Kathy, please gather their weapons and put them in the Talbots' trailer. Look for ammo, too. Melissa and Renee, please

20

transfer the stuff they looted from the house into her trailer."
Then, into the comms, "Susan."

"Yes?"

"Send Emily out here, please. She can help transfer supplies."

"She wants to bring her son out."

"I wouldn't advise it," I said, thinking of the three dead
bodies on full display.

"She says he needs to see things as they really are."

"Okay then."

Mother and son showed up a minute later, and I put them
to work helping Melissa and Renee. Emily walked past the three
dead men and said nothing, didn't even glance down at them.
The son stopped and stared at the three. '

"My dad always said that you reap what you sow," he said
aloud, staring at the bodies. "Thank you for handing out a little
justice."

"You're welcome. You'll need to watch your mom's back."

"Gramps told me to take care of mom. I'm gonna do that."

"Will you do something for me?" I asked him.

"Sure. Anything."

I took out the permanent marker and handed it to him.

"On each man's forehead, write *killer of innocents*."

"Sure."

"You know how to spell innocents?"

"Affirmative," he answered, and set off.

The pickups were soon empty of the looted supplies.

I walked over to Emily, said, "Seems a shame to have these
four working vehicles sitting useless. If Peter can drive, I suggest
you take this Power Wagon and have him follow you home. I'll
disable the other three."

"Peter drove his grandparents' ranch truck so he could
help with chores when he visited them. So yes, he knows how to
drive."

I opened the Power Wagon's driver's door. "It's a stick
shift. Is his grandparent's a manual?"

"It is."

I started the engine and checked the fuel level. "You've got half a tank left. Should be plenty to get you to Burns."

"Peter, come on over here," his mother shouted. He interrupted his writing and hustled over to us. His mother pointed to the Power Wagon, said, "Merry Christmas, Peter. You're going to drive this back to Burns. Stay close behind me."

"Seriously?" Peter asked, climbing up in the driver's seat, putting both hands on the steering wheel and his feet on the clutch and brake pedals.

It didn't appear that his legs were long enough to push down the pedals. "You have enough leg to push down the brake and clutch pedals?" I asked.

He had to scoot up toward the dashboard to do it, but was able to depress both pedals. "This is what I had to do when Gramps let me drive the ranch truck."

"Good enough." It wasn't as if he'd be encountering rush-hour traffic. I went to work on the remaining three vehicles, removing ignition keys, raising engine hoods, and pulling spark-plug wires. Then I pulled every other wire I could see. I finished them off by putting a bullet hole in all three gas tanks. I dropped the spent one and inserted a new magazine. Twelve tires received a round each.

Peter finished his writing and handed back the marker. I held out my hand and we shook. "Stay frosty, young man. I have no doubt you'll be able to take care of your mother."

"Thank you for helping us, sir," he said, his handshake firm.

"You're welcome. Continue being strong for your mom.

"Melissa, drive the Humvee over to Clint's driver's door and tell Kris to get in our ranch truck and wait for me. We'll top off the gas tanks by siphoning diesel from Clint's tank to the ranch truck and Humvee."

"The ranch truck's out of gas," Kris shouted across the distance.

"It's not. I'll show you the second tank's switch lever."

Emily and her son gave each of the ladies a hug, before it was my turn.

"Do you have any idea what happened to the power?" she asked as I disentangled myself.

I told her what we knew.

"Oh my gosh," she said, putting her hand over her heart. "This whole power outage is the result of an attack? And from the Chinese? After Putin was put away, I really thought we were on the path to reestablishing relations with them, but then when Pelosi felt it necessary to fly to Taiwan, she just lit the match that was waiting to ignite. I guess it's too late now for any kind of reconciliation. Oh well."

"What is it, Mom?" Peter asked, seeing his mother upset.

"I'll tell you when we're home, son."

To me, she said, "You treated your friend's wounds properly. The larger cuts can't be sutured closed—it's too late for that. She'll need to have those cuts cleaned and tended by a wound specialist. It's going to take some time. You've got her on antibiotics, so that's good."

"Thank you for checking," I said.

"The person that did that to her has been dealt with?" she asked.

"Yes," I answered, glancing at the snow-covered lump in front of the semi-truck. "He'll never harm another woman."

"Good."

Mother and son turned and walked back to the Bronco and Power Wagon. The engines started, and they were soon underway, merging left onto northbound Highway 78 toward Burns where they quickly disappeared into the snowy darkness. The deep growl of the Bronco's big V8 could be heard for a minute longer, and then it too was gone. The snow was coming down heavier than ever, sometimes blowing sideways with the stronger wind gusts.

We'd been there long enough. It was time to head out.

TWO

We finished gassing up forty minutes later. At one on the nose, we resumed our previous driving positions and got underway, merging onto Highway 95 East. Our convoy order went: Humvee, Cruiser, with Kris bringing up the rear in the ranch truck. Susan had returned Kris's night vision and comms to her, and I'd engaged the ranch truck's four-wheel drive and put it in high range.

I brought the Humvee up to thirty and left it there. When I turned on the running lights, I saw Renee had been right about the top few inches of the snowplow markers, for they lit up like crazy thanks to whatever reflective material they were coated with.

"Melissa and Kris, I've got my running lights on. Can you see the plow markers in your NVs from back there?"

"Perfectly," answered Melissa.

"This is going to work out fine," said Kris.

"Good. Keep your lights off. We've got about seventy miles to the Idaho border," I said over the comms. "Let's try and get there without stopping. We need to burn up as many miles as possible while this snowfall lasts. If it warms, and the snow starts to melt, and then freezes again, we'll be dealing with slippery, icy roads. And without snowplows and the salt they spread behind them, it would be very slow going."

"Are we going through any towns?" Melissa asked.

"Two. Rome and Jordan Valley. Both very small. They're on the map, but I'm not sure if they even qualify as towns per se. Once we cross into Idaho, we've got another twenty-five miles until we need to decide on which route to take. Both possibilities have some sharp elevation changes and if the weather warms and then cools, with ice forming on the roads . . . well, let's just say it will be difficult making forward progress, even with four-wheel drive."

As usual, when driving through soft, deep, virgin snow, the going was quiet, with none of the customary rattles or road noise. We continued in silence for several miles, passing four abandoned big rigs and double that number of passenger cars. None were blocking the highway and we saw no walkers on either shoulder.

"How's it going, Kris?" I asked.

"On uphill grades, the rear tires start spinning when I give it gas, even on the gentle inclines. But otherwise, okay."

Hoping to put the two drivers at ease, I said, "All three vehicles are four by fours and have mud and snow tires. We've got flat roads for the next fifty-five miles. According to the map, on the north side of Jordan Valley, there's a nine-mile descent. But we'll be fine—nine miles means it's a gradual descent."

"No matter how I play with the gas pedal, the rear end keeps sliding out," Kris said again.

Once we were on a level roadway, I slowed and came to a gradual stop.

"Kris, we need to put some weight in the bed of your truck. It's too light over the rear wheels."

"A few of those Hershey Kiss boxes should work," Kathy said. "They're heavy."

"Great suggestion," I said, putting the gear shift in park and setting the parking brake. I saw Kris open her door. "Let me do this, Kris. You can't be lifting anything."

"I have to pee," she stated sheepishly.

"Me too," from Renee. "That coffee we had back in Burns Junction flowed right through me."

"Okay. Everyone who needs to go, go. But one of you needs to be on overwatch."

Monica volunteered.

Greta jumped out with Renee and took the opportunity to take care of business.

While Monica provided overwatch, I carried ten boxes of Kisses from the trailer to the rear of the ranch truck. I lowered the tailgate, scooted the boxes in the bed, then placed them over the rear axle. Each box weighed roughly thirty pounds, and together, should do the trick. I covered the exposed boxes with a small spare tarp then secured the bundle with bungee cords.

We were soon underway and making good time—albeit at thirty miles an hour. But better safe than sorry.

"Putting the weight in the back has made a huge difference," Kris reported. "Thank you."

I keyed the comms, said, "Let's have a driving lesson. This is for everyone, so listen up. Driving in the snow takes some getting used to. I grew up in snow country and learned some basics early on. First, drive smoothly. The key is being smooth with your steering, accelerator, and brakes. Jerky movements will unstick tires. All adjustments of the wheel, gas pedal, or brakes must be deliberate, gentle, and gradual. This is the best advice I can give you—keep a constant pressure on the gas pedal, whether going up or down hill. You're in four-wheel drive, and you are not going to go fast down any steep hills. Once you start fiddling with the gas and brake pedals, you're headed for trouble.

"Second, look far ahead. Slow down for turns and allow triple the distance for stopping.

"Third, if you start to skid, look where you want to go not where you're going.

"Fourth and final. . . ah, what was the fourth? Oh yeah, control your skids. This is counter-intuitive and hard to master.

In a front-wheel skid, ease off the gas then aim where you want to go. But in a rear-wheel skid, turn the wheel in the same direction as the rear is headed and it will straighten out.

"And finally, Melissa and Kris, shift smoothly. Once you get in your final gear, stay in that gear. For these conditions go into third and stay in third—both up and down hills."

We passed a road sign that said we had twelve miles until we hit Rome, Oregon. Those twelve miles went quickly, traveling on flat, wide-open roadways. There were ranch and farm roads branching off the main highway, but we saw no tire tracks or other signs of recent activity. There were several abandoned passenger vehicles on the road and only two semi-trucks. Both semi's trailers' rear doors were in the closed position, but we passed them by, regardless—not wanting to take time investigating the contents.

Another road sign announced that we were passing through Crooked Creek State Natural Area.

Through the NVs, I could see we'd soon be crossing a bridge over Crooked Creek itself. The bridge looked to be a quarter-mile-long. A road sign showing a drawing of a car with two squiggly lines below it warned of possible slippery ice.

I keyed the comms, said, "We've got a bridge ahead. This is lesson five: when driving on a bridge in winter, especially when it's covered in snow, keep your steering wheel steady and unchanging pressure on your accelerator. Ice can quickly form on bridge roadways, and they can be very slippery."

Both drivers responded with clicks, and we crossed without incident.

Fifteen minutes later, and with headlights off, we entered the western outskirts of Rome, Oregon.

We came to a stop, and I scanned ahead with the thermal. I didn't expect to see anyone out this early in the morning, but I was wrong. One hundred yards up the highway, and off to the right, was a large building with a snow-covered tin roof. A few smaller outbuildings were scattered willy-nilly behind and to the sides of the larger building.

Three gas pumps shared an uncovered fuel island a scant twenty feet from the highway. Someone was sitting with their back up against the pump closest to us. He, or she, was facing in our direction, though I knew they couldn't see us through the falling snow and darkness. Another body, half-covered in snow, lay in front of one of those propane tank exchange lockers. Both bodies were dead, their heat signatures barely registering on the thermal's screen, but some heat remained, which meant that it hadn't been more than a few hours since whatever had befallen them had happened.

"We've got two bodies up ahead. Melissa and Kris, stay at the wheel. Renee, scoot over and drive the Humvee, please. Kathy and Monica, form a close-in perimeter, one on the Humvee and the other the Cruiser."

"What about me?" Susan asked, through the Humvee's open rear passenger door.

"Are you going to do this every time you feel left out of something?" I asked her, my frustration clearly showing.

"Yes, every single time."

"Well then, in the interest of maintaining group harmony, you can walk a close-in perimeter next to Kris's truck."

Once Susan was in place, I slowly made my way to the building and gas pumps. Ten feet from the body, I could make out two sets of half-covered tire tracks, one heading into the station from town and the other heading back to town. There was a mishmash of footprints around the pumps and bodies. A fuel nozzle lay in the snow and multiple sets of footprints led from the door of the building to the pumps.

The first body I'd seen was a man. He was jacketless, and according to the sewn-in name on his shirt pocket, his name was Luke. Luke had a bullet hole in his right cheek, blood dripping down onto the cement curb of the island. The blood had frozen when it landed, and a stalagmite had formed from the ground to his shoulder. Over the building's main entrance was a large round thermometer sporting a Coors Beer logo on its face. It read a chilly minus three degrees.

Fifteen feet from Luke, and lying next to the main building's front door, was the body of a young boy. He was face-down in front of the propane exchange locker, his hand still holding a long wooden stick with a key attached. He'd been shot in the back of his head. The locker was empty.

Likely scenario: the looters turned killers, had broken the front door's glass and forced Luke and the boy, who was probably Luke's son, to open the propane locker and unlock the gasoline tanks. Frustrated by the gas pumps not working, they'd shot Luke and, once the propane tanks were loaded up, shot the boy.

I risked a quick glance inside the store and could see tipped-over product displays and empty shelves. The glass-fronted beer coolers had been emptied as well. I didn't see any further bodies. I turned and made my way back to the front of the Humvee.

I keyed the comms. "Listen up. There are fresh tire tracks leading away from the station and headed east into town. I'm going to follow them on foot and make sure no one is waiting to ambush unsuspecting travelers. Renee, follow me in the Humvee but stay back fifty feet. Melissa and Kris, follow Renee. Kris, tell Susan to hop in with you. Kathy and Monica, one of you position yourself on the driver's side of the Humvee and the other the passenger side, then set a walking close-in perimeter."

Walking in the left-side tire track, I slowly made my way east on Highway 95. The tracks were three or four hours old, as new snow had filled in the first eight or nine inches of the twelve-inch-deep ruts. A quarter mile up, we crossed a bridge, and the tracks then turned left onto Rome Road where they disappeared from view.

"The tracks disappear off to the left. We're clear. Let's get out of Dodge, or in this case, Rome," I said into the comms. "Renee, catch up to me, please. Everyone else, resume your positions inside the vehicles."

"We could follow those tracks and hand out some—" Melissa started to say.

"Negative. Not our fight," I said, cutting her off. "We can't right every wrong we come across."

"Roger that," she replied.

The next thirty-four miles were mostly flat and straight with the occasional gentle curves eventually herding us northeast toward the town of Jordan Valley. The snowfall was lightening up the further east we traveled. The elevation hadn't really changed much, but the topography had, which I'm sure had something to do with the snowfall amounts. By the time we hit Jordan Valley, the snow had stopped falling all together and the roads were dry.

Downed power lines followed the road, and melted transformers still glowed brightly in the NVs. There was mile after mile of glowing hot spots, as if guiding us through the night.

Jordan Valley was larger than the previous town of Rome. Except for a lone dog crossing the road and many still-smoldering pole-mounted electrical transformers, the thermal scan showed no other heat signatures. There were a couple of coffee shops and an Arroyo gas station off to our right. The Comfort Rest Hotel was next door to the gas station. All had been looted, with windows and entrance doors broken.

There were a half-dozen bodies in front of the gas station and, further on, more bodies in the motel parking lot—more than I could count on two hands. The smell of blood, of bitter copper and iron, filled the air.

"Are those bodies?" Kris asked in a quiet voice. "And are they looters or residents?"

"Yes. And who knows," Renee answered.

"Pee-yew. What's that smell?" Kathy asked.

"Your typical warzone," I answered.

"Blood?" Monica offered up.

"Yes. Get used to it," I answered.

"There seems to be more trouble the further we go," Monica said.

"These super rural towns have low populations that wouldn't stand a chance against a determined crowd of looters," Melissa said.

"But looters would most likely be stranded travelers. And travelers usually aren't carrying weapons, right?" Kathy pointed out. "So, I'm guessing those bodies are looters who were shot by armed residents."

"Makes sense to me," Monica said.

"All the more reason for us to be ultra-careful," Renee cautioned.

The highway then took a hard left and put us on a northward path past Jordan Valley Elementary School and then the high school.

As we passed the high school, a powerful flashlight beam from the parking lot off to our left picked out the Humvee then illuminated the Cruiser and ranch truck. The beam was extinguished. I braced for bullet impacts, but none came. We picked up speed, and soon, only the dark outlines of ranch homes could be seen on either side of the highway.

The roadway was straight and dry. I gradually picked up even more speed, leveling off at fifty-five—an up-armored Humvee's top speed. "You guys doing okay back there?"

"Yep. No problems," Melissa answered.

"We're pretending none of this crap has happened and sharing what we'd eat for breakfast, lunch, and dinner," Monica said.

"We're doing fine," Kris reported. "I'm diggin' the dry roads."

"The Cruiser and ranch truck are still in four-wheel-drive high range. We'll change back to two-wheel drive during our next stop. Kris, tell Susan she can rejoin us in the Humvee then."

"We're just chatting away," Susan said through Kris's comms. "Girl stuff."

"Aren't they just Chatty Cathys?" Renee pointed out. Greta was sitting on Renee's lap receiving almost constant ear and chin rubs.

"You're going to spoil her," I said with a chuckle. "She's a specially trained military dog whose life mission is bringing down bad guys, not so much a lap dog."

"Whatever. She likes it and I like it."

I swear Greta looked over in my direction and grinned. I risked a quick glance in Renee's direction. "You know what I like?" I asked in a low, slow, husky voice.

"Uh oh," she said. "I know what that tone of voice means."

"Remember that time you flew into Seattle, and we spent a long weekend in Olympic National Park?"

"I remember it well. Or at least, I remember the lodge room well. . . we rarely left it."

"Remember the drive up the mountain?"

"Really? Now?" she asked, playing along.

"Why not? We're alone, except for Greta of course. But she won't say anything. We have a dry, straight road. And look at the room we have." I scooted the driver's seat-back and indicated the now abundant space between the steering wheel and me. "And it's nice and toasty in here."

"Okay, mister. But you better not disappoint," she said, after pretending to think it over. "Greta, in back." Once Greta was out of the way, Renee reached down, unlaced and took off her boots. Next off were her pants, panties, and plate carrier. She then reached over, unzipped my pants and brought me out. I sprung to life, as it were, and without letting go of me, she scooted over, straddled me and, facing me, guided me inside her. Together, we started moving in that age-old cadence.

"No foreplay? Right to the jackpot."

"Shut up, Kristen," she said. "I'm working here."

My comms came to life. "Why are you slowing down? Are we stopping?" Melissa asked.

Renee stopped what she was doing long enough to tell me to mind the road.

I flipped up my NVs and looked at the speedometer—forty. I keyed the comms. "Sorry, I was driving distracted. My bad," I managed to say. I lowered the NVs and brought us back to fifty-five.

With one hand, I attempted to raise her shirt and sports bra. Unsuccessful at the task, she took control of the situation, reaching down and pulling them up and over her breasts.

"Better?" she asked, both ample-sized breasts popping free.

"Much. Thank you," I said, my voice muffled as I sucked on one hard, erect nipple before moving on to its identical twin. "You know something? I think they *are* getting larger."

"Oh goody. I seem to be doing all the work here, not that I'm—" Renee started to say. She didn't finish the sentence, instead, she suddenly stopped moving, her body going taut in what I knew from experience was the prelude to her orgasm. She shook and then exhaled a lung full of air into my right ear. "Jesus, that came out of nowhere. And fast."

"I'm fairly confident Jesus had no part in that. But I'm glad I was here for it," I whispered in her ear as she resumed moving her rear end up and down. "I'm not going to last long, babe. Just an FYI."

"I feel another coming, Jon. Do. . . not. . . stop. Give me one more," she hissed, her body once again going taut and then shaking in orgasm. This time she wrapped her arms around my neck and hugged me so tight that the Humvee wandered into the opposite lane.

"What's going on with you?" Melissa asked over the comms, concern in her voice.

"Greta trying for ear rubs," I answered.

With me still in her, Renee leaned back and started the breast swaying and dangling, which she knew I loved. "Please, keep at least one eye on the road, mister."

I felt myself getting close, said, "Soon, babe." I took a hand from a breast and put it on her rear end to stop the motion.

I managed to stay on the highway as I exploded inside her.

"Wow," we both said, almost in unison.

"Good boy," Renee said a minute later. She planted a wet kiss on my lips, pulled down her sports bra and shirt, then lifted off me and scooted back to her side of the Humvee. A minute later, she was slipping her pants on. "Thank you for staying on the road," she said, while lacing up her boots. "But more importantly. . . for not disappointing."

"That was. . . very nice," I said, tucking myself away.

"The fact that the world is fucked up seemed to help with the intensity," she said. "It's Armageddon sex. In fact, I wonder if anyone has ever put those two words together in a sentence before? We could be the first."

"I'm sure that someone, somewhere, has used the word combination before," I said. "Though, this is probably the first time in history that it's actual reality and not fiction."

Renee went silent, staring out the window as the view her NVs provided passed by. She lifted her NVs up and looked across the cab at me. "I do love you, Jon. I need you to know that. I did before the possible baby came into the picture."

"And I love you, babe. Always and forever."

"I'm serious. I really mean it. I think I always have."

"Me too, Renee. Truly." I meant it with all my heart. "Both you and our child."

Renee slipped her plate carrier over her head and cinched it up. Greta was once again sitting on her lap receiving ear rubs.

Renee took hold of my right hand with her left as we drove on in contented silence.

THREE

We gradually climbed, then crested, a high-elevation hill. After that, it was a several-mile-long grade change leading down into a narrow river valley. A road sign told us we would be following the Succor Creek for the next twenty-five miles. We left the river valley when the highway turned east, and ten minutes later crossed the Oregon–Idaho border.

It started to rain, though not hard enough to leave the wipers on full-time. I slowed to twenty-five, opened the door a crack, and stuck my hand out. "It's really warming up. I'm guessing it's up into the high thirties or low forties."

"Would this be a good place to stop and take the Cruiser and ranch truck out of four-wheel drive?" Renee asked.

"Good as any," I answered, already slowing down.

I keyed the comms and told the group it was time to take a very quick break.

"I'll stand overwatch," Renee offered over the comms.

The column came to a stop, doors opened, and bodies piled out. Greta followed Renee, detouring to the side of the road to do her business. I took both Cruiser and ranch truck out of four-wheel drive and checked fuel gauges and tires. All was good, and after a few minutes of stretches and driver changes, we were back underway.

Susan was back in the Humvee, and she and Renee were soon talking non-stop.

I tuned them out and concentrated on driving. The highway followed the contours of the land, hilly and then suddenly bursting into long, flat valleys. In the valleys were ranches and farm access roads. I saw light burning brightly in one ranch-house window but saw no one outside. We passed many abandoned cars and a few semi-trucks. And something different here—the trucks' trailers had been opened and some emptied.

At two in the morning, we were a few miles south of the intersection of Highways 55 and 95. A decision had to be made. Turn left and continue on Highway 95, heading north almost to the Canadian border before turning east on Highway 2 toward Whitefish and home. Or turn right, and head east on Highway 55 to Highway 78 East toward Sun Valley Ski Resort, and then north on 93 up into Montana and home. Both routes pass through some formidable mountain ranges.

I called for a stop, said, "We need to make a decision as to which of two routes to take. Let's meet at the Cruiser. Susan, stand overwatch?" *That should placate her need to help the group.*

"You're not asking just to pacify me, are you?" she asked.

Jeeze, am I that transparent?

"Sorta kinda," I answered. What else could I say. Besides, the truth is always best.

"Well, okay then. Just so we're clear."

"Good," I said.

"Good," she replied quickly.

"If you two would stop acting like bickering ten-year-old siblings, we've got some decisions to make here," Renee stated firmly, sounding like the parent of incorrigible teenagers.

"Okay. Sorry," I said.

"Me too," Susan said, though in my opinion, somewhat half-heartedly.

"Go stand overwatch, baby," Melissa said, putting her arm around Susan and guiding her toward the rear of the Cruiser.

I spread the Idaho map out on the Cruiser's hood and replaced my NVs with a headlamp. Once Melissa had made her way back to the main group, I started in.

"We're here," I said, indicating the junction of Highways 95 and 55.

Using my finger, I traced the route. "We can turn left, which takes us north on 95, go all the way up to Highway 2, then east toward Kalispell, and finally a quick jog north to Whitefish."

I stabbed my fingertip on the small town of Marsing, Idaho. "Or, do we turn right, head east on 78 to 167, to 20, to 75 North to 93 North past Sun Valley Ski Resort and then all the way to Whitefish from there?

"I haven't added the actual mileage for either route, but I bet they're within fifty to a hundred miles of each other. And most importantly, both routes keep us a distance from Boise."

"Which route is fastest?" Kris asked.

"I'm guessing they're the same, though the latter takes us through fewer towns. And after Sun Valley, we've got some mountain passes to traverse, but the road is a good one. I've driven the Sun Valley route many times, and we shouldn't have much of a problem—even with snow on the roads."

"It's 2 a.m. now, which means we have another four hours of darkness left," Melissa pointed out. "If we want to stick to traveling in darkness, then we need to find a place to hole up before it gets light out."

"If we hustle, we can make it to Ketchum by the time daylight takes over," I said. "It's too cold to be pitching tents though. Besides, Sun Valley is full of condos and townhomes, which means there are probably a bunch of folks still hanging out and fighting for whatever supplies are left. While Ketchum, on the other hand, is mostly houses and ranchettes, and I bet we could find an isolated, vacant farm or ranch with a barn to spend the day in."

"What are we waiting for? Let's get a move on and get to Ketchum," Kris said.

Renee put her fingertip on Ketchum. "I second that."

"Monica? Kathy? You two good with Ketchum?" I asked.

"You betcha," Kathy answered.

"Sounds like a plan to me," Monica said.

"Melissa, please get Susan, and let's be on our way."

FOUR

Five minutes later, we came up on the intersection of 95 and 55. Across the street was a truck plaza with twenty to thirty semi-trucks neatly parked in designated spaces, exactly where tired drivers had pulled in for their government-required rest periods. Chances were, they'd been asleep when they were caught in the pulse. The plaza was full of night owls—three groups of people, both men and women, were gathered around barrel fires. Wooden pallets were stacked nearby, likely being used for firewood.

The truck plaza's main store lights were blazing away. I could see several people moving around inside, and there was no sign of looting or damage to the building.

The light from the store made its way across the parking lot and illuminated the entire intersection, not brightly, but certainly with enough light to make us clearly visible to the crowd in the parking lot.

And sure enough, before we could turn right onto Highway 55 and get past them, at least a dozen people abandoned their burn barrels and ran into the street. With practiced precision, they linked hands and formed a tight line across both lanes. None appeared to be armed, and unless we were willing to run them over, we were effectively blocked from going further than the hastily formed human line. A woman on the far right brought out a piece of white cloth and frantically waved away.

The only way to avoid them would be to turn left and head toward Boise, but that could be held in reserve as a worst-case scenario. I wasn't getting a bad vibe from these folks and decided that it wouldn't hurt to get out and speak with them. Then it dawned on me—*they see a military Humvee and assume we're military.*

"They certainly don't look dangerous. And I don't see any weapons," Monica said.

"Looks can be deceiving," Kathy cautioned.

"Melissa. Kris. Stay where you are. I'm going to go speak with them," I said. "Kathy and Monica, form a close-in perimeter. Have weapons ready but leave safeties on."

I turned to Renee and asked her to scoot over behind the wheel. "If it's all right with you, I'd like to take Greta with me."

"Of course."

"Greta, come," I said, opening the door and stepping out. Greta jumped to the ground and sat next to me, looking up in anticipation. She raised her snout and took in the scent that hung thick in the air.

"I smell it too, girl. Smells like freshly plowed fields. Earthy, even."

I looked up and saw that Renee was already in the driver's seat. She reached out a hand, grabbed the back of my head, and brought me in close.

"No heroics, mister," she said, right before kissing me hard.

"Never." I slung my rifle and freed my Glock's Velcro cover.

"Jeez, get a room, you two," Susan said.

I raised my NVs and keyed the comms onto the always-transmit position. "You all can hear what's said. Keep an eye out on the store and parking lot, please."

"Roger that," Melissa responded.

With Greta stuck like glue to my left side, I strode up to the line and asked who was in charge. They were mostly middle-aged and older. Several of the men had huge pot bellies, ample testimony to a trucker's diet of fast food and snacks. All of them, women included, wore hats sporting either trucking company logos or the American flag. Several wore stained and faded-red Trump MAGA hats.

The woman who had waved the white flag stepped forward, said, "No one's really in charge. We're more of a cooperative—stranded drivers, truckers, or folks headed up to Sun Valley for some Christmas break skiing. There's a bunch of kids and parents sleeping inside the building. The others on the line here, we're some of the original drivers that were parked at the plaza over there when the power died. Since then, stranded motorists and families have been streaming in—probably seventy or eighty the first few days. But we haven't had anybody show up the last two days."

"Until y'all drove up," the man standing next to the woman said.

"With the exception of them two Abrams on big-ass flatbeds that drove through late yesterday afternoon," another woman added. "Takes some powerful horsepower and torque to pull them things. Lots more than we ever done tow."

"Abrams? As in M1A2 Abrams main battle tanks?" I asked, astonished.

"Yes, sir. Along with two supply trucks, a fueler, and some kind of maintenance vehicle I never seen before," the flag-waver added.

"Don't forget them two Strykers that were escortin' 'em," the man on the far left shouted out. "Said they was from the Idaho National Guard in Boise and bringin' 'em to Mountain Home Air Force Base."

I had spent a good part of my military life inside a Stryker, and knew well the type of weapon systems they could carry. If we came upon them on our travels, they would undoubtably challenge us and soon discover we weren't military. The first question they'd ask: "where did you get the Humvee?" I didn't think they'd believe my answer even if it was the truth. Best to avoid them all together.

I carefully considered how I would ask the next question. "We're headed further north and need to fuel up. We hoped to do that at the base. But we're not sure where the main base entrance is."

The flag-waver answered for the group. "Up on Highway 167." She pointed behind her. "You drive down this road for two miles and you're going to hit Highway 78. Turn south, which means take a right, and after about sixty miles, give or take, you run into Highway 167. Go left and the base entrance is about fifteen miles up on the right. Where up north y'all going?"

"Northern Montana via Sun Valley and—" was as far as I got.

"You won't make it goin' that route," a man in the middle of the link said. Unlike the others, he was skinny as a rail with long white hair pulled back into a ponytail. His beard, slightly darker than his hair, was long, almost touching the second button from the top of his dark-blue flannel Carhartt work shirt. "Was headed south the night before the blackout and tried goin' that route myself. The ITD had 75 closed just south of Highway 93. Trooper said they had more than forty inches of fresh snow on the road and that the plows wouldn't start until the next mornin'. Which means it never did get plowed. It's been snowin' up there somethin' fierce, I'm sure. Probably four to six foot on the road by now."

"I appreciate the update. Thank you. I'm going to have to change our route," I said.

"I'd go east and get on Interstate 15," long-beard offered up. "That'll take you north to Interstate 90 and then on to anywhere in northern Montana. You only go over a couple of itty-bitty passes. Nothin' your three trucks over there couldn't handle."

"We're trying to avoid crowds, which is why we travel at night."

"You own the night and all that?" flag-waver asked, pointing to my NVs.

"Yes, ma'am. Exactly."

I tried to bring up the map in my mind. "What if we were to make our way over to 93 and bypass Sun Valley?"

"That'd work," the man on the line's far left said.

"You only have an incline starting at around Salmon and easing south of Conner," flag-waver said.

"Should be very passable all the way from Conner to north of Flathead Lake," long-beard added.

"Thank you for the advice," I said. "Why are you blocking the highway?"

"We're hoping you can tell us what's going on with the power," flag-waver answered.

"And why our trucks, cell phones, and computers died," long-beard added.

"Those military guys yesterday refused to tell us anything," a woman standing next to flag-waver said. "Scumbags, the lot of 'em."

"Well, gather around closer, and I'll tell you what we know," I said, waving them in.

Greta stood then growled at the approaching crowd. I put my hand on her back and said it was okay. She sat, and the group gathered in front of me.

Ten minutes later, I'd told them everything we knew. I also told them what we'd encountered on our travels. At no time did I tell them we weren't military.

Open mouths and hands flying to chests greeted my news. Then questions started flying at me.

"I'm sorry, but that's all we know."

"I told you I thought it was one of them EMP events," the link's last man said.

"What the hell you goin' up to northern Montana for? Nothin' military up there," long-beard asked, ignoring last link man.

"We're escorting a civilian VIP," I answered, which was totally true.

"When you get to the air base, ask 'em to take you there in a helicopter," someone suggested.

"They have working choppers?" I asked.

"Heard 'em. Haven't seen 'em."

"That's good news," I said, though it meant there were eyes in the sky. We did not want to be spotted with the Humvee.

I glanced over toward the truck plaza, said, "You seem to be doing well here."

"We have plenty of food and supplies—enough to last us months, if need be," flag-waver stated. "Lots of them trailers over there were destined for food distribution warehouses. We have more rice, beans, and dry goods than you can shake a stick at. Pete Higgins, the plaza's owner, has a twenty-five-hundred-gallon propane tank that fuels his coffee shop's stove and sixty-year-old generator, so no problem cookin', heatin' the place, and powerin' the lights."

"Protection?"

Long-beard crossed his arms across his chest. "This is Idaho. We're fine in that regard," he answered in a tone that suggested that particular topic was closed for discussion.

I understood his concern. Folks up in Montana feared the same thing: the government confiscating their guns, especially with Biden in office and Dem-controlled Congress intent on passing what they were calling "common sense gun laws."

My comms came alive. "Master Sergeant, you have a vehicle approaching your three o'clock. A thousand yards and closing," Renee said.

"Military or civilian?"

"Can't tell."

"That's gonna be Arbury," flag-waver explained. "One of our members had an emergency appendectomy last night. I hope it's them returnin'. They have a medical clinic in Marsing which they allow us access to. In return, we promised them we'd stay out of their town. That, and we're sharing a fifty-five-foot trailer full of medicine and medical supplies with them."

"Keep an eye on it, Corporal."

"Roger that."

"It looks like you're set for the foreseeable future. One piece of advice, though—don't form any more lines across the highway. There are too many bad guys willing to shoot you where you stand."

"We saw you was military, sir," long-beard said. "Normally, we got thirty weapons trained on anyone who comes up on us."

The comms came alive. "It's an old pickup truck, sir," Renee said.

The group heard the transmission, and several said it was Arbury coming back from Marsing.

"Good luck then, folks," I said, turning and heading back to the Humvee.

"Thank you for the information, Master Sergeant," flag-waver shouted after me. She joined the crowd as they made their way back to the warmth and relative safety of the parking-lot burn barrels.

I had Renee stay behind the wheel while I took the passenger side. Greta jumped from ground to floorboard to my lap and settled in. Renee turned the corner and headed toward Marsing.

Out of the corner of my eye, I saw a figure running toward us. "Stop, Renee," I said opening my door and stepping out. Over the comms, I told the others we were stopping and that there was no need to form overwatches.

Greta was right there next to me.

It was the flag-waver. We met at the Humvee's front bumper. She put her hands on her knees in an attempt to regain her wind.

"You okay," I asked, concerned.

"That was the furthest I've run since high school," she said, between gasps. "I'm okay. I wanted to let you know that Arbury was talkin' to someone at the hospital this mornin' who had brought in a gunshot victim. Seems a couple dozen residents got themselves a blockade up in a small town called Shoshone, which is up on 26 where it connects with 93. Highway 75 also starts there. They done blocked the road in both directions on the bridge over a little river or canal. The man's group off-roaded their way around it, but the asswipes done fired on 'em anyways. Nicked one of the passengers in the back seat, a young child. Fuckers."

"Let me get the map and—" I started to say.

"Don't need no map, hon. Only way around Shoshone now is by goin' 78 to 84 to 86 to 15 to—"

"How far out of the way are we talking here, ma'am?" I asked, cutting her off.

"Hundred and fifty miles, give or take."

"But the highway is clear from here to Shoshone?"

"Yes. As far as I know anyways."

"Thank you for letting us know."

"You're welcome. Thought you might wanna know," she replied, giving me a quick hug before turning and walking slowly back to the truck plaza.

I RELAYED THE INFORMATION TO the group.

"This is not good," I said. "And the only way we can avoid it is by detouring 150 miles. Besides the additional miles, the new route would take us on portions of interstate highways and through the city of Pocatello. That's not something I'm willing to do."

"So, we stick to the original route?" Kris asked.

"What about the blockade?" Monica asked.

"We'll deal with it when we get there," I answered. "Let's just chill and put some miles on the odometer."

"They seemed like good folks," Susan said, scooting up and speaking over my shoulder.

"Kinda restores my faith in people," Renee said.

"Shows what can happen when folks work together rather than trying to kill each other," I said, putting my seat belt on.

"I heard the man say the highway we planned on taking is closed. Which route are we taking now?" Kris asked. "I'm super confused."

I had Greta get in back with Susan and spread the map over my lap. Putting on one of Burt's headlamps, I studied the route then keyed the comms. "Highway 75 is the road that's closed because of snow. We're now going to stay on 78 until we hit 26, which is also Highway 93. We stay on 93 all the way up into Montana. But for today, I think we'll shoot for the town of Arco."

I started adding up the route mileage on the map and came up with a rough estimate. "Looks like we've got 230 miles, give or take a few, to Arco."

"Which means we're going to be running into daylight," Monica said.

"For an hour or so, which should be fine," I answered. "Unless we spot a place to settle in for the day while it's still dark. But there's not much out there."

"Except for the roadblock," Monica added.

"There is that. But it won't stop us for long. If it's still dark when we get to it, I figure it'll take less than ten minutes to get it cleared. And with this Humvee, clearing paths will not be an issue."

I glanced in the passenger-side mirror at the two trailing trucks and saw that Kris was lagging behind. "Tighten it up, Kris."

"Okay."

We passed a market on our right and then an Arroyo gas station, both unmolested. Other than charred power poles and transformers, and a few abandoned cars, the town appeared pre-blackout normal.

A road sign indicated Highway 78 was the next right.

"Taking the next right," Renee announced.

I checked the map and could see that we had open highway for the next sixty miles.

"We don't encounter another significant town until we hit Grandview," I said. "We have sixty miles of open highway. Let's pick up the speed to fifty-five."

It started to rain, though it was more of a heavy mist. The road was flat with farmland on both sides. The NVs picked up farmhouse after farmhouse. I could see giant farm machinery sitting in half-harvested fields, stopped in their tracks by the pulse. The strong scent of wet grass mixed with tilled soil filled the air.

A half hour later, we started to run parallel with the Snake River. We blew through Givens Hot Springs, Murphy, and then Grand View. Fifteen minutes later, we passed two churches, directly across the highway from each other, with burn barrels burning brightly in both parking lots. Cars were positioned like wagon trains surrounding the main buildings with several people standing inside the barricade of cars.

"Imagine the traffic jam here on Sunday mornings," Kathy said.

The roadway was flat and, for the most part, straight. When the road did change directions, it was gradual and easy.

Next was the town of Bruneau. We crossed over the Snake River, and for several miles traversed along the north side of the river. For the next thirty miles, the road was straight as an arrow, until it took a sharp turn to the north and dumped us in the town of Hammett.

Things had not gone well in Hammett—the post office had burned to the ground, the sign out front by the highway its only remaining identifying feature. Mom's General Store had been looted, the large plate glass windows and doors shattered. There were two bodies, a woman and a man, hanging from a tree limb in front of the store. Nailed to the tree trunk was a sign that said *Walkers, nothing for you here. Keep walking.*

"That's a warning not many will miss," Kathy said.

"Quick justice out in the wild west," Kris offered.

"Step on it and get us out of here. Quickly, please," Monica said.

"Good idea," Renee responded, stepping on the gas.

Once on the north side of town, we came to the first major highway in Idaho—Interstate 84.

Renee brought us to a stop.

"We have a road sign ahead: Glenns Ferry or Twin Falls," she said. "Which way, Mr. Navigator?"

"Turn right here. We need to go through Glenns Ferry and on to Bliss, Idaho," I answered, studying the map. "It's thirty miles to Bliss. At Bliss, or close by anyway, we get onto Highway 93.

"Renee, hold on a minute," I said. "Anyone need a quick break?"

Everyone wanted one, including Greta. I stood overwatch, and we were moving again five minutes later. Renee was still driving the Humvee, but Kathy had taken over for Melissa in the Cruiser, and Susan had gone back to keep Kris company. It was raining much harder now and visibility was becoming an issue.

The on-ramp was a long one. Where the ramp finally met the highway, there were two Idaho state police cars sitting where they'd died in the pulse. Both units sported dash-mounted radar units which I was sure had produced their fair share of revenue for the state and county coffers. All four doors and the trunk were open on one unit, and the other's trunk was open.

"Eyes sharp, ladies. Head on a swivel," I said. "We've got another thirty miles of this interstate before we're back onto safer roads."

The highway was four lanes, two in each direction, with a fifty-foot level dirt median between them. We encountered dozens of abandoned cars and trucks. None of the trucks' trailers had been opened.

"Now there's an opportunity if I ever saw one," Monica said. "Just ripe for the pickin'."

"It would take some organization and effort to get out here," Kathy said. "I doubt most of these folks could afford to leave their homes and towns undefended while out scavenging for supplies."

"They'll have to, eventually," Kris added.

We were gradually gaining elevation and my ears popped ten minutes into the climb. The rain was still coming down but the NVs were picking up the occasional snowflake.

We passed the off-ramp for the town of Glenns Ferry, but the road sign said the town itself was a couple of miles, via surface streets, to the south. The NVs picked up a line of cars and pickups blocking the surface street leading to town, but nothing was blocking the interstate, and we passed without incident.

A few miles later, we zipped past a rest area off to the left. There were a dozen semi-trucks and passenger vehicles parked in the lot, and the NVs showed several people huddled under the restroom building's roof overhang. Then we were past the town of Bliss off to the right. The snow was now constant but melting once it hit the ground. Up on the right was the interchange for Highway 26. We exited then went under the overpass and emerged on the north side of the interstate.

Highway 26 was two lanes and straight as an arrow. The ever-present downed power lines followed the road, and most poles were burnt and still glowing with heat. My best guess was that whatever preservative coating they applied to the wood poles was still radiating heat from the initial pulse.

We were gaining elevation, and snow was beginning to stick to the highway, though not enough to warrant stopping and putting the two trailing trucks into four-wheel drive.

Fifteen minutes later, we flew past the town of Gooding.

"Isn't Gooding where that deputy's wife's family is from?" Renee asked. "Deputy Stills, I think his name was."

"It is," Monica answered. "Hope he made it up here."

"He seemed like a pretty capable guy," I said. "And with his dad's help, they stood a good chance of making it.

"We're going to hit Shoshone in fifteen minutes," I told the women. "I'm not sure where the roadblock is, so we're going to do what we did in Rome, Oregon—I'm going to walk ahead of the trucks with the thermal and scout the road. Let's use the same drivers and outside watchers as last time."

"We passed a road sign a couple miles back that said the population is close to fifteen hundred. That's a lot of people," Melissa said, worry in her voice.

"Come on guys, we've done this before," I said, trying to defuse the tension in the air. "The only difference is, this time, we know, or at least think we know, there's something blocking our way. Trust me—we're not going to have a problem. Just do what I tell you, and we'll be fine."

FIVE

The ladies fell silent as we made our way closer to Shoshone. The snow was really coming down now, blowing sideways as it was buffeted by twenty to thirty mile-an-hour wind gusts. The outside temperature was going to be brutal thanks to the windchill factor.

The roadway was covered by five or six inches of snow with no visible tire tracks. There were quite a few abandoned cars and trucks, at least one every quarter mile or so. The ever-present downed power lines paralleled alongside us.

Even with the Humvee being in full-time all-wheel-drive, I could feel the tires losing traction, which meant the two trailing trucks would be having a tough time of it.

I keyed the comms, said, "Let's stop and engage four-wheel drives."

That accomplished, we were back up to speed, and a few minutes later, the first signs of the Shoshone business district appeared in the NVs. There was a junkyard, an auto parts store, auto repair shop, and two boat and RV self-storage lots. A mile further on and we were in Shoshone proper. The first building—or what was left of it anyway—was a burned-out

Idaho National Bank, the bank's vault and roadside sign the only recognizable and intact items remaining among the ruins.

Next door to the bank was the Shoshone Library, its glass entrance doors shattered and lying on the sidewalk out front. Four bodies were hanging from a lamppost that draped over the street in front of the library's main entrance. They were joined on the pole by joyous Christmas decorations proclaiming "Happy Holidays to One and All!"

"Not so happy for those four," Kathy observed.

"Look down the street, guys," Melissa said.

At every street corner was a streetlight hung with more Christmas decorations. And on every streetlight, more bodies hung alongside the holiday decorations. The executioners hadn't been picky—there were men, women, and children. All had their hands zip-tied behind them. Each face had the look of anguished death, with tongues out, and broken necks producing angled heads looking at the world with open, unseeing eyes. The bodies, too many to count, were swinging wildly, propelled by strong gusts of wind-driven snow.

"The fuckers killed children," Kathy hissed over the comms.

"If they didn't want outsiders coming into their town, and I'm assuming they're outsiders hanging up there, they could have posted signs warning this would happen," Kris said. "At least given them a chance to turn around."

"This could be a scene out of a horror movie," Renee said, eyes transfixed on the scene in front of us.

"Let's stop here," I said. I donned shooting gloves and a knit ski hat that covered my ears. I put NVs on over the hat and then pulled on a camo down jacket. I opened the passenger door and stepped out. It was bitter cold, probably close to five or ten degrees, and less than that once the windchill was factored into the equation. I attached the thermal to the rifle and booted it up. Greta had jumped into the vacant passenger seat and was looking at me with eager eyes. I told her to stay put.

"We're looking for Highway 93," I said, waiting for the thermal to cycle up. Vapor was forming in front of me with every exhaled breath.

"There's a sign up on the right that says 93 is one block up," Renee said.

"Good. I'm going to walk ahead. Monica, please take over driving from Melissa. Melissa and Kathy, put on your cold-weather outerwear and then form a close-in perimeter next to the Cruiser. Both of you on the passenger side, as it will offer you some protection from any shooters that might pop up in the buildings to our left. Susan, stick with Kris. Weapons charged, safeties off, and extra magazines in your pockets. They may have some type of choke point up ahead. Let me know when you're in place."

They were in position two minutes later.

The thermal's screen came to life. I raised the NVs, brought the rifle's buttstock up to my shoulder, and scanned the road ahead. Then to our right and left. Nothing. No heat signatures. I turned, looked at Renee, and waved her forward.

I walked under the first set of swinging corpses and then made my way across the intersection with Apple Street. There was a looted market on my right and then a small café next door which had been broken into, broken glass and trash everywhere.

Another scan with the thermal showed no heat signatures ahead. Walking under a second and third set of corpses, I could see an Idaho Best gas station ahead on the right. It appeared intact, but the thermal detected no heat. I brought us up to a hundred feet of the stop sign at the intersection with Highway 93. From here, we'd need to turn left and enter a block of solid storefronts. I put my fist up and brought the three vehicles to a stop.

I ran over to the far-left street corner and peered around the building. According to a road sign across the street, our next turn would be one block up and to the right. I raised my rifle and the thermal, and there they were: five heat signatures, right where we needed to turn. The five were standing in front of a

Parkman Brothers gas station. I ducked back behind the building and thought about what to do. But the decision was made for me.

Gunfire erupted behind us, coming from a couple of bolt action rifles as the rounds fired off every three to five seconds, about as fast as nimble hands could open, close, aim, and fire off a round.

"Two shooters, Jon," Melissa reported. "One in the alleyway behind your building there and the other up in the far-left upstairs window of the same building."

"Both of you hug the Humvee. Now!" I yelled.

Automatic gunfire then answered the single shots. Melissa was on full auto but in control, her return fire measured and coming in restrained bursts.

Kathy then joined in the response as I heard three-round bursts alongside Melissa's sustained automatic fire.

I risked a quick peek back around the corner. I raised the rifle, and the thermal showed all five figures running toward the corner—and me. They were half a block away and moving fast. I dropped a knee, selected full auto, braced against the brick wall with my left hand for barrel support, and settled the thermal on the far-left runner. Two seconds later, the thermal's sight glowed with red crosshairs. I fired a burst on full auto, moving from left to right. Four of the five figures fell to the ground. The fifth ran behind an abandoned car and huddled behind the front bumper. I selected semi-auto, brought the crosshairs to where I thought he might raise his head for a look-see, and sure enough, a head popped up where I thought it would. I fired a single round, hitting him in his lower jaw. Not sure of how many rounds remained in the magazine, I dropped it, inserted a fresh one, charged it, and stowed the expended mag in an empty vest pouch.

All firing had stopped.

"Both shooters down, Jon," Melissa reported.

I quickly swung the M1 around, scanned Kathy and Melissa, and then the road we'd just walked. Three heat signatures were two hundred yards out and advancing. The thermal's screen crosshairs glowed red.

The three shooters began firing on the run, little yellow heat signatures popping bright, and just as quickly disappearing from the thermal's screen. These three had semi-automatic rifles as they were firing as fast as fingers pulled triggers. They were also firing blind, because there was no way they could possibly see their targets in the blinding snow and darkness. They were as likely to hit their own people as us. Stupid.

"Kathy. Melissa. You have three shooters headed toward you on your nine. Move to the Humvee's front bumper and keep your heads down. I've got the three on thermal and will deal with them."

An errant bullet hit the brick wall five feet above me, bits of brick and mortar raining down on my head and shoulders. I kneeled, brought the gunsight back up, watched the scope reacquire the three shooters, and when the cross-hairs glowed red, fired three measured bursts. I watched the three heat signatures go down. I dropped the magazine and inserted a fresh one.

All gunfire had ceased.

I heard a woman moaning.

"I think Kathy's hit," Melissa yelled out, not bothering with the comms.

I ran back, heading toward the source of the panicked moaning. I reached the Humvee, rounded the rear bumper, and there was Kathy on the ground. She was crying while she frantically tore at her plate carrier.

I got behind her and, with my right hand on her vest's drag handle, lifted her into a sitting position. "I'm going to drag you to the Humvee's tire and sit you up. Understand?"

Kathy nodded. I dragged her ten feet across the snow-covered roadway and leaned her against the Humvee's passenger-side rear tire. Good news: there wasn't a blood trail.

I keyed the comms, said, "Melissa, get over here and provide overwatch while I check Kathy."

"What about the shooter in the—"

"Please come now," I said. "The rest of you stay where you are."

"Coming now," Melissa responded.

Melissa was there thirty seconds later. I handed her my rifle and told her to scan with the thermal.

While Melissa scanned for threats, I told Kathy I was going to remove her vest and check for wounds.

I leaned her forward and ran my hand along the rear of her vest and felt an indentation. I leaned her back and started loosening adjustment straps. "I'm going to lift this off now. I know it's difficult, but try and slow your breathing."

She nodded in understanding and took deeper breaths. I could see her chest settle down.

Once I had the plate carrier off, I ran my hands along her back and sides and felt nothing unusual. I leaned her back against the tire and visually checked her chest and stomach. And again, saw nothing. I held her vest up and turned it around. There was a neat little hole about seven or eight inches below the vest's rear neckline. I stuck my finger in and felt the ass-end of the slug. I took the Ontario and dug the thing out.

"Your vest took a round, Kathy," I said, holding up the collapsed slug. Her hands were clenched shut, and I pried open her left hand, placing the slug in her open palm. "That's a souvenir. We all keep our first stopped bullet."

"You were hit?"

"Yep. Five total. This vest stopped all five."

"You still have yours?"

I reached underneath my vest, opened my shirt pocket, and brought out the crushed bullet.

"Right here," I said, holding it up in front of her. "This was the first one."

She was looking at me with wide eyes.

"Your vest stopped the round. Looks to be a small caliber, most likely a twenty-two. You had the breath knocked out of you, and your body went into panic mode. That's totally normal. You'll have a bruise, but that's it."

"You're sure?"

"Absolutely."

"Okay. Thanks for checking."

I stood, but she grabbed my hand and held on.

I STAYED WITH HER UNTIL her breathing had returned to normal. I slipped the vest back over her head, cinched it, offered my hand, and helped bring her vertical.

I took my rifle back from Melissa, attached it to the sling, and slung it to the side. "Everyone okay?" I asked, taking out the Glock and walking toward the corner and my original five men. Not getting any responses, I told them to give me a comms check.

"I'm good," Melissa reported back. "I'll go check on our two shooters."

"Check your alleyway shooter and forget about the window shooter. Kathy, position close-in to our three vehicles. Melissa, I don't want you going into that building. It takes three to clear a building and we don't have time for that. When you're done with alleyway guy, please check on the three that came up behind us then form up with Kathy."

"Okay. Checking on the alleyway shooter."

"Checking in," Kathy responded, her voice cracking with pent-up emotion.

"I'm good," from Renee.

"They shot out my rear driver-side passenger-door window," Kris said, sounding truly pissed off.

"Is Susan okay?"

"She is," Susan responded through Kris's comms.

"We'll take care of that window once we're on the other side of town. Renee, as soon as Kathy and Melissa are in position next to the Humvee, drive up to me and turn left at the corner. I'll be fifty yards up from the turn. Monica and Kris, please follow her."

"Alleyway shooter is dead," Melissa said. "He was a teenager, no older than fourteen or fifteen. On my way to the other three."

I could see that three of the four I'd hit in the initial burst were unmoving and most likely dead. The fourth was trying to sit up but kept slipping in the snow. His rifle lay behind him. I kicked it aside. "Where are you hit?" I asked.

"In my left bicep. And man, it hurts," he said, tears rolling down his face. He was my age, skinny, and weathered as only an outdoor worker can be. "Two tours in the fuckin' desert, dozens of engagements under my belt, all without a scratch, and here I am, shot on Main Street in my own hometown. And my family and I survived Covid, Omicron, and all the other crap thrown at us. The town lost just under two hundred to the virus. . . most of them unvaccinated. Ended up having to burn the bodies. Fuckin' hurts. But I think it may have missed bone."

"How many of you are there?"

"Shooters?"

"Yes."

"Ten: us five here, three at four or five blocks back down the road, and two in this building behind us."

Which meant we had got them all.

"With two tours under your belt, you should have known better than to run down the middle of the street," I said. "You know to hug a building."

"Roger that, sir. Stupid on my part."

"What's up ahead?" I asked.

"Whadda you mean?"

"Roadblocks, barricades, more of your buddies? That's what I mean. On 93."

"Nothin', man. We're it."

"No barricade on a bridge up ahead?"

"No, sir. We took it down earlier this morning. Too much work and too fuckin' cold. Plus, there's no walkers out there anymore."

"The bridge is now clear? Nothing to block our path?"

"It's all clear."

"You responsible for those folks hanging from the lampposts around the corner?"

"Not me. That was the sheriff's idea. They were looters, killed by the store owners. Sheriff figured, since they were dead anyway, why not hang 'em up as a deterrent to others. Worked too."

"That's the first lie you've told me."

"I aint lying to you, I swear," he said, looking me in the eyes.

"The bodies had their hands zip-tied behind them. Why zip-tie dead people?"

"Zip-tied? Seriously?"

"Seriously. Those people were alive when they were strung up, including the children."

"Then the sheriff lied to me," he said. "I've been mannin' the bridge barricade for four days. Left my wife and two kids at home. I was told I had to help man the bridge or the sheriff wouldn't give us food and water. I truly had no choice."

"Why kill the kids?"

"I don't know. All I can say is the world's totally fucked up. And the fuck-ups are runnin' loose and carefree. You could have asked the sheriff, but that's the sheriff lyin' behind that car over there."

The three trucks came up behind us and stopped, exhaust vapor clouds billowing behind each one. The snow was falling as hard as I think I'd ever seen snow fall. The Humvee was a mere thirty feet away, but I could only make out a vague outline. Kathy took a knee and stood overwatch. Melissa strode over to where I stood over the wounded man.

"The three are dead. Who's this?" she asked, looking down at the guy on the ground.

"I had five running up to help the two that engaged you. I believe he might be the sole survivor. Could you check the other four and make sure they're out of commission?"

"Sure," she answered and left to check.

"I'm going to let you go," I said, reaching down and offering him my hand. He grabbed hold with his good hand, and I hauled him up. "Get home to your family. You have weapons at home?"

"I do. And not the pieces of shit that the sheriff gave me. I figured they'd come looking for weapons and ammo, and sure enough they did. I'd hid them in the garage."

A shot rang out. Melissa was standing over the sheriff and putting her Glock away. She saw us looking at her, said, "The rest are dead, but she was alive and suffering."

"The sheriff was a woman?" I asked him.

"Yeah. Mean as can be. She wanted to be queen of the valley and had the balls to make it happen."

"You letting him go?" Melissa asked, striding up to us.

"Yes," I answered her.

To him, I said, "Go, now. Back to the gas station."

"Thank you, sir. God bless you."

He turned and walked toward the Parkman Brothers station, then stopped and turned back to us. He pointed to the closest dead man. "He has a nice personal sidearm. May I take it? The sheriff confiscated the one weapon I had on me when they came knocking—my Glock."

I hesitated with my answer but could understand wanting a personal defense weapon to replace a government confiscated one. "Sure."

"You won't be able to remove that with one hand. I'll get it for you," Melissa offered. "Back up ten paces."

The man backed up as told and watched as Melissa removed the dead man's belt and holster. The belt had three additional magazines in a three-in-a-row magazine pouch.

Melissa carried the belt around the corner and was back a minute later.

"I put it on the sidewalk in front of the alley where one of your now dead friends tried to kill us. Good thing they couldn't shoot for shit. You stay right where you are until we turn that corner up there. If you make one move, you'll end up like your friends. Understand?"

"Yes, ma'am."

We turned and made our way to the waiting vehicles. "You're getting soft in your old age, tough guy," Melissa said, punching my arm.

"He said he was forced into helping the sheriff. I believe him. He's also got a family waiting for him at home. But wait one second—you're calling *me* a softie? You just removed a dead man's weapon belt for someone you don't even know. I half expected you to put a bullet through his head or, at the least, make him strip and walk home naked."

"Hey, I can be forgiving on occasion," she said, with a chuckle. "And as for stripping, he's a he, not a she. I didn't want to see his skinny ass, did you?"

"Nope."

"I didn't think so. You want me to gather up their weapons?"

"No. But thanks for asking. Normally, I'd say yes, but I just want to get on our way." I keyed the comms and told the women to load up.

I walked around the Humvee's front bumper and opened the front passenger door. I raised my rifle and performed one last scan with the thermal. Seeing no heat signatures other than the four dead attackers and the wounded man, I climbed in.

I keyed the comms and asked if Kathy and Melissa had retrieved their dropped magazines.

"Yes," Melissa answered.

"Ah, no," from Kathy. "Sorry. Let me get them."

We waited for the word from Kathy, and when it came, Renee took off, swinging wide right to avoid running over the bodies and the man I'd spared. I watched in the sideview mirror to make sure that the two following trucks were with us. Renee took an immediate right and we were on 93 and getting up to thirty-five, as fast as I thought safe in the deepening snow. A minute later, we passed a True Value hardware store on our right. It appeared to be untouched by looters. I saw a candle flickering in one of the large plate glass windows and a figure staring out at us.

And then we were driving between two ancient lava fields that stretched away for miles.

"Kris, we'll fix your window once we cross the bridge they had barricaded."

"Thanks, it's friggin' cold in here," Susan shouted over the sound of rushing wind. "Snow is actually accumulating on the seats."

"What's that? I can't hear you over the sound of all that wind," Renee said.

"Not funny," Kris shot back.

To me, Renee said, with a wide grin, "I thought it was."

We passed the Shoshone Cemetery on the left and then crossed the bridge thirty seconds later. An old yellow school bus blocked the right-hand lane, but the left was clear. An almost new Ford Expedition that had probably been used to block the westbound lane, had been pushed aside.

I removed the thermal from my rifle, brought it up, and scanned ahead. Clear.

"Let's stop here, Renee.

"Okay, Kris. I'll fix your window now. Obviously, I can't replace the glass, but there's plenty of cardboard I can cut to size. I'll wrap the cardboard in a plastic garbage bag and use duct tape to hold everything in place. Should work fine.

"While I'm doing that, Melissa and Kathy, reload your empty magazines. Monica, please stand overwatch."

Renee, followed by Greta, got out of the Humvee and stretched. "Jon, give me your empty mags and I'll load them for you."

I handed Renee the two empty mags. "Thanks, babe."

"You're welcome. Do I have time to boil some water for coffee and a quick Mountain House meal?"

"We can always make time for coffee," I replied. "And a warm meal sounds great. Don't forget we still have those sandwiches Molly made for us."

"It's too cold for sandwiches. Hot Mountain House meals sound much better.

"Everyone, I'm boiling water for coffee and a freeze-dried meal. Place your orders!" Renee announced over the comms.

Greta must have sensed it was mealtime for she was dancing and prancing around Renee. Renee got her water and food bowls and filled both. She placed them on the ground next the trailer and Greta attacked the food first and then lapped up the water.

On my way to the ranch truck, I spotted Kathy behind the Cruiser loading her magazines.

"It's not every day you get in a firefight, let alone get hit in one. How are you?" I asked her.

She kept loading her magazines, answered, "Better now than right after the firefight. That was some scary shit… I've never been more scared in my life. But you know what's weird? I wasn't scared during the fight. Just afterward."

"It's not weird, it's normal. There's so much going on in an engagement, your mind goes into hyperdrive and your body just kind of follows suit. Just so you know, I feel the same way after a firefight."

"Really? You're not just saying that."

"Nope."

She nodded and continued loading.

"Thank you, Kath. You did good back there. I like knowing I can count on you."

Thirty minutes later, with window fixed and meal eaten, I took a fresh cup of coffee and relieved Monica on overwatch.

Once Monica had eaten, we packed and got back underway. The road was ruler-straight, but gently undulated up and down—as if we were on one of those kiddy county-fair roller coasters. The roadway wove its way mile after mile over the contours of the lava flows.

It was still snowing without letup. There was a good foot of fresh, powdery snow on the roadway. The shoulder had narrowed and there was a ten-foot drop to the surrounding landscape. As a precaution, I had Renee reduce our speed to thirty.

The roadway eventually leveled off, and there was no more roller-coaster effect. We were passing quite a few abandoned cars and pickups, and I had to remind myself that in these more rural agricultural areas, folks were up and out of the house hours before city folks had even opened their eyes for the day.

Fifteen minutes later, we drove past the town of Richfield, Idaho. The town itself was located north of the roadway, but the businesses on the main highway appeared intact. On the east end of town, we passed an LDS church on the left. There were several burn barrels burning brightly in the parking lot, and at least a dozen people were huddled around them for warmth. There was a break in lava fields, and for the next thirty miles, we passed dozens, maybe even a hundred farmhouses. And like the area around Marsing, the huge, and now useless, farm-equipment giants were sitting dead in the fields.

It was now five thirty, and the first rays of daylight would soon start to show over the eastern horizon.

We passed without incident through the town of Carey. There were several retail stores, churches, and a post office on the main drag. All appeared intact and unmolested. And big surprise, the number of abandoned vehicles east of town dropped dramatically. But then you really couldn't farm lava fields. Because that's what was out here. . . nothing but lava fields.

A few minutes later, we passed a viewing area turnout for the Craters of the Moon National Monument. A quarter mile past the viewing area was a sign saying the Craters of the Moon Visitor Center was eight miles ahead.

"You see that sign?" Monica asked over the comms. "It might be a good place to spend the day."

"I second that," a tired-sounding Kris said.

"No harm in checking it out," I said.

Ten minutes later, we were approaching the entrance road to the visitor center and campground.

I could see the center up on our right. "Renee, pull over and stop. I want to scan the building and surrounding grounds with the thermal."

Once stopped, I stepped out and scanned a full 360 degrees, giving extra time on the visitors' main building and parking lots.

"Nothing shows on the thermal," I reported over the comms, as I got back in the Humvee. "And there are no tire tracks in the snow. Kris and Monica, stay here on the highway. Susan and Melissa, set up a close-in overwatch. Renee and I are going to drive up and check out the building and surroundings. I'll let you know when it's okay to join us."

I had Renee turn right onto the entrance road. We drove slowly through the center's main parking lot and then drove around to the building's rear parking area.

"Stop here, Renee. I'm going to check it out on foot. With Greta's help, of course."

I opened the passenger door and Greta jumped to the ground, circled four or five times, then sat next to me waiting for the fun to begin. I reached back in and retrieved the M4.

"Is it too cold for Greta?" Renee asked before I could shut the door. "Will the snow be too cold on her paws?"

I looked at Greta and she seemed unconcerned with the cold. Vapor formed with every breath she exhaled, but she wasn't whining or shivering.

"I think she'll be okay," I answered, as I attached the M4 to the sling. "I'll get her back to you as soon as possible. But I really could use her help in clearing the building."

"Go check. I'll keep the engine and heater on for you. Be careful."

"Will do. Let's go, Greta."

I lowered the NVs and started the search by checking the building's rear doors. All were locked. We made our way around the building's southern side and stood in the main parking lot facing the center. The building's façade was mostly glass with some dividing walls made of brick or stone. I brought the thermal up and scanned every inch, and again came up clear.

The main entrance door had been shattered, but all the other glass windows and doors were intact. I worried about Greta's bare paws on the broken glass, but approaching the door, I could see that it was tempered and wouldn't hurt her. I tried opening the door, but it was locked. I turned sideways and slipped through the opening. Greta followed, looked up at me waiting for the search command, and after receiving it, took off.

The building was long and narrow, the front all glass with a ten-foot-wide corridor running the entire length of the building. Exhibit rooms, a gift shop, and manager's office were set to the left, with their entrances off the corridor.

I watched Greta enter then exit each room. Twenty seconds later, she emerged from the furthest room and ran back up the corridor to my side. Her tail thumped and she remained silent, which I took to mean all was clear. I reached down and rubbed behind her ears.

I retraced Greta's path and, sure enough, found the building empty. Besides the front door, the only other damage I found was an overturned and emptied vending machine in the gift shop.

The building's interior was cold, but as it was protected from the wind, much warmer than outside. We could set up the propane space heater in the gift shop, shut the doors leading to the corridor, and get it quickly warmed. There was plenty of floor space for sleeping pads and bags. And best of all: overwatch could be done from inside the building and out of the wind.

I had a good view of the Cruiser and ranch truck idling out on the highway. I keyed the comms, said, "Monica and Kris, drive up and park next to Renee behind the building. Try and drive in the ruts the Humvee made. If this snowfall keeps up, our tracks will be covered in a couple of hours."

"Roger that," Monica responded.

I made my way to the rear of the gift shop and opened the exit door. The Humvee was parked ten feet away. I opened the passenger door and waved Greta in.

"It's going to work out fine," I told Renee, watching Greta jump to floorboard to seat to center console. "We'll set up in the gift shop. It's a large space which will allow us plenty of room to lay out our sleeping pads and bags, though not so large that our space heater will have a problem warming it up."

"Good, because I'm ready for a nap."

"Go ahead and unload what you think we'll need for the day. There's a loop road and campground further down the access road that needs checking out. I'll be back in twenty minutes or so. Show the ladies the door I came out of and have them set up in that room. Okay?"

"Sure. You want some company on your stroll?"

"Thanks, but you go ahead and get set up. Then warm up."

I made my way out of the parking lot. The Cruiser and ranch truck drove by, and I watched them park next to the Humvee. All three engines shut down and an eerie silence fell over the place. I suddenly felt something strange come over me. I shook off the heebie-jeebies, turned left out of the parking lot, and made my way down the hill. There were no tire tracks or footprints in the snow. The road was narrow, barely two lanes wide, and wove between black, snow-covered lava flows. I passed the guard shack and noted that the gate arm was up.

I turned right past the guard shack and, with the thermal, scanned the road ahead. A hundred yards down the road, I came to a football-field-sized open area which a signpost said was for the use of group campers. The NVs picked up at least a dozen large semi-trailers and the same number of camper trailers—all Airstreams. On the side of each semi-trailer was the name, Century Five Productions, Burbank California.

I'd stumbled upon a film production location. I took a knee and thermal-scanned the entire meadow. Nothing. The place was empty. I did a quick search and found no bodies on the ground or in any of the travel trailers, though the Airstreams had been ransacked. I heard a squeak behind me, turned, and saw that one of the semi-trailer's doors was swinging back and forth in the wind. I made my way to the trailer, swung open the door, and wished I hadn't. For inside, stacked six-foot-high, were too many bodies to count. If I had to guess, I'd say sixty to seventy. The bodies that were visible had been torn apart by bullet impacts. Bullet holes, too many to begin to count, riddled the three sides of the trailer, from knee height to ceiling. The only round that could inflict the kind of damage I was looking at was the .50-caliber. I felt objects under the snow, kneeled, and swept away almost a foot of snow. A couple of hundred empty .50-caliber rifle cartridges littered the area in front of the trailer doors. These people had been herded into the trailer and then executed.

I climbed into the trailer and checked the bodies closest to the doors. The bodies were frozen solid and had formed a solid mass of intertwined arms and legs. I tried—but found it impossible—to move them. I cut my search short as I knew I wasn't going to find any survivors.

I jumped to the ground, shut the doors, and searched the other semi-trailers. All held location equipment, except for two: a dormitory and the canteen. At fifty-four-foot-long and having to feed sixty plus folks three meals a day for who knows how long, the kitchen canteen must have held a lot of food supplies. It had been stripped bare.

I keyed the comms. "Who's on overwatch?"

"Monica is in front and I'm in back," Melissa answered.

"Kathy, can you take over for Melissa? Melissa, drive the Cruiser down the access road and I'll meet you at the guard shack."

"Will do," Melissa answered.

"Everything okay?" Renee asked.

"For us, yes. For others, not so much," I answered. "I'll explain when I see you."

"Very cryptic, but okay. Be careful, babe."

"Always."

SIX

I met Melissa at the guard shack and had her drive to the clearing. I showed her the trailer with the bodies and then the canteen truck. We drove the loop road with me thermal-scanning the entire time. We found no one or anything of interest. We were back at the visitor center thirty minutes later.

The women had the space heater blasting and the room was toasty warm. The sleeping pads and bags had been set up and water was boiling for meals and coffee for those who wanted some.

I brought in Kathy and Monica and relayed to the group what I'd found.

"Sixty people?" Renee asked in obvious amazement.

"Yes," Melissa answered. "Maybe more. You can't really count them; they're frozen, and all the arms and legs are intertwined—it's one big mass of bodies."

"How long do you think they've been in the trailer?" Monica asked.

"No idea. How long does it take for a human body to freeze?" I asked. "It's a pure guess, but at these temps, maybe two days. I don't know."

Kris, sitting in one of the camp chairs, asked, "So whoever killed them is most likely long gone. Right? And won't be coming back because there's nothing here?"

"Correct. There is nothing left of value. They won't be back."

"Good," Kris said in obvious relief.

"Do we want to take one of the Airstreams?" Susan asked. "I mean, it's an Airstream. And you can't get better than Airstream. Did the killers take the propane tanks? And what about clothes and stuff on the inside?"

"As far as taking one of the trailers goes, I like the idea, and would if we were closer to the ranch. But we're too far away. If at some time in the future, we find ourselves in need of extra living quarters, we can always come back and get them. And we can check the propane tanks later today. Let's set up our usual overwatch rotation, starting now. Set up in the corridor down at this end. Get the binoculars, and glass the highway and access road. No one is coming at us from the back."

"Before we hit the sack, I want you to show me the death trailer," Renee said.

I told the other women what we were doing and asked if they wanted to come. I had no takers, and who could blame them?

We took Greta with us and walked the hill down to the field. Fifteen minutes later, we were on our way back to the center when Greta whined, broke off from us, and circled the guard shack. She disappeared behind the small building, and a few seconds later, we heard her whimpering.

We found her sitting next to two bodies that were jammed up against the shack's rear wall, underneath the roof's eaves.

Greta looked up at us and whimpered again. "Why is she whimpering?" Renee asked.

"Let's find out," I said, kneeling for a closer look. There was a man's body half-lying atop a woman, his arm wrapped around her waist. Both were fully clothed, though the man only wore a long-sleeve sweater on his top half. The man was nearly frozen, and I was careful when I moved him. Once I had him rolled off the woman and onto his back, his arm remained in the same frozen looped position.

"I've never seen a frozen body before. Have you?" Renee asked.

"Once, in the mountains of Afghanistan. But he'd been hit with a grenade and was almost unrecognizable as human."

I removed my gloves, felt for a pulse on the man's neck, and found none. The woman was on her back and lying on an outdoor lounge cushion. She was fully dressed and also wrapped in a man-size parka—*probably this man's*. Greta stood, lowered her head, and licked the woman's cheek. The dog sat down again and looked up at us.

"What the heck is she doing?" Renee asked.

I felt for a pulse and found none. I flipped up my NVs and dug in my pocket for one of Burt's headlamps. I turned it on and could see that the woman's skin, lips, and fingers had colored to a bluish tint. I took hold of her hand to check for a pulse in her wrist. I was ready to give up when one of her fingers wrapped around one of mine and wouldn't let go.

"She's alive, Renee. Though I can't feel a pulse."

"She's probably suffering from hypothermia."

"Definitely. And a severe case at that. Do you want to try and save her?" I asked. "If so, we're looking at a full day or two. Most likely longer."

She answered yes without hesitation.

I keyed the comms and explained the situation. I asked for Melissa and Kris to drive the ranch truck down to the guard shack.

I looked at Renee. "We'll put her in the back seat and take her up to the visitor center. She's probably too far gone but—"

"We have to try, Jon. I've seen too much death these past few days. It would be nice to actually save a life rather than take one."

"Agreed." I keyed the comms, said, "Susan, look around and see if there is some type of cushion that we can use as a mattress. Bring in the extra sleeping bags and zip two together. Bring the water filter kit in and the largest pots we have. We need to be heating water constantly for the next day or so. We'll need the medical kit, too."

Melissa and Kris soon showed up in the ranch truck.

"We need to place her on the rear seat. According to my physician sister, moving a person suffering severe hypothermia is one of the worst things you can do, but we need to bring her up to the visitor center. Melissa and I will lift her mid-section. Renee, put your hands under her head and don't let it hang. Kris, you grab ahold of her ankles and lift, and if you feel strain on your wounds, say something and we'll stop."

It wasn't pretty, but we managed to lift her up and place her in the back seat. We drove to the center's back door and reversed the loading procedure. Susan had found eight couch seat-cushions for use as a mattress. We placed her on the cushions and stepped back. The cushions made a mattress that looked to be about queen-sized. Perfect.

"Kris, in the medical kit there should be a pair of cutting scissors. Find it and start cutting her clothes off. Everything."

"Why not just take her clothes off?" Kathy asked.

"Too much movement," I answered. "Listen, everyone, I watched my sister save a ranch hand's ten-year-old daughter suffering from hypothermia. She'd fallen through the ice in a winter lake and was in the water for close to thirty minutes before being pulled out. She was in the same shape as this woman. We can save her but keeping her still is imperative. Too much movement can cause cardiac arrest. My sister kept telling us it's all about blood movement. Warming up the body is just a way to get blood to the heart."

"Cut her clothes off, Kris. Susan, please get all the stoves going and heat as much water as you can. Empty three water bottles into a pot and save the bottles and tops as we're going to reuse them. Get the water filter out—it's going to become a giant hot water bottle."

I found an old-fashioned thermometer in the medical kit and placed it under the woman's tongue. Kris removed the last of the woman's clothes while I waited for the thermometer to have enough time for a good reading. I visually checked for entry wounds and didn't see any. The woman looked to be in her mid-thirties, five foot six or seven, 130 pounds, and with very long brunette hair.

"Was there any identification in her pockets?"

"Nothing," Kris answered.

"Her temp is eighty-five," I said aloud. "That's low, for sure, but survivable. If it was in the mid to low seventies, she would need an emergency room fully equipped to handle hypothermic cases. But at this temp, I think we can help her."

"At least we're making an attempt," Renee said.

The water was just starting to steam. "Susan, turn the stove off, and carefully fill the filter bag. Then fill the three empty water bottles."

I turned back to the other women. "We need to slide the sleeping bag under her."

We got that done, and I asked for the first two volunteers.

Blank stares greeted my request. "We need two of you to strip and climb into the sleeping bag with her—one in front and one in back," I explained. "Bare chests, so jog bras off. You can leave your underwear on."

Continued silence greeted my request.

"Now is not the time for modesty—she needs your body heat. There's nothing you'll be showing me that I haven't seen before. We'll put her on her side and you'll both need to mold your bodies to hers. The water bladder goes on her chest and one water bottle under each armpit. The third bottle goes on her groin."

"I'll do it," Renee said, taking her jacket off.

Monica held her hand up. "I'll do it, too," she said, slipping her boots off and starting to undress.

"I'll take the next shift," Melissa said, "as long as I can be in front.

"I'll join you, Melissa," Susan said, "and I'll take her back."

I put pillows down. "If you can, sleep. She's not going to move."

We gently moved the woman onto her side. Renee slid in front and Monica behind.

"My God she's freezing cold," Monica said. "I've never felt anyone this cold before. And believe me when I say I've shared a bed with more than a few pairs of cold feet."

I gathered the woman's hair, grabbed a towel, and wrapped it around her head, leaving her face free of any covering. I took the three water bottles and placed them under her armpits and between her legs. Susan handed me the water filter bladder, and I placed it between the woman chest and Renee's. Kathy then zipped up the sleeping bag.

"How is it?" I asked the two volunteers.

Both answered "Cold".

"You'll warm up. Give it a few minutes. We'll refill the bottles and bladder every hour. Oh, and don't massage her skin. That's a very bad thing."

"Why would that be a bad thing?" Monica asked.

"Blood will flow to the massaged area and not the heart."

"Okay. Sorry, no massage for you," she whispered in the woman's ear, imitating the Nazi Soup character from *Seinfeld*.

I smiled at the attempt to lighten things up. Monica had always been a rock in stressful times at work, and it was no different now.

I made coffee for those that wanted some. "I'm going to stand overwatch," I announced.

"I'll relieve you whenever you're ready to come in," Kathy said.

"Sounds like a plan. Don't forget to keep those bottles filled with warm water. And take her temp at the same time you change the water."

It was now a little after eight in the morning.

DAY SEVEN

MOVIE STAR. WOMEN IN CHARGE. AMBUSH & REVENGE.
PJ & JANE. PLANE. EX-FIANCE. LOOTERS. RANCH.

SEVEN

As far as overwatches go, the one here had to be the most comfortable I'd ever manned. I'd rolled the facility manager's desk chair to the western most section of the glass-walled corridor and found an unopened carboard carton of plush bears in the gift shop's small storeroom and used it as an ottoman. The inside temperature was cold, for sure, but this far away from the broken-out door, I was comfortable in my down jacket, gloves, and wool beanie hat.

The snow was still falling, and if possible, seemed to be falling heavier now than before. Our tire tracks were completely covered, which was a good thing, but I was beginning to worry that there might be too much on the highway for us to make our way through.

I brought the binoculars up and glassed the highway and access road. I could barely see the highway through the falling snow.

It was now noon. I was bone-tired and needed to close my eyes for a few hours. I'd been checking the ladies at the top of every hour. They'd been refilling the bottles and filter bladder with hot water hourly and had taken the woman's temperature four times now. The latest reading was eighty-nine. Renee and Monica switched out with Melissa and Susan. But before I let Susan climb into the sleeping bag, I cleaned her wound and applied a new bandage.

"Susan, put a clean T-shirt on. I'm worried about bacteria getting in the wound," I told her as I packed up the med kit.

"Isn't it supposed to be skin on skin?"

"It should be, but with your wound, you need something between you and her. A T-shirt will be fine."

"Okay."

"Thank you."

"You're welcome."

"Don't you two start that tit-for-tat bullshit again," Renee admonished.

"Yes, Mommy," Susan said, slipping a T-shirt over her head and zipping her side of the bag closed.

Kathy relieved me on overwatch.

I walked through the gift shop and let myself out the back door. I stepped up onto the Cruiser's passenger-side running board and unlocked the Thule cargo box. The rear sprang up, and I reached inside, taking hold of a small, black faraday bag. I unzipped the bag and took out my old iPhone, a small Bluetooth speaker, and three backup battery power bars. I resealed the faraday bag, then shut and locked the cargo box.

Back inside the gift shop, all eyes followed me as I connected one of the power bars to the old iPhone 8, put my thumb over the phone's power button, and holding my breath, watched as it powered up. *Hell yeah!* I hit the music icon and selected the purchased playlist. I clicked shuffle and the opening to Sting's "Fields of Gold" started up, which brought smiles and thank-yous from all those present.

I hit the power button on the external Bluetooth speaker, hit the iPhone's settings, and clicked the Bluetooth speaker icon. Music filled the room.

I lay down and, listening to Sting's mellow voice, fell instantly asleep.

───────────

"WAKE UP, JON." I FELT my shoulder being rocked and opened my eyes to see Renee kneeling over me. I brought my watch up but was having a hard time seeing the dial. I heard Led Zeppelin's "Going to California" playing in the background.

"It's five o'clock in the afternoon," she said. "You've been sleeping for five hours." She leaned over and brought her lips to my ear. "You are never going to believe who our semi-frozen patient is."

"Who?"

"Dawn Tillman."

"We're talking about *the* Dawn Tillman? The actress?"

"Yep. One and the same."

"How do you know?"

"Well, she's no longer blue, so I recognized her. She then told us her name."

"She's awake?"

"She is now. Yes."

I looked over at the makeshift warming bed and could see Kris on one side and Kathy on the other.

Renee saw me looking. "I changed Kris's bandages and got her a clean T-shirt."

"Thank you, hon. What's our patient's temp?" I asked.

"Ninety-five point something."

"Wow, she's really warming up. Is she slurring her words?"

"A little. And she's confused about things."

"That's normal. Okay, let me get up."

I swung my feet around and realized I'd fallen asleep with my boots on. And my vest. My rifle was leaning against a wall near the bottom of the sleeping pad next to a sleeping Greta.

Renee handed me a cup of coffee, said, "Just made it."

"You are a godsend," I said, cupping my hands around the mug and kissing her. "I might have to keep you around."

"Well, I hope so, mister."

"Who's on overwatch?"

"Susan. For about two hours now. We want to know if we're leaving tonight?"

"Let me look at her, and then we'll discuss and decide. Deal?"

"Deal."

"Does she know that she's suffered hypothermia?"

"We told her. While you were asleep, Melissa and I gathered the empty gas cans, drove down to the production company trailers, and siphoned diesel from one of the semi-trucks. The ranch truck and Humvee's tanks are full. And the jerry cans are full too. We found twenty full gasoline jerry cans in the generator trailer, so now the Cruiser is gassed up as well. We also took the full propane tanks off the Airstreams. We now have eleven full, grill-sized propane tanks in our trailer."

"You two did all that?" I asked a smiling Renee.

"We did. We also found Dawn's trailer and put together a backpack with some of her stuff. She now has clean clothes to put on."

I smiled up at her, draped my arm around her waist, and brought her down onto my lap.

"You're amazing, babe," I told her. I planted a long kiss on her lips, all the while holding my coffee mug steady. "I love you."

"Not nearly as much as I love you," she said.

"Jeez louise, you two," Melissa said from two sleeping bags down. "You could write dialogue for some cheesy daytime soap opera."

From across the room, I heard a voice I vaguely recognized, say, "I think it's cute."

I patted Renee's behind and lifted her up off my lap. She stood, and together, we made our way over to the three women in the sleeping bag.

"Kris and Kathy, you two can crawl on out of there now," I said. "Thanks for donating some much-needed warmth."

"Yes, thank you. I can now say I've been in an all-female threesome," Dawn said, smiling.

While they extricated themselves from the sleeping bag, I stuck the thermometer under the actress's tongue. She sure looked like the famous actress now.

"You two get any sleep in there?" I asked, addressing the question to Kathy and Kris.

Both confirmed they had slept.

"Monica, will you heat some water? Once it starts to steam, pour some in a mug and then put six or seven packets of sugar in it."

"I can make tea or coffee if you want," she answered.

"No, water is good. Nothing caffeinated." Then. "I need to check you. May I do that?" I asked Dawn.

She nodded her assent.

I gently unwrapped the bath towel from her head. I checked both her ears. Normal color had returned to both. Her eyes followed my every movement.

"Your ears, lips, and skin have returned to a normal color. When we found you, your color could best be described as Smurf-blue."

I lowered the sleeping bag to her feet and asked her to lie on her back, which she did. I checked her toes and had her wiggle them. I removed the bottled water from between her legs and then the two under her armpits. I took the makeshift hot water bottle off her chest and checked her overall color. Her breasts were vivid white and contrasted with her general overall tan. I covered her back up.

I removed the thermometer. "Ninety-six point five. That's close to my normal temperature. By the way, I'm Jon. Have you met the rest of the group?" I asked.

"Nice to meet you, Jon. And I have met them."

"Can you tell me their names?"

"Kris, Kathy, Renee, Monica, Susan, and. . . and. . . ah. . . Melissa. Was that a test? Did I pass?"

"It was and you did. You feel like sitting up?"

"I do."

"Let me help you sit—"

"I'd like a T-shirt first," she said, smiling that world-famous grin at me. "Although you've already seen all the goods."

"Jon, stand aside. Let me help her," Renee said.

I stood aside. "Your limbs will probably be sore. Go slow," I said.

Renee helped her get the T-shirt on, then stood behind her, and with a hand under each arm lifted her into a sitting position against the wall. Monica then handed her the warm sugar water.

She took tentative sips, then gulps, and had the cup emptied in no time.

"Are you military?" Dawn asked.

"No," Renee answered. "None of us are."

"Jon is retired Special Forces and the rest of us are his loyal civilian warriors," Kathy explained.

"And fighters, each of you," I said.

"Cool," she replied. "And all the gear and weapons?"

"My good friend and his dad own a gun and tactical store in Las Vegas. He set us up. The idea was that we appear to be military so that we're more likely to be left alone."

"We had free rein to take anything we wanted," Monica said. "What you see here is just a small fraction of the gear he set us up with."

"Let me tell her a few things, guys," I said, and waited for them to quiet down. "My sister is an emergency room physician. A few years ago, I watched her work on a young girl who was suffering severe hypothermia, so I sorta kinda know what to look for. First off, you're going to be fine. You'll be stiff and sore for a couple of days. You will also be slurring and confusing your words. But other than that, you should be good to go. Keep hydrating. We have plenty of bottled water, and you need to drink as much as possible. You're one very lucky woman. If Greta, the lovely lady sleeping over there, hadn't found you, you'd have died. Do you remember anything about what happened to you and your group?"

"The power had gone out, our generators had stopped working, and none of the vehicles would start. All our cell phones were dead. We knew something was terribly wrong when the production company's satellite phones failed to turn on.

"The weather was okay for the first couple of days, then it started to rain and got very cold. The Airstreams' heaters still worked though, and we crammed everyone into the twelve trailers. The film's director and twelve of our crew set out to get help in a town called Arco. They were confident there was safety in numbers. They never came back. Then it started snowing and got super cold.

"I'm not sure which night it happened—my sense of time seems to be messed up—but a group of men and women showed up with guns. I was walking the loop road with one of the other actors when we heard gunshots. We hid behind the guard house. Those people stayed here for two days while we stayed hidden behind the building. People would drive in and out all day long. Tony, that's the guy I was walking with, gave me his coat and tried to cover me the best he could. And that's all I remember."

Renee placed a camp chair next to Dawn and filled her in on everything we knew about the pulse and subsequent blackout. She then recounted what we'd seen and experienced on our journey. Shock was replaced with emotion when Renee told her about the trailer and its contents.

"They killed every last one?" Dawn asked, tears flowing down her cheeks. "I'm the only survivor?"

"That we know of. Yes," Renee answered. "I'm so sorry."

"Oh my God. They were all such wonderful people. Accomplished people. Caring people."

No one said anything for several minutes. The only sound was Lifehouse's "You and Me" coming out of the Bluetooth speaker.

Dawn was the first to speak. "The power is not going to come back on for a decade or longer? Seriously?"

"Probably longer," Renee answered.

"What about Canada? My work takes me all over the world, but I call Vancouver Island my home. Is the power on there?"

"At this point, we don't know how far north the pulse reached," I answered. "But doesn't most of Canada's power come from southern Canada? If so, the southern Canadian grid is down, which means that most of Canada is probably dark. Yesterday, I spoke with my folks via ham radio, and the power was out there. Our ranch is less than sixty miles from the Canadian–US border."

"Do you have family in Vancouver?" Renee asked.

"My little sister Cassie lives with me and attends college there. My mom and dad live outside Paris, and my older sister lives down on St. Thomas in the. . . the. . . ah. . . darn it, I forget where that is."

"US Virgin Islands," Melissa said, sliding a chair next to Renee and sitting.

"Don't you live with Cory Danns?" Kris asked, as she was lacing up her boots. "*People* magazine did an article on industry couples, and you and he were highlighted."

"That article was published a couple of years ago and is old news. Robert Preston Jones lives with me now. At least he did up to a few days ago when I talked to him last—although he did say he was flying to Hawaii to start filming there, but I'm not sure of the timing."

"You live with Robert Preston Jones?" Kathy asked. "The actor, Robert Preston Jones?" Her voice was filled with amazement—I'd never seen Kathy display astonishment before.

"Yes, for the last three months or so," Dawn answered with a grin. "I'm a lucky woman."

"No shit," Melissa said from across the room.

The conversation then turned more in the direction of Hollywood gossip than Dawn's current medical condition. Renee looked at me and nodded her head toward the corridor.

"I'll be right back to help you get dressed," Renee told Dawn. I followed her out and shut the door behind us. The sky was darkening, and the snow had stopped falling.

"We need to bring her with us," Renee said in such a way as to make it abundantly clear that there was to be no discussion. "If we leave her here, she'll be good as dead. Can you imagine a group of men stumbling across her and what they would do to her?"

"Unfortunately, I can. We won't leave her here. There's plenty of room for her at the ranch. Make sure you tell her where we're headed and that she knows there's a place for her."

"Thanks."

"No problem, babe. I'm going to talk with Susan."

"Okay."

Renee went back in the gift shop, and I turned and walked down the corridor toward Susan.

"Hey," she said.

"Hey back. See anything other than a bunch of snow?" I asked, as I glassed the far western horizon. It was clear sky as far as I could see.

"Nothing. It's been very quiet."

"It's certainly beautiful out there," I said. "But if it doesn't start snowing again by tomorrow morning, the sun will melt the snow on the roadway."

"Which means ice will form tomorrow night."

"Yep, which could be a big problem."

"Then we should probably get a move on. Time for a meeting?"

"Yeah. Let's go."

We found Dawn standing next to the makeshift mattress, Kris and Renee supporting her under her elbows, and Melissa sliding a pair of baggy sweatpants on her.

I brought over a camp chair and set it behind Dawn. Dawn looked at the chair and laughed. "That thing will collapse as soon I sit in it. It'll never hold my weight."

"It will. Trust us," Monica said, and with help from Kris and Renee, Dawn slowly sank down into the chair's comfortable support.

"Let's gather around for a quick meeting," I said.

Once the women were seated, I started in. "Renee, did you explain to Dawn where we're headed?"

"I did, and she'd like to come with us."

"Thank you, Jon, for the offer," Dawn said.

"You're welcome. And just for the record, my mother and two sisters are your biggest fans. When we show up at the ranch be prepared to be smothered with attention. Hell, that goes for each of you."

"That's nice. I look forward to mee. . ." Dawn sputtered out. After a few seconds of silence, her brow curled in concentration. "I'm sorry, I forgot what I was saying."

"What you're experiencing is normal after suffering hypothermia. You'll need a day or more of rest for your body to get back to normal. But enough questions. For now, just relax."

I turned my attention back to the group. "The sky's cleared and it doesn't look like there's going to be any snow falling for the next several hours."

"If there's no snow falling during the daylight hours, then chances are the sun will be out. If that happens, we're looking at melted snow on the roadway," Susan explained. "Then the melted snow will freeze overnight, and the next day, the roads will be almost impassable. It's to prevent this formation of ice that snowplows spread salt behind them."

"Which means we need to pack up now and get going," I said. "We've got another 480 miles to go. Under normal conditions, meaning dry highway with no road construction, we could make that in ten hours. Now? Maybe twelve or thirteen. But it's doable."

"Yay! Non-stop to the ranch," Kathy shouted out. Everyone joined in, and the next few minutes were spent yakking and high-fiving. I let them carry on for a few minutes longer, but then stopped the fun and had them start packing up.

I walked over to Renee and told her I'd be back in thirty minutes. "I've got something I need to take care of. I'm taking the ranch truck."

"Okay. I'll get the Humvee packed and ready to go. And thank you for setting up the music. We all appreciate it."

"You're welcome. And thanks for packing up," I said.

I grabbed the keys to the ranch truck and left the group to their packing. I stopped at our trailer, took out two gasoline jerry cans, and put them on the ranch truck's back-seat floorboard. I drove down to the trailer containing the bodies, parked, and opened the trailer's swinging doors wide. I gathered up every bedsheet and blanket I could find and soaked them with gasoline. I piled anything burnable underneath the trailer and soaked it all in gasoline as well. I threw the soaked sheets and blankets over the bodies, left a thirty-foot trail of gasoline and set it on fire. I watched as the gasoline quickly ignited and whooshed its way underneath the trailer and up and into the interior.

I stood back and watched the fire build. I'd been concerned that the fire wouldn't spread in the cold and frozen environment, but my concerns soon vanished. The bodies were engulfed in a building inferno, fueled in part by the fire beneath the wooden-floored trailer.

I drove back to the visitor center and parked. Renee saw me drive up and opened the driver's door.

"Are you okay?"

"I'm fine."

Renee pointed to the smoke drifting up into the sky. "Is that your doing?" she asked.

"Yes. The bodies. I couldn't leave them there like that."

Renee hugged me and didn't let go. "You are a good man. I love you, Jon Kristen."

"WHERE SHALL WE PUT DAWN?" Renee asked.

"In the Humvee with us," I answered. "In the back seat. It's the safest place for her."

Renee and I took Dawn's elbows and walked her out the back door to the Humvee.

"Hello, Humvee. . . Whoa, look at that thing!" Dawn exclaimed. "I did an action movie a few years ago that took place in Iraq, so I know what a Humvee is, *and* I know what that gun up there is, too. Does it actually work?"

"Oh yeah," Renee answered. "Are you hungry?"

"Starving."

"It's too late to heat up a freeze-dried meal. We do, however, have some sandwiches and chips."

"A sandwich sounds great. Thank you."

Once Dawn was belted in and eating one of Molly's sandwiches, we quickly finished loading. We were ready to head out a few minutes later.

"Everyone weaponed-up? Have extra mags? NVs on? Fuel tanks full? Give me a comms check, please," I said.

Each checked in, and we were good to go.

"I want to get to Highway 75 without stopping. That's almost a hundred miles. Does anyone need a last-minute potty break before we head out?" I asked.

"I'm good, Daddy," from Monica.

After the laughter had died down, there were no takers.

I drove out the rear parking lot and over the first of two speed bumps. "Whoops, sorry, I've gotta tinkle—it's been like three days," Dawn said. "And that speed bump just brought it on."

"Stopping," I said.

"I need to sorta hurry," Dawn said. "Sorry. I'm so sorry."

"No need to be sorry," Renee said, hustling to help her out of the back seat. Renee supported Dawn while she did her business, then helped her climb back in.

Once back in the front seat, Renee thermal-scanned the highway and reported it clear.

The roadway was covered with at least eighteen inches of fresh snow. It was light, fluffy powder, and not at all the hard crusty stuff it would have been had it had a chance to melt and freeze.

The road was level and straight. I brought our speed up to thirty and kept it there. We hit the town of Arco twenty minutes later.

A Sinclair gas station on our right marked the beginning of town. It was intact and unmolested. There was no light showing and nobody out and about.

"I just saw a grove of pine trees," Melissa said, with actual excitement in her voice. "We must be getting close to the mountains."

"I'd much rather look at pine trees than barren desert, any day," Kris said.

Renee completed another scan. "The thermal is clear," she reported.

We passed an RV and trailer park on our right and then a sports bar further up on the same side of the road.

"I've got a bunch of people standing in the bar's parking lot," Renee reported.

"Heads on a swivel, people," I said.

From the parking lot, a beam of light settled on the Humvee and followed us until we were well past. It was then extinguished.

A quarter of a mile up, Renee reported another group of people on both sides of the road: the right side in a motel parking lot and the left in the parking lot of a tire store. None tried to stop us.

"Those folks further back down the road and these two groups up here create a classic choke point," I said. "The first group spots the target and the next two corrals them in. Whoever organized these folks has had military experience."

"I bet they think we're military and don't want to tangle with us," Melissa said. "I mean, who in their right mind would fire on an armed, up-armored Humvee?"

"Those folks back in Shoshone did," Monica answered. "What were they thinking?"

"Not much, obviously," Kris said. "They were young, after all, and probably felt invincible."

"You're both right," I said. "About them thinking we're military. And Kris saying they were kids. This town is well protected and seems to be in good shape. I bet we find the same thing at the other end of town."

The road curved to the right and I could see a stop sign ahead. A road sign indicated that access to Highway 93 required a left turn. Renee declared the intersection clear of any heat signatures. I went ahead and made the turn.

Highway 93 was now four lanes. There were too many tire tracks in the snow to count. They all looked recent.

"Multiple heat signatures ahead on the right next to those grain-silo-looking things," Renee reported over the comms. "And even more in the Mobil station parking lot across the street on the left. I count eleven in the Mobil station and seven by the silos."

One man left the Mobil station and planted himself in the center turn median. He put a palm up in a stop signal, opened his jacket, slowly turned in a circle, then put both palms up which I took to mean he wasn't armed. I slowed to a stop.

"Renee, scan beyond him and on both sides, please."

Over the comms, I asked the women if they could see anyone other than the groups ahead of us. "Look behind and up on rooftops as well."

"All I see are the two groups ahead on the left and right and this guy in front of us," Renee said.

"Nothing back here," Melissa reported.

"Same. Nothing," from Kris.

I took the microphone for the loudspeaker hailer, turned the volume up, said, "United States Military. You folks next to the silos and in the gas station, set your weapons down, walk to the curb, and sit your butts down with hands behind your heads. Once that happens, you there, in front of us, can approach. We have information to share with you."

"Shall I set up a close-in perimeter overwatch?" Monica asked.

"Yeah. Good idea. Set up on the left side and Kathy on the right. Keep eyes on them. I think we're good here as I'm pretty sure they're after information, not anything else. Plus, this is going to be a quick conversation."

I could see the man in front of us pointing to the group in the gas station parking lot. He was indicating with his hands to put their weapons on the ground. They walked forward, sat on the curb, and placed hands behind heads. He then turned to the silo group, and they also complied.

"There's one heat signature still at the gas station," Renee announced. "Looks to be a lone female with a rifle, hiding behind the bagged-ice vending machine."

I keyed the hailer, said, "Ma'am, step out from behind the ice machine, put your weapon down, and join your friends on the curb. Now!"

The man in the center median turned toward the station and yelled something I couldn't make out. The woman hesitated but put her weapon down and joined her buddies on the curb.

"Keep scanning, Renee."

I stepped out of the Humvee, reached back in for the rifle, and attached it to the sling. I switched comms to always-transmit so the group could hear what was said. "Renee, turn your volume up so Dawn can hear."

"Roger that."

I yelled for the man to approach. "Hands up and keep them where I can see them."

The man put both hands up with palms facing me as he continued toward us. Through the NVs I could see he was older, short, and heavy. He had the standard cowboy hat on his head and wore jeans with a matching Levi jean jacket. A smile was planted on his face.

He was twenty feet away when I told him to stop. I flipped up the NV's.

"Hello, sir, my name is—" the man started to say, the smile never wavering. *He's got to be a politician.*

"I have one question for you, sir, and I don't want to hear a bullshit answer," I said.

"Well, all right. Ask away," he said, sounding mystified. A frown had replaced the politician smile.

"Two or three days ago, a group of folks left Craters of the Moon Visitor Center and walked toward your town in search of answers and maybe some help. I want to know what happened to them."

The man's eyes grew wide, and his brow furled in concentration. He took two steps back, half-turned, and I thought he might run back to the gas station.

"It's not a trick question, sir," I said, watching his body language.

He turned back to me, said, "I take it you're talkin' bout those movie people?"

"I am."

"They're dead," he said, then quickly added, "but we didn't kill 'em."

"Tell me."

"We didn't really organize until yesterday. Before that, we were just kind of waitin' around for the power to come back on. Most folks here are Mormon and have some food stocks in their pantries, so we aren't super worried about where our next meal is gonna come from. Anyhoo, this group of folks you're askin' about, showed up lookin' for help. But what they really wanted was some water and were hopin' for answers as to what happened to the power and whatnot. We couldn't answer their questions, but we're good people here and were in the process of gatherin' some water for them when a group of armed mountain people from southern Montana showed up. We'd driven the film folks down to the RV park south of town—you passed by it on your way here—and told 'em to stay put while we gathered them some supplies."

"This story is taking too long to tell. Summarize please," I said.

"Okay. Sure. Anyhoo, this mountain group got hold of the film people, killed them for the supplies they had on them, then drove down to Craters for the supplies there. Two days later, they drove back through town and kept on goin' north. Don't know nothin' about what happened at the visitor center."

"Where are the film people now?"

"Buried. There was discussion about burning the bodies, but the ground isn't frozen yet, so we used Stan Howard's old backhoe and dug a trench."

"How do you know that's how it happened?"

"I watched them dig the hole, sir."

"No, I mean, how do you know that's how the group met their end?"

"Oh, one of the folks sittin' on the curb over there is my sister. She lives next door to the RV park and witnessed the killing. She says the killers was mainly after food."

"Still clear, Master Sergeant," Renee reported.

"How do you know they're mountain people? You stop one and ask? And how many were there?"

"I know four of the guys—I spent a summer doin' court-ordered highway trash pickup with 'em. And we got a hold of a straggler. Uh, what was the other question?"

"How many were there?

"Oh yeah. There were probably eighty or ninety that blew through here in a bunch of older-model pickups and cars. The straggler told us that their original number was closer to six hundred, but armed militias from Kalispell and Missoula have banded together, and after several encounters, had reduced that number to what came through here. According to the straggler, this Kalispell–Missoula force has established a roadblock south of Lolo. Which of course means that quite a few of those eighty or ninety can't get back to their homes and supplies. Which is why they ventured this far south."

"Why do you think it is that Arco residents didn't have their supplies taken?"

"Don't know. Don't care. After seein' what they did to that movie group, we gone ahead and mobilized. Anyone tryin' to come through Arco's gonna have to go through both sets of choke points. We're just waitin' for those yahoos to try somethin' here. We're gonna put 'em in their place downright quick, too."

I waited for him to fist bump his chest, but he didn't.

"One last question for you," I said.

"Shoot."

"Did the straggler say where they were headquartered?"

"In Salmon, Idaho. Just north of the bridge that crosses the Salmon River. They took over a hotel right there. Don't know nothin' else."

"Can I speak with the straggler?"

"Perhaps in the afterlife, sir."

"Ah, okay. Thank you for the information. Here is what we can tell you regarding the power," I said.

"Just one second, sir," the man said, holding a finger up. "My memory isn't so good—probably why I never finished high school. If it's okay with you, I'd like to bring up one of the town's schoolteachers. Sue's the smartest person I know and remembers everythin'."

"Sure. Bring her up."

The man turned to the silo group, cupped his hands around his mouth, and yelled for Sue to join him.

Sue ran over and stood next to the man, said, "What trouble have you gotten us into now, Frank?" Sue was a good twenty-five years younger than Frank, was at least six inches taller, maybe even nine inches, if you factored in the cowboy boots she wore. Frank shrunk back, and it was obvious he was afraid of her.

"Nothin', Sue. I swear," he said, looking up at the woman towering over him. "I want you to hear what the man has to say. You know I can't remember nothin'."

"It's nothing, Frank," she said, correcting him. "Nothin' is not in any dictionary I know of." She then turned her attention to me.

"Master Sergeant, I'm Sue Cleary. I'm the Arco High School principal and sixteen-year Idaho National Guard member." She took two large steps forward and extended her hand in greeting. "Master Sergeant Kristen," she said, eying my name patch. "How is it that all your electronics are working?"

"I'll get to that," I said, shaking her hand. I started in on the news.

"Jesus fuckin' Christ," Frank exclaimed at the first mention of the word nuclear. He then stared up at the night sky.

They both remained silent as I told them what we knew. I fudged the story a little by saying I'd been given the Humvee out of the pulse-protected Henderson Depot, and that we'd been ordered to escort a civilian out of Vegas. But from Vegas on, I told it exactly as it had happened.

"China," she said. "I knew that they'd make a move someday. But not this kind of move. If they think the US is going to roll over and play dead while the little fuckers come on in and take over, they have it all wrong. I bet we've already destroyed their satellites."

"I don't know anything further than what I've told you," I said. "If I were to say anything else it would be pure speculation."

"Pure what?" Frank asked.

Sue leaned over toward Frank and told him to relay the information to the two groups.

"Gather them together, Frank, and tell it just as Master Sergeant Kristen here just said it. And don't forget to tell them it could be a decade or longer before the power comes back online."

"Okay, Sue," Frank said. "And thanks for the intel, sir."

"You're welcome," I said. "Good luck to you."

We watched Frank slip and slide his way through the snow and wave in both groups of people off the curbs.

"He's not the brightest star in the night sky, but he is the richest. His great-grandfather founded the town, and his family still owns most of the better farmland for fifteen miles in every direction. He's head of the chamber of commerce, though it's more honorary than an actual functioning position."

"He told me a group of ninety or so fighters from up north killed that film crew and then drove down to the visitor center. Is that true?"

"Yes. We were in the process of putting together a care package for them when it all went down. I didn't see the fighters when they first showed up, but I did see them drive through a couple of days later on their way north. They have a half-dozen working trucks and cars. Two trucks had what looked to me to be a .50-caliber machine gun mounted on tripod swivels in the beds. Reminded me of what the insurgents had in the back of their shitty little Toyota pickup trucks."

"And another militia from further north reduced their numbers to ninety from over six hundred?" I asked. "If that's the case, then it must have been a hell of a battle."

"According to a straggler we nabbed, yes, it was. He said they call themselves the Montana Protection Force, or MPF for short. He described this MPF as an overwhelming force. He said they even have an airplane. The two forces had collided two or three times before with minimal damage and casualties, but the latest clash, up by Lolo, was by far the most damaging. The southern force, although they refer to themselves as being a militia, have retreated to Salmon, Idaho. They've taken over a hotel on the north side of the bridge that spans the Salmon River."

"Is that the only area on 93 they control?"

"If the straggler was telling the truth, and I'm pretty sure he was, then yes, that's it," she answered. "Highway 93 between Lolo and Salmon, Idaho is what some are saying is the neutral zone."

"Does the southern group have a leader?" I asked. "And how were they able to organize so quickly?"

"The leader's name is Eric Lassman. And they were already organized—had a six-year head start before the blackout. They're a white supremist group. As you might know, Montana and Idaho are rife with right-wing extremist groups."

"Have any towns between here and Salmon gotten folks together like you have?"

"Yes. Although quite a few have since come down here and joined us. We have men and women from as far north as the town of Ellis. We've got twenty or so from Mackay, the largest town south of Salmon. Since Lassman blew through here and Mackay the other day, Mackay has now formed a first reaction force of forty-five men and women. They act as a buffer between the southern group and us down here. They also provide us with advance warning."

"Advance warning? How does that work?"

"Road flares. Mountain peak to mountain peak communication—a series of eight of them. They're stationed above the town of Salmon and run all the way south to us here. We'll get at least ninety minutes warning of them leaving Salmon and thirty minutes warning that they've rolled through Mackay and are headed toward us."

"Road flares. That's pretty ingenious. Unless the clouds are low."

"Nothing is perfect, but it worked for the Indians, didn't it? Look, what I think you probably want to know is will you encounter any problems between here and Salmon. Right?"

"Yes, ma'am."

"Then the answer is no. You'll have smooth sailing between here and Salmon, though Mackay will have a roablock in place. When you arrive, get on that hailer and ask for their leader, Melinda Hughes. She's ex-military, a retired colonel no less. She's Air Force, but I don't hold that against her."

"Did you organize the choke point at the other end of town?"

"Yes."

"Nicely done," I said. "How did the first group warn you that we were coming through? Road flares?"

She answered by reaching in her parka's front pocket and bringing out an old dark-blue Motorola TALKABOUT radio. "Put them in a faraday bag years ago. And surprise, the bag worked as advertised. Don't suppose you have an extra set of those NVs lying around, or one of those?" she asked, pointing to the M4 I was cradling."

"Sorry, ma'am. We don't."

"Well, can't blame a gal for asking. Tell me, Master Sergeant Kristen, is it really as bad out there as you told it?"

"Worse, ma'am. A lot worse." I then told her about the film crew and trailer back at the visitor center.

EIGHT

I wished Ms. Cleary the best and we were on our way. The highway was covered by a least a foot of snow, but it was still the light, fluffy variety, and we had no problems making our way north. We encountered no tire tracks, which meant no vehicles had recently passed before us. Four lanes turned into two, and our constant companions, the ever-present burnt power poles, accompanied us mile after mile.

"I'm sorry about your film crew," I said, turning around to look at Dawn in the back seat. "I know it hurts to know what happened to them."

"Better knowing than not, I suppose," she replied, wiping an errant tear away. "When they didn't return, we figured something bad had happened. So, I guess I was expecting the worst and it's what I got."

Greta was sleeping with her head on Dawn's lap. Dawn was giving her ear rubs, and Greta's leg was moving in rhythm to her hand. "Looks like Greta has a new friend, Renee," I said.

"Traitor," Renee said, laughing.

I keyed the comms and told the group we should have a quiet ride for the next two or three hours. "Next stop is the intersection of Highway 75 and 93, roughly seventy-five miles north. We'll take a stretch break there. Keep an eye out for wildlife on the roadway. Hitting a deer is no laughing matter, even in a Humvee."

The moon was out in full force, and I really didn't need the NVs to navigate. I turned them off and put them on the center console. Renee saw me do it and did the same.

"Do you want me to continue to scan with the thermal?" she asked.

"Yes. Probably don't need to, but this close to home, why chance missing something ahead. Warn me if you see deer in the road."

"I can see mountains on both sides of us," Kris said over the comms. "Does the highway start to climb at any point ahead?"

"I've driven this section of 93 many times, and I don't remember any significant elevation change. It should be pretty much flat all the way into Montana."

We passed the town of Moore off to our left. Then Darlington, which consisted of a collection of abandoned bars and trailers. On the northern outskirts of Darlington, we passed several ranch houses with candles and lanterns burning in windows. It was early evening, and we saw several people standing in kitchens preparing meals.

"Looks almost like normal times, doesn't it?" Dawn said, continuing to scratch behind Greta's ears.

"Especially at night," Renee said.

"Not sure when we'll see normal again," I said.

Renee brought the thermal up and immediately said, "A bunch of deer on the shoulder. . . 200 yards ahead on the left."

"I see them. Thanks."

"What do you call a bunch of deer that have gathered together?" Renee asked.

"Is this trivia night?" I asked.

"Could be," Renee answered.

"You described it correctly in your question," Dawn said.

"I did?"

"Bunch of deer is correct. You can also say a herd, mob, or parcel. And, ah, one more, but. . ."

"A rangale," I finished for her.

"What's a rangale?" Renee asked.

"A bunch of deer," Dawn answered.

"Okay, I give up," Renee said, laughing and throwing her hands up.

Twenty minutes later, we passed through Leslie, Idaho. There were a couple of long-shuttered RV parks and a cemetery on the northern outskirts of town, but not much else.

"Next up is Mackay," Renee said, studying the map between thermal scans. "Looks like it could be substantially larger than the last few towns we've been through."

"That woman back in Arco said it was safe up to Salmon," Dawn said. "Shouldn't we be okay?"

"After what we've seen and been through for the past few days, I don't feel comfortable taking anyone at their word," Renee said.

I keyed the comms and told the others that we'd soon be hitting the town of Mackay. "Be watchful and pay attention to your sides and sixes," I said. "There's supposed to be a friendly roadblock ahead."

We started seeing warehouses, single and double-wide trailers, and small, rundown motels. I reduced our speed to forty through the several-blocks-long downtown.

"We've got a bunch of people stretched across the highway," Renee reported. "Six hundred yards ahead. They've got what looks to be sawhorses blocking the road with no way around them. There are more people in a motel parking lot on the left side of the highway. And the funny thing is, they're standing on our side of the sawhorses and looking north. It doesn't appear that they're concerned with their six. They haven't seen us."

"How can that be," Dawn said. "The moon's out, isn't it?"

I glanced up and could see clouds moving in from the west. "Looks like clouds are rolling in, which is great news for possible snow, but they're obscuring the moon up ahead. Renee, let me know when we're 200 yards out, please. You other ladies, check to our left and right. This could be a choke blockade like Arco had in place."

"I don't see any heat signatures to our sides, only those ahead of us," Renee said.

"We've got people blocking the road ahead," I announced over the comms. "We're going to stop 200 yards south of their barricade. Monica and Kathy, please set up a close-in perimeter. If they fire at us, return fire but do so over their heads. Fire off a full clip. The thermal shows no one other than those ahead of us. But keep sharp."

"Two-hundred-twenty yards out, ten, and now 200," Renee said.

I brought the Humvee to a stop. I grabbed the NVs, cycled them up, and put them on. I waited a full sixty seconds to make sure Monica and Kathy had enough time to ready their weapons and take up their overwatch positions.

Through the NVs I could see the line of folks standing behind the sawhorses. There were twelve behind the barricade and another ten a few yards away in the motel parking lot. I took the microphone for the hailer, turned the power on, and set the volume to maximum. I clicked the microphone three times in quick succession and watched the reactions to the night suddenly becoming filled with electronic clicks. Cigarettes were thrown to the ground and rifles brought up to the ready position, moving from right to left as they searched the darkness for the source of the clicks.

I let the silence grow for a full minute, just enough time for them to question if they'd actually heard what they thought they had. Several had lowered their weapons, shrugged their shoulders, and lit fresh cigs.

"US Military behind you," I said over the hailer. "Do not fire your weapons."

Several men at the barricade dropped a knee, raised weapons in the ready position, and pointed them in our direction but didn't fire. I watched the balance of the men from the motel parking lot join their fellow members at the barricade.

"Lower your weapons, now!" I said with as much authority as I could muster. Being the good soldiers they were, it was an order they ignored. "What's coming is a warning, folks."

I keyed the comms, said, "Ladies, fire a full magazine over their heads, please."

A full thirty-round clip, fired in three-round bursts, makes for a very impressive noise, especially when the bullets are flying over your head, because each passing round makes a sucking noise—one of the most terrifying sounds you will ever experience.

"The next time I ask them to fire, they'll be aiming much lower. Point your weapons down. We're not here to harm you. We're looking for Melinda Hughes. Ms. Hughes, if you're there, please identify yourself, walk forward twenty paces on this side of the barricade, and stop."

A woman in combat fatigues came forward and, with her hands, motioned for weapons to be lowered. She pointed to those that hadn't complied, and soon, all were lowered.

She then turned and strode the twenty paces as instructed.

"Thank you, ma'am," I said. "I'll join you momentarily.

"Monica and Kathy, you inserted a fresh mag?"

Yes, from both.

"Kris, Melissa, you good?" I asked.

"Good," Kris replied.

"Couldn't be better," from Melissa. "Though I'm sitting behind a steering wheel and missing all the fun."

I turned to Renee. "This won't take long. Scoot on over behind the wheel. Keep scanning with the thermal, and if you see something say something." Greta jumped from the back seat to the comms console and looked at me in anticipation.

"You want to take her?" Renee asked.

"Sure." I opened my door and stepped out into the cold night, Greta right behind me. I attached the M4 to the sling and checked that the Glock was ready to fire.

I walked the 200 yards with Greta hugging my left side, coming to a stop in front of the woman. I raised the NVs and offered her my hand. High-ranking military, such as the one standing before me, have been taught and understand proper decorum, which meant she had to shake it. She did.

Melinda Hughes was five-five, one hundred pounds max, black hair held in place in a severe bun tied at a forty-five-degree angle to the top of her head. Her black high-top combat boots were shined to a seemingly impossible military-approved sheen. She was impressive-looking. And very pissed off.

"What gave you the fucking right to fire your weapons at us?" she shouted, spittle spraying the air between us.

Greta stood and growled a warning. I put my hand on her back, said, "Easy, girl." Greta sat but never took her eyes off the woman. "Your people pointing weapons at us is what gave us the right," I replied calmly. "Based on what we've been through and witnessed the last eighteen hundred miles, I think we showed incredible restraint, ma'am."

"That's debatable, soldier."

"It's master sergeant, Colonel Hughes, ma'am."

"Are we through with the dick waving, Kristen?"

"Yes, Colonel. Though I know mine is most definitely the larger of the two," I said, with a smile planted on my face, "ma'am."

Ignoring Greta, the colonel stepped toward me, put her hand on my chest, pushed me backward, said, "Well I would fucking hope so."

And with that the ice was broken, the chain of command dismantled, at least for the duration of this visit.

"Since you asked for me by name, I assume you spoke with Sue Cleary down in Arco."

"Affirmative."

"Do you have any information that you can share with me about what's happening with our power and electronics?" she asked.

"I do," I said, and over the next several minutes told her about the nukes and all the rest, excluding of course, the truth of how we came to acquire the Humvee.

"Master Sergeant, the thermal has picked up a bright heat signature up on the ridgetop to our northwest," Renee said over the comms.

The colonel heard the exchange, turned, and glanced toward the mountains to the west. The flare was easy to spot. "That's our early warning system," she said, "which means we've got sixty minutes, give or take a few, before those yahoos from Salmon reach us."

"What's your plan, Colonel?"

"Choke point there," she said, pointing to the barricades. "We'll put some folks back up the highway and come in behind them."

Which was exactly what I thought she'd say.

"Won't work. Meaning no disrespect, Colonel, but your experience is from high in the sky. I'm a ground grunt and have seen similar situations unfold many times."

"Continue," she said. "I'm listening."

"I'm going to assume that Lassman doesn't have comms, so he'll send a couple of scout vehicles ahead of the main force. And you could easily take care of them, but if one of the scouts doesn't double back and give the all-clear signal, then the main force won't come into town in a neat and organized manner. They'll split their force in half and walk in on foot, which is going to render your plan. . . well, unworkable."

A good officer is a smart officer and is one who has learned to listen to those below her. She listened.

"What do you think we should do?"

"I saw a church on the south end of town. Send a quarter of your force down there and have them stay out of sight. The remaining force needs to take those barricades and get them put away. Then have them hide in those last six motel rooms that face the highway. Break out the windows and put as many shooters in the windows that can fit. Put five or six up on the roof, too—it's flat so won't be an issue staying up there. Pull all your vehicles to the motel's rear parking lot. I'll put our vehicles back there as well. After that second recon vehicle doubles back to the main force, I'm going to wait for the main force to come rolling through. I'll then reposition the Humvee in the front parking lot."

"They have ninety-plus men," she said. "Clearly, the odds don't favor you."

"I have a weapon system in our Humvee that more than evens the odds," I said. "We have an M134 Minigun, ma'am."

"No shit. Really?" she said excitedly, almost dancing-in-place excited.

"Yes, really. You want to go with my plan or yours?" I asked her. I probably sounded like a smartass, but it wasn't intentional.

"Yours, of course. Tell me what you want done."

"Like I said, get a quarter of your force down to that church. You have working vehicles?"

"Yes, four older pickup trucks, an old VW Bug, and believe it or not, my next-door neighbor's old Ford Edsel."

"Gotta love those old cars, especially now. Okay, put a quarter of your force at the church and have them get out of sight. The trucks too. Let those two scout vehicles go by and then let the second double back. Once that second scout turns around and goes back north to give the all-clear, bring your men out and create that choke point. You'll have to deal with that first scout later. If for some reason, remnants of the main force slip through, the church becomes the second offensive line.

"Put a man up on the north end of the motel's roof and have them watch for the main force. Once that main force appears, and the middle of the column is level with the motel, I'll reposition the gun so we'll have a full one-eighty-degree field of fire. There's nothing across the street but open fields, so we're good there."

"Anything else, Master Sergeant?"

"No. Have them do it now, and quickly. They might have sent a recon foot patrol, so we need this area to appear empty."

"I think you might be giving these mountain folks a little too much credit. Foot patrols, forward scouts? But, hey, you never know."

"Look what the mountain folks in Afghanistan accomplished," I said. "Who's in control of that country now?"

"True that." She smiled, turned toward the barricades, and started shouting orders.

"Colonel?"

"Yes," she answered, turning back to me.

"You know what that weapon will do to those men," I said. "Do you want to try and reason with them first?"

"No," she answered without hesitation. "It's too late for that bullshit." She then turned and walked back to the barricades, issuing commands the entire way.

I PUT GRETA BACK IN the Humvee and had the ladies drive our three vehicles behind the motel. "Face them toward the street," I said. "Renee, put the Humvee close to the motel corner so we can move it to the front parking lot when it's time. Melissa, please come with me. Kathy, take over for Melissa. Monica, set a close-in perimeter overwatch and cover the ranch truck and Cruiser while being mindful of your six and sides. Kris and Susan, stay put in the ranch truck."

"Roger that," Monica said.

"Will do," Kris replied.

I waited for Susan to bitch about being told to stay put, but she remained uncharacteristically quiet.

While Melissa provided overwatch, I climbed into the back of the Humvee and doubled-checked the belt feeding into the delinker. I'd done it properly and the gun was ready to go. After the demonstration back at Sig's place, I'd fed the gun from the largest of the remaining ammo cans—actually, a wood crate, holding a thousand rounds. I'd be able to fire several two-to-three-second bursts. Even one long, non-stop sustained burst. Plenty for this job.

"Is there anything I can do to help?" Dawn asked. "I'm feeling better. Really."

"If you're truly up to it, when I start firing, make sure the belt doesn't get snagged as it leaves the crate," I answered. "Like this." I put my hands under the third fold from the top and lifted the entire group. "Keep doing this, until the can is empty. The belt needs to flow into the feed chute. Once the belt is in the feed chute, it's smooth sailing."

"I can do that."

"Renee, when the time comes, and I say go, drive to the halfway point between street and motel," I said. "Point the front end at ninety degrees to the street, put it in park, and set the parking brake. I need to be able to fire from the nine o'clock to three o'clock positions. And leave the engine running—that's critical."

"Will do."

I flipped switches and powered the system. I listened to it cycle up and waited for the green light to appear. While waiting, I released the brake on the turret and rotated it a full 180 degrees. Satisfied, I reset the brake, removed the gun's weather cover and stowed it below. I grabbed my ear plugs and hung them on one of the two trigger handles. Thirty seconds later, the weapon's green ready light lit up, and it was ready to fire.

"Renee, do you have your ear protection?"

"Yep, right here," she answered, opening the center console and taking out a headset. "I have an extra for Dawn, too."

The top of the Humvee's gun turret was no more than two feet below the motel's rear roof. I took the thermal from Renee, and climbed from the top of the turret onto the motel's flat roof.

"Melissa, hop up here with me," I said. "Climb onto the top of the turret and step up to the roof. Hand me your rifle and give me your hand."

Once Melissa was on the roof, we made our way to the northern corner facing the street. I handed over the thermal. There were already several of the colonel's men lying prone on the roof's edge.

"We're going to get one chance with the Minigun," I said. "I'm the only one who knows how to reload the thing, and it would take too long for a repeat performance."

"Then we need to get it right the first time," she said, lying prone, taking five magazines out of her cargo pockets and placing them next to her.

"Yep. And we will. You're going to let what we hope are two recon vehicles drive through and wait for the returning one to pass back north and give the green light to proceed. When you see the main group of vehicles approach, keep an eye on the first one in line. Let me know when it gets to the second driveway to our right. At that point, Renee will drive the Humvee from behind the building and stop halfway to the street. I'll fire from our right to left and hopefully we'll hit the entire group of them. Got it?"

"Yes."

"You heard the woman from Arco say she thought this group coming our way had two trucks with swivel-mounted .50-caliber machine guns in the rear beds? Those trucks and the gun's operators are our main focus. Once those two are out of commission, then zero in on the other vehicles. If one of the .50-cal trucks is the last in the convoy, then fire at the shooter in the back of the bed. I might not get to him before he returns fire."

"Okay."

"Once I'm done firing the Minigun, use your rifle to take down any runners. Give us sitreps when you can. And don't let that thermal out of your sight."

"Copy that," she replied, moving the thermal directly in front of her.

"What if they don't send scouts out ahead of the main force?" she asked. "What if they come down the highway as one large force?"

"Not a problem," I answered. "Tell me, and we'll deal with it. Okay?"

"Okay."

"Thanks," I said, patting her on her shoulder and running back to where I could hop back down to the turret.

I was back on the ground and making my way to the Cruiser and ranch truck when the colonel spotted me. "Master Sergeant?" she shouted out.

"Yes, Colonel?"

She was now cradling an AR15 on a single-point sling and had a black plated vest on. "We're set up. Twelve of our people should be at the church by now and know what to do."

"Excellent," I said, looking at my watch. "If your original ETA is accurate, those scouts should be driving by in ten to fifteen minutes. Where are you positioning yourself?"

"I thought I'd be most useful in one of the motel rooms."

"Good choice. Close to all the action, but not too close. An excellent officer-like decision."

"Any last-minute advice you'd like to give me?" she asked. Her voice was shaky from pre-engagement nerves. "This is my first on-ground action."

"Sure. First, let me do my thing before you or your people get involved. If events go to plan, you won't have to fire that weapon. Breathe, stay calm, and keep your head down. Have extra magazines close by for quick reloads. Other than that, don't be a fucking hero. The town needs you."

"Good advice. Thanks," she said, letting out a deep breath.

"I'll hit the motel's roof with a rifle butt when we spot movement. Please make sure that your people know to let the scouts pass and return. That is critical to the plan's success."

"Understood. I'll talk to you after it's over." She turned and ran around the side of the building toward the motel's front parking lot. Once there, she stopped, shouted out commands to those on the rooftop and in the windows. "Do not fire until that Minigun has done it job. Got it? I'll personally shoot anyone that blows it."

I heard lots of "yes ma'am" and "got it."

I nixed double-checking the Cruiser and ranch truck—*I've got to trust them to know what to do.* I climbed up onto the Humvee's hood and then dropped into the turret. I ducked down and asked Renee and Dawn if they were ready. Both said they were.

"Comms check, everyone," I said, releasing the turret brake.

All checked in.

"Now we wait," I said.

"HOW MANY TOURS DID YOU do in the Middle East, Jon?" Dawn asked.

"Four. Two each in Iraq and Afghanistan," I answered. "And more special ops than I care to remember."

"Where did those take you?" Renee asked.

"I shouldn't really say, but I suppose all that secrecy bullshit is now out the window. I've been in South and Central America more times than I have fingers and toes. Same for Eastern Europe and Africa. And once in the Arctic, of all places."

"What was in the Arctic?" Dawn asked.

"The Chinese military had started construction of what they said was a research facility. In reality, it was a full-blown FOB. They never finished it."

"What's an FOB?" Renee asked.

"Forward operating base—for housing military equipment and personnel."

"You blew it up?" Dawn asked.

"No. Not every mission ends in *booms*. That facility was dismantled after two consecutive crews came down with mysterious headaches and other unexplained illnesses."

"Sounds like the same thing that hit some of our embassies over the last few years," Dawn said.

"Yep, what's good for the goose is good for—"

The comms came alive. "We have two southbound vehicles, six hundred yards out," Melissa said.

"Roger that," I replied. I hit the motel roof several times with my rifle butt.

"Three hundred yards," Melissa reported. "Two pickup trucks. I have a heat signature of a person standing in the back of one."

"That's going to be one of the fifties," I said. "I hope it's the one that backtracks to the main group. Otherwise, the church group's job is going to become much tougher."

"Passing by and now three hundred yards down the road. The second truck has a gun mounted in the back," Melissa said.

"Any sign of the main group?" I asked.

"Negative."

"Monica, watch your six," I said. I was still worried that they might have sent an advanced recon foot patrol.

"Roger that."

Five minutes passed. Then ten.

"We've got a vehicle headed north at high-speed. It's the .50-cal truck. Passing now," Melissa announced.

I leaned down and told the two women to get ready. I put my ear plugs in and lowered the NVs into place.

"Returning," Melissa said, three minutes later. "The .50-caliber is leading a convoy of vehicles. They'll be at the driveway in five, four, and now, Jon."

"Go, Renee," I said.

Renee drove to the front parking lot, coming to a stop halfway between the motel and road. I could see the entire convoy from this position. The leading .50-cal truck was followed by another four pickups, five passenger cars, and an old VW Microbus. The last vehicle in line was the second .50-cal truck. It was trailing the other vehicles by at least 200 yards. Which was a problem, but not insurmountable—I'd fire from left to right instead of the other way around. It was the empty two hundred yards I was worried about. I'd have to stop firing, to avoid wasting hundreds of rounds while I moved over the empty space.

I flipped the fire-switch safety cover up as I brought the gun to bear on the trailing .50-cal. Before I could press the trigger, I heard Melissa fire several bursts at the trailing .50-cal truck and could see strike sparks flying off the truck's front bumper. I swung the gun back to the right and aimed in the general direction of the lead .50-cal truck. "Dawn, here goes," I said in warning.

"Ready," she answered.

"Firing," I yelled. I pressed the trigger and watched as tracer rounds hit low. I quickly corrected for elevation and the first truck burst into flames, doors and windows exploding and flying off the truck's frame. Keeping pressure on the trigger, I swiveled to the left and continued firing as I moved down the line. I watched in the NVs as truck after truck, car after car, disintegrated in the nightmarish green glow. Every four rounds spitting out of the Minigun was a tracer round, and the night lit up with the sound and light of a laser beam death dance. I was moving the barrel from the VW Microbus to the trailing .50-cal truck when the barrels spat out their last round. The barrels came to a stop a few seconds later, steam rising from all six barrels into the cold night air. Hundreds of spent shell casings were slowly melting into the snow beside the Humvee.

Melissa must have hit the .50's driver, for the truck slowed, hit the curb with its right front tire, and gently bounced backward. Melissa continued firing, and I watched in the NVs as the .50's operator was hit and tumbled to the ground. I don't think the .50 got off a single round, so fast and furious was the ambush.

Several fleeing survivors of the Minigun's onslaught were soon cut down by the colonel's people.

Fifteen seconds after it had begun, it was over. Except for the trailing .50-cal truck, all the vehicles were on fire. The lead .50-cal truck was burning, but for now, the flames were confined to the cab and engine area. The bed, and the .50, appeared to be intact.

I watched as the colonel and her men, a few women among them, emerged from the motel's front-facing rooms.

"Colonel, you may want to retrieve that .50-cal from the lead truck," I yelled, pointing to the leading pickup. "The fire hasn't made it to the bed yet. A .50-cal and its ammo could be a future lifesaver."

"I hear you, Master Sergeant," she answered. She then pointed to three men, explained what she wanted done, and off they went toward the lead .50. She then brought in the remaining fighters, and soon four two-man units split off from the main group and set up overwatch positions. A last group, comprised of eleven fighters, split up, each member walking up to a burning vehicle. Handguns were brought out and single shots fired into the heads of dead or wounded opposition fighters. Weapons that weren't burned were gathered and brought back to the colonel. The wounded driver of the trailing .50-cal was dragged out of the cab, dumped on the ground, and shot. The truck was then driven to the colonel, and the confiscated weapons loaded into the rear bed.

I shut off the power to the Minigun, jumped to the ground, removed the earplugs, opened the Humvee driver's door, and handed them to Renee.

"You two, okay?" I asked.

"Just peachy," Dawn answered. "Not really, no. I've never seen anything so awful. And it was so quick, and. . . I guess, the word I'm searching for is: final."

"I can't believe I'm going to say this, but here goes," Renee said. "You get used to it. After you understand that, in these kinds of encounters, it really comes down to them or us. And once you've accepted that, this kind of thing becomes a memory."

The wind changed direction, and thick black smoke from the burning vehicles blew directly at us.

"What's that smell? Dawn asked. "It's terrible."

"Kris, Kathy, Monica, drive up behind us," I said over the comms. "Melissa, come on down from the roof. There's a ladder on the rear of the building."

There was no way to explain the smell away, so I answered with the truth. "What you're smelling are burning human bodies. Lots of them," I said. "Burning hair smells like sulfur, skin smells like charcoal, and iron-rich blood still inside blood vessels gives off a coppery, metallic odor. Burning human body fat smells like a side of fatty pork on the grill."

"I'm going to be sick," Dawn said. She opened the rear passenger-side door and dropped to her knees retching.

I was walking around the front of the Humvee to help her when the colonel yelled out my name. "Can you come over here for a minute?"

"I'll help Dawn, Jon," Renee said. "See what she wants."

The Cruiser and ranch truck pulled up behind the Humvee as I made my way to the colonel. She was standing twenty feet to the right of the fourth burning pickup truck.

A man and woman were on the ground surrounded by five of the colonel's fighters: four men and a lone woman. The man's left leg was missing below the knee, and he was trying to cinch a belt above the stump. No one was helping him accomplish the task. The woman with him was a young teenage girl and appeared to be unharmed. She was pleading with her captors, telling them she was a victim of the man lying next to her, and that she was not an accomplice.

The wounded man was in his late thirties, very overweight, and dressed in desert fatigues with white high-top sneakers. His face was white, probably from blood loss. He was also bald, but not naturally so—shaved. Covering his entire head, from the top down around all sides to just above his ear tips, was the largest Nazi swastika tattoo I'd ever seen.

"This guy is their leader, Eric Lassman," the colonel said, nodding toward the man on the ground. "The woman helping guard them, Bonnie, went to high school with him. She was ready to finish him off when she recognized him."

"And the girl?"

"She's telling us a pretty convincing story about how she was kidnapped from her friend's house on the third day of the power outage. She says he's been raping her daily and then letting his friends use her. It's not a fairy-tale story."

"You believe her?" I asked.

"I do."

"Me too. We've witnessed rapes and kidnappings on our journey, and her story sounds all too familiar. How old is she?"

"Fourteen," she answered.

"Oh boy. Take her away from the guy. Now," I said. "Let her know she's going to be safe from him."

The colonel nodded, walked over to the girl, reached down and offered the youngster her hand. She then led the girl back to where I was standing.

"What's your name, hon?" I asked.

"Darlene Edwards, sir," she replied.

"Where's your home, Darlene?" the colonel asked.

"Leadore."

"That's northeast of here on 28," the colonel explained. "And forty miles, give or take a few, southeast of Salmon."

"You're done with him," I said. "He won't be hurting you anymore."

"Thank you, sir," Darlene said, eyes shining.

"Question: did you witness the shooting of the film crew back in Arco and then the larger group at the visitor center?"

"I did. I'm sorry they did that."

"Why'd he get them to do it?" the colonel asked.

"His initial reason for the raid was to get their supplies. When he found out they didn't have any, he said they were a bunch of Jews, blacks, and Asians, and was going to do what he couldn't do before the power went out."

"You mean kill them?" the colonel asked.

"Yes, but he used the word exterminate," she answered, looking down at the ground. "He is truly an evil person, ma'am."

"Was he the one that gave the order to kill those people?" I asked, pointing to Lassman. "Both the group in Arco and the larger group at the visitor's center?"

"Yes, sir."

"Thank you for answering. And I'm sorry you had to be there. Just a couple more questions. Did he leave any fighters in Salmon?"

"Only three. All older women. Old, but very mean women. They held me down on the bed while he. . . you know. . . did what he did to me. They're at the hotel on the river. They sleep on cots in the lobby. They start drinking when it gets dark and are usually passed out by eleven or so."

"The road from here to Salmon, are there any of his fighters stationed along the way?"

"No, they looted and burned everything worth having from Salmon down to Challis. There's nothing left to guard."

"Where were you headed tonight?" the colonel asked.

"Arco and maybe as far south as Butte City. He was considering stopping here on the way back to Salmon, but it depended on what he got out of Arco and Butte."

"Why did he bring you along on his looting and killing sprees?" the colonel asked.

"The killing excited him and he wanted me right there to . . . you know, like. . . service him."

"I'm sorry this happened to you." I turned my attention to the colonel. "You'll make sure she gets home?"

"Yes."

"Sir?" Darlene said.

"Yes?"

"There's more women and girls at the hotel. He's, like, holding them in a big meeting room. He picks six or seven of them every night and gives them to his fighters to use. My mother is one of the women they're holding."

"What's her name?"

"Rebecca Edwards. She goes by Becky, though."

"Okay. Where in the hotel is the meeting room?" I asked.

"Off the lobby. Behind where the three old women sleep."

"Do you know how many girls they're holding?"

"I was kept in Lassman's room, but the guards walked me through the lobby once, and the meeting room doors were open. I looked in and saw a bunch. . . like, maybe twenty or thirty."

"Jesus Christ," the colonel said. "We gotta get them, Master Sergeant."

"And we will," I said. "Thank you for the information, Darlene."

"Thank you again, sir. You'll let my mom know I'm okay?"

"I will. Colonel, can you have someone walk her back to the motel for now?"

"Sure. What's going on?" she asked.

"I need to bring someone over, and Darlene shouldn't be here to witness what's coming. I'll be right back. Don't let anything happen to Lassman while I'm gone, Colonel," I said.

"Nothing will happen. You have my word. By the way, Master Sergeant, the rifles we were able to save from the fires were all military-issued M4s."

"Fully automatic?"

"Oh yeah."

"Those auto .50-cals are not available to civilians, and the military keeps a very close eye on those puppies. I bet Lassman raided a National Guard armory. They're lightly guarded during the best of times, but with the blackout, might have been completely unguarded."

"I bet you're right," she said.

"If these are from an armory, then there's got to be more weapons and ammo than what you found here. Maybe up in Salmon."

"We'll check."

"Ask Lassman," I suggested.

"Good idea."

―――――――

I HEADED BACK TO THE Humvee. I opened the rear passenger door and asked Dawn to step out and follow me.

She didn't question me, just gave me her hand and let me lead her to where the colonel waited.

The colonel's mouth hung open in surprise at seeing who I was bringing over.

"You're Dawn Tillman," she said.

"I am."

"Dawn, this is Colonel Melinda Hughes. Retired Air Force."

"Colonel," Dawn acknowledged.

"Hello Ms. Tillman. Like you suggested, Master Sergeant, we asked Mr. Lassman where he's storing his weapons and ammo. He admitted raiding an armory but wouldn't tell us which one or where he's storing what he took."

"I figured he wouldn't say anything."

I pointed to Lassman lying on the ground, said, "Dawn, that man is the leader of a white supremist group based in Montana. He personally ordered the killing of your people in Arco and the crew camped at the visitor center. He killed them for your production company's supplies, but also because some of them were Jewish, black, Asian, or Mexican. He's going to die in the next two minutes for what he did to those people. The only question is who's going to do the killing?"

"What do you mean?" she asked, looking from me to the colonel.

"Those were your friends that died on his orders. I'm giving you the opportunity to hand out a little justice."

"You can say no," the colonel added. "No one will think less of you because you declined."

"I don't mean to put you on the spot, but here we are, right now, and this needs to get done," I said.

And then she surprised the hell out of me by saying yes. "But only if we do it together. You stand behind me and we both hold the gun."

I removed the Glock from its vest-mounted holster and led her over to the man who was still trying to staunch the flow of blood from his missing leg.

"Back off, folks. Let Ms. Tillman have some space," the colonel said to the guards surrounding Lassman.

The fighters stared at the actress in disbelief, but backed off, leaving Lassman sitting alone on the ground.

The Glock had a round in the chamber and was ready to fire. I put the gun in her hand and, leaving my hand on hers, stepped behind her. I wrapped my arms around her and had both of my hands over hers. "Put your finger on the trigger but don't pull it," I said. Once she did that, I told her to aim the Glock at his chest. "When I say fire, you pull the trigger and then again. So, two in a row."

"You mean a double-tap?"

"Yes."

Then she surprised me again, by saying to Lassman, "Asshole, you have murdered dozens of my friends. They were good people. People who would give you the shirt off their backs if you needed it. They did not deserve to die. But you do, and now it's your turn. Any last words?"

"Yeah. I have," he said, in a squeaky, weirdly high-pitched voice. "How about, fuck you, cun—"

Boom. Boom. And then a third *boom.* Eric Lassman slumped over, two neat holes placed dead-center mass, blood pumping out of both. She'd fired the third round into his right eye.

"No. Fuck you, you piece of shit," she screamed at the dead man.

Hand shaking, she continued to hold the Glock in a death grip.

"Finger off the trigger and let go of the weapon, Dawn," I said. "It's done."

She released the gun.

"Thank you for letting me do that. It helped having you behind me. I don't think I could have done that alone," she said. She then turned toward the colonel and shook her hand. Then did the same with the other fighters, several saying, "Well done."

Dawn then walked back to the Humvee, hopped in and shut her door. I saw Greta jump over the center console, sit on Dawn's lap, and receive more hugs and kisses than she's had in her entire life.

I turned my attention back to the colonel. "I'll free those women and girls at the hotel. Can you arrange to get them to their homes?"

"Of course. I'll get a couple of trucks together. They'll follow you, by two or three hours."

"Thanks. I hate to leave you with this mess, but we really do need to get going," I said. "You still have to deal with that first scout truck, but it shouldn't be a problem."

"It won't be. And we'll let these fires burn themselves out," she said.

"This may sound a little gruesome, but strip the bodies of the dead, take anything useful, like shoes, socks, belts, coats. . . hell, anything. Then throw the bodies in the fires."

She nodded, brought over a fighter, and turned my suggestion into an order.

"Yes, ma'am," the woman said, who turned and ran over to a group of people gathered in the motel parking lot.

"I may know some of the men that lead the Kalispell and Missoula force," I said. "They call themselves the MPF. I can speak with them and see if they might want to combine forces with you here, and with Sue Cleary down in Arco."

"That's a great idea. And yes, please have them come down and talk with us. Tell them I'd like to discuss the possibility of creating a much larger group, one that would encompass all of Idaho and Montana. And what does MPF stand for? Montana something something?"

"Montana Protection Force. And I'll mention your idea. I'll suggest they come down fourteen days from today. It may be a day or two off , but let's say in that time frame. Good?"

"Works for me," she said, closing the distance between us, sliding her rifle to the side, and hugging me. She released me and stood back. "I know hugging isn't considered good officer conduct, but fuck it. Thank you for making our lives safer. Without your help, I truly believe our town and inhabitants would have been in grave jeopardy."

"You're welcome. Perhaps I'll see you in two weeks," I said.

"I hope so, Master Sergeant. By the way, I never asked, what brings you and your men up to this neck of the woods?"

"Escorting a VIP."

"Ms. Tillman?" she asked, sounding surprised.

"No, someone else," I answered, thinking of our unborn child.

———————

BACK AT THE HUMVEE, I fed the Minigun from a fresh ammo can, after double-checking that I'd secured and shut off power to the gun. I also made sure there was a round in the trailing link. I spit on the barrels and it instantly fizzled, so I knew it was still too hot to put the cover back on. Melissa handed me the thermal.

"You did an outstanding job up on the roof," I said. "Your fire was controlled and accurate. The sitreps you gave us were spot-on. Your performance under pressure is off the charts. Thank you for your help."

"Ah shucks, boss," she said with a laugh. "Do I get a gold star along with a pat on the back."

"Get out of here," I said, wrapping my arm around her shoulders and giving her a quick hug. "Actually, it should be two gold stars. Where are you going to ride?"

"I'll ride with Kris and Susan. That okay?"

I smiled, said, "Sure, but no hanky-panky in the back seat."

"You're one to talk," she said, a wide grin planted on her face.

She turned and was walking back to the ranch truck before I could come up with a reply.

I keyed the comms and told the ladies to load up. "We've got fifty miles to go until we hit Highway 75. We'll stop for a break there. Let's get a move on."

I walked over to Eric Lassman's body and wrote *killer of innocents* on what was left of his forehead.

NINE

We were on our way a couple of minutes later, Renee driving, with me sitting shotgun and scanning ahead with the thermal. The road was snow-covered, but flat, and I felt comfortable having Renee hold us steady at forty. This road was one of the main highways leading to Highway 75 which would then feed south into Sun Valley Resort. We only slowed as we passed abandoned, looted semi-trucks and passenger cars with skis still in locked roof-mounted racks.

We were a scant five minutes north of Mackay when the first snowflakes appeared in the NVs. The Mackay Reservoir and campground were off to our left, farmland with giant moving irrigation monsters dominating the landscape to the right.

Then the farmland was gone, replaced by scrubland and mountains looming up a quarter mile beyond the shoulder of the road. The snow was really coming down now, and Renee wisely slowed to thirty.

We crossed the Salmon River an hour later, the intersection and beginning of Highway 75 up on our left. We pulled into the parking lot of a looted and partially burnt gas-station-slash-general-store which was situated directly across from the intersection.

I stepped out, scanned, and came up empty. "Clear. Melissa, please stand overwatch."

"Copy that."

I crawled up into the turret and tested the barrels for any remaining heat. They were warm to the touch, but not hot enough to damage the cover. I covered the Minigun and jumped to the ground.

There were hundreds of spent .50-caliber casings littering the parking lot. I could now see a dozen or more bodies inside the still-standing station's service bay. Each had been shot once in the back of the head. They must have been herded in, made to line up and kneel, and shot execution-style. Most looked to have been skiers and snowboarders as the majority were wearing ski clothes. These folks must have walked from their abandoned vehicles to the shelter of the station, only to be executed by Lassman and his thugs.

"Once you're finished taking care of your personal business, I need your help picking up these spent cartridges," I said. "The ranch has a reload room, and I could reuse these. Please grab a cooking pot and start picking them up."

Dawn, probably wanting some privacy to do her business, walked around the building toward the back. It was Kris who told her to come back and stay in sight of us. "It's a rule with us, and we're all safer that way," she said.

Dawn shrugged and went along.

Twenty minutes later, we'd cleared the parking lot of spent cartridges.

"Looks like we gathered you close to five hundred rounds," Kris said.

"Five hundred .50-caliber rounds—what a monumental waste of ammo," I said. "Whoever sent those rounds into this building was a sick and twisted fuck. They'd already killed those innocent people, why go to the trouble—let alone use up all that valuable ammo—on shooting up a building?"

"Because they could?" Kathy answered.

"I think you're right," Monica said. "Maybe they have a bunch of ammo so burning through five hundred rounds means nothing to them."

"It truly does seem like society has slipped into an anything-goes mindset," Kathy added.

"What I simply can't wrap my head around is how fast people have abandoned the laws and norms of society," Renee said. "I mean, it's been like, what, six or seven days since the power went out?"

"Think about the dozens, if not hundreds, of conspiracy and white supremist groups that have sprung up since Trump green-lighted them and the Republican leaders turned a blind eye. These groups have been chomping at the bit, just waiting for something like this to happen," Dawn said, "so they could use it as an excuse to go into hyper-vigilantism."

I took a gasoline jerry can out of our trailer and doused the pile of bodies with half the contents. I left a trail of gas leading out of the service bay and under one of the large roll-up bay doors.

"Everyone out," I said. With the women standing safely behind me, I threw a waterproof match on the trail of gas and watched as it whooshed its way to the pile. We stood watch to make sure the fire wouldn't go out before burning the structure to the ground.

The service bay's walls collapsed ten minutes later.

"Let's go," I said.

The comms beeped as we pulled onto the highway. "What towns are next?" Susan asked.

"We've got Challis and Ellis. Then nothing for forty miles until we hit Salmon," I answered.

"Don't forget those three women Lassman left at the hotel in Salmon," Melissa said.

"I haven't forgotten."

We drove through narrow canyons with mountains rising on both sides and then through wide-open valleys. The road, however, stayed fairly level, and driving through the snow at a decent speed wasn't an issue. We passed several semi-trucks whose trailers had been opened and emptied. Passenger cars had been abandoned, most headed south toward Sun Valley Ski Resort. As always, burnt telephone poles marked our path ahead.

A few minutes later, we hit the town of Challis. Every main-highway business, whether market, hotel, restaurant, or auto parts store, had been looted and damaged. Some had been burned to the ground, either by the pulse or by Lassman.

I'd been scanning ahead with the thermal and hadn't seen a soul, not even on a front porch. It was still early evening and someone, somewhere, should be out and about. *They're probably too afraid to come out of hiding.*

I took the microphone and powered up the hailer. "Time for a public service announcement," I said. "Ever done a PSA, Dawn?"

"Once, during the height of Covid infections. I did a thirty-second spot asking people to mask up. This was when Trump refused to wear a mask and most of the White House staff came down with the virus."

"Want to give it a shot tonight?"

"I can do that. What's the gist of the message?"

"Three things. First: we're US Military. Second: Eric Lassman and his followers are dead and it's now safe to come out. Third: tell them the power is out because nuclear warheads exploded over Colorado and Ohio which resulted in an electromagnetic pulse. The power will likely be out for a decade or more. Those are the main points. You can adlib anyway you want around that."

I handed the microphone to her. I showed her how to use it and then turned the volume to max.

"Renee, slow down to fifteen." I keyed the comms and told the others what we were doing. "Dawn, start speaking—slow and clear. Say your message, wait thirty seconds and repeat. Keep doing that until we're on the other side of town."

Dawn nodded, cleared her throat, and began speaking. "Attention residents, this is the US Military. Eric Lassman and his followers are dead. It is now safe to move about. The power is out due to nuclear explosions over Colorado and Ohio, which resulted in an electromagnetic pulse. The power could be out for a decade, possibly longer." She waited thirty seconds and repeated the message. She broadcast it another five times.

The message had been received. I scanned the highway and side streets ahead and could see people emerging from their homes. A trickle at first, but by the time we reached the northern outskirts of town, and despite the cold, dozens were lining the main highway, most clapping and cheering us on.

"That's cool," Renee said. "Great idea, hon. And nicely done, Dawn. If they had an award for best public service announcement, you'd be a shoo-in for another Oscar."

"Well, thank you, Renee."

"According to the map, Ellis is the next town and is seventeen miles up the highway," I said over the comms.

After seventeen miles of following the Salmon River and driving through several narrow canyons with the river only a few feet from the roadway, we passed the only building on the highway through Ellis—the US Post Office. It had been looted, but not burned.

"The next town is Salmon, Idaho. It's forty-one miles. We'll be following the river the entire way," I said. "Passengers, keep your driver alert. Otherwise, settle back and enjoy the ride."

———

THE HIGHWAY FOLLOWED THE WINDING contours of the Salmon River. During the day, the scenery would be spectacular—mountain hillsides touching the narrow shoulder of the roadway on one side, then the wide, rushing river mere feet from the roadway's edge on the other. To the left of the river, steep hillsides reaching up hundreds of feet into the air. But now, in the dark of night with snow falling as heavy as ever, driving had become a challenge.

"Renee, slow to thirty. Kris and Monica, we're slowing to thirty. Even though the road is flat, it's narrow and winding. Remember to keep your steering wheel and accelerator actions smooth."

"Lucky for us there's snowplow markers, otherwise we'd likely be swimming in the river," Renee said.

The snow was quickly accumulating on top of the twelve inches or so already on the roadway. "Turn your running lights on, Renee. We need to be able to see the reflection off the top of the markers."

"Slow to twenty-five, Renee," I said, a few minutes later, then repeated the new speed over the comms.

"I grew up outside Toronto, Canada," Dawn said. "I learned to drive in snowstorms. I would be happy to spell you."

"If Jon agrees, I could use a break after we hit Salmon," Renee said.

"Done," I said. "But let's get to Salmon first. An hour's drive has now turned into a two-hour slugathon."

We drove on in silence for the next hour. Kris then broke the silence.

The comms came alive. "How are you going to deal with the three women at the hotel?" Kris asked. "Asking for a friend."

"We're going to find a safe place to park as close to the bridge as possible. Then Melissa and I are going to cross the bridge on foot and free those women and girls. This snowfall makes for perfect cover."

"I want to go with you guys," Susan said into Kris' mic.

"Susan, I have no doubt whatsoever that, when you're healthy, you're more than capable of handling yourself," I said, trying to keep my cool. "But a one-armed Wonder Woman is still one-armed. In the months and years ahead, you're going to have plenty of opportunity for action—count on it."

In the background, I heard Melissa tell Susan to let it go. "Okay," Susan said. "Just want to help where I can."

"Understood. And I appreciate your desire to help. But you can help by getting better. And by standing overwatch once we're stopped in Salmon."

With no further comments from the ranch truck, we fell silent as we continued to follow the contours of the river. An hour later, the roadway parted ways with the river, its rushing water disappearing west into the darkness.

We soon hit the southern outskirts of Salmon. On our right, we passed a shed and tractor store that appeared intact. A quarter mile up on the right was the burnt-out shell of a Bureau of Land Management building, a wooden roadside sign the only surviving evidence of what had once stood there.

"Why burn a BLM building and not the tractor store?" Monica asked.

"Maybe something to do with the BLM being government while the store is independently owned?" Kathy answered.

"Anti-government sentiment might be pretty prevalent in this area," Monica said.

"As a native of Montana, I can attest to the general mistrust of the Feds in this part of the country," I said.

"We've got bodies in the parking lot of the gas station up on the right," Renee said, lowering the thermal scope. "And more across the street in the motel parking lot."

"Looks like a group put up a fight," I said. The plate glass fronting the station's quick mart had been shot out, swinging glass entrance door still on its hinges, but minus the glass. Vehicles had been positioned wagon-train-circle-style and had been shot to hell. They resembled Swiss cheese more than cars or trucks they had once been.

"Fifty-cal rounds pass through car and truck skin like a knife through soft butter. These folks never stood a chance," I said.

"Man, oh man," Monica said, "there has to be fifteen or twenty bodies out there."

"Do you think the young girl was wrong about the town being left in the hands of three elderly women?" Dawn asked.

Renee handed over the thermal. I brought the scope up and scanned both gas station and motel parking lot. "These bodies have zero heat signatures and have probably been dead for two or three days. And they're covered in six to eight inches of snow. So, no, the girl probably wasn't wrong. But only one way to find out, and that's by checking the hotel, up close and personal."

Dawn thumped her chest with her fist, said, "Oorah."

I turned in my seat and gave her a surprised look.

"What? In a film I played a Black Hawk helicopter pilot in Afghanistan and must have done and said that a half-dozen times in the movie. Didn't I do it right?"

"No, you did it perfectly."

"I had an actual female active-duty Marine helicopter pilot who worked with me during shooting. She made me practice that dozens of times."

"I always admired those women pilots," I said. "Piloting slow-moving flying targets takes guts and determination."

"She told me the higher-ups would only use her if a male pilot wasn't available. She was more often than not a supply and equipment mover. Pissed her off."

"Someone has to ferry equipment. Renee, slow to fifteen and let me scan ahead," I said.

We had made it a half mile further north and were at the parking lot entrance of Hometown Store and Pharmacy when Renee keyed the comms. "Stopping. We have bodies twenty feet ahead that are blocking the road with no way around."

Through the NVs, I could see that they were covered in snow and had probably been there for quite some time.

"I'll check," I said, handing the thermal to Renee and stepping out. "Running lights off, babe."

"Setting up overwatch," Melissa said.

I walked the twenty feet and stood over a line of eight bodies. They were facedown with their hands zip-tied behind their backs. I brushed snow from the heads of two and found bullet holes to the back of both. I walked down the line and could see that there were four men and four women. All appeared to be late twenties to mid-thirties. The middle four seemed squished somehow—flattened would be a better word. Then the answer came to me—they'd been driven over. Repeatedly. Fresh snow had almost covered them up, but I could see vague outlines of tire ruts running north up the highway.

I keyed the comms, said, "These eight were executed, like the folks at the gas station across from Highway 75. The middle few have been runover several times."

"Scumbags. All of them," Kris said. "Not these folks, I mean Lassman's people."

"Now dead scumbags," Renee pointed out.

"We're not going to drive over them," I said, then asked Kathy to help me move them to the side of the road. "You good to do some lifting? If your back hurts from the bullet hitting your vest, just say so."

"I'm good." We each took a foot and started the job of dragging them to the side of the road.

"They're almost frozen solid," she said, as we dragged the first, a woman, to the curb. "I'm happy to help you, but this is just plain sad."

"Sorry, but you're the strongest of the bunch, and hauling a dead weight like a body is more difficult than most people imagine. Besides, might as well put all your weight training to use."

"Not complaining. Just can't believe I'm hauling dead bodies off a road in. . . Where are we again?"

"Salmon, Idaho."

"Yeah, Salmon, Idaho," she said. "Once we're at the ranch, will we be able to go two or three days in relative safety, or is it always going to be fighting and killing, and running into bad guys? Like it's been since we left Vegas?"

We set the body of a woman down and made our way back to the last remaining corpse, a man.

"The ranch will be a safe haven, I promise. My father's been preparing for an event like this for years. He has a faraday room which should have protected all kinds of remote sensors which will probably already have been set in place. And by now, drones are most likely flying programmed grids 24/7, looking for trespassers."

"Your dad has drones and remote sensors?"

"He does. My father is a kindhearted man who would do anything to help someone in need. He loves his family, his animals, and his ranch, though I'm not sure in what order. But piss him off and watch out. But you'll see for yourself soon enough."

With the last body removed from the roadway, we walked back to the vehicles which were now obscured by heavy snowfall, even in the NVs. I keyed the comms, said, "Once we're settled in, I'll give you a tour of the ranch, and fill you in on the security that's been set up. But a huge safety feature is the fact that the ranch house is set four miles from the closest road. And that road's a very remote road that dead-ends a couple of miles further on. It's so remote, there's absolutely no reason for anyone we don't know to be anywhere near our place."

"I can't wait to get there," Kathy said. "And I know the others are worried and concerned about what the future might hold for us."

"It's natural to be concerned about the unknown, but you haven't met my father. Just wait."

"Look forward to it."

"Keep it slow, Renee," I said, once we were back underway.

We crept along at ten miles an hour, which gave me enough time to fully scan ahead with the thermal. We passed a motel on our left and a Two Brothers gas station on the right, both empty and looted. The highway then ended at the intersection for Highway 28. We turned left onto Main Street and continued north on 93. There was a looted and burned Burger Palace on our right and another motel on the left which appeared intact. We then passed an Idaho State Liquor Store on our right. It had been looted but was still standing.

The comms chirped. "I bet that was the first place they ransacked," Kathy said as we passed the liquor store.

"No doubt. Too bad we're late to the party—I could really go for a rum and coke about now," Melissa said.

"I haven't seen anyone, alive that is, in the thermal," I said. "It's Challis all over again."

"Dawn needs to do her PSA here," Renee said.

"And she will. As soon as we've delt with Lassman's old crones."

There were more retail stores that appeared to have been looted. We passed two more gas stations and four restaurants but saw no more bodies. The snow was really falling, and the NVs' range dropped remarkably. Though diminished, it still reached out a good hundred yards or so.

A few minutes later, the NVs picked up the beginning of the bridge which crossed over the Salmon River. The hotel where Lassman and his fighters were living was the first building on the other side.

"Turn right at the next street," I said. "The sign says it's a museum. They must have a parking lot in the rear."

There was. Renee pulled in and parked next to an abandoned minivan, the museum's name on a magnetic sign on the van's rear flank: *Lemhi County Historical Museum.*

"Kathy, Susan, and Monica, please set up a wide perimeter overwatch," I said. "Monica, go to the parking-lot entrance and watch the street."

The women were on station in less than forty-five seconds.

I took the thermal, walked out into the street, crossed to the furthest point west without actually crossing the bridge, and scanned. Nothing. The fact that Lassman hadn't put a guard on the one logical place—the bottleneck at the bridge's choke point—showed just how cowed the residents must be.

Back at the Humvee, I collected the M4, checked it and the extra magazines. I pulled the Glock and made sure it was loaded with a round in the chamber. Melissa watching me, followed the same routine.

"Turn your NVs on, Lis," I said. Once she was finished with her weapons check, I leaned in and kissed Renee. "See you two in a few."

"Where's my kiss," Dawn said from the back seat.

"When we get back. I promise."

"I'll hold you to it, buster. Be safe, you two."

With weapons up and at the ready, we started slow running across the bridge. The sound of the river flowing beneath the bridge masked any noise we made. Once back on land, we came to the hotel's parking lot. I took a knee, and Melissa did the same to my right.

"We're going to hug the sidewalk that runs in front of the first-floor hotel rooms," I said. "The sidewalk ends underneath the main entrance portico, and if memory serves me right, it looks very much like the hospital entrance in Battle Mountain. We'll then make our way to the outside rear lobby exit. If there's a sentry, I'll take care of it. Then we both enter the lobby and render the three women harmless. If we get confirmation from the hostages that it's the three older ladies Darlene says helped Lassman rape her, we'll deal with them."

"Roger that. I'll be right behind you."

I brought the rifle up and ran along the hotel's first-floor rooms. We came to the end of the sidewalk, then turned right toward the river. The hotel lobby was up on our left. There were no sentries. I tried the door and found it unlocked. I felt Melissa's hand on my shoulder as I opened the door, and we both stepped through. Melissa took hold of the door and quietly closed it. We were inside a large lobby, and it was darker than the darkest cave. The NVs picked up the details: the check-in desk to our left; directly in front of us, some fifty feet away, the three women sleeping on hotel roll-a-way beds. To their right were two large double doors which presumably led to the conference room Darlene said held the captives. A wooden broom had been placed through the two doors' handles, effectively locking them shut.

I brought my attention back to the three sleeping women. Alongside boots, backpacks, clothes, and assorted booze bottles, I could see AR-style rifles.

Melissa had seen the weapons as well. She leaned in close, whispered, "Let's take their weapons, stand back, and wake them up."

I gave her the thumbs-up. We crept up to the women and retrieved their rifles and backpacks. We stepped back ten feet to their rear, put their stuff on the floor behind us, then I shouted at the top of my lungs, "Wake up!"

And did they. All three shot up and looked around for the source of the rude awakening. Three heads swiveled but not to the rear.

"Back here, bitches," Melissa shouted. "Hands on the back of your head."

The women on the left and right did as they were told. The woman in the middle reached beneath her pillow and brought out a small handgun.

"Drop that weapon or I'll put you on the ground," Melissa shouted out. "Your choice."

The woman hesitated but dropped the gun. Melissa stepped forward and kicked it to the side. "Good choice," she said. "Now, the three of you lay facedown on the floor with your hands behind your heads."

Once they were on the floor, Melissa patted each down. "They're clean."

Darlene had said they were old women, but these three were in their mid- to late thirties. *I guess age is in the eye of the beholder.*

"Jon, I'll watch our guests here if you want to check on the women and girls."

"I can do that," I said, thinking my days of watching over Melissa had come to an end.

I turned and walked to the set of double doors. I removed the broom handle and opened the right-hand door. The conference room was at least thirty-foot deep by fifty-foot wide. The floor was carpeted but there was no furniture save for one king-size mattress in the far right-hand corner. The room was as dark as the lobby, but the NVs picked up a group of at least two dozen girls and women cowering together in the far corner of the room. There was a five-gallon bucket in the left-hand corner of the room that was serving as a toilet—the space reeked of urine and excrement.

"I'm here to free you, not harm you," I said, fighting off gag reflexes from the stench. "My friend is out there guarding the three women and they, nor any of Lassman's fighters, will ever harm you again. Lassman and his fighters are dead. Each and every one of them."

The group digested the news in silence, then the crying started. Some started clapping.

"Who are you, mister?" a woman asked, over the noise of the celebration. She had her back against the rear wall of the conference room and the other women and girls were gathered around her.

"I'm Jon Kristen and my friend's name is Melissa. What's your name, miss?"

"Becky Edwards."

"Becky, your daughter Darlene is alive and will be here in a couple of hours. She is the sole survivor of a skirmish down in Mackay that killed every one of Lassman's fighters. She's the one that told us about this hotel and you women and girls being held here."

Becky Edwards started to cry and joined the rest of the women in clapping. I took off the NVs and put on one of Burt's headlamps. I turned it on, and the room was bathed in bright light. Too bright, the women shielding their eyes from the sudden glare. "Sorry." I turned the light to the lowest setting, which they were able to tolerate.

A young girl, no more than twelve or thirteen, barefoot and dressed only in dirty T-shirt and shorts, stood and asked, "What about my mother and father, Tim and Tara Bruner? I was taken from them in front of the Hometown Store and Pharmacy. I haven't seen them since."

Another young girl stood and asked the same question. And then two more.

I had a terrible feeling that the bodies we'd recently moved off the highway were probably the girls' parents. "I don't know," I answered truthfully.

There were seven or eight adult women in the room, but none at this point seemed fully functional. They were still cowering in the corner and most seemed frozen with fear.

"Becky, do you know how to handle firearms?" I asked.

"I do," she answered. "I'm a rancher, Mr. Kristen, and own several."

"Come with me, please," I said. I took her hand and walked her out of the room and into the lobby. "Becky, this is Melissa. Melissa, Becky." The ladies shook hands and said hi.

My headlamp settled on the three prone women. "Are these women part of Lassman's group?"

"Yes," she answered.

"Darlene told us three women took turns holding her down while Lassman raped her. Are these the three?"

"I didn't have no part in that crap," the center woman said.

"Yes, these are the three," Becky answered. "Her included. And they held the rest of us down as well. It took all three of them when Lassman's friends gang-raped us."

"Not me. No way," center woman said.

Melissa raised her rifle and stood over the three women.

Uh oh.

"Melissa, back off," I said. "This is not something you're going to finish."

Melissa frowned, but stepped back. She then walked over to where we had dropped the women's rifles, selected one, and walked back. She dropped the mag, ejected a round, then slapped the magazine back in and charged the weapon. She handed the rifle to Becky and stood back.

I took a jacket from the pile of stuff we'd taken from the three women. "Becky, put this on. And find a pair of boots that fit—it's cold outside."

I approached the captives who were now streaming out of the conference room. "I'm taking Becky outside, but we'll be back in five minutes. Stay in the lobby. The bathrooms are over to your right. Not sure if the water is still flowing, but it's worth a try."

One of the women's boots fit Becky. Once she had laced them up and put the jacket on, I said, "Follow me."

I led her out of the lobby and into the cold night air. The snow was falling harder than ever and was quickly piling up. "I was beginnin' to think I'd never breathe fresh air again," she said, taking in deep breaths.

"Folks from Mackay are driving up here in a couple of hours. They're led by a woman, Melinda Hughes, who is an actual colonel and someone you can trust. Darlene will be with them. They'll help you and the others. We need to be on our way, and you'll have to keep the rest of the women and girls safe until they arrive."

"I can do that. What am I supposed to do with the three assholes in there?" she asked, pointing toward the lobby.

"What would you like to do with them?"

"Um. . . I don't know."

"If you do nothing, then the group that's driving up to help you will deal with them. But that means you won't have the opportunity to take care of them yourself. Do you know them? Are they from here?"

"All three are from Montana. So no, we don't know them."

"I didn't want to mention this in front of the girls, but we carried eight bodies off the road a mile or so back in front of Hometown Store and Pharmacy. I'd be willing to bet those are the parents of the four girls that asked about them."

"Oh God, I know those girls and their parents well. They're good people," she said. "I'll make sure someone identifies them. If they are the parents, we'll find relatives or families that will take the girls in."

I nodded thanks.

"We can take care of this for you," I said, pointing to the three women. "Just say the word."

"Okay, take care of it for us."

"Stay here," I told her.

I went back inside. Melissa must have found zip ties because the women's hands were now tied behind their backs.

"Let's take them out front," I said to Melissa.

I grabbed them by their wrists and lifted each into a standing position.

"Ouch, that fuckin' hurt, asshole. What you goin' to do to us?" center woman asked. The other two hadn't said a word.

"Walk out front," I said. "And if you think Lassman and his fighters are going to rush in and save you, think again. They're dead. Every one of them."

Once out front, I had them walk out into the falling snow and turn right toward the far north end of the parking lot—I didn't want the girls to see the bodies.

"Kneel," Melissa said.

The center woman yelled, "Fuck that," and with hands zip-tied behind her, took off, awkwardly running toward the highway. She'd made it onto the highway when Melissa sent a round into her right buttock. The woman screamed and fell face-first onto the roadway. Melissa walked out, took the woman by her hair, and half-dragged her back to where her two accomplices were kneeling.

"You fuckin' shot me, bitch," the woman screamed at Melissa. "I didn't do nothin' to you."

Becky had watched us walk the three women out of the lobby and had stood back while the one had run.

"I've changed my mind. I'll do it," she said.

"Please, don't kill me," center woman pleaded, looking up at Becky with terrified eyes. "Eric made us do it. It was either that, or be part of the harem."

"Harem?" Melissa asked. "Seriously? He actually used the word harem?"

"He did," Becky answered.

"Please, let me go," the right-hand woman said. "You'll never see me again. I swear."

"Too late," Becky said. "You helped those disgusting pigs rape those young girls. They're only thirteen years old for Christ's sake. And the older teens and women didn't deserve to be passed around like whores. Me included."

"I'm so sorry, ma'am," the woman on the left said. "We deserve whatever judgment you pass out. I know even God will have a hard time forgiving me."

No one said a word for a full minute. *I mean, what could you say?*

"Let the one on the left go," Becky said. "God would want me to be lenient with at least one of them."

Melissa looked over at me and I nodded. Melissa took out her knife and cut the zip ties. "Get the fuck out of my sight."

The woman turned to go back inside, probably for her things.

"Oh no you don't," Melissa shouted out. "Take off, now."

"Wait one," I said. "Are there girls being held anywhere else?"

"Check out a home on Second Street," she answered. "It's a yellow house with brick front steps. Lassman was using it before he took over this place. I'm not sure if anyone is still there, but it's worth checking out."

"You know where that is, Becky?"

"Yes."

"Okay. Go," I told the woman.

But the woman hesitated. "I know something you'll want to know. In exchange for the information, I'd like my boots, clothes, and backpack. At least I'll stand a chance of getting home to my kids."

"Tell me the information and I'll consider it," I answered.

"Lassman kept all the food and supplies in the first six self-storage units across the street there," she said, pointing to a large self-storage complex. "He's been stockpiling and buying weapons and ammunition from a military base in Wyoming for years. He moved the lot of it down here after the last skirmish with the militia from Kalispell and Missoula."

"Okay. Get your stuff," I said.

"Really, Jon?" Melissa asked.

"Yes, really. Go with her and make sure she only takes what's hers."

Melissa stood her ground.

"Melissa. Please just do it."

Melissa scowled, then grabbed the woman's elbow and led the way back inside the lobby. They emerged three minutes later. Once outside the lobby, the woman, zip tie removed, started running north past us and into the night.

Becky watched the freed woman run down the road and eventually disappear into the darkness of the falling snow. She turned her attention back to center woman, raised the rifle, and aimed for the back of the woman's head. The rifle started to shake and wobble. A fully loaded AR is heavy, but it wasn't the weight alone that was causing the weapon to shake. It was second thoughts.

"I can't do this," she finally said, lowering the rifle. "I don't have it in me to kill someone."

"Thank fuckin' Christ," the wounded woman said, sagging in relief.

Melissa quickly raised her rifle and put a round though the woman's heart. Center woman fell face down in the snow. Pumping blood quickly turned white snow into pooling red puddles resembling cherry Slushies.

Before Melissa could bring the barrel behind the last woman, Becky moved between the woman and Melissa.

"I want to let her go as well," Becky said.

"You sure?" Melissa asked, hesitating then backing off.

"Yes, I am. Let her go. Please. Enough of the killing. This one has paid the price for all three of them," Becky said, pointing to dead-center woman.

I cut the woman free. She thanked Becky, turned, asked if she could get her stuff. I nodded, and she was running north two minutes later.

"Becky, you need to have someone check out the yellow house on Second Street," I said.

"As soon as I see someone I know, I'll send them."

I keyed the comms, said, "Ladies, we're good here. Please drive over the bridge and into the hotel parking lot. We'll be waiting out front."

Each responded and drove up to us two minutes later.

Renee hopped out and greeted me with a kiss and a hug. Then Dawn did the same, though her kiss landed on my cheek.

"You're Dawn Tillman," Becky said, sounding truly astonished.

"Guilty as charged," Dawn replied.

"What're you doin' up here in Nowheresville?"

"Got caught up in things down by Arco."

"Oh my God, you must have been part of the film crew," Becky said, putting her hand on her chest. "I heard them bragging about killing all those poor people. I'm so sorry."

"Thank you. Lassman and his band of assholes are dead and literally burning their way to hell as we speak," Dawn said.

"Renee. Dawn. Now might be a good time to head to the south of town, turn around, and start your PSA announcement," I said. "Dawn, there are a bunch of young girls and women inside that need to be reunited with parents, husbands, or boyfriends. Add something to your message that lets the residents know where the girls are waiting. Melissa, please go with them and use the thermal just to be safe. The rest of us will wait here for you. We'll head out once you're back."

The three drove off in the Humvee, and I watched as they headed back across the bridge. It was the first time since Las Vegas we'd been apart, and I was already experiencing a mild case of separation anxiety.

"What's a PSA announcement?" Becky asked.

"Stands for public service announcement," I answered. "We came up with it in Challis. We started broadcasting it on the south side of town, and by the time we hit the northern outskirts, people were lining the streets."

"What's the announcement?"

"You'll hear it soon," I answered.

I heard a commotion coming from inside the lobby. The swinging lobby doors opened and out came the former captives, including the older women who'd been huddling in fear. Like Becky had done earlier, each was taking deep breaths of fresh air. Then they started rubbing their arms to stay warm.

"It's cold out here, Becky," I said. "I saw a flashlight sitting by one of the beds inside. Why don't you take the girls and find the hotel's linen closest? Look for blankets. If there's none there, start searching the rooms."

"Good idea. Follow me, ladies. Let's find us some blankets and food."

She turned and led the procession back inside the lobby.

"Becky, one more thing," I said to her retreating back.

She and the procession stopped. Becky turned, said, "Yes?"

"There are two more rifles in the lobby. Give those to two of the older girls or women that know how to handle them. We're leaving soon, and you'll be on your own for a couple of hours. I don't think there are any more of Lassman's fighters alive, but let's be cautious and have them stand watch."

"Okay. Good idea. Thanks."

"Those girls are only fourteen or fifteen years old," Susan said, watching the group make their way back inside the lobby. "Did Lassman and his fighters rape them all?"

"Continually, since day three or four of the blackout," I answered. "The older teens and women, too. Not only individually, but Lassman had daily group sex."

"Seriously? What sick fucks," Kris said.

"Those bodies we took off the road, Kathy? Four of those girls told me they were taken from that same store."

"You really think those were the girls' parents?" Monica asked.

"I do. There were four sets of male and female," I explained.

"And about the right age for having kids that young," Kathy added.

"Ah, man. Those poor girls," Susan said.

I heard something and put my finger up asking for quiet. In the far distance, I could just make out Dawn repeating her PSA message:

"Attention residents, this is the US Military. Eric Lassman and his followers are dead. It is now safe to move about. The power is out due to nuclear explosions over Colorado and Ohio which resulted in an electromagnetic pulse. The power could be out for a decade, possibly longer. If you are missing daughters, wives, or girlfriends, please make your way to the River Hotel on 93 at the north side of the Salmon River bridge. There are survivors waiting for you."

Fifteen minutes later and having been repeated a half-dozen times without Dawn missing a single word, the message had been received loud and clear, for the residents of Salmon were emerging from their homes. Thirty seconds after the last message was sent out over the hailer, the Humvee pulled into the hotel parking lot.

Residents on our end of town must have heard the first few messages, for dozens could be seen outside their homes, hugging neighbors, and walking the streets. Several couples and three men ran up to us and asked if we had found their daughters, girlfriends or wives.

"Stay right here," I said. "Let me get someone to help you. Melissa, please have Becky come out."

Melissa ran inside the lobby and emerged a minute later with Becky and the former captives in tow.

"Carly!" a woman screamed, running up and hugging one of the girls.

"Dad! Mom!" a young girl yelled out, jumping into her father's arms.

One of the older women I'd seen cowering in fear, spotted her husband and fell to her knees. "I'm sorry, Brad. I tried to fight them off, but they took me from Mom's house," she said. "I'm so sorry."

The husband kneeled and embraced his wife. "I love you, Franny. And you have nothing to be sorry for. I tried to get you back, but they shot at us. Bill Evans was with me and was hit. He died later that night."

All told, there were seven happy reunions over the course of the next ten minutes.

Becky gathered the remaining girls. "Your parents are probably on their way. Let's go back inside and warm up while we wait for them."

"Any of the happy reunions happen to be ones that asked about their parents?" Kathy asked, after the girls had gone back inside.

"Sadly no," Becky answered.

Two of the remaining men looked to be capable, and I told them that help would be arriving soon. I had them go inside and take the two rifles that the girls had so they could stand watch until help arrived.

"One of you watch the front and one the back. And don't shoot the help when they show up. Melissa, will you go with them and make sure the weapons are functional and that these two know how to handle them?"

Melissa motioned to the two men to follow her inside.

"Maybe we should wait for the colonel to get here," Renee said.

"Do you really want to wait here for another two or three hours?"

"No. Not really."

"Neither do I. It's time to move on. We're done here."

"But I'm not sure those two guys can handle—"

"They're gonna' be fine," Kathy said. "Let's get going."

Then I remembered the self-storage units across the street. *Shit!*

"Hang on a minute. Lassman stored his supplies and ammo in those storage units across the street," I said. "Before we leave, let's check and see if they have any .50-cal rounds. Renee, please stand overwatch here while I get the crowbar. Kathy, come with me, please. You too, Dawn, if you're up for the walk."

I took the crowbar out of the Cruiser, and the three of us walked across the street and up a slight incline. The chain-link drive-through gate was open, and we walked right up to the first of the six street-facing storage units. There was a cheap lock on the roll-up door, and the crowbar easily snapped it in two. Inside the twenty-by-forty-foot unit was enough food to feed an army of six hundred for months. The next four units held more food, clothes, medical kits, and other supplies.

The sixth unit was the largest, about the size of a three-car garage. It held the ammo and weapons, crate upon crate of ammo, containing both NATO 5.56 rounds and belted .50-cal rounds for the auto fifties. Tens of thousands of rounds of each caliber. The wooden crates were stenciled in yellow, indicating the contents. The .50-caliber cans' lids had two cartridge shapes embossed, one on each end, to indicate the direction of loading.

Lined up in six neat rows of twenty were military-version M4s. The rifles were fitted with military-issue ACOG sights and would have survived the pulse. I had relied on ACOGs on my duty rifle during all four deployments.

Stacked up against the back wall were boxes of M870s, the military version of the civilian Remington 870 12-gauge shotgun. These shotguns were an invaluable asset when

LARS H. LARSEN

operating in urban environments. Most Special Forces units had adopted the M1014, a variant of the Benelli M4, a semi-auto shotgun, and the National Guard were evidently being supplied with first generation shotguns. Next to the shotguns was a pallet of .50-cal ammo cans containing 12-gauge shotgun ammo.

Stacked to the ceiling were twelve cardboard master cartons of 5.56 magazines. Each carton held 144 magazines.

And for the grand prize: sitting by themselves, still in their original wooden transport crates, were four fully automatic Browning M2 .50-caliber machine guns. In separate crates were three M3 fixed tripod mounts and one suspension spring system for use in helicopters and open-door aircraft.

Each crate was stenciled with black lettering designating the Wyoming National Guard and describing the crates' contents.

I glanced back to the hotel and, through the snow, could see Melissa standing with one of the men she'd recruited as an armed guard. I keyed the comms, said, "Melissa?"

I watched her reach up to her shoulder and key her mic. "Yes?" she answered.

"Are those two men going to be able to look after things?"

"Affirmative. One is ex-military and the other is a hunter."

"Good. Ladies, drive all three vehicles over to the self-storage unit across the street." I held up a hand and started waving. "See me across the street and up the hill from you?"

"Yep."

"I'm worried about the snow and getting out of here, so drive through the gate and approach me so that you're pointed back downhill. Renee, park the trailer next to the roll-up door behind me, driver's door next to the unit. Melissa, come too, please."

I watched all three vehicles exit the hotel parking lot and cross the street. Even though it was snowing heavily, the NVs picked out twenty to thirty residents running up to the hotel and reuniting with some of the girls and women.

150

"We going to take some weapons and ammo?" Kathy asked, taking a visual inventory of the storage unit. "There's a ton of stuff in here. No, make that tons of stuff."

"We are," I said. "Those .50-caliber machine guns are priceless."

"How many we taking?" Dawn asked, lifting the lid off one of the Browning's and looking inside.

"Two. Plus, as many crates of ammo as we can fit in the trailer and in the bed of the ranch truck. And we'll take forty each of those M4 Rifles and M870 Shotguns. Oh, and three cartons of the 5.56 magazines."

"We have room for all that?"

"Maybe, but it's the weight I'm really concerned about," I said. "We may have to lose a few of those Hershey Kisses cartons and for sure all those grill-sized propane tanks."

"You'll get some pushback on leaving the Kisses behind," Kathy said in all seriousness.

"Bullets are much more important than Kisses," I pointed out.

"You have Hershey Kisses?" Dawn asked, her voice sounding more than a little excited.

"A bunch. More than we could eat in a year. Maybe even two," Kathy answered, giving Dawn two thumbs-up.

Renee brought the Humvee and trailer to a stop next to the roll-up door, the Cruiser and ranch truck stopping close behind. I brushed six inches of snow off the tarp and removed it from the trailer. I studied the trailer's contents and, more importantly, their placement. Most of the weight was over the hitch, like it should be, but there was room over the dual axles for considerably more.

The women were gathered around the back of the trailer. Each was weaponed-up, but no one was standing overwatch. "I know it seems safe, but someone needs to stand over-watch, "I said.

Kathy raised her hand and said she'd do it. "I'm going to need you to help load."

"Let me," Susan said. "With one arm, I'm not much use to you carrying heavy ammo cans."

"Sounds good. And thank you."

"You're welcome," Susan said. "Can I talk to you for a sec? Over here."

I followed her to the far-left roll-up door. "What's up?"

"I thought you should know that Kris has not been taking the antibiotics you gave her."

"Any idea why not?"

"Nope."

"How's your wound?"

"Melissa checked it the last time we stopped. It's healing nicely."

"Good. And thanks for telling me about Kris."

Once back with the main group, I said, "Okay, here's the situation: we have the opportunity to supplement the ranch's armory. I say armory simply for lack of a better word." I then went through what I wanted to take. "We're talking considerable weight here, probably more than this trailer was designed to handle. The trailer was made to carry four ATVs, which I'm guessing weighed a total of three thousand pounds or so. With the gas and water cans, ammo, Kisses, and the gear already in there, I would say we have roughly eight hundred pounds to start. With the—"

"We are not going to leave the Kisses behind," Renee said, "if that's where you're going with this."

"We might have—" I managed to get out.

"No," Kris said.

"No. No. And no." This from Monica.

"I'm with them," Dawn said, smiling and pointing to the other women.

"Listen, bullets are—" I said.

"Listen, mister, the answer is still no," Renee said. "We can leave the propane tanks we took from the Airstreams."

"I like Kisses as much as the next guy, but bullets can save lives. Do Kisses?"

I had them with that. But the women looked crestfallen. Then Kris said, "How about this: we load as many Kisses as possible in the back seat of the ranch truck. What doesn't fit gets stacked up next to the trailer and when the weapons and ammo are loaded, if there's extra room, they go. If not, they stay. How's that?"

"That works for me." I gave the women a thumbs-up.

"Where shall we start?" Kathy asked, rubbing her hands together. "I need a workout."

"Let's empty the trailer and start over. But we need to hurry. I want to get all this loaded and covered by the tarp by the time the colonel gets here. I hate to say this, but we're going to have to wait for her—we can't leave these storage units unguarded.

"Renee, please fill the gas tanks of all three vehicles— careful you put gasoline in the Cruiser and not diesel. And it's diesel in the Humvee and ranch truck and not gasoline. Monica and Dawn, get those Kisses out of the trailer and fill the ranch truck's back seat with as many cartons as possible. Kris, you can't lift anything heavy, so how about taking dinner orders and making us some chow?"

"I can do that," she answered.

"Kathy and Melissa, we're going to empty the trailer then load those two machine guns. We'll then redistribute stuff around and start loading the M4s and shotguns. Then we'll start on the ammo and finish up by loading our stuff."

An hour later, the vehicles were gassed up, and the two Brownings, forty rifles and forty shotguns had been loaded. We'd removed the dozen propane tanks taken from the Airstreams which freed up both space and weight. Renee questioned leaving the propane, but I assured her there was propane up the wazoo at the ranch. Monica and Dawn had squeezed fifteen master cartons of Kisses into the back seat of the ranch truck. We'd then taken a fifteen-minute break to eat.

Renee fed Greta who wolfed it down and promptly fell asleep on a crate inside the ammo storage unit. With Monica and Dawn helping us, we were able to fit in twenty wooden crates of 5.56 ammo, for a total of 33,600 rounds, one hundred cans of .50-caliber, for a total of 10,000 rounds, and fifty cans of shotgun shells, for a total of 2,500 shells. The three cartons of 5.56 magazines also fit in the trailer. We threw the tarp over the trailer and secured it with the bungee cords.

I stepped back and studied the trailer and hitch. It looked okay to me. The tops of the trailer's tires weren't touching the wheel wells, and actually had three or four inches of clearance. The trailer was level, and maybe even tilting toward the Humvee. Which was a good thing.

To the delight of the women, we took the Kisses out of the ranch truck's back seat and put every single carton in its eight-foot bed. We took an extra tarp and bungee cords and covered the sweet treasure, protecting it from the elements. Those Kisses were heavy, and after stepping back and eyeing the bed, I could see the truck was now sagging in the rear. The truck was an old F250 heavy-duty model and was built to carry and pull heavy loads, so I wasn't overly concerned.

We were ready to head out and were only waiting for the colonel to show up.

———————

DAWN WAS STILL DRESSED IN the sweatpants Renee had found for her at the visitor center. "Dawn, I saw boxes of uniforms in storage unit number three. Renee, why don't you help her find a set of fatigues that fit. Then search through the other storage units and see if there are any boots and any other gear she needs. Keep an eye out for rifle slings, too."

While Renee and Dawn searched the storage units, I sat my ass down on a wooden crate next to Greta and watched the town come alive. Several hundred residents were walking the streets and a few dozen had stopped at the hotel. An old VW Bug, with comical-looking foot-long bouncy eyelashes above the headlights, drove up and stopped in front of the hotel's lobby entrance. I saw Becky emerge through the entrance doors and stick her head in the passenger-side window. A minute later, she patted the car's roof and it took off, tires spinning in the snow.

Dawn and Renee returned a few minutes later. Dawn was now in MultiCam pants, T-shirt, long-sleeve shirt, winter jacket, boots, and her hair was pinned up underneath a boonie hat, identical to the ones the women were wearing.

Renee dropped a large cardboard carton at my feet. "Your slings, sir."

"Thank you. That was a good idea," Dawn said, twirling around and showing off her new attire. "It's much warmer."

"Looks better, too. Let's go check on Becky," I said to Renee, stowing the box of slings underneath the trailer's tarp.

Kathy had relieved Susan on overwatch, and after checking in with her, Renee and I started walking across the street. Greta must have had built-in warning sensors, for as soon as Renee started walking down the hill, she jumped down from her sleeping perch and was at her side.

The guard Melissa had armed stood just inside the lobby and blocked our path.

"Who are you?" he asked us. He had the bearing and stance of an ex-cop or soldier.

"Let me put it this way," I answered, "had I been one of the bad guys, you'd be lying on the ground with a hole in your chest. But today is your lucky day—you're still breathing."

The man thought about it then stepped back and waved us in. "Sorry, dude. I'm not thinking clearly," he said. "The girl in the black sweatshirt helping cook—that's my daughter, Margo. You've got to be their rescuers. Thank you." He stuck his hand out and we shook. He pulled me in for a shoulder bump and there was an embrace for Renee.

"You're welcome. A group of folks from Mackay should be arriving soon," I said. "Please don't shoot them."

"I won't."

Becky and six girls were cooking over three backpacking stoves sitting on top of the check-in desk. Several candles were burning, providing illumination.

"Hey, guys," Becky said.

"Hello. Smells good," I said, raising my NVs. "You're making chili mac?"

"Wow, good nose on you. Yep, chili mac it is. The assholes had a room off the lobby full of freeze-dried meals," Becky said. "I'm talkin' hundreds. You'd think they coulda' shared a few with their starvin' sex slaves. You guys hungry?"

"We just ate—thank you, though," Renee said.

"Have more girls and women been reunited with loved ones?" I asked.

"Let's step over there," Becky said, indicating an area off to our left. She handed one of the girls her spoon. "Keep stirring, honey. I'll be right back."

"The four girls that asked if you had information on their parents—none of the parents have shown up. I've asked someone to check on those bodies you mentioned earlier and hope to hear somethin' soon. I also had someone check the yellow house on Second Street. It's empty.

"Two of the older women are from towns further north on 93, Conner and Darby. If we give you their names, can you include them in your public service announcements as you drive through their hometowns?"

"Great idea," Renee answered. "Consider it done. What are their names?"

"April Townsend is from Conner, and Jenny-Mae Duncan is from Darby."

"We drive right through those two towns. Why don't we drop them off at their homes?" I said. "As long as we have room."

"That would be awesome. Thank you. The others have been reunited with their families. But why are you still here? I thought you guys needed to get back on the road."

"Decided to wait for the colonel," I answered. I didn't mention what we'd found in the storage units—let the colonel decide what to do with the supplies and weapons.

One of the younger teens left the food prep area and made her way over to us. "Can I pet your dog?" she asked Renee. She was wearing a dirty Jonas Brothers T-shirt and even dirtier khaki pants. Tears were streaming down her cheeks. "I have a dog. His name is Blankets, 'cause he likes to snuggle under blankets with me. I really miss him."

"Sure, sweetheart. She likes to be rubbed behind her ears," Renee said.

The girl kneeled down and started rubbing behind Greta's ears. Greta licked the tears off the girl's cheeks.

"There are another five young girls that are from towns further east or west of here that haven't been reunited. But we'll make sure they get home."

"Becky, three pickups just pulled up," the guard shouted from the lobby entrance.

"That's going to be the colonel. Let me go meet them," I said, already headed toward the lobby entrance. Greta looked at me and decided the ear rubs were better than cold snow on her paws.

Once outside, I saw the two passenger doors open on an old, rusty four-door Chevy crew pickup. The colonel stepped out, spotted me, and waved.

Next out was Darlene Edwards. She waved as she ran past me and into the hotel lobby.

"That's going to be a hell of a reunion," the colonel said as she watched eight of her fighters spread out and form a protective ring around us. "All she talked about on the drive up here was seeing her mother again."

"Better that than talking about her captivity," I said.

"I guess. Is that your doing?" she asked, pointing to the dead woman in the parking lot. Several inches of snow had accumulated on the body, but it was pretty obvious it was a recent fatality.

"Did I fire the shot? No. Did I okay it? Yes."

The colonel shrugged, said, "I assume she was one of the three guards?"

"Affirmative."

"Well, she made her choice. And the other two?"

"Gone."

"Gone as in dead? Or gone as in left or ran away?"

"The latter."

The colonel looked at me funny and smiled, not unlike a parent to a child caught letting the dog out of the backyard and not chasing after it.

I smiled back and said nothing.

"Okay. What's the status of the females?" she asked, sounding like a woman in command.

"All but eleven have been reunited with their families. We're pretty sure that the parents of four of the eleven are dead. Two of the women we're going to drop off in towns along our route. The rest are from out of the area but are going to be taken home."

"I saw the bodies on the south side of town. Looks as if residents made a last-stand effort to rein in Lassman," she said, brushing snow off her head and shoulders.

"It must have been a slaughter," I said. "Like sticks and stones against nukes. Lassman had .50-cals and automatic weapons. Like I said—a slaughter."

"And there are no more of Lassman's people here? Other than the three that were guarding the girls?"

"Pretty sure they were it, though I haven't searched the town. If there are any of Lassman's followers still in town, they'll be flushed out soon enough."

She nodded and stayed silent, finally asked, "What now?"

"You're the colonel. You tell me. You've commanded thousands of people in harsh, hostile environments. You're a military-trained, forward thinker. Me, I'm just a ground grunt who removes obstacles that stand in my way."

"It's pretty clear to me that you're not just a ground grunt."

"Let's take a walk. There's something I need to show you," I said, turning and starting to walk toward the storage facility across the highway.

"How far are we walking?"

"Just across the street and then up that itty-bitty hill," I said, pointing to the storage units. "I know you're used to choppers and airplanes for transport, but welcome to my world."

"It's not that—my fucking boots are killing me," she said, a grimace on her face. "I haven't worn these since I retired out, and I have blisters the size of silver dollars on both heels."

"You want me to carry you, Colonel? What do you weigh? A hundred pounds?"

"Would you? And I'm 103. But I'm kidding about you carrying me."

"I'm not kidding," I replied. "Blisters are not something to ignore." I keyed the comms and told Renee what I was doing. I stopped, turned around, and presented the colonel my back. "Hop on."

And she did. She slung her rifle behind her, hopped up, and wrapped her legs around my waist. And off we went, her arms around my neck. I wouldn't say she was light as a feather, but there were many times I'd carried battle gear that matched her weight.

"Did you strip the clothes off the bodies of the dead back in Mackay?" I asked as we made our way up the incline.

"Yep, it's all in the bed of the pickup truck we drove up in."

"Good. There's bound to be a pair of shoes or boots in your size. Better yet, there may be a pair for you behind one of these roll-up doors. And I'll treat those blisters for you."

"You're a medic, too?"

"I was taught to take care of my men, ma'am."

"Don't call me ma'am. That just doesn't seem right when you're carrying me on your back up a hill. My first name is Melinda. Can I call you Jon?"

"Please do," I answered, stopping in front of the far-left storage unit. I set her down and called the women she hadn't met over for introductions.

Introductions made, Kathy resumed overwatch as I raised the door on each storage unit.

"Wow, did he take this from residents, or did he actually buy all this stuff and store it?" she asked, after checking out the contents of the fifth and last single-sized unit.

"I don't know about the first few storage units, but I'm pretty sure I know where he got most of the contents of this last one," I said, rolling up the door on the three-car-garage-sized storage locker and illuminating the contents with a flashlight.

"Oh my," Melinda said, taking it all in. Despite the pain from the blisters, she walked through the storage unit, opening and inspecting the various crates and ammo cans.

"Look at all those M4s and shotguns," she said, picking up a rifle and inspecting it. "These are priceless. With these babies, we'll be able to defend ourselves from just about everything but an Abrams or one of my old A10s."

Melissa, trailing Melinda, said, "You haven't seen the really good stuff yet. Check out the crates on the far back wall."

"I see the .50-cal ammo cans," Melinda said. "Wait one. . . they're belted, which means it's meant for machine guns."

"Keep walking," Melissa said, urging her on.

And then Melinda spotted the two Browning crates. "Holy mother of God, there are two more fifties?"

"Plus, close to fifty-thousand belted rounds," I added.

"These were originally the Wyoming Guards'," she said, her hand running along the stenciled name on the wooden crate. "He either stole or bought them from someone in the guard, because the tracking system would have to have been fiddled with at the local level."

"I'm going with stole," Melissa said. "Lassman didn't strike me as someone who would know how to handle an organization's finances, let alone save up enough for all this."

"Regardless of how he acquired it, it's now yours," I said. "Keep it safe and disperse the food and supplies as you see fit. And full disclosure: we've already taken some weapons and ammo. We took two fifties along with a tripod stand and a suspension cradle. We also loaded up a few M4s, shotguns, ammo for each, and three cartons of 5.56 magazines. We didn't touch the food or other supplies."

"If you hadn't, I would have suggested you did," she said. "Thank you for staying and safeguarding it."

"We've got a present for you, Melinda. Ladies," I said.

"Don't tell me, you found a dozen Javelins. Or maybe a few Stingers," she said, hope clear in her voice.

"Better," I said, laughing, as Monica, Kathy, and Kris emerged from behind the ranch truck. Each was carrying a carton of Kisses.

Once the ladies were close enough for Melinda to read the carton markings, she said, "Much, much better. Kisses? Hell, yes!"

"We thought you might like them. Now, find yourself a pair of boots, and then we'll take a look at those blisters."

TEN

Thirty minutes later, we were headed north. The two women we'd offered to drive home had joined four of the colonel's fighters who were returning to their own homes further north on 93. They'd left in one of the group's pickup trucks a few minutes ahead of us.

I was driving the Humvee, as I wanted to make sure all was good with the added weight we'd piled in the trailer. It was as if nothing had changed. The big turbo-charged diesel didn't strain one bit with the added weight. Kris had reported that with the extra weight of the Kisses cartons in the truck's bed, the front end was higher than before. While she said it was weird driving with the front elevated, it didn't seem to have altered the handling much.

The next town, twenty-one miles up 93, was North Fork.

"Dawn, when we reach North Fork, you can take over driving. After North Fork, it's twenty-four miles to Gibbonsville. After Gibbonsville, we cross over the Idaho–Montana border on our way to Darby, some fifty miles north of the state line."

"Sounds good," she said, petting her new BFF behind her ears.

It was wide-open valleys and straight highway north of Salmon. Barren, snow-covered fields lined both sides of the highway. We encountered abandoned and looted semitrucks and dozens of passenger cars, most with skis and snowboards sitting in racks on car roofs. We had to slow and make our way around the trucks as there was virtually no shoulder the further north we traveled.

The road meandered along the contours of the Salmon River, which we followed all the way into North Fork. On the left, we passed the River's Edge Lodge and then the River's Edge general store, both burned to the ground. We came up on the Village at North Fork, and through the NVs, I could see twenty or thirty people standing out front. The NVs didn't show any weapons, so I pulled into the parking lot and stopped. I stepped out and called the crowd over. The smell of burnt wood and trash filled the air.

"I have something to tell you," I said, and waited for them to move in closer. I then told them everything we knew. "Lassman and his fighters are dead. The women and girls he abducted have been freed. Sorry, but we don't have any further information. We need to be on our way. Good luck to you."

Dawn took over driving and had it down pat after only a few miles. The snow was coming down heavily, the wind blowing hard enough that Dawn was fighting the wheel.

I keyed the comms, said, "Let's slow to twenty-five and, if safe, a bit faster on the longer straightaways."

We maintained twenty to thirty miles per hour into Gibbonsville. We crossed the Idaho–Montana border and the Continental Divide. Once across the border, there was a road sign warning us that, for the next seven miles, we would face a winding, twisty road. Dawn safely navigated her way through seven miles of hairpin curves and emerged in front of the US Forest Service building in Sula.

It was now four in the morning, and even at this early hour, there was quite a crowd milling about in the parking lot, a mix of all ages, men and women, young teen to older-looking grandfathers and grandmothers. I had Dawn stop one hundred yards out. The NVs showed that most of them were armed. I turned the hailer on, said, "US Military convoy behind you. We have information to give you, but you will need to set your weapons down before we pass along the information. It's for your safety as well as ours."

We watched in the NVs as chaos and then spirited discussion ensued. "You have thirty seconds to comply or we're moving on. Your choice."

The desire for information was apparently stronger than the desire to fight, as they finally complied. Five minutes later, we were back on the highway and headed north. The roadway followed the Bitterroot River which was flowing on the west side of the highway.

"Next town is Darby," I said, studying the map with a flashlight. "It's fifty miles north, and it, along with Salmon and Hamilton, is one of the three larger towns on 93."

This section of the highway I remembered well from weekend skiing trips to Sun Valley. It had us driving through narrow gulches—the mountainsides touching the eastern side of the highway, the highway itself, and then the river and hillside to the immediate west of the river. Then we were bursting out of the narrow canyons into wide, short valleys—at most one or two miles long. These valleys contained homes, farms, fishing resorts, and campgrounds. Then it was back into the narrow gulches. These gulches had names, like: Spring, Coyote, Elk, Franklin, Billy Goat, Whiskey, and Robbins.

In the valleys, most of the business entities had been looted or burned—who knew whether by the EMP or the hand of Lassman. Dead power lines lay alongside the highway, and the wooden power poles' top two or three feet were burned. Most individual homes had been spared and a few had candles burning in windows.

In one particularly narrow canyon, we encountered an abandoned Mayflower moving van. With no shoulder to pull off onto, the truck's driver had stopped in the northbound lane.

Its cab took up most of the southbound lane as well. With less than a foot to spare, and rushing water below, we barely squeaked by.

Dawn performed her PSA announcement in each valley. She said taking sixty seconds to pass along life-changing information was the least we could do.

An hour later, we hit the southern outskirts of Darby. Most businesses along the main highway had been looted or burned, one building after another in ashes.

"What the heck?" Kris asked over the comms. "I'll never understand why these businesses were burned. For what possible purpose? I understand the looting part, though I don't condone it. But the burning?"

"Lassman was a sick fuck," Melissa responded. "He probably burned ants with a magnifying glass when he was a kid."

"We have a bunch of people ahead," Dawn yelled out, bringing the Humvee to a quick stop. "They're in the parking lot of the motel up on the right."

"Stopping," I said into the comms.

"They're running away," Renee said. "They must not know that Lassman and his fighters are dead."

"The colonel's truck with the two freed women should have arrived an hour ago," Kathy pointed out.

"Maybe they're dropping the one woman off outside town," I said. "I think her name was Jenny-Mae something. Dawn, it's time for your PSA. You want me to drive?"

Dawn laughed, said, "I can chew gum and talk at the same time."

"Then start talking. Wait sixty seconds and repeat. And keep at it until we're on the other side of town."

"Yes, sir, Master Sergeant, sir." Dawn then executed a perfect military salute.

"Snap to it, Private," I said with as much authority as I could muster, but regardless of my attempt to remain serious, I burst out laughing. Soon Renee and Dawn were laughing as well. Dawn had forgotten to release the mic button on the hailer, and the town of Darby was flooded with the amplified sound of laughter.

———————————

DAWN *WAS* ABLE TO DRIVE and recite her PSAs at the same time. She was accelerating up to cruise speed, when I spotted a roadside sign advertising a veterinary hospital ahead on the right. It sat alone at the end of a quarter-mile-long tree-lined driveway. There was an old-fashioned, red wooden barn sitting behind the house and a smaller metal-sided equipment building sitting to the right of it. A pasture, outlined with white wood fencing, ran from the street, along the entire length of the driveway and was a good three-hundred-foot wide. There were no animals present. A hundred years ago this would have looked like an all-American working farm or ranch house. I could see candles burning in two of the house's upstairs windows.

"Slow down and turn in the next driveway on the right," I said. "It's a long shot, but let's see if we can buy or barter ourselves some dog food for Greta."

Dawn quickly slowed and was able to complete a controlled right-hand turn into the hospital's parking lot. The Cruiser and ranch truck followed us in. I saw a curtain open and quickly close in one of the windows on the second floor.

"There's someone home," Melissa said. "Curtain moved in the second-floor middle window."

"I saw it too," Kris said.

"Why leave a candle burning in your windows?" Monica asked. "That's like advertising the fact that someone's home."

"Almost every retail building has either been looted or burned to the ground. Why was this one spared?" Kathy asked.

"Good question. Let's be careful, everyone," I cautioned. "Dawn, drive up and then park so that we're facing the highway."

Renee scooted up from the back seat, said, "Why don't we get on the hailer and have Dawn do her PSA then ask whoever's inside to come out? It could be that they think we're part of Lassman's group."

"I'll overwatch," Melissa said.

"Thanks, Melissa. And that's a good idea, Renee." I powered up the hailer and turned the volume down. I handed the mic to Dawn, and she started right in on her PSA.

Before she'd finished, the front door opened inward and then the screen door outward. A young girl, perhaps thirteen or fourteen, and holding a golden retriever by a short leash, stepped out onto the front porch. The dog was tugging with all its might, and the girl was using both hands and most of her body weight trying to keep it in check.

"My mom is upstairs working on a cat," she shouted. "She says to wait five minutes and to not leave. She told me to say 'do not leave' twice to make sure you understood."

The girl had long, blonde hair that almost touched her waist. She was tall and thin, with a big smile. The NVs showed white teeth glistening with metal braces.

"Renee, let's you and I go introduce ourselves to the young lady," I said.

"Shall we let Greta come with us?" she asked.

I stepped out and opened Renee's door. "Sure, why not. It's a veterinary hospital, after all. But let's ask first."

A plaque above the screen door read, *Large Animal Practice—little ones welcome, too.* The plaque must have been made with a CNC machine for, above the words and carved into the plaque, were intricate, three-dimensional carvings of cats and dogs.

"Hello, I'm Jon and this is Renee. What's your name?"

"Jane," the girl answered, finally getting the dog under control and sitting by her side. "And this is Payton. She just turned eight months old yesterday." Payton was panting and her tail wagging three or four hundred beats per minute.

"Jane, we have a dog too. Her name is Greta," Renee said. "Would Payton mind if we were to let her out of the truck?"

"Gosh, no. She'd love it. Payton loves other dogs."

Renee patted her thigh, and Greta jumped from the back seat to the ground and immediately hugged Renee's side. Greta's focus fell on Payton, thumped her tail once, then returned to looking up at Renee.

Jane released her hold on the leash and Payton bounded down the front steps and sprinted toward Greta. Payton, trying her best to get Greta's attention, danced around Renee and Greta. Greta would have nothing to do with the dancing youngster.

It was now close to six thirty and light enough to not have to use the NVs. I flipped mine up and told the others to shut theirs down.

The screen door opened behind Jane, and a woman emerged cradling a tiny black-and-white kitten in her arms. The woman was medium height and build, with long, curly red hair. Her face was a freckle factory to go along with the red hair. She was wearing pale blue surgical pants and matching short-sleeved shirt with a black long-sleeved T-shirt under that. She had pale white skin, so pale I would bet she'd have to lather on extra amounts of sunscreen to venture out in the sun for even short periods of time.

"That's a Belgian Malinois, Jane, and has obviously been trained to not react to other animals. So, please get Payton back on the porch," the woman said. She then brought her attention back to us. "Excuse my manners, I'm Pamela Jane Calhoun. People call me PJ. I'm the town vet. The power really not coming back on?"

"It's not," Renee answered.

"Does that Toyota or Ford have a hitch on the back?"

"Yes, ma'am," I answered. "Both do. We stopped in hopes of—"

"What you said about Lassman and his fighters being dead—is that really true?" she asked, walking down the steps and approaching us.

"It is," Renee answered.

"Well, hell, that's the best news I've heard since the fucking lights went out."

"Mom, stop with the bad words," Jane shouted down the steps. "Remember, if you say them, then I get to say them."

"Sorry, honey. I forget sometimes."

The Hummer's driver's door opened and out stepped Dawn. PJ's eyes widened in either disbelief or excitement.

"Mom, she sure looks like that movie star you love: Dawn Tillman," Jane said.

Dawn smiled, said, "I look like her because I am her. We stopped, PJ, in hopes that you might have some dog food we could buy or trade for."

PJ was now standing in front of Renee and I. Dawn closed her door and came around the front of the Humvee and put out her hand toward PJ. The two women shook hands.

"Listen, you guys," PJ whispered, "I don't want Jane to hear this. My ex-husband and Jane's dad, Lawrence, was one of Lassman's right-hand men. A couple of days after the power went out, Lawrence, the douche that he is, stole a neighbor's bike and pedaled over here, supposably to check in on Jane. But on his way out, he swiped the keys to my old truck and took off, leaving Jane and I stranded. This town, and others nearby, are well aware of who my ex is and the reason why this building is still standing while theirs probably isn't. I—"

"PJ, we stopped for dog food. Do you have any?" Renee asked again. "Yes, or no?"

"Yes. A bunch," PJ answered, waving her hands in dismissal. She must have realized that she was being dismissive, for she apologized. "I'm so sorry, I know I'm sounding bitchy, but Jane and I have been working non-stop getting our cargo trailer loaded with most of the practice's equipment and supplies. And dog food is definitely among the supplies. I've been waiting for Lawrence to show up with my truck, but after hearing your message, I have a feeling he might be dead. Just between us, the loss of the truck hurts more than the possibility of him no longer being among the living. Are you headed north? Tell me you are!"

I figured I knew where this conversation was going and wasn't sure I was ready for the question that was sure to come. But we were headed north, and I had both Dawn and Renee standing next to me, so lying or even bending the truth a bit wasn't going to work. So, I did the right thing and answered truthfully, "We are."

"I hate to ask you, but you're our last hope," she said.

And here it comes, I thought.

"Please let me hook up the trailer to one of those trucks and go with you. I don't think that itty-bitty Land Cruiser will handle the trailer's weight, but that white Ford should have no problem. It's a diesel? Right?"

"It is," Renee answered.

I had doubts about pulling another trailer and saddling the group with two more people. I guess my face showed what I was thinking for PJ said, "The town is going to come for us, even though I had absolutely nothing to do with Lassman. In fact, I didn't even know my ex-husband had anything to do with him until a neighbor told me a few days ago, but it's guilt by association. They'll kill us for sure. I have family in Kalispell that we can stay with. Please take us. Please."

"Jon, why not?" Renee said.

"I've got twelve years of large animal veterinary experience under my belt. I've treated thousands of cattle, horses, goats, pigs, and every farm animal that walked off Noah's Ark. I would be a valuable addition to any town or large ranch," she said. "Just not here."

"Let's at least pull her and her stuff up to Kalispell," Dawn said.

I watched Jane playing with her golden retriever on the porch, then turned back to Dawn and Renee where I was faced with two hard stares, and I knew that I'd just lost another battle thanks to weaponized female will.

———————

I SIGHED IN RESIGNATION, said, "Renee, take Greta and Kathy and clear the house."

"There's no one in there," PJ said.

"It's how we do it," Renee explained. "It's for your protection as well as ours. Do you have any weapons in the house?"

"Yes, a shotgun and a Glock handgun. Both are sitting on the kitchen table."

"Renee. Kathy. Please check now."

"Does this mean you're going to take us?" PJ asked, watching as Greta and the two ladies climbed up the front porch steps and entered her home.

"Melissa, I'm going to go look at her trailer. There's a possibility that unhappy town residents may visit this woman and her daughter. So, be alert. Susan, stay with Melissa on overwatch. Monica, go back down the drive toward the street and watch the road. Dawn, get back in the Humvee, turn on the engine, and be ready to take off."

"So, *are* you?" PJ asked.

"Maybe. Show me the trailer," I said, as I watched the ladies spread out to their respective positions. "Monica, you see anything coming our way, let me know."

"Roger that," she replied, before two-timing it down the driveway toward the street.

"It's in the barn. Follow me," PJ said, turning and heading toward the barn. "Jane, stay on the porch with Payton, please."

I followed her across the gravel area between the house and barn. She slid open the barn door and there was her trailer. It was an enclosed cargo trailer, a big one, with triple axles, at least eighteen foot long and seven foot wide. It had single opening doors on both sides and two swinging doors on the back with a pull-out ramp for driving things up or herding animals in. It was tall enough for a horse to stand up in. The name of the vet practice was painted on both the sides and rear of the trailer: *PJ Calhoun, Large Animal Veterinary Medicine.*

It was packed full, from floor to ceiling. Their suitcases were sitting inside and would likely be squished when the two swinging rear doors were closed.

I walked up the ramp and stood on tippy toes trying to see what she'd loaded in.

"What's packed in here?" I asked. "I can't see anything beyond the first row of boxes and totes."

"Mostly animal meds. I'm the Idaho, Montana, and Wyoming small-practice distributor for the country's top five animal pharmaceutical companies," she explained. "Three days before the blackout, I received a complete restock from all five, getting inventory ready for the new year. Which means I've got vaccines for livestock, poultry, and pets. I've got anti-parasitic drugs, fertility management drugs, gastrointestinal, respiratory, and cardiovascular medicines. And not just a little of this and that. I'm talking multiple cases of each. And we stuffed our entire inventory in here. Plus, our animal food. There's dog, cat, horse, and a little bit of cattle feed. My medical and surgical instruments are in. Don't ask me how they survived the power blackout when nothing else did, but I have a Philips portable ultrasound imager and an Amadeo portable X-ray machine. They both work."

"How do you know they work?"

"We have a generator and had power for the first day and a half after the blackout. We ran out of propane and that was the end of that."

"Where did you store the two working machines?"

"In an enclosed and locked metal security cage."

"The cage most likely acted as a faraday cage. Did you have other electronic items in the cage?"

"No. Just the two. They're super expensive and the cage was for those two items only."

"That was lucky," I said.

But back to the task at hand—towing this big girl. If need be, the Cruiser could pull it. But the ranch truck could pull it across the country without breaking a sweat.

The comms squawked. "House is clear, Jon," Renee said. "And I have the weapons."

"Thanks. We're going ahead and will be taking them and their trailer with us. The ranch truck will tow it. "

PJ had heard, smiled, and was dancing a jig in place.

"Monica, all good up there?"

"Affirmative. Nothing moving."

"Melissa, you and Dawn need to take half of the Kisses from the back of the ranch truck and put them in our trailer... I don't care where. Just cram them in and cover with the tarp. Then have Kris drive the ranch truck to the barn and back in the main door."

I turned my attention to PJ. "You have ten minutes to gather any last-minute things. You'll ride in the back seat of the white Ford. Your dog and the little cutie in your arms there, too. You have any other animals in your care?"

"No, Jane and I were about to take our annual Christmas trip to my dad's place in Kalispell. We closed the practice the day before the blackout, so all our boarders and patients were picked up."

"I'm glad that worked out."

PJ stood there smiling at me. I reached out and ran my finger over the kitten's head. "Go. Now!" I told her. "Times ticking down."

"Thank you," she said, putting the kitten under my chin and releasing it. "It's a girl, by the way." She turned and ran back to the ranch house. I held the blue-eyed kitten out in front of me, its little kitten paws reaching out for me.

"You ready for a journey, little girl?" I said to the kitten who was wiggling and extending and retracting her paws.

The kitten meowed. And then again.

I smiled, brought her under my chin, said, "You just got a name, young lady. Your new name is Journey." I could feel and hear her purring away.

ELEVEN

A few minutes later, Melissa and Kathy had finished transferring half of the Kisses to our trailer. Kris then backed the ranch truck into the barn. I connected trailer to truck, cranked the support wheel up to the travel position, and watched the truck's rear sag as the wheel left the ground. I stood back and studied the level of both truck and trailer. The trailer's tongue and truck's hitch were low, which was exactly how you'd want it. I didn't connect the trailer's seven pin into the truck's receiver, so there wouldn't be any taillights or brake lights working. I inspected the trailer's tires and all six looked good.

I walked to Kris's window, said, "Hop out and come with me, please."

Kris followed as I led her into the barn's equipment room. I shut the door behind us and asked her to pull her shirt up so I could check her wounds. She did, and I could see that several were showing early signs of infection. I leaned in, took a whiff, and sure enough, the odor was unmistakable.

"Have you been taking the antibiotics I gave you?"

"I took two and then stopped. They made me sick."

"Several of the cuts are infected. You need to take the meds, Kris."

I put my hand on her forehead and could feel more than normal heat. "You're running a temperature. Your body is trying to fight off the infection and I'm not equipped to handle this. We need to get you to a doctor as soon as possible."

"I'm fine."

"Bullshit! You're not fine," I shouted. "If we weren't so close to the ranch, I'd force those pills down your fucking throat."

"Good thing we'll be there later today. Cute kitty, by the way."

I looked down and spotted Journey's head poking out. I'd put her in one of my jacket's large front cargo pockets. She looked around, craned her head up, spotted me, and meowed.

I was as upset with Kris as I'd ever been. There was only one way I knew to motivate her to take the drugs. "You want to see your kids again?" I asked her. "Then take the fucking pills."

"Okay, Okay. Don't get so upset. I'll start taking them."

"Good," I said, though I doubted she would. "Now get back in the truck and pull forward so I can close the barn door."

PJ, Jane, and Payton walked up, and after introductions were made, I put them in the ranch truck's back seat.

"I have baby bottles and formula for the kitten," PJ said, climbing in and scooting over to make room for Payton and Jane. "She's probably starving about now. And I have these for Greta." She held out a yellow tennis ball and a rope toy with two heavy-duty knots on each end. "She's a military canine, so she most likely had one of these as a reward object."

I took the two and said thanks then handed Journey to Jane. "Her name is Journey," I said.

"I like it," PJ said. "Good job."

"You get everything you wanted out of your house?"

"I think so."

"Do you want to do a last-minute walk through to be sure?" I asked. "I'll give you another few minutes if you want."

PJ glanced at Jane who shook her head. "We're good. We're both ready to go."

I nodded, stepped back, and shut the driver-side passenger door. "Kris, you ever tow a trailer or boat before?"

"Yes. When you were teaching us how to drive the Cruiser."

"That's right. Which you already knew how to drive but didn't tell us."

"I'm sorry about that. Truly."

"You think you can drive with this large trailer behind you?"

"I can. Swing wide. Allow plenty of time to stop. And keep the speed under fifty to avoid trailer sway."

"I'm impressed. You did listen," I said.

"I'll drive and we'll see how it goes."

"Okay," I said and started to walk away. Then thought of something and turned. "One more thing. A trailer this size usually has trailer brakes. They're not connected, so give yourself plenty of time to stop."

"Will do. Thanks."

PJ rolled her window down, said, "I've been towing this trailer around Montana for six years using the same size truck and transmission. I'd be happy to drive."

"Thank you for the offer," I said. "Let's let Kris drive, at least initially, and see how it goes."

I keyed the comms, told Renee to hop in the back seat of the Humvee. "Dawn, pull the Humvee a hundred feet toward the highway. Melissa and Susan, you're in the Cruiser with Melissa driving. When we get to the end of the driveway, stop and pick up Monica."

"Roger that," Melissa said.

"Monica, you hear that?"

"Yep."

I sensed I was missing someone. I keyed the comms, asked, "Who am I forgetting?"

"Me," Kathy answered.

"Sorry. Ride shotgun with Kris in the ranch truck."

"Roger that," she replied.

"Greta? Where is she?" I asked. "I've got a couple of presents for her from PJ."

"She's next to me in the Humvee," Renee answered.

I watched as Kathy climbed into the ranch truck. "Kris, drive up behind the Humvee. Melissa, you'll follow the ranch truck and watch our backs."

"Will do," she answered.

I ran to the Humvee and jumped in. I keyed the comms, said, "Let's roll. We're getting close to home, so easy does it. As long as there's snow on the road, keep back at least two hundred feet from the truck ahead of you."

I turned and faced Renee and Greta. I held out the tennis ball and rope toy. Greta looked at the two toys and gently took the rope toy in her mouth. She set the rope down in front of her and barked.

"She just barked!" Renee shouted. "It's her first bark."

It was now seven fifteen in the morning. We'd spent forty-five minutes at PJ's.

THE ROADWAY WAS COVERED WITH two to three inches of freshly fallen snow, but driving conditions were manageable. Snow was falling, but lightly, and I could see rays of early-morning sunlight sneaking past some of the thick clouds over the eastern mountain range. The western skies were dotted with light cumulus clouds, which likely meant the snow would soon stop falling.

"We've got what looks to be clearing skies ahead," I said over the comms. "If the snow stops falling, we could be pulling into the ranch by late this afternoon."

"If it stops snowing, won't the roadway turn to ice?" Kris asked.

"Yes, but only after a full day of sun turns it to mush and then freezes overnight," I answered. "We should be at the ranch before nightfall."

"How far is it to the ranch?" Monica asked.

"Two hundred miles, give or take a few."

"Whoopie!" Kathy said. "We're so close I can taste it."

"Taste what, exactly?" Melissa asked.

"Safety," Kathy answered.

"Amen to that," Renee said.

"Two hundred miles of uncertainty," I said, bringing the women back to the now. "Keep alert and your head on a swivel. Watch your nines, threes, and—Melissa—our six."

"Roger that," Melissa said. "Watching our six."

Each time we faced a new stretch of highway, I scanned ahead using the binoculars.

The Bitterroot River appeared on our right, and we followed its bends and curves for the next seventeen miles. Railroad tracks matched the contours of the highway and were on our right all the way to a few miles south of Hamilton. We'd passed through several smaller towns without slowing down. On the north side of Como, the snow stopped falling altogether. There were still clouds in the sky, but the sun was sending beams down to the ground. I watched as the beams of light raced across the landscape, keeping pace with the moving clouds above.

"It's beautiful here," Kris said. "I love all the trees and seeing the snow-covered mountains in the background."

"God's country for sure," Kathy said.

"I agree, it is beautiful," Melissa said, "but it's too remote. I'd rather have people around me than trees, meadows, streams, and other Mother Nature shit."

"I love the nature shit, as you call it," Kathy said. "We leave Seattle once a month and backpack trails surrounded by Mother Nature."

"I hate to burst your people bubble, Melissa, but the ranch is remote as remote can get," I said. "But there will be a lot of folks living there. Just close your eyes and pretend you're in Seattle."

We crossed over the Bitterroot River and the southern outskirts of Hamilton came into view. We passed the Cast a Line fishing lodge on the left and then the Caught One lodge. The highway went from two to four lanes, and the pavement was wet, but no snow showed on the highway. We passed the burnt-out skeleton of a Montana Brother's gas station on the right.

"Dawn, slow down and let's start the PSA announcement," I said, leaning over and powering up the hailer. I handed Dawn the mic. I keyed the comms, said, "Ladies, we're slowing to twenty, and Dawn is going to start her PSAs."

Dawn had just ended her third PSA when I spotted a large group of residents in a Domino's Pizza parking lot up on the left. There were thirty to forty men and women, all armed. Several men were huddled over a map spread out on the tailgate of an older-model Dodge four-by-four truck.

I keyed the comms, said, "We've got a large group of armed folks two hundred yards ahead in the Domino's Pizza parking lot. We'll stop a hundred yards out. When we stop, do not form a perimeter overwatch—I'll let you know when."

"Roger that," from Kathy.

"Waiting for the okay," Melissa said.

The group had noticed us, and half their number were streaming onto the highway and headed our way. They were walking, not running, which I took as a sign they were friendlies. Their weapons were not in the ready position.

I keyed the hailer mic, said, "Stop your advance. We have further information to relay beyond what you've heard over the hailer. Again, stop where you are. Send one person toward us, unarmed. Set your weapons on the ground and take three steps back. This is for your protection as well as ours."

"Kris, ask PJ if she knows any of these people," I said.

A few seconds later, Kris responded. "She does—three, possibly four, of them. She says they're local ranchers, and she's treated their cattle and horses. She doubts they're part of Lassman's group. She says they live in outlying areas and almost certainly don't live in town. Which means they weren't hit by Lassman," she added.

I watched the advancing group consult with an older man who pointed to the ground. The fighters set weapons down and stepped back. The older man released his rifle from a sling, set it down on the pickup's tailgate, and started walking toward us. He was wearing desert combat fatigues, pants tucked into tan-colored boots, winter camo jacket, and had on a plated vest like mine. I could see a black handgun in a vest-mounted holster. He was on the shorter side, maybe five-seven or -eight, and built like a pro wrestler—all muscle. He looked to be in his late fifties or early sixties, with short gray hair and sporting a thick black mustache.

"Okay, Melissa and Kathy, set up a close-in perimeter now, please."

I watched the ladies exit their vehicles and take a knee. I stepped out of the Humvee and walked toward the advancing man.

We met halfway and stopped. I stuck out my hand and we shook.

"My name is Jon Kristen. Might you be Ted Mitchell?"

"I am," he replied. "But how could you possibly know that, Master Sergeant?"

"Colonel Melinda Hughes down in Mackay. But she thought you'd positioned your people up in Lolo," I said.

"We decided to move south and incorporate Hamilton. We arrived this morning and are working out the details with these folks," he said, turning and pointing to the people behind him.

"Colonel Hughes is in control of Highway 93 from Salmon on the north to Arco on the south," I said. "She would like to combine her fighters with yours and Eddy Taylor's. I took the liberty of telling her that you and Eddy would meet with her in Mackay in fourteen days' time."

"We can do that. Lassman and his group are really dead?" he asked. "We got a large portion of them in our last engagement, but quite a few managed to slip away."

"We dispatched them earlier this morning. They're all dead."

"Were they on the receiving end of the Minigun?" he asked, nodding toward the Humvee and its weapon lying underneath the weather tarp."

"Yes. It was most effective."

"I bet. I should have mentioned it before, and I apologize for that, but I know who you are, Jon. We've been expecting you. A few days ago, your sister Abigail told us there was a chance you'd show up on 93." He looked at his watch, an old wind-up Timex, said, "In fact, she should be getting here in the next ten to fifteen minutes."

"Abs will be here? In Hamilton?"

"Yep, she flies in and lands any place with enough room. She did the same thing in Lolo. She's one of the most competent pilots I know."

"Is she flying the Beaver?" I asked. If true, then getting to Seattle and Vancouver just got a hell of a lot easier.

"I think that's what it is," he said. "It's got those huge tires on it and clear plexiglass bubble windows on the sides. She says she has floats, or maybe she called them pontoons. Whatever they're called, she says she can land on water."

"That's the one."

My father bought the Beaver new in '62 for getting to remote areas of the ranch, carting hunters and their gear into inaccessible national forest land, and for hauling supplies to the ranch. And those tires were thirty-five-inch tundra tires. It was a 1962 de Havilland Beaver with a three-bladed prop. Three years ago, my father had had it restored by Vintage Air in Victoria BC Canada. It was totally original, except for an FAA-mandated communication system. But everything else was as it was when it rolled out of the assembly hangar. . . including the original radio. Being an early sixties model, it had no modern electronics in it other than the GPS unit and the new comms.

"Why does she fly in?" I asked.

"She delivers food, ammo, and other supplies," he answered. "It can hold a lot of weight in the back. She flies people in and out. She even acted as an air ambulance after our engagements with Lassman. She and I have done reconnaissance flights together. Without Abigail and her plane, I'm not sure we'd be standing here today."

"Do you know if one of the plane's radios works?"

"It does. Or it did. Up in Lolo, one of our members has an old two-way in his pickup, and they coordinated timing of supplies and whatnot. No reason I can think of that would have suddenly rendered it inoperable."

"Excuse me a minute, Ted." I keyed the comms, said, "Renee, will you please power up the radio, then push the all-channel transmit. Then transmit asking for Abigail."

"Abigail?"

"Abigail is my sister," I answered, as I released the Humvee's two ten-foot whip antennas. "She's also the pilot of our plane that's landing any minute now."

"You never told us you have a plane," Melissa said.

"It's not my plane. It's the ranch's plane. And I never mentioned it because I wasn't one hundred percent sure it had survived the pulse. Which evidently it has."

"Was the plane going to play a part in your plan to get to Seattle?" Kris asked.

"Yes. And Vancouver, Canada for getting Dawn to her sister."

"Very cool," Kathy said. "Do you fly?"

"Used to. Never learned water landings though. My license expired while I was in the military.

"Ted, I guess we should probably move our vehicles off the highway and give her some landing room," I said.

"Park across the street in that parking lot," he said, pointing to the burnt-out remnants of a gas station. "She doesn't need much highway to land or takeoff, plus there are no light poles or other obstructions along this section of highway. There's no airport close by and I figured this was safer than landing in a vacant cow pasture."

"The Beaver is the original STOL aircraft," I said.

"What's STOL stand for?"

"Short Take-off and Landing. She can land and takeoff almost anywhere—even lands and takes off from gravel riverbeds. All with a full load of fuel, people, and their gear."

On the off chance that Abs was close by, I keyed my mic and asked for Abigail. And got nothing.

"She said she'd be here at eight this morning," Ted said, glancing at his watch. "She's got another ten minutes, which means she's too far out for your personal comms to reach."

I keyed the comms and told the drivers to park in the lot across the street. I watched as the Humvee, followed by the ranch truck, followed by the Cruiser, parked in the gas station's lot.

Dawn had pulled in and parked facing the street. She left the engine running, opened her door, and stepped out. She wasn't wearing a boonie hat and her hair was down in all its glory. She was known for her long, thick hair and was the celebrity spokeswoman for an international hair products company—before the pulse, I'd see two or three of her commercials on network television nightly.

Ted's facial expression was priceless as recognition set in.

"You are the spitting image of Dawn Tillman," he said. "Sorry, excuse my manners, I'm Ted Mitchell." He extended his hand, and they shook.

"Nice to meet you, Ted Mitchell. I'm Dawn Tillman."

"No way," he said, eyes lighting up.

"Way. Since the day I was born," she said, smiling the famous smile.

"Wow. I've never met a movie star before."

"Then I'm glad I'm the first."

The comms came alive. "John, your sister responded and is on channel twenty-eight."

I removed the radio from its vest pouch and switched channels. I keyed the mic, said, "Abs?"

"Reading you loud and clear, Jon. Have Hamilton in sight. ETA two minutes."

At the top of the Humvee's whip antennas are thin black pieces of fabric. Both were pointing east, which indicated a west to east wind.

"Abs, wind is five, gusting to ten, blowing west to east. Roadway runs north and south. We're on the southside of town right after the highway straightens out. Ted is here, too."

"Roger that. I see you."

A few seconds later, I heard the Beaver's engine as it changed rpms for landing. I spotted Abs heading straight for us at fifty feet.

Like every smart bush pilot, she was checking out the landing spot before attempting to land. She flew by, turned and circled back, touching down twenty feet past where we were standing. She came to a stop, turned on a dime, taxied back to us, and turned again so that she faced north. The engine continued to run for twenty seconds then stopped, propeller winding down and finally stopping.

Abs released her seat belt, opened her cockpit door, and quickly climbed to the ground. She opened a small cargo hatch door, took out a set of plastic wheel chocks, and placed them around both wheels. She then ran into my arms. I lifted her off the ground and spun her around. I set her down and smiled—setting eyes on my little sister was wonderful.

She stood back, said, "We've all been worried about you, brother. We thought you were heading north and then east, and I've flown out there twice looking for you, obviously with no results."

"Change of plans. We had to make a choice back in Nevada, and the snowfall made it for us. I was concerned we wouldn't have been able to head east over the mountains into Montana. Ended up heading east further down south then headed up north on 93. Snowed all the way, but never dumped enough to stop our progress—luckily all three vehicles have four-wheel drive."

"Well, I'm just happy you're safe," she said, hugging me again. "And those two flights weren't a total waste of fuel. I spotted a large convoy of civilian vehicles traveling north on 95 near Coeur d'Alene. I flew low to check them out, and instead of a friendly wave hello, they fired on me. I flew out that way the next day but didn't see them."

"Has Eddy Taylor set up roadblocks?" I asked.

"He has, they're at—"

My little sister Abigail, Abs to our family and close friends, was anything but little. She was five-eleven bare-footed, slim, but muscled-up from ranch work since she was ten years old. She had blonde hair cut long enough to support the almost constant ponytail that sticks out of her beat-up, tan-colored Stetson. Like me, she had the Kristen blue eyes. She still sported a work-outside-summer-and-fall tan, that was in vivid contrast to her light-blue eyes. She was truly beautiful, but the strongest, toughest individual I knew—man or woman. She was a tomboy through and through, but call her that, and you'd find yourself sitting on your ass and not knowing how you got there. She had been in many relationships, none of which had lasted more than a few months—she said she wouldn't settle for anyone that couldn't be her equal.

She had lived on the ranch her entire life, only leaving for college, a six-year stint at Cornell University to study hotel and resort management.

Today, instead of the usual jeans and long-sleeve flannel shirt she generally favored, she sported a full set of camos—pants, shirt, jacket, and combat boots. She had a plated vest on, though a lightweight model, and wore mirrored aviator glasses. She had a Glock resting in a thigh-mounted holster. Looking at her reminded me of those Norwegian female special forces soldiers that had trained with us in Afghanistan.

"—Marion on Highway 2 west of Kalispell and Olney further up 93 north of Whitefish. That's in addition to the barricade he's got set up northeast of Kalispell on Highway 40 at Columbia Falls. Ted over there, has barricades set up west and east of Missoula on Highway 90 at Frenchtown and Clinton."

"That's good progress," I said. "Ted can fill you in on what we've encountered down south that will create a very large safe zone."

Hearing his name, Ted stepped up and shook hands with Abs.

"Abigail," Ted said, craning his neck and looking up at her.

"Theodor," she answered coolly. "I've got your ammo in the back," she said, pointing to the Beaver. "I loaded it, but I'm not going to unload it too. Have a few of your people unload, please."

"Can you have four of your people stand overwatch, as well?" I asked.

"They're already in place and have been since we arrived this morning," he answered tersely, turning and walking away. "And I'll get some guys to unload for you, Abigail."

We watched as Ted left to gather up an unloading party.

"He's mad at me," Abs whispered. "Last week he asked me to stay overnight with him in Lolo and I told him in no uncertain terms that I wasn't interested and never would be. I didn't tell him so, but what guy do you know has a mustache? I mean, seriously. He looks like a short version of Magnum PI."

"Ouch. He must be twice your age and very confident in himself," I said. "But then again, dark times call for bold measures."

I keyed the comms and asked my team, along with Dawn, PJ, and Jane, to make their way to the plane.

A minute later, I was introducing my sister to the group.

Abs shook hands with each as they were introduced.

"Leave it to my brother to show up with a movie star," she said, after being introduced to Dawn. "It used to be stray dogs, cats, and Canadian geese he brought home. Now it's movie stars."

Dawn laughed and told Abs how she wouldn't be alive if it wasn't for us getting her blood flowing and her body warmed up. "And it's all thanks to Greta for finding me."

"Greta?"

"This is Greta," I said, leaning down and giving her ear rubs.

Abs kneeled in front of Greta and using both hands rubbed under her chin. "Aren't you the beautiful one," she said.

I was saving Renee for last. "Abs, this is Renee, my very significant other."

"It's very nice to meet you, Renee. But you are much too pretty for the likes of my brother," she said, a big grin on her face. "Just kidding, bro. My mother is quite anxious to meet you, Renee. So be prepared. She's already spruced up the Roosevelt cabin for you two."

Renee put her arm around my waist and hugged me tight. "Please tell your mother I'm looking forward to meeting her, too," she replied. "And your father and sister as well."

"You may regret those words," Abs said. "Our parents are characters."

"What's the weather like ahead?" I asked, stepping away from the ladies.

"Clear skies all the way to the ranch."

"On the flight down, did you see anything on the ground I should worry about?"

"I flew directly over 93 the entire way in the hopes of spotting you. I saw nothing in the way of trouble. There's an abandoned pass-through barricade a mile south of Lolo, but that's it. Roads are dry except for a few patches of snow where the sun can't reach."

"Speaking of roadblocks and barricades, are they screening people trying to get in?"

"You mean, are they asking if they're doctors, nurses, dentists, farmers, and or engineers? And the answer is yes. After you contacted us, it was dad who suggested they start doing that. It's resulted in letting quite a few in and having more deciding to stick around and contribute, in exchange for food and shelter."

Six of Ted's men started unloading boxes of ammo.

"Where did the ammo come from?" I asked, watching the men empty the cargo hold.

"Eddy Taylor," she answered. "Ted is under the mistaken belief that Eddy took most of the spoils collected after the last battle with Lassman at the barricade outside Lolo. But this is from the Montana National Guard. Eddy has an agreement with them."

"Eddy didn't take Lassman's supplies," I said. "We found Lassman's cache of weapons, ammo, and supplies down in Salmon. But Lassman and every one of his fighters are dead. We, along with a group of fighters down south, ambushed him in Mackay. We met a woman down there who oversees the local fighters. She's a retired air force colonel and a natural leader. She wants to combine forces with Eddy and Ted to create a state-wide militia. She's good people, Abs."

"Well, heck, brother, that's wonderful news about Lassman. He's been a pain in our ass since the blackout. Eddy is worried about the folks I spotted yesterday, and with Lassman and his fighters out of the picture, he can fully concentrate on this new group. We're going to fly out there later today in hopes of spotting them—can't easily hide a hundred-plus working vehicles."

"One hundred? Seriously?"

"Seriously. You heard right. One-hundred-plus. I stopped counting at eighty."

"I can't get over how fast things are falling apart, Abs. While I don't condone it, I can understand individuals reverting to looting in order to provide for their families—it's basic survival instinct. But one of the things I've learned about

Lassman, is that within two days of the blackout, he had gathered his group together and was on the move."

"We know, he started his looting and killing spree at a Walmart Supercenter further north up 93 in Missoula. We were totally unprepared for him."

Abs was looking behind me at the Humvee. "What's that on top of the Hummer? Under the cover."

"A Minigun."

"Is that the gun Arnold Schwarzenegger's character shoots the jungle to pieces in the movie *Predator*?"

"It is."

"No shit? How did you come by a Minigun?"

"Down in Battle Mountain, Nevada. Spoils of a home invasion gone bad. Can I fill you in on the answer to that and other questions once we're at the ranch?"

"Of course."

"Is Asta at the ranch today?"

"She is. She was driving up to the house as I was leaving for the airstrip. She pulled a two-day shift at the hospital, and I'm sure she's still sleeping."

"Are you flying directly back to the ranch?"

"Yep. Meeting Eddy later this morning at the airstrip. Why? You want a ride?"

"Not me, but two of our group are injured and need to see a doctor. Susan suffered a gunshot wound and Kris has a dozen or more infected knife cuts and hasn't been taking her meds. Can they ride back with you?"

"Of course. Can they be ready to go soon? I plan on leaving once this load is off the plane," she answered, turning to see how the unloading was progressing. "I don't like having the Beaver sitting on the ground and exposed for long."

I spotted Susan and Kris and waved them over.

"What's up?" Susan asked.

"I'm sending you two to the ranch with Abs," I said. "My other sister, Asta, is home today. As I mentioned before, she's an emergency room physician and will treat your wounds. Get your backpacks and take a seat."

"On the plane?" Kris asked.

"Really?" Susan asked. "Can I bring my weapons on-board?"

"Yes, to all questions," I answered. "And please hurry—she's anxious to get back in the air. Kris, give your vest to Dawn and your comms to PJ."

"Cool," Susan said, turning to retrieve her backpack from the Cruiser. "I have dibs on shotgun."

"I really don't like flying on small planes," Kris said, undoing the vest's side retaining clips and slipping it over her head. "I'd rather drive the rest of the way."

"Listen, Kris, those cuts are infected and need to be looked at as soon as possible. While we should be at the ranch tonight, you know full well that shit happens, and we might be delayed. So, you're flying with Abs. Go get your backpack and meds," I said. "You can be pissed off at me now, but you'll thank me once you're hugging your kids in Seattle."

Kris nodded, took her comms and vest, and handed them to Dawn and PJ. She turned and walked slowly back to the ranch truck.

"Kathy, please search Kris' backpack. Look for weapons and make sure the key to the ranch truck stays in the ignition. The last thing we need is a hijacked plane and useless truck."

"Roger that," she said.

The men who'd been unloading finished up and waved to Abs as they walked back to their group.

"You need to keep an eye on Kris, Abs. She stole that white truck from a ranch in Nevada, and I don't trust her. Once she's at the ranch, restrict her to the ranch house or lodge room, and have her escorted should she have a good reason to venture further beyond the front porch of either building. I'll explain everything in detail tonight."

"Okay. We'll see you later today," she said, giving me another long hug before climbing up and into the pilot's seat.

"I'll follow 93 home. If I see something fishy, I'll fly back and update you via radio once I'm in range. Keep your comms on."

"Thanks for that. Is it okay if Susan carries her weapons onboard?"

"Sure."

"One more thing, Abs," I said, with as much seriousness as I could muster.

"Yes?" she answered, clearly concerned.

"Aren't you going to give a goodbye kiss to your boyfriend?" I asked as she cinched her seatbelt tight.

She smiled and gave me the middle finger. I watched as she primed the cylinders with fuel by pushing down and up on the plunger located to the left of her seat. She fiddled with fuel mixture levers located in the center of the instrument cluster. "Get the chocks for me, bro," she said. She closed her door, and a minute later, I heard the starter crank over. The prop spun five or six times to clear the oil in the bottom two cylinders. She engaged the mags, and the engine roared to life, white smoke surrounding the engine housing quickly whisked away by the wind.

I removed the chocks and stowed them away. I rapped my knuckles on the cargo doors to let her know they'd been removed and stowed.

Susan was first at the plane, and I told her what I'd told Abs about Kris. "Keep a close eye on her," I shouted in her ear.

"Happy to," she yelled back. I helped her up and into the co-pilot's seat. I got the seatbelt around her, snapped it into place, and snugged it up. Abs took a set of headphones and helped put them over her ears. Before Abs could plug them into the intercom system, Melissa was pushing me aside and planting a kiss on Susan's lips. Susan responded, and Abs and I were witness to a very long kiss. A rather obvious French kiss at that.

Abs looked at me from over Melissa's shoulder and silently mouthed *What the fuck?*

I grinned and shrugged. I then grabbed Melissa by her collar and gently led her to the ground. Kris showed up a minute later, and I helped her up and into the rear passenger seat. I tried to help her with her seat belt, but she swatted my hand away, said, "I absolutely hate it when you're right."

Happily retreating from an angry Kris, I closed the two starboard-side cargo doors and stepped back. I joined the remaining ladies, and we watched as the Beaver accelerated down the highway and quickly took to the air. I expected Abs to do a flyby, but she continued north toward home and was soon gone from view.

TWELVE

"Okay, let's head out," I said. "Dawn, Renee, and me in the Humvee—you two decide who drives. Melissa and Monica in the Cruiser, again, you two decide who drives. PJ, Jane, and Kathy in the ranch truck—PJ drives and Kathy provides security. Where's Journey?"

Jane opened one of her jacket pockets, took out the sleeping kitty, and handed her over. I held her up at eye level and one of her eyes opened and stared at me. She meowed and promptly fell back asleep. Greta heard the meow and trotted over to investigate. She stood on her two back legs and put her snout up to Journey's rear end.

"Why do animals do that?" Renee asked. "I've often wondered."

"Anal glands back there tell one dog a lot about another," PJ answered. "Just one of nature's many wondrous ways of helping to identify friend or foe."

"Can you imagine humans sniffing one another's butts?" Melissa said.

"They do. What's it called when you stick your face between someone's butt cheeks and the person moves their ass back and forth?" Kathy asked. "I saw a guy do that to a girl on that HBO show *Girls.*"

"Maybe motorboating?" Monica offered.

"Motorboating is when a guy, or a woman, puts their face and mouth in a well-endowed woman's cleavage and moves their head rapidly in a side-to-side motion while blowing out," Renee explained. "The resulting sound is akin to that of an outboard motor."

"I can attest to the accuracy of Renee's statement," I said sheepishly. "But I don't know what they call doing that between butt cheeks."

"It's called booty-boating."

We turned to see who had offered up the answer. And there was Jane, a big grin on her face.

"What? You guys think you're the only generation that knows this kind of stuff?"

"I hate to think what else you know," PJ said, a frown planted on her face.

"Don't worry, Mom. I think it's gross."

I handed Journey back to Jane and set out to find Ted Mitchell. I found him in deep discussion with five fighters back at the pickup's tailgate.

"Ted, we're going to head home now," I said, sticking out my hand. "It was nice meeting you, and we'll see you again in a couple of weeks when we head down to meet with Colonel Hughes."

"Look forward to it, Jon. Safe travels."

I turned and headed toward our three-vehicle convoy.

"Jon?" Ted asked.

I stopped and turned, said, "Yeah, Ted?"

"Not sure I said it before, but thanks for putting down Lassman and his fighters. Makes our job a lot easier knowing our home territory is safe, now that that group out west could become an issue."

"You're welcome. See you soon."

With no snow on the road ahead, I spent the next few minutes taking the Cruiser and ranch truck out of four-wheel drive and back into two-wheel drive. Once that was done, I walked around the front of the Humvee and settled into the passenger front seat. Renee was driving with Dawn in the back seat. Greta was lying next to Dawn with her head in her lap and the rope toy a few inches away.

I keyed the comms and asked for a check.

"Hear you fine," from Melissa.

"Ditto," from Kathy.

"PJ?" I asked.

"Oh. . . fine. I hear you," she answered.

"All good," from Monica.

"What are we waiting for? Let's get home," Renee said.

THE ROADWAY SURFACE WAS DRY except for the narrower portions of highway with tall trees lining both shoulders. The sun would only shine on the roadway from late morning to early afternoon, and the snow, while slushy, was still there.

I had Renee bring us up to fifty and hold steady. I knew from having driven this highway dozens of times, that we had no sharp or hairpin turns ahead of us. We were making great progress and only slowed twice to avoid dead semi-trucks. The Bitterroot River made an occasional appearance in the distance off the right-hand shoulder.

I keyed the comms and asked PJ if the trailer behind her truck was behaving.

"No issues so far," she replied.

"Cool. If you start to see any sway, slow down and let me know."

There were retail businesses on both sides of the highway, though separated by a mile or more of open space. None had been looted or burned. We passed a winery, numerous churches, auto repair shops, propane suppliers, and every other service provider a town might need. We even passed two working sixties-era pickups headed south. They flashed their lights at us and waved in greeting.

"Folks are venturing out," Dawn said. "It's good to see."

"Feeling safe does that," Renee said. "I know I'd want to check things out if I had a working vehicle and thought it was safe."

We slowed, and Dawn performed her PSA in the town of Victor. A group of residents were gathered in front of Wrangler Chow and Brewery, and we were greeted with friendly waves and lots of thumbs-up.

The Bitterroot River was off to our right once again.

"These highways are in great shape," Melissa said. "I mean, I don't think I've ever driven on such smooth roadways."

"Montana spends a bunch of money maintaining the more important, well-traveled highways," I said. "That's why, if you drive through Montana in the summer, you're always running into roadway construction."

"Well, whatever, it's nice driving on a smooth surface," Melissa said. "And these passing lanes every few miles are nice, too."

"Lots of RV's and tourists in the spring and summer means traffic jams and impatient drivers near and in towns."

Stevensville, Montana was next up, but the town itself was a mile or two off to the right and we saw no signs of activity.

We passed by the Lee Metcalf Wildlife Refuge on our right. The Bitterroot River flowed only a few feet from the right shoulder. Fifteen minutes later we entered the town of Florence. We slowed and Dawn broadcast her PSA as we passed the local Ace Hardware store.

We were soon past Florence and on our way to Lolo, a set of railroad tracks on our right accompanying us the entire way.

According to the colonel, Lolo was the site of the latest battle between the MPF and Lassman's so-called Montana

Militia. Lassman had suffered a staggering loss and had retreated south to Salmon, Idaho, evidently bringing with him his cache of weapons and ammo.

On the southern outskirts of town, we came upon the impressive barricade set up by the MPF. It was built of flattened cars and pickups piled three high and stretching across both lanes of the highway. In front of the pile were six-foot-high steel plates with firing slots cut out. *I'll have to ask Abs how they were able to transport flattened vehicles to the site… let alone stack them.*

To the left of the barricade was a steep hillside which afforded no passage and gave the defenders the very advantageous high ground from which to rain fire down upon the invaders. To the right was a deep drainage ditch with steep sides, which would be impossible for anything less than an Abrams tank to navigate.

In the very middle of the wall of cars was an opening the size of a large semi-truck. Once inside, I guessed you'd have to turn sharp left, then sharp right, and then sharp left again before you got out of the maze—from all appearances, it was the same system and set-up we had used in Iraq and Afghanistan. Except instead of crushed vehicles, we had used fifteen-foot-high concrete walls.

They had built it in the perfect spot—the only way past this wall was through it. Which had proved impossible for Lassman and his fighters. Twenty to thirty of Lassman's cars and trucks were still sitting where they'd been shot to hell. Most had flat tires and shattered windshields. I could only imagine the human carnage that had taken place here. Why Lassman had thought his fighters could possibly overcome the impressive barricade and its superior high ground would remain a mystery and go down in Montana lore as the stupidest thing Lassman ever tried. It had also been the beginning of the end for his group.

The impressive barricade, while now unmanned, still presented us with a challenge: getting the trailers through. The sharp "S" turns inside the barricade were just so. . . sharp. In Iraq and Afghanistan, the barricades had been designed and built by the Corps of Engineers, and built to allow the passage of large semi-trucks, tanks, and armored personnel carriers. Here, not so much.

"Renee, bring us to a stop, please." I keyed the comms, said, "we're stopping here and I'm going to check the interior. I'm concerned that we may not be able to get the trailers through. Monica and Kathy, set up a close-in perimeter next to your vehicle."

"Why do you think we can't fit through?" Melissa asked. "The opening looks to be plenty large enough."

"You familiar with a slalom ski race?"

"Yes."

"That's what's inside that structure. There are "S" turns that we may not be able to get the trailers through. I need to check it out."

"Got it," Melissa said.

"I'll be right back," I told Renee and Dawn. "I'm taking Greta." I opened the rear passenger-side door, and Greta jumped to the ground. She took up her standard position on my left, and with her hugging my side, we walked the hundred yards to the twelve-foot-high wall of metal.

I put my hand out and told Greta to search. She took off and disappeared inside the barricade. Fifteen seconds later she was back at my side, which I took as an all-clear sign. Together we walked the "S" turns and were in the clear on the north side of the barrier a few seconds later. We reversed the course and, using my boots as a twelve-inch guide, measured the distance from one turn to the nearest interior barrier wall. Thirty-five feet. The two trailers were about the same length: seventeen feet. Add to that the length of the hitch and tow vehicle and we were looking at almost forty-five feet. If I remembered my high school geometry, primarily angles: acute, right, and obtuse, we'd make it through. But many years had passed since Mr. Arbuckle's geometry high school class. I stood back and eyed the angles—doable. Especially with swiveling trailer hitches. I hoped, anyway.

I keyed the comms, said, "I think we're good. Renee, go ahead and drive up and into the entrance. Once inside, stay to the right, make your turn and stay to the left and so on. I'll walk alongside and guide you through it."

"Roger that," she replied and started her approach.

Once inside the barricade, I had her hug the right side. When the trailer's right front tire was even with the barricade, I had her turn the Humvee's wheel hard left. The Humvee turned left, and the trailer swiveled left on the hitch ball. The trailer obediently followed, clearing the left-hand side of the entrance by two feet.

"Now stay as far left as you can. Go forward. More. Two more feet. . . and stop. Now turn a hard right." And again, the trailer cleared by two feet. Renee repeated the process one last time, and she was free of the barricade with open highway ahead.

The Humvee's rear passenger-side door opened, and Dawn whistled for Greta. Greta looked at Dawn and then up at me.

"Go ahead, girl."

Greta ran for the open door and jumped up onto Dawn's lap.

"Sorry, Jon," Dawn said, before shutting the door.

"Yeah, I bet," I said, under my breath.

I walked back through the barricade and waved PJ up.

"Stay to the right and stop when I—"

"I heard you guide Renee through," she said. "I've got this."

And she did. She was a pro at hauling a trailer, and we were headed north once again in no time.

HIGHWAY 93 THROUGH LOLO WAS lined on both sides by strip malls and the odd retail store and service provider. We passed a McDonalds, a casino, a Tractor Supply Company, and at a Dairy Queen on the right, we spotted a large group of folks cleaning up broken glass and covering broken windows with sheets of plywood. They waved and gave us the thumbs-up as we drove by.

"Shall we do a PSA announcement?" Dawn asked.

"I think we're done with the PSAs," I answered. "I have a feeling these folks already know the news."

The comms chirped. "Do you think the DQ is up and running?" Melissa asked. "I'm suddenly craving a vanilla cone."

"I'd go for the Reese's Extreme Blizzard," PJ chimed in. "And Jane likes the Chocolate Dipped Cone."

"I'd take any ice cream," Monica said.

Up ahead, on the left, was a Cruise America RV rental station. There were thirty or forty RVs of various sizes parked neatly on the small lot. Most, if not all, had people standing in front of them who appeared to be living in them.

"What a great solution for housing stranded travelers," Melissa said over the comms.

"It is, isn't it," Renee responded. "Might not have electricity, but they provide shelter from the elements, a bed, and heat if they have propane in the tanks. Good enough for the short term anyway."

From the back seat of the Humvee, Dawn said, "In total, I've probably spent months, maybe even a year of more, living in trailers and RVs on shoot locations where hotels weren't close by. I like 'em. Especially the Airstreams. Could I live in one full-time? If I had to, you bet."

"Before the blackout, Bradley and I were about ready to purchase a Winnebago Revel," Kathy said over the comms. "The Revel is an RV built into a nineteen-foot-long Mercedes Sprinter Van. It's got four-wheel drive, a bed that lifts up which provides a ton of storage in the back, hot and cold water, a toilet, shower, refrigerator, stove top. . . Heck, pretty much everything our house has but obviously on a much smaller scale."

"A house with wheels," PJ added.

"A house that could climb steep mountain trails," Kathy added.

"Bet you're glad you didn't buy it," Renee said.

Kathy laughed, said, "You're right there. It would've been a $160,000 hunk of useless metal. But heck, we could have always slept in it."

"Renee, let's take advantage of the clear roads and make up some time," I said. "Take her up to fifty and keep it there, as long as it's safe, even through towns." I keyed the comms and informed the drivers behind of the new speed.

I reached over and took ahold of Renee's hand, said, "Hi, babe. We're almost there."

"Hi back. You know what's the first thing I'm going to do once we're in our cabin?" Renee asked.

"Do I need to cover my ears before he answers?" Dawn said from the back seat.

"I'm sure I'll be happy to go along with whatever it might be," I said, laughing.

"And we'll do whatever you're envisioning, for sure. But not till after I take a long hot shower," Renee answered. She then looked at me with a worried expression on her face. "Wait, is there going to be hot water at the ranch?"

"Sadly, no. Remember, we're in survival mode. Water is for drinking and cooking, not for hot showers. Even short ones. We have plenty of body wipes though." I'd said all that with a serious face to match my serious tone.

My answer was met with total silence—from the back seat as well as the front.

"Oh," Renee finally said.

"Oh, is right, Renee," Dawn said. "We can always start a fire and boil some water for a warm-water rinse-down."

Renee released my hand and turned to look at me, said, "I guess. And that second thing we were going to do, mister, will have to go on the back burner. So sorry. But feel free to go solo."

"Ouch," I said. "I guess I'll have to take that long hot shower solo."

"But you just said there was no hot—"

"I think he's fucking with you," Dawn said, interrupting Renee.

"Are you?" Renee asked, a hopeful plea in her voice.

"Yes," I answered, no longer able to keep up the charade.

"You suck," Renee said, smacking the top of my hand. "That hand isn't getting anywhere near me for. . . well, a few hours anyway."

"That was just plain mean," Dawn added, reaching forward and whacking the side of my head.

"Sorry, guys, it was just so much fun watching your reactions."

"So there really is hot water for showers?" Renee asked. "Like at Sig's place?"

"Yes, like at Sig's place. The ranch has propane up the wazoo. Years ago, right after I was born, the lodge ran out of propane for hot water, and Dad had to face a bunch of pissed-off New York City lawyers and their spouses. They'd paid a bunch of money to play cowboy for two weeks, and while they didn't mind getting dirty during the day, they wanted that hot shower after getting off the horse at the end of the day. Dad had the tank refilled the next day, but later had the thousand-gallon tank replaced with a mammoth thirty-thousand-gallon model. And taking it even further, each of the cabins has their own thirty-five-hundred-gallon tank. The main ranch house, where my parents and family live, has a thirty-thousand-gallon main tank and an eighteen-thousand-gallon backup. Recently, my father has invested heavily in geo-thermal systems to both heat and cool buildings and water. Chances are, he'll save the propane and use the geo-thermal.

"So hot showers, for the next few years at any rate."

"Hot water forever."

"Your ranch has a lodge and guest cabins?" Dawn asked.

"It does."

"Is it named the Double T?"

"Yes," I answered, surprised she knew the name. "The official name is Kristen Double T. I'm surprised you've heard of it."

"I have. Quite a few of my actor friends have been guests at your ranch, some quite frequently. It's on the 'A' list of places to escape for a little rest and relaxation between film projects. And you're known for absolute discretion. You even have a long runway in the middle of nowhere, which means private jets can land with no paparazzi taking pictures. But why didn't you mention it before?"

"Since I was a little kid, my parents have stressed how important it is to not mention who our guests are. It's been drummed into us to the point that I never mention it to anyone. If I were to mention it, I think it would sound like I was bragging."

"Well, okay. I understand that. However, I would like to reserve the Aspen cabin for the duration of the apocalypse."

"The Aspen cabin?" Renee asked.

"The Aspen cabin is one of the lodge's nicest," I answered.

"If you call a photo of the Aspen cabin's exterior on the cover of one of last year's *Architectural Digest*s, and the Double T Lodge and Ranch being named one of the top five lodges in North America by *Conde Nast* being *nice*," Dawn said.

"Abs is the one that made the lodge and conference center into what it is today," I said. "And the ranch is still that: a viable working livestock and land management concern."

Renee looked over at me, said, "You failed to mention any of this to me. And then there's the plane."

"Eyes on the road, please," I said, pointing a finger at the road ahead.

"What else haven't you told me? Huh?" she said, sounding pissed off.

I thought for a moment, then said, "I told you I love you. Doesn't that count?"

"Girl, you need to quit while you're ahead," Dawn said. "He's got you there, sweetheart."

Renee laughed and pointed a finger at me. "Just fuckin' with ya."

————————————

ONCE NORTH OF LOLO, WE were again accompanied by the seemingly ever-present Bitterroot River on the east side of the highway. We passed by the occasional wooden power poles with burnt tops and downed lines. The closer we got to Missoula, the more often we encountered dead trucks or cars. Every semi-truck with a trailer had been opened and emptied.

"It's ten miles to Missoula," I told the group. "It's by far the largest city we've encountered, but lucky for us, the state built a bypass road south of town that will take us northwest and directly to Interstate 90. We'll be on 90 headed west for five miles when we hit 93 North again. Once we're back on Highway 93, we're looking at roughly 110 miles to Kalispell."

"And it's safe from here to the ranch?" Monica asked.

"Abs flew over this route this morning and didn't spot any problems. And Lassman and his group are out of the picture, but there's still going to be the lone individual who needs to provide for himself and family. At this point, people are going to be running short on food and water, even those folks who were somewhat prepared with a well-stocked pantry. Desperate people are dangerous. Then there's the neighborhood groups that have banded together and are bound to be out foraging. What I'm saying is: we can't let our guard down."

The comms fell silent and the three of us in the Humvee were content to watch the beautiful Montana winter scenery pass by.

We'd passed a U-Haul center on the left when PJ keyed her comms. "A mile up on the right is a pet hospital owned and operated by Katie Fitzhugh, a friend of mine. We attended and graduated vet school together at University of California, Davis. Can we stop for five minutes so I can check in on her? The building is on the highway."

"Ten minutes only, please," I said. "Drivers, park on the highway and keep the engines running. Monica and Kathy, please provide a close-in perimeter watch."

The building appeared ahead on the right, and Renee slowed to a stop directly in front. Monica and Kathy set up their overwatch position. We watched as PJ ran across the parking lot toward a set of double glass doors. She tried to open the door and found it locked. She tapped her knuckles on the glass and, with her hands cupped and shielding her eyes, peered inside. She turned to us and shook her head. She had started walking back to the ranch truck when a woman appeared behind her at the front right corner of the building. The woman was holding a shotgun at the ready position then lowered the barrel as recognition must have set in. The two women embraced and disappeared around the side of the building.

Greta whined for a potty break. Dawn opened her door, and Greta circled the Humvee twice, came to a stop at the point she originally touched ground, circled in place four times, and finally peed. She sat and waited for the door to open. The door opened and she jumped back onto Dawn's lap.

"Greta, I love you, baby, but you need a bath," Dawn said. "Heck, we both do."

Two men and a woman walked out of the motorcycle dealer next door to the pet hospital and approached the Humvee. They appeared unarmed so I let them walk up to the Humvee's driver's door.

I opened my door, stepped out, walked around the front bumper and stood next to the driver's door. I undid the Velcro strap holding the Glock in place and kept my hand on the grip, ready to pull it out if need be.

"Jon?" Monica said.

"Walk to the back of the trailer, driver's side, and let them know you're there."

"Roger that."

The woman came to a halt and stuck out her hand. I took it and we shook. Her grip was strong and confident. She was perhaps a couple years older than me. Both men were giants. One was at least three inches taller than me, and the other maybe five inches. Obviously, there are taller guys than me in the world, but I don't often come across them.

"Hello, Master Sergeant," the woman said. "My name is Patty Green and these big guys behind me are my brothers Matt and Peter."

"Nice to meet you, Patty. Gentlemen. Are you armed?"

"No, sir. We left our weapons in the shop," the taller of the two answered.

"Which brother are you?" I asked him.

"Peter, sir."

"You own the shop, Patty?"

"Yes, sir. For the last few years, anyway." She pointed to the Humvee, said, "I spent three years of my life drivin' the same identical up-armored Humvee in Afghanistan. I was an MP at Bagram. I mostly pulled perimeter duty and spent twelve hours a day, seven days a week sittin' my ass in one of those uncomfortable seats. Finally bought a pillow at the base exchange and saved my ass. We didn't have a Minigun, though. We did sport a .50-cal, however. Shame that the base is now swarming with Al-Qaeda."

The comms squawked alive. It was Monica. "Master Sergeant, we've got an old pickup truck approaching from the south. A half mile out."

From the corner of my eye, I saw PJ and her friend emerge through the hospital's double glass entrance doors. The two women hugged. PJ then turned and ran back to the ranch truck. The woman stepped back into the clinic and watched PJ until she was back at the truck. She then closed and locked the double glass doors behind her.

"Monica, let it pass on by," I said.

"Roger that."

"That's Paul Stafford. He owns the U-Haul rental center down the road a bit," Patty said, watching the truck approach.

The sixties-era Ford pickup slowed and stopped next to the four of us. The passenger window rolled down revealing a man driving with a young girl in the passenger seat. The man leaned over, said, "Morning, Patty, boys. Does the man know what's goin' on with the power?"

"Haven't gotten that far, Paul. Hi, CeCe," Patty said.

"Hi back," the girl said, smiling. She had shiny metal braces like Jane's.

"Well, sir, can you tell us what's happening with the power?" Paul asked.

"There was a—" was as far as I got.

The comms squawked. "There are two more old pickups headed our way," Monica said. "Half mile south and moving fast."

We all looked back down the road. It was Paul Stafford looking in his rearview mirror who recognized them. "That's gonna be Mark Perdue and his daughter Rebecca. They own and manage a bunch of apartment buildings in Missoula and Kalispell. Mark's company is the largest commercial and residential construction firm in Montana. And Rebecca is a former Miss Montana and runs the rental side of things."

My heart suddenly skipped a beat. "Let them on by," I managed to say.

The two pickups slowed to a stop behind Paul's pickup. Both drivers got out and walked over to us.

"They're both armed, Jon. Handguns in belt holsters," Melissa said.

"It's fine, guys," I said. "They're good."

Rebecca Perdue was indeed beauty-pageant beautiful. Tall, with long jet-black hair cascading from beneath a black Stetson hat. With dark-green eyes, light-olive skin, she looked to have some Native American heritage in her bloodline. She wore tight wrangler jeans, a long-sleeve black T-shirt under a half-zipped Levi jean vest, revealing an impressive bust beneath. She was walking on well-worn Justin boots.

Rebecca Perdue was my sister Abs's best friend. And my ex-fiancé.

"Good morning, y'all," Rebecca said with a smile and friendly wave. "I was right, Dad. That is Jon's Land Cruiser."

"Mornin' Rebecca," Patty and the brothers replied in unison. The brothers stood taller and sucked in their stomachs.

"Hi, Jon," Rebecca said. She followed the hello by walking up to me, placing her right hand behind my head, and pulling my head down a few inches to more easily plant a kiss on my lips. The kiss lasted at least ten seconds; nine seconds longer than proper protocol allowed.

"Hi, Becca," I said, ending the kiss and pulling back. I was the only person besides her grandmother that she allowed to call her Becca. "You haven't aged a day since I last laid eyes on you. Hello Mr. Perdue."

"Mornin', Jon. Good to see you again. Been a few."

"Yes, sir, it has. Maybe ten years. You were at the ranch giving my dad some quotes on a remodel."

"That's right. If memory serves, we won that job. In fact, I was at your ranch yesterday. Your dad wants me to build a large dormitory-slash-bunkhouse. He also asked if we wanted to stay at the ranch. We're taking him up on the offer, and we're on our way there now. He also filled me in on the conversation you two had a few days ago. Is it true about the power and China's involvement?"

"The power grid will be down for years," I answered. "As to the Chinese involvement, it's pure speculation at this point. All we know for sure is that the missiles came from North Korea."

"We all know North Korea doesn't have the technical—" he started to say.

"We're going to be ranch-mates—just like the old days," Becca said, interrupting her dad and changing subjects. She took a step back and looked me over from head to toe. "You look great in your battle gear, Jon. Are those the same camos you were wearing in that picture you sent me a few years ago? It was the one with Burt standing next to you and you were both kitted out with your vests and the other stuff. How is Burt, by the way?"

"Burt is doing fine. He's married." I silently cringed, for I was always tongue-tied around Becca.

"I know," she replied, well aware of the effect she had had, hell, was having, on me. She came in close, close enough that her jean vest was touching my armor. She put her hand on my upper arm and started lightly rubbing. "If you recall, we went to the wedding. I'll never forget that wonderful week we spent together in Las Vegas."

I heard the Humvee's driver door open behind me. Renee stepped out and Dawn was soon at her side. Both had taken their boonie hats off and their manes were flowing in all their glory. I looked from a beautiful Becca to an equally beautiful Renee and Dawn, and I just plain didn't know what to say.

Renee stepped in and put her left arm around my waist. Dawn was on my left and put her right arm around me.

"Hi there," Renee said. "I'm Renee."

"And I'm—" Dawn started to say.

"Dawn Tillman," Mark Perdue sputtered out.

"Hello," Dawn said, extending her hand toward Mr. Perdue.

"The night before the blackout, we rented *Restless Moon* from Direct TV," he said, shaking her hand. "We loved you in that movie, didn't we Rebecca?"

Becca nodded but said nothing. She had adopted a sullen look and crossed her arms, looking from Renee to Dawn, trying, I figured, to work out which woman I was with.

"To my knowledge, I don't think we've ever had a movie star come through town," Patty said, putting a hand over her heart. She shook Dawn's hand. "You're even more beautiful in person."

"Well, thank you. That's very kind of you to say."

Becca didn't appear happy to have the attention taken away from her.

"Renee, Dawn, this is Rebecca Perdue and her father Mark," I said. "Our two families go back several generations. Becca and I grew up together."

"And were engaged to be married," Becca added. "Don't forget to mention that bit of information."

Renee looked at me, said, "Really?"

"Rebecca, no sense in bringing up the past," Mark Perdue said.

"I'm thrilled that we have a movie star in our midst, but I'm still waitin' to hear what happened to the power," Paul Stafford said, his fingers drumming the top of his steering wheel impatiently.

"Well, folks, it's like this," Dawn said, and proceeded to tell them everything we knew about the blackout. "The power isn't likely to be restored for a decade. Perhaps longer than that."

"Christ almighty, those friggin' Chinese!" Patty's shorter brother Matt exclaimed. "First it's the fuckin' Covid-19 that escaped from their weapons lab. Yeah right—more like injected into Chinese agents and sent to us in the form of Asian airline passengers. That killed a million plus of us here in the States after the Delta variant's sixth surge went wild. Stupid anti-vaxxers 'bout kilt us all. Then Omicron hits us, and we lose another couple hundred thousand. We get that under control, and then China sends four missiles, two of which get through and detonate, and takes out the country's power grid. That'll probably kill a million more."

"More than that," Renee corrected. "We figure almost sixty percent of our population will die over the course of the next year."

"That's almost two hundred million deaths. Mostly from starvation, lack of clean water, disease, and scarcity of medicines," Dawn said.

"And let's not forget the deaths that'll come at the hands of our fellow citizens," I added. "You wouldn't believe the things we've seen in the last few days."

"I find those figures hard to believe," Paul Stafford said.

"Well consider this then," Renee said. "Between South and North Korea, seventy-five million are probably already dead from the nuclear fallout from the missiles we sent back at 'em."

We were all silent as we digested that huge number. It was CeCe who broke the silence. "Dad, she said the power won't be back on for ten years, maybe longer. Is that possible?"

"Who knows for sure, honey buns," Paul Stafford answered. "Let's get on home and tell your mom the news."

CeCe waved goodbye as Paul Stafford sped off.

"We should probably get back to the store and start making some long-term plans," Patty said. "Thank you for the information, Master Sergeant. Good luck to you all."

"You by chance have a working ATV you want to trade for?" I asked. "One that would be good on-trail and off."

"I don't have a working ATV, but I do have an old—and I mean very old—Honda XL350 motorcycle I could trade," she said. "It's designed and built to be both on-road and off. It has good-sized knobby tires on it, too."

"Runs really good," one of her brothers said. "Rebuilt the motor myself. Got some surface rust on the paint, but that don't matter none. I mean, who gives a shit, right?"

"Right. As long as it runs. And the tires are decent."

"You have food to trade?" Patty asked.

"We do. I'll give you twenty-one Mountain House freeze-dried meals. Twenty-seven, if you throw in extra tubes, tires, and flat tire patches."

"Fifty. And I don't want any of their Chinese Stir Fry."

"Thirty-three. And I'll throw in five gallons of water. I'll add three more meals if you have a front or rear fork basket that will fit on it."

"Basket?"

"Like a bicycle basket that you'd put grocery bags in. Or a little dog."

Patty thought it over, then said, "Matt, that three-foot-by-two-foot black wire basket on the new Honda ATV might work. You put it together yet?"

"I haven't. Like, why would I? It aint gonna' run anyways. And the cargo carrier is what you're thinkin' of. I can install it for 'em if you want, Patsy. Won't take but a couple of minutes."

"Thirty-six Mountain House meals and the water. Done. Matt, install the cargo carrier, then fire the thing up and ride it back so the master sergeant here knows it runs. And bring the extra tires, tubes, and a few patch kits."

I knuckle-bumped Patti, said, "Good. Mr. Perdue, we're also headed to the ranch. If you want, you're welcome to slide in between that white truck with the trailer and the Land Cruiser. Might be safer than your two trucks alone."

"Sounds like a plan to me. Thanks."

"You two have more weapons besides those two handguns sitting on your hips?" I asked.

"We do. We both have shotguns and an AR-15 with lots of loaded magazines."

"Good. How was the trip up to the ranch yesterday? Any issues?"

"None. I took the bypass around Missoula, both there and back, with no problems. I did see quite a few folks out and about, but none approached me. I did drive pretty fast through town though."

"Good to know," I said. "We have one stop to make, and that's north of Kalispell. The woman driving the white Ford truck with the large trailer behind it is a veterinarian from Lolo. We're getting them and their trailer to her father's place. We have comms, but no extras to let you use. So, if you see something fishy, honk your horn three times and we'll stop. Leave plenty of space between you and the truck ahead of you— at least a hundred feet. You good on gas?"

"We have full tanks—got it from one of our construction sites."

"Renee and Dawn, will you get the Mountain House meals out of the trailer, please. No Chinese Stir Fry. And get one of the blue water jerry cans, too."

"Sure," Renee said.

"Come on, let's get them," Dawn said, taking Renee's hand and guiding her away. Becca was directly in their path and showed no signs of stepping aside. Mark Perdue took hold of her elbow and scooted her out of their path.

A few minutes later, we all heard a motorcycle start up. Matt appeared from around the far side of their building. He had extra tires around his neck which looked like black hula hoops. The motorcycle appeared tiny beneath his huge frame. It looked like he was riding a child's tricycle, for in order to get his feet on the pedals, his knees stuck out comically to the sides. It might have been a dark-blue when new, but now had blended-brown spots from surface rust. He leaned back, goosed the throttle, and performed a wheelie—it might have been rusty, but there was nothing wrong with the motor. He cut the engine and coasted up to us. The black wire cargo carrier was mounted in front of the handlebars.

The bike would be perfect for its intended use.

"Where you want it?" Matt asked.

"Let's put it in the back of the white pickup on top of the boxes," I said. "The tailgate has room to go down, but we'll have to load it sideways because of the trailer."

"Come on, Peter, let's load this up for the man." Matt lowered the tailgate and hopped up into the bed. Peter lifted the front wheel, and Matt easily lifted the machine up and into the back. He laid it on its side and on top of the Kisses cartons, hopped to the ground, and shut the tailgate.

"You're good to go, sir," Peter said.

"Thanks, guys. It's kind of loud. By any chance do you have a quieted-down muffler that I could have. I need it to be stealthy. I can install it."

"We have just the thing," Matt said, looking at his sister for the okay to grab it.

Patty nodded her assent, and Matt took off at a fast trot. He disappeared into the shop and reappeared thirty seconds later holding a short, stubby chrome muffler in his right hand. "This will really keep the noise to just a few decibels," he said, handing it to me. "It's very restrictive and will knock down a couple of horsepower, but if you want stealth, then that muffler is exactly what you want."

"Thanks."

Renee and Dawn were back with the Mountain House pouches a minute later, and once the meals and water had been handed over, we regrouped to our vehicles. Mr. Perdue and Becca drove their pickups round and got in line behind the ranch truck.

All three Greens waved goodbye, turned, and walked back toward their motorcycle shop.

I looked over at Renee in the driver's seat and smiled. She didn't smile back. *Uh oh.* She made no move to put the Humvee in gear and head out.

"You ready to go?" I asked her.

"When were you going to tell me you'd been engaged?" she asked coolly, turning her head to stare at me. It sounded more like an accusation than a question.

"Will you please start driving," I said. "We can talk while you drive." I was starting to lose patience, but managed to say please again.

"Renee, we need to get going," Dawn said.

"Yeah, you're right, the both of you. Sorry."

I keyed the comms, said. "It's ten miles to the southern outskirts of Missoula and then another hundred miles to Kalispell. We're going to be driving through five or six miles of packed city streets. There are almost eighty thousand people living in Missoula, which means it's got more potential for danger than any other town we've driven through. So, keep a very sharp eye out. Especially Melissa and Monica in the Cruiser."

"Didn't your sister say the roads were safe?" Monica asked.

"She did. But she's looking down from three or four thousand feet. She can't see individuals or small groups of people. Remember, that's eighty thousand people, and most were totally unprepared for any kind of disaster let alone a decade-long power outage."

"Bring it up to fifty, Renee. Faster the better," I said.

"Less time for the bad guys to react?" Dawn asked.

"Yes."

We soon crossed over the Bitterroot River and entered a more heavily developed area. We had to slow and make our way around dead cars that had died at numerous traffic signals. We passed dozens of boarded-up commercial buildings and restaurants—some burned to the ground. An Applebees looked to have been looted, but the Walmart a bit further back in the same shopping center seemed intact. There was a line of people waiting to go inside, with armed guards controlling the crowd of several hundred.

"Well, that's good to see," I said. "It means there is some type of working authority here."

"It's weird driving this road and seeing people everywhere. Like everyday life in a big city, but without cars or power. It's as if everything is frozen in time except the people," Melissa said.

"Like a *Twilight Zone* movie," PJ added.

We fell silent as we made our way north. We passed Toyota and Ford dealerships on the left, hundreds, perhaps thousands, of brand-new cars and trucks destined to remain parked for the rest of time. We saw dozens of people at a Super 8 Motel sitting or standing in front of its rooms.

Bicycles were the main source of transportation. We saw dozens of people pedaling with backpacks strapped to their backs, making their way in the direction of the Walmart store.

I keyed the comms, said, "We turn left at the next signal, which takes us onto South Reserve Street."

The intersection was a major one on this side of town. There were at least thirty dead cars and three semi-trucks clogging all four lanes. Renee slowed, navigated her way around the backup, and turned left. I watched in the sideview mirror as the rest of our convoy negotiated the turn behind us.

A golf course was on our left, and on the right, retail strip malls, one after another. Most intersections had been controlled by traffic lights, and more often than not, a line of abandoned cars and trucks slowed our progress. Soon, both sides of the road were lined by strip malls. We continued through this thick commercial environment for several miles. The road eventually left the commercial section of town and we entered a residential area.

We crossed over a river and there was another Walmart Supercenter on our left. Again, there were armed guards allowing people to enter for supplies. There were many older vehicles in the parking lot that appeared to have been fired on. Most were burnt-out hulks with visible bullet holes in doors and along their flanks. *This must have been one of the battle sites with Lassman.*

We were again driving through a heavy commercial retail zone. There was a Panera Bread, Walgreens, Wendy's, and a Chipotle Mexican Grill, each closed and boarded-up. There was a WinCo Food Store that appeared to have been looted—the front windows shattered, both sets of entrance doors off their hinges and lying in the parking lot, the trash, debris, and abandoned shopping carts scattered about, looking like many of the third world countries I'd been in. The next three miles was more of the same. We passed by every fast-food franchise and travel motel chain available in the United States. *How many fast-food joints and motels could a city this size support?*

We passed a Costco, and like Walmart, there were armed guards controlling crowds. There was a short line of working vehicles waiting to get gasoline at the Costco Gas Pumps, a cardboard sign letting people know that gas was available, but with a limit of three gallons per week per vehicle. The sign also said the premises were under the control and protection of the MPF. I could see a man hand-pumping gas into his sixties-era pickup, again with an armed guard watching over things. *I wonder if they're giving gas away or bartering?*

We'd driven another mile through more heavy commercial strip malls, hotels, and restaurants, when I saw the Interstate 90 overpass ahead. We drove under the freeway, and Renee was preparing to make a left onto the on-ramp when I spotted a short line of people outside a Starbucks up on the right.

"Delay the turn, Renee," I said. "Get to the right and stop in front of the Starbucks. Park on the street so we can easily hang a U-turn and get on the freeway."

"You really think they're up and running?" Melissa asked.

"I have both hands together and I'm praying to the coffee gods," Monica said.

"Let's find out," I said. "Monica, Kathy, please set up a close-in perimeter.

"Renee, want to go with me?"

"You bet."

"I'd ask you too, Dawn, but your presence would create a frenzy."

"I'll drive again," Dawn offered.

"Great," I said. "Renee, put your hair back up and under the boonie hat. We want to look military. Get your rifle, too. While you're putting your hair up, I'll go back and fill in the Perdues."

Becca was standing next to the driver's door talking with her father. I told them the plan and asked if they'd be interested in a coffee. Both said yes. Becca gave me a six-item ingredient list and I said I'd try but made no promises.

Renee was waiting for me back at the Humvee. We walked together across the parking lot toward the line of people. There were seven people in line. I tapped the last person in line on her shoulder.

"They really serving?"

The woman was elderly and had a young child by the hand. "They are. The manager and one other person opened a couple of hours ago and are going to make 'em until they run out."

"How are people paying?" Renee asked.

"They want ammunition, but will take food or alcohol in trade."

"How long have you been waiting?" I asked.

"A minute before you arrived."

"They only have three items from the menu, so they're makin' 'em fast."

"Let's wait in line, Jon," Renee said.

"Okay."

"Do you know what happened to the power? And why our motorhome died?" the woman asked.

"We do have some answers," Renee said. Several others in front of us in the line turned toward us and waited to hear what she had to say.

Renee started telling them what we knew. I keyed the comms and asked for a status check.

"All good, Jon," from Melissa.

"Also, all good," from PJ. "Salivating in place here."

"Good to go," from Monica. "I can smell the coffee out here in the street."

"An A-okay," from Kathy.

"And that's all we know," Renee said, finishing up with the news.

Three people who'd been waiting in line, turned and walked away. One of them, a pregnant Asian woman, started to cry as she walked toward the Best Western Motel next door.

The door to the Starbucks opened and a couple and another person walked out holding a cardboard tray with six coffees. They had smiles on their faces.

A young man, no more than seventeen years old and wearing a tan Starbucks shirt and a green visor, held the door open for the woman. Seeing no one behind us, he waved us through as well.

His coworker, a teenage girl about the same age and dressed in identical clothing, said, "We have three items on the menu this morning: cappuccinos, Cinnamon Dolce Latte, and Café Mocha. We have cream and sweetener. That's it." She rested her hand on the butt of a black semi-auto handgun that was sticking out of a tan leather, belt-mounted holster.

"We'll take ammunition in trade. If you don't have that, we'll settle for food or alcohol," the young man said.

"I have a half a bottle of Kahlua you can have," the woman ahead of us answered hopefully.

"First things first," I said. "Take your hand off that handgun, young lady. Now."

The girl looked surprised by the order, but complied.

I smiled and said thanks. "NATO 5.56 rounds work for you?" I asked. "And I'll cover the lady's drink, too."

The girl's coworker took a long hard look at us and must have figured we had cases of ammo out in the Humvee.

"Ten rounds per drink."

"Two. And the young lady in front of us gets hers for free," Renee said, putting her hand on the older woman's shoulder.

"Seven," the Starbucks girl countered.

"Three. And that's our final offer," I said. "What's it gonna be?"

"How many drinks are you going to order, sir?" the girl asked.

"Ten," Renee answered. "All Café Mochas. And we'll give you the ammo already in a magazine."

"Done," the girl said. "David, go get their order started. Where's the ammo?"

Renee took a loaded magazine out of one of her vest pouches and held it up for inspection. "This is a thirty-round clip. You'll get it when we have the drinks."

I looked at Renee with newfound respect as to her negotiating skills.

"How is it that you're able to open up?" Renee asked the young barista. "I mean, seems like most people are scrounging for food and here you are making Café Mochas."

"I decided to bring my grandfather's old generator in and see if I couldn't get at least some of the non-computerized machines up and running," she answered. "I live pretty close by and have a key to let myself in. There's water in the back, and we were able to get at least the three menu coffee drinks available. The day of the blackout, I brought the store's cream home and stuck it in our garage storage freezer. It stayed cold this entire time.

"We're doing this in hopes of getting ahold of some ammo. We have weapons at home, but we burned through more than a thousand rounds out on BLM land last month and hadn't had a chance to replenish. The 5.56 is what I was hoping to get." She turned and helped her coworker with our order.

We chatted with the woman ahead of us. We learned she, her husband, and granddaughter, had been headed to Calgary, Canada when their RV had quit sometime during the night in the parking lot next door. They were doing okay, but she worried about what would happen to her husband when his extensive list of medications ran out.

Our order was soon finished. David loaded them into three cardboard carriers and slid them across the counter. The woman thanked us for the coffee, and she and her granddaughter turned and started back toward the motel. Renee handed over the loaded magazine, and we were distributing the steaming drinks a minute later.

Becca and her dad were still chatting when I brought them their coffees.

"Here you go," I said, handing each a very hot cup of coffee.

"Thank you," Becca said. She took a tentative sip and uttered an "Ahhhh."

"Thank you, Jon," Mark Perdue said, raising his cup in mock salute. "Much appreciated."

"Tell me, Jon, which woman are you sleeping with?" Becca asked, tilting her head and raising her eyebrows. "Movie-star-woman or the hot-blonde-next-door?"

"Enough of that, Rebecca," her father said, pointing a finger at his daughter.

"It's okay, Mr. Perdue. Becca and I have history, so I guess she's entitled to ask me questions. And I'll always answer honestly."

"Thank you, Jon," she said. "That's good to know."

It was time to have some fun. "I'm sleeping with both of them," I answered. "Usually at the same time."

I lightly touched Becca's arm, turned, and strode back to the Humvee.

I couldn't hear Becca's response, but I did hear Mr. Perdue say, "Well, you did ask, honey."

THIRTEEN

Dawn had one hand on the wheel and the other holding a cup of the precious liquid. She completed the U-turn and took the freeway entrance for 90 West. We drove in silence, savoring the joy of what could be the very last cup of a morning Starbucks coffee.

Being an interstate highway, and the major east–west route through Montana, there were dozens of dead and abandoned semi-trucks and autos. Most had coasted to the shoulder, but there were a few that blocked a lane. We weaved and dodged our way around them. Most of the semi-truck trailers had been opened and, those that had held usable supplies, emptied.

A few miles further on, we passed the eastern boundary of the Missoula Montana Airport. To our left, and a half mile from the freeway, was the end of the runway. Two planes, one a Boeing 737 and the other a twin-engine prop commuter plane, were sitting there as if waiting their turn to take off. The 737 appeared in position for takeoff and the other was still sitting in the taxi lane. Both planes' doors were open and the Boeing's emergency slides were deployed and still inflated. *At least these two hadn't fallen out of the sky.*

The comms chirped. It was Melissa. "The coffee is wonderful. Thanks!"

"This very well could be the last Starbucks I'll ever have," PJ said. "Thanks again."

"It almost feels like it's a normal workday and I'm driving to the office with my morning Starbucks," Monica said.

"Except there are people who want to kill you at every other corner and bend in the road," Kathy added.

I was surprised by how organized things had seemed. Other than armed guards at the gas stations and the two Walmart Supercenters we'd passed, the dead and abandoned cars and trucks, downed power lines, and the occasional burnt-out building, things seemed normal here.

"There's a bunch of people at the airport off-ramp and they're moving to block the road," Dawn shouted out.

So much for normalcy.

This stretch of interstate was four lanes, two in each direction and divided by a grass median. Running the length and equally centered between the eastbound and westbound lanes, was a wrist-thick wire acting as a last defense against vehicles crossing over the median and into oncoming traffic. To our right was an interstate embankment rising up at a forty-five-degree angle from the shoulder and clearly impassable. We could perform a U-turn, but with the trailer it would require several back-and-forth maneuvers which we didn't have time for. There was no place for us to go except straight ahead—right toward the crowd.

"Bring us to a stop, Dawn," I said. I keyed the comms and warned the other drivers we were stopping.

The size of the crowd was anywhere from two to three hundred. There was no way of counting, so thick was the mass of people now running toward us. Many were armed with red-handled fire axes, golf clubs, and ski poles. There were men and women in business suits and dresses, mothers holding babies in their arms, some with small children hanging onto Mom's or

Dad's belts as they were led along, and lots of folks with backpacks with wheeled luggage trailing behind them.

They were now three hundred yards out and closing. As they neared, I could hear them yelling for food and water.

"Kathy. Monica. Set up a close-in perimeter. Safeties off. Red dots on. Fingers off triggers until I say otherwise—ASAP, please. Drivers, stay behind the wheel and keep the engines running."

I powered up the loudspeaker, grabbed the microphone, stepped out onto the roadway, said, "Stop where you are! If you advance any further, we will fire!"

The crowd continued surging toward us. Clearly, a verbal warning wasn't enough. I raised my rifle, aimed a few feet over the advancing crowd, and fired a full clip on automatic. Nothing like thirty bullets whizzing a few feet over your head to bring some clarity to your sudden bravado. Without taking my eyes off the crowd, I dropped the empty magazine, inserted a fresh one, and charged the weapon.

I watched the crowd stop in its tracks, most dropping prone to the pavement and covering their heads.

Two remained vertical: a woman and a man. The woman turned and tried to wave the mob back onto their feet to resume the march. After thirty seconds of effort, the woman gave up, shrugging her shoulders and dropping her hands. The crowd stayed put.

"Thank you for stopping," I said. "We have information to give you. Wait one." I handed the mic to Dawn. "Go ahead and give them the message, minus the news about Lassman. These are probably stranded passengers so the name Lassman wouldn't mean anything."

Dawn delivered her PSA. I could see the crowd digest the news—hands covering their mouths in disbelief, heads shaking, hands over hearts, and sudden consolation hugs. Even from two hundred yards away, I heard many echoes of *No* and *It can't be true*. Many sat on the roadway, those with children bringing them close for reassuring hugs.

"Dawn, let them know that there's relative safety in town. But first, tell them we have no food or water for them and have them retreat to the off-ramp to let us pass. Tell them to gather their belongings and walk east, or the direction we just came from, to the second exit which is North Reserve Street—they'll see a Cracker Barrel on the left. Go right, which is south, and they'll see a Walmart Supercenter and a Costco. They're guarded by the Montana Protection Force, and they'll be let in for supplies."

"Will they really be let in?" Dawn asked, not sounding convinced. "And why were these people left on their own for this long?"

"I don't know. But when I speak with Abs, I'll ask her to get ahold of Eddy Taylor about granting them access. It'll take these folks three or four hours to walk that far, so we may have time to make it happen. The barricade is a few miles west of the airport, so at least they're inside the safety zone and should have safe passage to Walmart."

Dawn broadcast the message, and we watched as the crowd filtered back to the airport off-ramp. A few minutes later, the highway was clear.

With Monica and Kathy back in their respective vehicles, Dawn resumed heading west.

Before we passed the off-ramp, the man who had remained standing broke from the crowd and sprinted toward the center of the two lanes. It was clear that he would be there before us. Dawn moved left and the man mirrored our move. It didn't appear that he would let us get by without first running him over.

"Slow down and bring us to a stop," I said. "Let's see what he has to say. The rest of you keep an eye on that crowd and the surrounding areas."

The man was in his early thirties, unshaven, unkempt, and his clothes filthy. He was dressed in tan-colored khaki pants, light-blue button-down shirt, a dark-blue blazer, and once-white New Balance sneakers.

Dawn brought us to a stop ten feet in front of the man. I stepped out but left my door open, said, "Good morning, sir. I take it there's something you didn't understand in our message." *Tough guy, I am.*

The man started to walk toward us.

"Do not get any closer, sir."

The man stopped, said, "We are a group of 182 stranded passengers. We have lost eighteen of our number since the day of the blackout, six yesterday alone. Some died because of non-working pacemakers, but most from dehydration and lack of medicines. We drank the last bit of water two nights ago. We have scavenged the aircraft pantries, terminal restaurants, and snack bars. We've also raided the retail stores from the surrounding area, but armed looters and other scavengers beat us to it or threatened us away. We melted snow for drinking, but then the snow melted away. There is no more water or other drinkable liquid to be had. Well, that's not strictly true, Master Sergeant. We forced open a small liquor cabinet in one of the restaurants, but we hesitate to have a seven-month-old drink Jack Daniels. I understand you need to be on your way, sir, but can you spare any water? Even a few bottles would help us get to the off-ramp your message has us walking to. We have snacks and some crackers left, but it's water we're in dire need of."

"Are you ex-military, sir?" I asked. It would take a fellow soldier to recognize the badges on my arms and know their respective ranks.

"Yes. Did eight years in the Air Force, with two tours of Afghanistan at Bagram. I was on one of the last transports out after we turned the base over to the Afghans. Mustered out three months ago as an E-6 technical sergeant. I worked the tower as an air traffic controller. My name is Scott Powell. My wife is Katie, and the seven-month-old I mentioned is our daughter Myra. I was here at the airport for an interview as a controller in the tower. I brought my family with me so my wife could check out the town. And Montana."

"Where are you living now, sergeant?"

"With Katie's parents in Spokane."

"Did you get the job?"

"I did. We were on the plane for the flight back to Spokane when the aircraft simply shut down—it's a small prop job. It's still out there on the taxiway."

"Hold on one second, Mr. Powell," I said as I slid back into the Humvee.

I keyed my comms and asked if anyone knew how much water we had left.

"We have four of the five-gallon water cans and maybe six cases of bottled water left," Melissa answered.

"Kathy, Monica, and Renee, grab three of the water cans and five cases of the bottled waters. Leave us with one each of the water cans and one case of bottled water. Place them to the side of the trailer."

"Hey," Dawn said, her hand up and waiting for a high five.

I slapped her hand, stepped back out, and walked toward the sergeant. I stuck my hand out and we shook. "We're leaving you with some water. It's pretty much all we have left, save for a small reserve. It's not much, but should be enough to get you and your people to town."

He visibly relaxed, said, "Thank you, Master Sergeant."

I watched as Renee and Greta jumped out and helped uncover the trailer. Greta left the two women and sat at my side.

"We had quite a few of those beauties at Bagram," he said. "Smartest animals I ever saw."

"She's a great asset," I replied, leaning down and petting her behind her ears.

"Must have been multiple warheads to bring down the entire American power grid," he said.

"You'd be right. Two got through—one exploded over Colorado and the other over Ohio. They came from North Korea, though the Pentagon thinks that China was behind it."

"The Chinese. . . figures. There was talk among the intel specialists at Bagram that the Chinese were in serious talks with the Taliban soon after the ex-president released those fighters."

The comms chirped and it was Melissa. "Pickup approaching our six. Half mile and closing fast. Looks like a single driver, no passenger."

"Let it pass," I said.

An old Dodge Ram pickup, driven by a gray-haired man, clearly older than the truck, slowed as he drove around us. He waved and then accelerated away.

"That's a beautiful Land Cruiser in the rear of your column," Powell said, holding his hands above his eyes in an attempt at reducing the late-morning-sun's glare. "I've got an old International Scout back in Spokane I'm restoring. Got the rebuilt engine in it the week before we flew out here. Started it up and it actually runs—first time I ever rebuilt a motor."

"V8?"

"Yeah. Gutless, but lots of torque in low range."

"All done, Jon," Renee said, pointing to the pile of water. "Tarp is back in place."

"Thanks, ladies. Go ahead and load up." I turned to the sergeant, said, "We've got to get a move on. Good luck to you and your family." I held out my hand and we shook. "Let us pass before you bring your people over here."

"Will do. And thank you again, Master Sergeant."

I held the door open for Greta and she took her patrol position on top of the center console.

We were soon back up to fifty. The Humvee's radio was still on channel 28 and I tried Abs several times without success. I set the radio to auto-transmit on all channels and let it do its thing.

"Shouldn't this radio be able to reach out quite a distance?" Renee asked from the back seat. "I mean, it's military-grade and all. Right?"

"It is. But I really don't know," I answered, buckling my seat belt. "Communications wasn't my area of expertise or responsibility—weapons, my men, and advising and taking newly commissioned second lieutenants under my wing was. We had a radioman in our squad that followed on my heels wherever I went. I knew how to press the mic and talk. The rest was up to the radioman."

"How refreshing," Dawn said, "a man who admits he doesn't know everything."

"Dawn, take the next exit and go north on 200."

We exited Interstate 90 and took a gradual right onto Montana Highway 200 which was also Highway 93.

There was a Taco Bell and a Flying J on the left and a Conoco on the right. The Taco Bell was a burnt-out shell and all three were littered with abandoned dead vehicles, but hand-written signs at the gas stations said gas was available for trade. Although there were currently no customers, armed guards were standing next to the extensive lineup of pumps.

We passed a Days Inn Motel on the right and a McDonalds on the left. Both appeared deserted, but intact. Further up on the right was a Peterbilt truck dealership. The showroom and service buildings had burned to the ground, and I could see exploded electrical transformers on poles behind both buildings, which might have explained the fire. Five or six of the two dozen trucks appeared to be housing several families in their sleeping cabs.

A mile further on were dozens of expensive RVs and trailers in the Boulder Ridge Resort RV Park, sitting where they had died a quiet death in the pulse. We were soon past any retail enterprise and in open country. The roadway was four lanes, and the going was easy and steady.

I told Dawn to keep it at fifty.

"Roger that," Dawn answered.

I glanced in the side-view mirror and could see the ranch truck, the Perdues' two trucks, followed by the Cruiser. PJ was trailing too close to us and Melissa too close behind Becca. I keyed the comms and had both drivers back off. I watched in my side-view mirror as both increased the distance.

"Good. Thanks," I said.

We were now in hilly terrain and more rural. The homes we passed were five- and ten-acre ranchettes, some with bundled-up owners out front waving at us in greeting.

"It's good to be home, or close to home," I said over the comms.

"I'm tired," Kathy said. "It's been a long day."

"Soon enough," I said.

"Dad lives on the north side of Kalispell," PJ said.

"Whereabouts?" I asked her.

"You familiar with Northern Spruce Golf Club?"

"I am. I played there several times during summer breaks from college."

"That's where he lives. He and a buddy of his developed the golf course and the surrounding housing development. Sold twenty, one-acre lots, and his buddy built and sold the homes. Dad is a veterinarian and owns a practice right across the street from the course."

"I'll get us there and then you guide us to his home."

"Will do," she replied. "And thank you again for taking us."

"What are these bridges we're driving under with a forest growing on them?" Dawn asked.

"Those are wildlife bridges," I answered. "Or sometimes referred to as wildlife crossings. They're overpasses built exclusively for wildlife, allowing safe passage for deer, elk, moose, and other animals that were frequent moving targets for cars and trucks. Where you see these overpasses, and there are a few of them in Montana, the area would have seen a high number of collisions between animal and vehicle. The outcome for humans and animals is usually not a good one. There is also special protective fencing along miles of Highway 93, although you can't see it, it's there."

"How cool is that?" Melissa said. "Not only are these highways beautiful, but they're also safer for both humans and wildlife."

We steadily made our way north. We traveled through narrow passes then emerged into surprisingly wide valleys, the land on both sides of the highway plowed and appearing ready for planting that may or may not ever happen.

"With the exception of the Big Sur Coast, I don't think I've ever seen such beauty, and it just seems to go on and on," Monica said.

"I've never been, but I've seen pictures of Switzerland," PJ said. "Every time I drive this route, I'm reminded of those pictures and think how similar it seems. Especially with the tall, snow-covered mountains in the background."

We fell silent as we ate up the distance. Soon, we were in Arlee, Montana and Dawn performed her PSA in front of the Arlee Post Office. A mile north of the tiny town of Ravalli, Highway 200 split off to the west and Highway 93 continued north.

Next up was the town of St. Ignatius. The town itself was a half mile off to the right of the highway and Dawn broadcast her PSA from the shoulder. I didn't see anyone, but I knew they were there as a thick haze hung over the town from the dozens of chimneys billowing smoke as folks tried to keep warm.

We passed by a large body of water on our left that, as a youngster, I thought was an ocean. I knew it now as the Ninepipe Reservoir. As a kid, our class had enjoyed annual field trips in the fall to watch and identify the millions of waterfowl that used the place as a resting spot on their annual migration south. *It still looks as large as an ocean.*

The comms chirped. "I'm so sorry, but I really need a potty stop. I'd hoped to make it to my father's place, but I'm ready to burst," PJ said.

"I second that," Melissa said. "The coffee. . ."

"Me, makes three." Renee said from the back seat.

The highway was straight as an arrow for several miles in both directions and this was as good a place to stop as any— we'd be able to see anyone approaching several miles out.

"Bring us to a stop, Dawn. I'll overwatch," I said, grabbing the binoculars and stepping out. Greta did her three circles around the Humvee then did her business.

The ladies piled out of all three vehicles, pulled pants down and did their thing. Becca opened her door, looked around at the other women, shrugged, then did the same. Mr. Perdue joined me at the head of the column.

"Those folks at the airport exit weren't on the highway yesterday when I drove through," he said. "What did you tell them?"

"I passed on the information we have regarding the blackout. Then I told them to head two exits down and make their way to Walmart or Costco."

"Those are under the control of the MPF. I'm not sure they'll like seeing a few hundred hungry and homeless travelers approaching their food supply."

"I get that. I'm trying to get ahold of Abs as we speak. I'll ask her to contact Eddy Taylor and have them allowed in."

"Good luck with that, Jon. They've been busy getting stranded travelers to leave, not allowing more in."

"They owe me," I said, thinking of the ambush we had set up that had wiped out Lassman and his followers.

"Looks like rain moving in," he said, pointing to the west.

I looked to the west, and sure enough, dark clouds were headed toward us.

"Looks like it, but it's not cold enough for snow. Good chance for later this afternoon though," I said, watching the shadows cast by the clouds move across the water of the reservoir. "And there was no way I was going to leave those people to die of thirst, Mr. Perdue."

THE TOWN OF RONAN WAS next. Dawn performed her PSA in front of an intact McDonalds on the south side of town and again at a Dairy Queen on the north. The Exxon gas station was selling gas and allowing two gallons per person per day. A large crowd, working on a half-dozen older cars and pickup trucks in the parking lot of the Napa Auto Parts, waved as we passed by. Dawn honked in response.

We passed a road sign which let us know we were traveling through the Flathead Indian Reservation. Flathead Lake, with its billions of dollars of shoreline real estate, was twelve miles ahead.

Open farmland on both sides of the highway stretched for miles in all directions. Almost all available acreage had been plowed and made ready for spring seeding. Those fields that hadn't been plowed, were ready to be tilled, and many had tractors, with huge tillage machines still attached, sitting where they'd been rendered useless by the pulse.

We drove past the small town of Polson on our left and started gaining elevation. A few miles further on we passed the Flathead Lake Scenic Turnout. Flathead Lake now lay before us.

"It's beautiful," Kathy said over the comms. "And huge."

"It's the largest lake in the western United States, outside of Alaska," I said. "And the seventy-ninth largest freshwater lake in the world."

"Those other seventy-eight lakes must be humongous, because I can't see the other side of this one," Melissa said.

"You normally can, but not today. Too much smoke from chimneys," I said.

"I've heard of Flathead Lake," Dawn said. "Some of my friends have second homes here."

"It's become a very popular place," PJ said. "Though not all native Montanans are happy to see out-of-staters migrating here and changing the cultural landscape. Not to mention raising property values and property taxes."

We passed a Walmart Supercenter on our right and then a Safeway supermarket. Both were open and guarded by armed sentries.

The lake was now on our right, and there were several rowboats a few hundred feet offshore. Each was filled with fishing poles in the hands of their hopeful occupants.

We passed a closed and boarded-up Starbucks. A Subway next door was also boarded-up.

There were still the ever-present dead and abandoned cars and trucks on the road. Power lines were draped alongside the roadways and power poles with burnt-out transformers, the usual melted molten mass pooled on the ground beneath, were also there.

We came up on a casino resort called Kwataqnuk, its parking lot full of older pickups and cars. Fifty or sixty armed residents were standing together and most turned toward us and waved. All were smiling. *I wonder if Abs told them of our pending arrival.*

Past the Kwataqnuk Resort was a quarter-mile-long bridge spanning the headwaters of the Flathead River.

Dawn brought us to a stop on the bridge, said, "Look ahead, Jon."

Halfway across the bridge, blocking both westbound and eastbound lanes, was a barricade consisting of a couple of dozen wooden sawhorses. The barricade was manned by six armed guards.

"Go ahead and drive up there," I said. I figured they'd move those to the side and allow us through.

Even before Dawn had taken her foot off the brake pedal, the sawhorses were moved to the side and two of the guards were waving at us to drive through.

"How'd you know they'd move those aside," Renee asked, accelerating toward the makeshift barricade.

"They knew we were coming," I answered. "Too many people waving as we drove past, and no one running into the street to ask us questions."

The guards smiled and waved as we drove past.

"Seeing smiles and waves is remarkable after what we've seen and experienced these past few days," Monica said.

"No hangings or rapes here," Melissa said.

"Or at least none that we've seen," Kathy added.

"If things like that happened here, they happened soon after the pulse hit and before Eddy Taylor organized things," I said. "Try something like that now, and I bet you'd be in a world of trouble."

The highway broke away from the lake and we started climbing the surrounding hills. We were now driving north through thick forests of pine trees. Even though we were sitting behind the thick glass of the bulletproof windows, I could smell the heavy scent of pine.

"Smells like home," I said.

Renee put her hand on my shoulder, said, "I can't wait to see the ranch and meet your parents and your sister, Asta. And I'm sorry about the whole engagement thing."

"It was a very short engagement. She broke it off the day after I enlisted. She couldn't see herself as an army wife. I can't say I blame her."

I put my hand on Renee's. "I look forward to having you meet everyone. And you too, Dawn. I hope you know that you're welcome to live with us at the ranch. If you decide to stay, we'll make our way to Vancouver and bring your sister back. Promise."

Before Dawn could say anything, I said, "I have a confession to make, you two. Earlier Becca asked who I was sleeping with—the beautiful movie star or the hot blonde from next door."

"Uh oh. You answered by saying me, right?" Renee asked.

"No. I said I was sleeping with you both. Sometimes at the same time."

"Oh boy," Dawn said.

"I was messing with her."

"But that might be fun. . . the three of us," Dawn said. "You know us Hollywood types go in for the group sex stuff."

"I would have to—" I started to say.

"Ask me," Renee answered for me. "And the answer would be—"

"I'll think about it?" Dawn finished for Renee.

There was an uncomfortable silence in the Humvee.

"She'll figure it out soon enough," Dawn said, breaking the silence. "In the meantime, let her stew."

Renee didn't take her hand away. I figured that was a good sign.

"She really said the hot blonde from next door?" Renee asked.

"And don't forget the beautiful movie star," Dawn added.

FOURTEEN

We lost elevation as the highway turned east toward the lake. We were soon driving along the shoreline and passing by the beautiful Big Arm Resort on our right. The US Post Office came up on the left; the only thing untouched was the sign out front and the usual power pole with the melted transformer out back. Further on were lakefront homes with one-acre lawns, now a winter brown. There was mile after mile of these lakeside, multimillion-dollar homes.

We drove through the lakeside town of Elmo, with its mix of residential and commercial buildings. We curved back to the east as we followed the contours of the lake, and again, it was mile after mile of multimillion-dollar lakefront homes. We passed through the shoreline towns of Dayton, Rollins, Lakeside, and Somers.

It was on the north side of Somers that we finally left the lake and headed northwest.

The highway was again four lanes, two in each direction, but with no grassy median. Commercial businesses lined both sides of the highway. Used car lots, RV sales and repair, self-storage units, propane, stone and tile outlets, and appliance stores were predominant. Heck, just about every kind of business enterprise could be found along this stretch of highway. Flathead Lake powers-that-be didn't want this kind of commercial clutter near their pristine lake and had evidently deemed this area more suitable.

We were nearing the regional FedEx ground facility, when the Humvee's radio came to life. "Jon, copy your broadcast," Abs said. "Look up, brother."

I looked up, and there she was, three hundred yards out and closing fast. Really fast. She was fifteen feet off the ground and headed right for us.

"Jon?" Dawn said, questioning-panic in her voice.

"Keep driving. She'll pull up."

I grabbed the mic, said, "Hey. Wanna play chicken?"

"Don't tempt me," Abs said, pulling up at the last second. I could see Eddy Taylor sitting in the co-pilot seat staring down at us in terror as Abs banked to the left. His hands were gripping the instrument panel, his mouth open in what must have been a primordial scream.

"Are you taking the Alternate 93?" Abs asked.

"Affirmative."

"I'll land right after the turn. See ya in a few."

I clicked the mic in response.

"Take the next left, Dawn," I said.

Abs completed her one-eighty, continued northwest, and started her descent onto the highway. I lost sight of her behind some pine trees.

We turned left and there was Abs, taxiing toward us. I had Dawn bring us to a stop. Abs was no more than twenty feet away when she turned on a dime and brought the Beaver to a halt. She left the engine idling. *I love the sound an idling Beaver makes. A deep and rhythmic bass sound.*

Eddy Taylor opened the cockpit passenger door and climbed to the ground. I thought he might drop to his knees and kiss the ground, but he opened the compartment aft of the starboard cargo doors and came out with another set of wheel chocks, this set bright-yellow. He placed them and then patted the fuselage. Abs opened her door and climbed to the ground. She turned and walked toward us. She waved at Eddy to join her.

I keyed the comms and told everyone to stay put. I pointed to the Perdues and put my palm up in a stay-where-you-are motion.

I joined Abs and Eddy in front of the Humvee. I shook Eddy's offered hand, and we buddy-bumped shoulders.

"Good to see you," Eddy half-shouted over the engine noise."

"And you as well."

Edward Taylor—Eddy as he's called by family and friends—and I had known each other since we were little kids. My parents considered him their unintended second son. We attended grade through high school together. We played high school football, Eddy the quarterback and me his favorite receiver. His father is a retired army general who, through a sitting Montana US Congressman, was able to get Eddy into West Point. After four years at West Point, he graduated as a commissioned officer and served an additional fifteen years. He retired as a lieutenant colonel and was now the national news media's favorite go-to-expert when they were in need of a presentable ex-military talking head. Both conservative and more liberal networks used him as he was always careful to be non-partisan in his comments. With the recent issues in the South China Sea, Taiwan, and Ukraine having led most of the pre-pulse news, he'd been very busy—I'd seen him almost nightly on many of my favorite all-news networks.

Eddy was two inches shorter than me at six-two, had longish black hair with a sprinkling of salt mixed here and there, olive-colored skin from his mother's Italian family, and had maintained his military leanness. His most remarkable features, however, were his piercing, light-blue eyes—almost like the blue eyes of an Alaskan Malamute.

Eddy was wearing a long-sleeved, blue-checked flannel shirt with a black T-shirt underneath. Over that was an old dark-blue down vest I could have sworn he had worn in high school. He wore faded blue jeans with light-tan cowboy boots.

"Thanks for landing, Abs, though we could have spoken over the radio."

"We flew over Idaho earlier and found those assholes just north of Bonners Ferry," Eddy said. "I asked Abs to fly lower, and sure enough, they started firing at us. I couldn't be one hundred percent sure, but I thought I saw a .50-cal mounted in the back of a pickup truck. Afterward the radio started acting wonky, fading in and out."

We all turned and looked at the Beaver. "No wonder—my fucking antenna is gone," Abs said, pointing to what was left of the antenna, a stub where once a two-foot-long dangly metal job used to be. "Fuckers."

"Let's fly her over to Kali airport," Eddy said, "fill her up with gas, and scavenge around for an antenna. There's like, what, fifty or sixty dead airplanes sitting on the tarmac and in hangars? We're bound to find something that will work."

"Okay," Abs said.

"Listen, Eddy," I said, and told him about the couple of hundred stranded passengers at the Missoula Airport. "Can you take them in and get them situated?"

"Not a problem, Jon. I'll do one better and have our guys drive out toward the airport and pick them up—we have three old sixties-era school buses we got running again. We'll bring 'em back to Costco and supply them. We can put them into one of several motels that we've been meaning to press into service. Once they're up to it, and want to, we can drive them as far as our roadblocks. From there, they can start making their way home."

"Awesome. Thanks. Abs, how are Susan and Kris doing?"

"Mom is very happy to have someone to fawn over. Asta was starting to look them over when we took off."

"How are your parents?" I asked Eddy. Eddy's parents' place was down the hill from the ranch, spitting distance off Highway 93.

"Dad is not doing well—his pacemaker quit working after the pulse. Mom is like a rock and holding everything together. Your mom and Asta stop by every other day and check in."

"Sorry to hear about your dad."

"Shit happens and we move on," he said. "Especially now."

"You going to head back to the ranch after you're done at the airport?" I asked the two.

"Yep," Eddie answered.

"Hang around until we get there," I said. "We should be pulling up to the ranch house in a couple of hours. I've got something to show you."

"Sure," he answered, staring at the Humvee. "Is that what I think it is?"

I thought he might be referring to Dawn, but she was not an "it". Then I figured he meant the Minigun.

"Yes."

"I forgot to tell him," Abs said, shrugging her shoulders. "Sorry. My bad."

"Please tell me you have ammo belts for it."

"A bunch," I said. "I'll fill you in later. Wait for us. Okay?"

"I'll be happy to. Your mom was baking a Dutch apple crunch pie when I showed up at the ranch this morning. Hopefully there's a piece left. I'll see you later, bro," he said, offering me his hand. "And a big thank you for taking out Lassman for us."

"My pleasure," I said, shaking Eddy's offered hand. "It was a group effort."

I watched Abs climb into the pilot's seat. Eddy removed and stowed the chocks, and a minute later they were airborne and heading toward the Kalispell City Airport less than three miles to the north.

We were soon headed north ourselves.

"The folks from the airport—they're going to be picked up and taken to Costco and then put up in a motel. When they're up to it, they will be taken to a roadblock and can be on their way," I reported.

"Who was the guy?" Dawn asked.

"He's kind of a hunk," Renee said.

"A very handsome hunk. Almost beautiful," Dawn added. "Is he single?"

"He is single," I answered. "His name is Eddy Taylor and he's co-leading the MPF along with Ted Mitchell. I've known Eddy since grade school. We were best buddies until we graduated high school. He went to West Point, and I went to the University of Utah. We've kept in touch and try and get together every couple of months."

"Your sister and Mr. Taylor there make for a great looking couple," Renee said. "Anything going on between them?"

I didn't answer right away because it wasn't something I'd ever considered. "Eddy and Abs are more like brother and sister. Although, I wouldn't mind if the two of them were a couple."

"But as far as you know he's fair game?" Dawn asked.

"Don't know for sure. He could have a new special someone. Other than a couple of quick phone calls, it's been a few weeks since we've really spoken."

"Okay then," she said. "I'll find out soon enough."

"Didn't you say something about having a live-in boyfriend in Vancouver?" I asked. "Or was that said while you were half frozen."

"I don't remember saying anything," she answered, looking at me with a mischievous smile. "You said my memory could be sketchy for a few days."

"Really?" I said, clearly not believing her. "Yet you remember me telling you that."

From the back seat, Renee said, "You told us that Robert Trent Jones was your current live-in boyfriend."

"Okay, okay. I give up. He is. Though he flew to Hawaii to start work on a new film, and Hawaii might as well be on the far side of the Earth. Besides, we were more friends with benefits, than being full-on committed to each other."

We encountered the first of three traffic circles I knew we'd be hitting.

A fifteen-foot-high concrete sound-barrier wall was to our right, newly built housing developments crammed in behind it like sardines onto once pristine grazing land. The concrete wall went on for miles; the only breaks were for off-ramps leading to retail strip malls. Huge, newly built apartment complexes, probably built by Mr. Perdue's company, were scattered along both sides of the highway. A few miles further on, we passed a large strip mall containing Cabela's, Michaels, Home Depot, and Pet Smart stores. It was just past Pet Smart where we rejoined the original Highway 93.

I had Dawn turn left. We crossed over the Stillwater River and passed the local cemetery on the right.

"My dad's place is a mile or so up on the left," PJ said over the comms. "Take the first left past the golf course. It's Wild Pine Drive. Wild Pine Drive also serves as the club's entrance."

Dawn was ready to turn into the golf course when I had her come to a stop.

"PJ, I've played the course several times but have never driven further than the clubhouse. Give me the lay of the land," I said. I wasn't going to take us into an area I wasn't familiar with.

"We turn left here and the street curves to the left past the course clubhouse. We turn right on Quail Circle and enter a cul-de-sac. There are five homes on an acre each. There are homes on the two corners, one house next to those, and then my dad's place between those two. There's a bunch of space between houses. . . maybe two or three hundred feet from one driveway to the next."

"Any other streets?"

"Yes, instead of turning right onto Quail, you can turn left on Wild Pine Circle. There are another fifteen homes there."

"Any exits other than this one spilling out onto 93?"

"No, this is it," she answered.

"Okay. Thanks for the information. Melissa and Monica, I want you to stay here on the highway. Monica, set up a close-in perimeter. The Perdues will stay with you. Please let them know the plan."

I watched Monica exit the Cruiser and walk up to the two Perdue trucks. She then walked back to the Cruiser and took a knee next to the driver's door.

"Dawn, turn left and take it slow, walking-pace slow. I don't want to plow headfirst into something we can't get out of. PJ, follow us at forty feet."

We were going past the clubhouse parking lot entrance off Wild Pine Drive, when I caught sight of the main entrance to the clubhouse. Someone had forced it open—the front door was hanging off its hinges, the door's glass shattered and strewn about the entrance portico. There were also what appeared to be full cardboard cartons of Mountain House product piled high, apparently waiting for a truck or trailer.

"PJ, the clubhouse has been looted. Looks like they're waiting for a truck or trailer to haul this stuff away."

"I see that. Dad and his business partner own the golf course and clubhouse. He uses a large storage room to the rear of the kitchen to store all kinds of long-term provisions. No one other than Dad, his business partner, and I have access to that room. Those provisions are what I was counting on to keep the three of us going."

"Dawn, bring us to a stop. I'm going to check it out, and I'm taking Greta."

Greta jumped to the floorboards and then to the ground. She took up her standard position on my left side, looking up at me waiting for commands.

Renee opened the rear passenger door, reached back in for her rifle, attached it to the sling already around her neck, and quietly closed her door. "I'm going with you."

"No, you are not," I said. "But I could use you here on a close-in perimeter watch."

She looked like she was ready to argue, but said, "Okay. Be careful."

"Always, babe."

Renee grabbed me by the neck and kissed me hard, drew back, and said, "I love you."

"Always and forever," I said, kissing her in return.

Greta and I made our way to the clubhouse front entrance. Glass from the missing front doors was strewn everywhere, but we managed to make it to the exterior wall to the right of the doors without making much noise. Full cartons of Mountain House meals were stacked six high. There were at least twenty stacks sitting in front of the broken doors. There were also piles of five-gallon tubs of Emergency Essentials rice, black beans, pinto beans, rolled oats, and freeze-dried meats and vegetables. There were enough long-term provisions there to feed a large family for two or three years. I stuck my head around the door-frame and peered inside. There was no one visible but I did hear male voices.

"I told you I heard somethin' out front," a male voice said from the rear of the building.

"Sandra, go check it out," another male voice said. "It's probably Bobby and the others back from checkin' out the houses further down the road."

I keyed the comms, whispered, "We've got people inside the clubhouse. Not sure how many. Melissa and Monica, drive behind the Humvee and set up a close-in perimeter." I turned down the comms' volume, placed the rifle on the ground, and took out the Glock.

A few seconds later, a woman walked out of the broken front door. She spotted the Humvee and let out a quiet oh. I reached out and covered her mouth with my gloved hand and brought her to me so that her back was against my chest. She was now facing the Humvee. I held the Glock in front of her face so she would be sure to know I had it.

She was in her late twenties to early thirties. She had blonde hair, now greasy and dirty. She stank to high hell.

"Keep quiet, don't fight me, and you'll live," I whispered in her ear. "How many are inside?" Her mouth moved under my glove as she tried to answer, and I told her to use her fingers. She raised her left hand and held up three fingers.

"And how many are with Bobby?"

She held up both hands and put seven fingers up.

"How many vehicles?"

Two fingers.

"Are they all armed?"

She gave a thumbs-up.

"How about the three in here?"

Another thumbs-up.

"You armed?"

She nodded her head.

"Hand it over." I took my right hand off her mouth and held up my hand.

With her right hand, she reached under her jacket and took a black Glock out of its in-the-waistband holster and placed it in my hand. I put it in my right front pants cargo pocket. I placed my hand back over her mouth.

"Sandra, you see anythin' out there?" a male voice yelled out from the interior of the clubhouse.

"Answer him by saying no." I pressed the Glock against her right temple. "I'm going to take my hand off your mouth. You say only the word 'no.' Understood?"

She nodded.

I took my hand off her mouth. She yelled, "No."

"Excellent. Take one step forward." She did. I took the butt of the Glock and hit her right below her right ear. She dropped to the ground like a rock. She'd wake up with a hell of a headache, but she'd be alive.

I keyed the comms, whispered, "We've got three bad guys inside the clubhouse and seven more checking out houses further down the street. Renee, Melissa, Monica, and Kathy, form a firing line next to the Humvee. Get prone—you know the rest. Face the housing development. Renee, tell Dawn to turn the Humvee to the side to afford some protection to the ranch truck behind."

"Sandra, where are ya, baby?" a male voice shouted out from further inside the clubhouse.

I risked a quick glance inside and saw a man walking toward the front door. He saw me looking, raised a handgun, and let loose with several unaimed rounds. I went to my knees and then to my stomach. I was flattened against the concrete of the entrance way and the exterior wall. I could feel Greta hugging my side.

The wooden doorframe where I'd been standing disintegrated from several direct hits. I took the Glock with my left hand, stuck my head out, quickly sighted in, and fired two rounds into his center mass. He fell back onto the reception desk and slowly slid to the floor. I got to my feet, kicked his gun away, and ran past. I took a position against the wall which led to the restaurant. Greta was glued to my side. I could feel her tense up, just waiting for the command to go to work.

"Is everyone in position?" I asked.

"We are," Melissa answered. "You want some help in there?"

"Negative. Those shots could have been heard by the other group. They may be coming into view shortly. Melissa, run toward the houses and hide behind something. Let them go on by you. If they start firing, then go ahead and return fire from a flanking position."

"Roger that. Moving," she said, her breathing coming hard and fast through the mic. Twenty seconds later, she said she was in position.

"Clive, everythin' all right?" a man asked from the kitchen just beyond the restaurant. "Whatcha shooting at, dickhead?"

I flattened on the ground and poked my head around the corner. A man was standing midway through the restaurant, carrying a five-gallon bucket in one hand and a black semi-automatic handgun in the other. "Clive? Fuckin' answer me, dude." He still hadn't seen me.

I brought the Glock up, and using two hands fired one round, hitting him under his chin. He fell face-first to the ground. Eleven rounds left.

I caught movement further on in the kitchen. A round whizzed over my head, and another hit the wall to my left.

I was pinned here, unable to get to my feet without presenting a hard-to-miss target. "Greta, go get him, girl."

The man had time to get one errant round off before Greta launched herself through the air and latched onto his shooting arm. The gun dropped, and the man spun around, desperately trying to dislodge the determined Greta. Greta was in the air, with all four feet off the ground, being whirled around as if she was on a county-fair ride. I got to my feet and ran into the kitchen. The man screamed for me to make her stop.

"Greta, stop." I didn't know what command to give Greta, but I needn't have worried, for she let the arm go, landed on all fours, and sat watching the man.

"Sorry, man. I'm really—" he began to say, rubbing his arm.

I fired one round into his left temple. Ten rounds remaining.

"Greta, let's go," I said, running back to the front entrance. The woman was still out cold. I kneeled next to her, did a quick body search, and told Greta to guard. Greta sat next to the prone woman.

"Thank you, girl. You saved my butt," I said, quickly rubbing behind her ears.

She thumped her tail once and brought her attention back to the prone woman.

I retrieved my rifle, ran to the Humvee, and took a knee next to Renee. I keyed the comms, asked, "Melissa, you see anything further down the street?"

"Negative."

"Did you hear the gunfire from the clubhouse?"

"Barely," she answered.

"Okay. They're not coming to us, which means we'll have to go to them. PJ, you and Jane leave the ranch truck where it is and get in the Humvee. But first, lock it and bring the keys with you."

"Melissa, do you have the keys to the Cruiser?"

"I do," she answered.

I ran back to the Cruiser, locked the doors, and then ran back to Renee.

I keyed the comms, said, "PJ, I'm walking toward the houses. Tell me when we get to your dad's street. Have Dawn follow me. Melissa, when we get parallel to your position, join us. Monica, Kathy, Renee get behind the Humvee's trailer and follow. If needed, I'll tell you when to form a firing line. Safeties off, fingers off triggers, and red dots on. Three-round bursts. Let's go," I said, and started walking toward the houses. Melissa joined me at the head of the column a minute later.

"I figured you could use another full-auto up here," she said.

I pointed to the opposite side of the street and told her to walk along the curb but to not get ahead of me.

We came upon the first intersection which was Quail Circle, PJ's father's street.

"Stop," I whispered in the comms. "Wait for me here."

I crossed the street, ran past Melissa, and headed toward the corner house on the north side of the street. I pressed against the wood siding and came to the corner facing the cul-de-sac. A waist-high juniper bush gave me some cover. I peeked around the corner and saw two sixties-era pickup trucks. One was backed into a driveway one house in from the opposite side's corner home. The other was backed into the driveway of the house I figured was PJ's fathers. Both trucks had what looked to be fifteen-foot dual-axle utility trailers behind them, both in the process of being loaded. Both garages had two car-sized roll-up doors and one golf-cart-sized one. The trailers had been backed up to the first of the two car-sized doors.

I continued watching and finally got a head count on how many looters were working each truck: three on PJ's father's house and four on the other. They were walking through the opened garage doors and loading the trailers. After dropping off their loads, they retreated back into the garage, and I assumed back into the interior of the homes. I looked for sentries but saw none.

I ducked back. "There are two homes being looted. PJ, your dad's is one of them. The other is the house next door to his on the left. There are three looters working your dad's place and four in the other. They're carrying all kinds of stuff—pots and pans, blankets, household things, anything useful or barterable. Does your dad have weapons or ammo in the house?"

"He does. He's got a secret room behind the pantry in the kitchen that has all of that. The neighbor to the left of dad's is a widower, Mr. Kaiser. Mr. Kaiser is a gun collector and has dozens of firearms. Dad tells me he's a prepper like him. He lives alone."

A plan was forming in my mind. "PJ, what's behind these homes?"

"The tenth fairway."

"Are there fences?"

"No. Fences aren't allowed."

"Does your dad have any pets?"

"Yes, a geriatric German shepherd that's almost blind. Though he's an ex-police dog. His name is Marty. And an FYI— the house you're at now and the one to its right are probably empty as their owners have winter homes in Palm Springs and Naples, Florida."

"Thanks for the information. It helps."

I peeked around the corner and timed the comings and goings of the men working PJ's dad's place. Roughly every thirty seconds a man would emerge from the garage, deposit whatever he was carrying into the trailer, then head back into the garage. There was another thirty seconds when no one was present. Then it started up again. The other home had four looters and there was only fifteen to twenty seconds when no one was present. We could easily shoot two of the seven as they were loading the trailers, but that would leave five shooters inside the homes. We could be stuck here for hours dealing with that. Better we take them out one at a time. Quickly and quietly.

"Melissa and Monica, come up here next to me," I said, sticking my head out and watching the two homes.

Both women were soon kneeling next to me.

"Here's the plan. I'm going to the backyard of this house and then make my way backyard to backyard until I get to PJ's father's place. I'll get to the front of the garage and put down each of the three looters. I'll then do the same at the other house. I'm hoping that the looters stay focused on the job at hand and don't glance over at the other house—there's a least fifty yards from one garage to the other. But just in case, I want you, Monica, to run across the street and position yourself at this same corner of the house across the street and provide me cover for PJ's dad's house. Melissa, you watch over the other home. Both garages are no more than 150 yards from either position, so you shouldn't have any issues with taking the shots. Just make sure you've got the magnifier up and in position behind the red dot. When that red dot moves onto your target pull the trigger. Set the selector to semi-auto. Got it?"

Both nodded.

"Monica, get yourself ready to run when I tell you."

I stuck my head out and watched both houses. When both homes had empty driveways, I told her to go. She took off and was kneeling at the home across the street five seconds later.

"I'm moving now," I said. I ran back toward the rear of this home and then ran through the backyard and through the next-door neighbors. The landscaping behind both houses was fully mature and provided plenty of cover. I was soon at the back of PJ's father's garage.

On the back patio were two men, one lying on a lounge chair and the other face down in the grass. Both had been shot in the head. Lying next to the man on the grass was a large

German shepherd, also shot. This had to be PJ's father and Mr. Kaiser, the neighbor. I did a quick check of both men and neither had a pulse. *I'm so sorry, PJ.*

"I'm at the back of your dad's house, PJ," I whispered. "There's no other way to say this—there are two men and a dog in the backyard. All three have been shot. They're dead, PJ. I'm sorry."

"Oh no," she said. "Dad. . ." I could hear her gasping for breath as her emotions took over.

"Someone please stay with PJ."

"I heard you," Jane said. "I'm here."

"Thanks."

I ran along the side of the garage toward the street, stopping just short of the front corner. Keeping myself hidden, I keyed the comms, asked, "Monica, anyone in my driveway?"

"There is. He's turning back toward the garage and is now inside," she said. "Go now."

I sprinted across the width of the driveway and positioned myself with my back against the closed golf cart garage door. I holstered the Glock and took out the Ontario.

"You see me, Monica?"

"Yes."

"Let me know when the next guy is on his way out of the garage and is ready to step onto the driveway. Got it?"

"Yes."

"Melissa, tell me when someone walks out of the garage next door."

"Roger that."

Twenty seconds later, Monica said, "Now!"

An older man with stringy, long, gray hair and a matching gray beard stepped out of the garage. Both hands were full of bedding and pillows. He was ready to step onto the trailer's loading ramp when I came from behind and wrapped my left arm around his neck. With my right I plunged the Ontario into the side of his neck, withdrew, and plunged the blade in two more times. With blood spurting away from me, I dragged him around the garage and dumped him behind two large, black, plastic, wheeled garbage cans. The old guy stared at me in wide-eyed terror as he tried to stem the blood spurting out of this neck. I took four steps and was back in position next to the garage opening. It had taken no more than ten seconds to put him out of commission.

"Man walking out of the other garage," Melissa said.

I crouched low and went still.

"He's back in the garage," Melissa reported.

"Man in your garage and stepping out. . . now," Monica said.

I came out of the crouch and caught the guy by surprise. This one was in his late teens and put up a struggle. But with his hands full of pots and pans, he was unable to stop me from dragging him backward and into the bushes. Using all my strength, I slit his throat from one side to the other. Blood gushed out and sucking air sounds was all the noise he made. He dropped his pots but luckily, they landed on the mulch-covered ground and made no noise. I dumped him next to the old man and now both were staring at me in terror as they tried in vain to stop the blood loss. Both had black automatic handguns in belt-mounted holsters. I removed both and tossed them to the side.

"You've got another guy next door," Melissa said.

I was behind the trash cans and stayed put.

"He's gone back inside," Melissa said.

"Dad? Kevin? Where are you two?" a man yelled out from inside the garage.

"A man carrying a rolled-up rug is walking out of the garage. . . now," Monica said.

The man must have spotted the bedding and pillows on the ground, for he dropped the rug and immediately had his hand on the butt of his gun. Before he could remove the handgun from its holster, I came up from behind, put my leg next to his, and flipped him onto his stomach. I kneeled on his lower back, placed both my hands on the Ontario's hilt, and pushed down with all my upper body weight. The tip of the Ontario slipped into the nape of his neck. He went limp, dead as soon as the tip of the knife pierced his brain stem. This guy was middle-aged and could have been the father of the younger one and the son of the older man. *I might have just wiped out three generations of the family tree.*

Not wanting to waste time, I left him on the driveway, ran to the back of the house, turned left at the corner, and ran past PJ's dad, Mr. Kaiser, and Marty. Less than a minute later, I was behind Mr. Kaiser's garage.

I keyed the comms and told Melissa that I was going to do the same thing here as I'd done at the other house. "Tell me when they're ready to step out of the garage and onto the driveway," I said as I ran to the outside corner of the garage. "Let me know when I can cross the driveway."

"Cross now," she said, three seconds later.

I ran across the opened garage door and positioned myself hard against the garage's exterior wood siding.

"A man is in the garage and stepping out now," Melissa said.

The man was actually a woman. She was in her sixties, short, skinny as a rail, with gray hair pulled up and covered by a black San Francisco 49er beanie hat. In each hand, she was holding the knotted ends of a full black contractor's trash bag.

I got behind her, covered her mouth with my left hand, and with my right plunged the Ontario into her neck. Before I could drag her out of sight two men came out of the house and into the garage. They were carrying a large one-hundred-pound propane cylinder. It was at least four feet long, and a man was positioned on each end. I dropped the Ontario and then the woman. Seeing me, they dropped the tank. I was first to get a weapon out, and I fired from ten feet away. I caught the lead man under his left armpit and the trailing man center chest, both probably dead before they hit the ground. Eight rounds left.

The propane tank was rolling toward me, and I stepped aside as it rolled past. As I was reaching down for the Ontario, I heard two rifle shots and watched the wooden doorframe surrounding the door between the garage and house disintegrate. A figure ran back into the house, what was left of the door slamming shut behind them.

"It was a woman, Jon," Melissa said over the comms. "She was reaching for her weapon, and I fired. She's young, probably early teens."

The old woman I'd first encountered was lying face-up on the driveway, her right hand trying to staunch the spurting blood. Her mouth was moving like a dying fish, opening and closing fast, trying to breathe in oxygen that wasn't there for her. Her eyes were wide and full of fear, no doubt she knew what was in store for her.

I watched as the life slowly left her, then kneeled beside her and gently closed her eyes. *I'm sorry it came to this.*

I looked down expecting to see the front of my vest and pants covered in blood, but I'd somehow managed to avoid the blood spray.

Someone barricaded inside a house was the situation I feared the most. Clearing a home or building, when someone's inside, was the most dangerous part of military or police work, especially when they were armed.

I gathered weapons and walked back to the Humvee. I opened the front passenger door, leaned in, and took out the hailer mic. "Power it up, Dawn."

"To the young woman inside the house. Please come out. We don't want any further loss of life. You have our word that you will not be harmed. We have another member of your group, a woman named Sandra in custody. The other ten are dead. We'd like you to join Sandra. You have two minutes to come out, or we're coming in. Come out and live, or stay in and die. Please make the right choice."

Turning off the hailer, I keyed the comms. "Melissa, please come on over here and try and get ahold of my sister on the

Humvee's radio," I said. "Have her ask Eddy Taylor what they're doing with captured looters."

"Will do," Melissa said, running back to us at the Humvee.

"Kathy, please run up to the highway and let the Perdues know what's going on. And on your way back check in on Greta and our other female looter."

"Roger that," she replied.

"Can I trust you?" a female voice yelled out from inside the house.

"You can, miss. We've seen enough death in the last week to last a lifetime. We have no desire for more."

"Why'd you kill my family and friends?"

"They killed our friend's father and neighbor. And they were looters."

Several minutes passed with no word from the woman.

"I'm going to trust you, mister," the girl finally shouted out.

"You can. First, open the front door and throw your weapon out. Then walk out of the house, get on the ground face-first, and put your hands on your head."

Which she did.

"Monica, Renee, cover me, please," I said as I walked up the driveway and onto the front porch. I patted the woman down and found no other weapons. I stood back and told her to stand up and put her hands behind her head.

She was much younger than I had initially thought. She couldn't be much older than sixteen or seventeen. She was filthy—both body and clothes. Her longish brown hair was matted and greasy and hadn't seen a comb or shampoo in. . . well, probably since the pulse hit. Like Sandra, she stank to high hell, and I stepped back in a vain attempt to avoid the rank odor.

"Walk to the Humvee and put your hands on the hood."

"What are you goin' to do with me?" she asked, once she had her hands on the hood. She was shaking and could barely speak.

"I don't know yet. What's your name and where are you from?"

"I'm Janice Watkins," she answered, voice quivering. "The woman you're holdin' is my aunt Sandra. We're from Kila. We ran out of food and water two days after the electricity went out. My uncle got two of his old trucks workin' again. They hooked up two ATV trailers, and we drove to my grandparents in Kalispell. We ran out of food and water there yesterday. Their neighborhood has banded together for security, and we were unable to scavenge any of the houses in their development. So last night we started drivin' north and came upon this neighborhood early this mornin'."

Kila was a small town about ten miles southwest of Kalispell on US Route 2. I've driven through the town on my way to cattle auctions in Marion, Montana, and there can't be more than two or three hundred residents.

"Who are the people here with you?"

"You got Sandra and me. The others are my dad, brother, grandmother, grandfather, uncle, and four cousins. That's all there is."

"Where's your mother?"

"She's watching our place in Kila."

The comms chirped. "Jon, the woman is awake and is sitting up," Kathy said.

"Can she walk?" I asked.

"She heard you and says she can."

"Walk her back to the Humvee. Tell her we have Janice."

Janice was staring at Dawn sitting behind the Humvee's steering wheel. Her eyes widened in surprise. "Is that Dawn Tillman behind the wheel?" she asked.

"It is," I answered. I didn't feel the need to explain any further.

"Are you really the military, mister?"

"No. We're civilians. I'm ex-military."

"Do you know what's goin' on with the power? And why aren't cell phones workin'?"

"There were nuclear explosions which created an electromagnetic pulse. They knocked the power out for ten years or more. It also killed anything with a computer chip in it."

"That's exactly what my mom thought might have happened. Dang, she was right. Everyone poopooed her."

"Who killed the two men in the next-door backyard?"

"That was my grandfather. He killed the one man to make the other man talk. It worked because he told them about the storeroom full of food in the clubhouse."

Melissa stepped out of the Humvee's front passenger door. "Can I talk to you, Jon? In private?"

"Stay right where you are, Janice. Do not move one inch."

"I won't. Promise."

We walked twenty feet away. "I got ahold of your sister," Melissa whispered. "Anyone caught in the act of looting is given no trial. They're taken to the Kalispell police station and held there until they have ten or more in custody. Then the group of them are taken to a police shooting range outside the town limits and shot. They've dug a pit with an old excavator. If there are no witnesses to the looting but they're caught with spoils that clearly don't belong to them, they're given a trial and the town council decides their fate. According to your sister, the town council usually has them escorted to a barricade and released."

While Melissa was relaying the message, I watched as Kathy and Greta led Sandra toward the Humvee. Sandra walked up to Janice, both crying at the sight of each other. After a long hug, both put their hands on the hood.

Kathy reached into her pants cargo pockets and retrieved four black semi-auto handguns. She put them on the front passenger seat of the Humvee. Greta sat and watched the two women captives.

"Thank you, Kathy. And thanks for checking, Melissa." I keyed the comms and told everyone to converge on Melissa and me. Once we were together, I told them what would happen to the two women if we handed them over.

"PJ, these people killed your father and his next-door neighbor. Neither of these two women pulled the trigger. It was the young girl's grandfather that did that. If we turn them in, they'll be executed, no trial. PJ, this is your call," I said.

"Mom, you can't kill them. There's been enough of that. Mr. Kristen, what would you do if it was your dad?"

All eyes fell on me. "The man responsible is dead," I said. "Believe me when I say he died a slow agonizing death. Nine other members of his family are dead. I would let these two go. I'd give them one of the trucks, some rice, beans, and water. Then send them on their way. The young one's mother is alive and waiting for her."

"Then that's what should happen," PJ said, hugging Jane to her side. I heard a meow and Journey stuck her head out of Jane's pocket and let out a loud whine.

"She's hungry," PJ said. "Jane, go back to the truck and feed her. Now, please."

Jane frowned and handed Journey to her mother. Jane walked off and headed toward the two women.

"Jane, what are you doing, honey?" PJ shouted after her daughter.

"You'll see," Jane said without looking back.

"Hey, you, the young one," Jane said to Janice.

Janice turned to face Jane.

"This is for my grandfather," Jane yelled, and with a solid-looking right hook, punched Janice on the side of her head. Jane had put all her weight into the swing and, after the hit, had lost her balance. She landed on her butt, which didn't stop her from yelling, "And to both of you: fuck you!"

PJ handed Journey to me and went to help her daughter get back on her feet.

"Everyone good now?" Dawn asked.

"I'm sorry, ma'am," Janice said, rubbing the side of her head. "And to you," she said to Jane. "I deserved that."

"I want those two to dig three graves in Dad's backyard," PJ said, once Jane was out of earshot. "It's soft sandy soil and will be easy for them."

"Good idea," Dawn said.

"I'm not sure I want to remain at Dad's house," PJ said, tears running down her cheeks. "But we can't go back to our house in Darby—it's far too dangerous for us there."

"You can come with us to our ranch," I said. "I know my parents would welcome you. Not sure where Mom would put you and Jane up, but I do know there's plenty of room."

"His ranch is really really nice," Dawn said.

"You truly mean that?" PJ asked, looking right at me. "No bullshit?"

"Truly. Jane will love it."

"I'll trade vet care for room and board," she added. Her eyes suddenly grew wide. "Wait, your last name is Kristen. Is the ranch we're talking about the Kristen Double T?"

"That's the one," I answered.

"I've been to your ranch. In my third year of vet school, I summer interned with my father. A large animal vet from Whitefish asked him to go out to your ranch with him and give a second opinion. I tagged along. I met your dad and his foreman—I think his name was Billy. . . Ah, that's all I remember of him."

"You're thinking of Billy Egan, our ranch foreman. And the Whitefish vet was most likely Christopher Woodbridge."

"Yes, that's the vet. Your ranch is incredibly beautiful," PJ said. "Its ranch house is something out of a movie. And—"

I put my hand on PJ's shoulder, said, "I'm sorry to interrupt, but we've got a lot to do here."

"Sure. I get it. Sorry."

"Do you want to see your father before we bury him?"

She thought for a beat, then said, "No, I want to remember him alive."

"Renee, can you round up two shovels from either garage? Then escort both women to PJ's father's backyard and have them start digging. Holes should be six feet long, two feet wide, and at least four feet deep. We'll put the dog at Mr. Calhoun's feet. Keep watch over them, but stand back at least ten feet."

"Okay," Renee said and left to gather the shovels.

"PJ and Monica, please knock on the doors of the other homes in the cul-de-sac and see if anyone's home. If so, ask if they need anything as far as food and water. Then start unloading those trailers of anything other than food, water, medical supplies, or ammo, and put them back into the garages. We can always come back for them later."

Renee was back with two shovels and a pickaxe. We walked together to the Humvee. The women still had their hands on the hood.

"You two are going to dig two graves. Dig them—"

"Please don't kill us, sir," Sandra wailed at the top of her lungs. "Please let us go. We promise you'll never see us again. Please!"

"Whoa there, ladies. The graves are not for you," I said. "They're for the two men your people killed."

Sandra collapsed at my feet and hugged my legs. "Thank you. Thank you. God bless you."

"Aunt Sandra, get up," Janice said, gripping her aunt under her armpits and helping her stand. "He promised not to hurt us."

I took the shovels and pickaxe from Renee and handed them to the two women. "You two go to the backyard of the house there," I said, pointing to PJ's dad's house, "and dig those graves. We'll wrap the two bodies in blankets and help you place them in the graves. Once that's done, you're going to strip the bodies of your family members and help us bring them out to the street here. Then we're going to let you take one of your trucks and take off. You'll be sent on your way with some supplies to take with you. I suggest you drive straight back to Kila. All clear?"

"Yes, sir," Janice said. "Crystal clear. Thank you."

The two women turned and headed to the house, Renee trailing twenty feet behind, her rifle at the ready. Greta was right with her, hugging her left side.

"Kathy, let's gather up the weapons and put them in our trailer."

We heard tires on pavement and watched as both Perdues drove up.

"Good timing," I said to Mr. Perdue. I then explained what we were doing and asked him to provide overwatch.

"You betcha', Jon," he said, getting out of the truck and reaching back inside for his rifle.

Becca was staring at the two driveways. "Are those bodies in the driveways?"

"Yes."

"Did you do that?"

"Yes."

She nodded, said, "I've never seen a dead body before."

"Be glad for that, Becca," I said.

"Kathy, let's start unloading those trailers."

Over the next hour we unloaded the trailers of non-food items. I'd started both trucks and picked the best for us to drive to the ranch. It was a battered old Chevy two-door with a loud, but smooth-running, diesel engine. The fuel gauge read a little less than half a tank—plenty. The other truck was an even older Dodge. The Dodge looked better, but when I turned it over, it ran unevenly, continuous black-and-white smoke coming from the exhaust. I unhitched the trailer from the Dodge and drove and parked the truck on the street. I then backed the Cruiser to the trailer and hooked it up.

PJ and Monica were back and reported the other homes in the cul-de-sac unoccupied. PJ then showed us her father's secret weapon room behind the kitchen pantry. There were a few hunting rifles, all quality, top-of-the-line, and a bunch of ammo for them. We got those loaded up as well as his neighbor's gun collection—PJ and Monica loaded those, so I wasn't sure what was there.

The two women had the graves dug shortly after we were done loading the trailers. With blankets from the house, we wrapped both men and the dog, and gently placed them in the graves. We found more shovels, and we all helped fill in the graves. We brought PJ and Jane over. PJ then gave a brief grave-side eulogy.

Using two wheelbarrows, we loaded the dead looters' bodies and dumped them in the middle of the cul-de-sac. I had them leave the grandfather off the pile, and I wrote *killer of innocents and looter* on his forehead. I doused the rest with gasoline and set them on fire. We stayed until we knew the fire wouldn't go out. We didn't strip the bodies as the ladies said they were too dirty and bloody. Good decision. We did relieve them of their holsters and boots.

We locked both houses and secured the garage doors. It was time to drive up to the clubhouse and load what we could into the trailers.

"Monica, drive the Chevy up to the clubhouse entrance. Janice, you and your aunt get in the bed of the Chevy and stay there until I tell you otherwise. Got it?"

"Yes," Janice answered, hopping onto the tailgate and then helping her aunt climb up beside her. Neither woman had looked at the fire.

"Melissa, drive the Cruiser, PJ the ranch truck, and Dawn the Humvee. Mr. Perdue, if you would, please, drive up there and stand overwatch while we load up. I'll follow in a few minutes.

"Renee, you want to try and drive that old Dodge up to the clubhouse?"

"I'll try." She got in and turned the key. A couple of gear grinds later, she let the clutch out and, leaving it in first gear, left the cul-de-sac and turned left toward the clubhouse.

I looked down and there was Greta.

"I don't blame you, honey. I wouldn't want to be in that thing either," I said, leaning down and rubbing behind her ears.

REACHING HOME

Greta and I were alone with the burning bodies. A few minutes later, the wind shifted direction and blew smoke toward us.

We started a slow jog toward the clubhouse.

FIFTEEN

We loaded as much food as we could into both trailers. We then loaded what would fit in the Perdues' trucks. There was still a ton left—literally, a ton. PJ's dad had been a serious prepper and had had the money and time to do it right. We'd have to come back for the rest. Luckily the door to the storage room hadn't been forced open, instead being opened with a key provided to the looters by PJ's dad. To disguise the door, we piled furniture and kitchen stuff in front of it. We also dragged the three dead bodies into the kitchen in the hope that any future looters would leave well enough alone. I wrote *killer of innocents* on each forehead.

We gave Janice and her aunt three five-gallon buckets of rice, two five-gallon buckets each of black beans and pinto beans. We also gave them three five-gallon plastic water jugs from the storeroom. If rationed, it was enough food to last three people for several months.

Addressing Janice and Sandra, I said, "I hope this thing makes it to Kila. We spared you today. But if I ever lay eyes on you again, I swear I'll put a bullet in your heads. You two understand?"

"Yes, sir," they answered in unison.

"Good. Then go. And good luck to you."

"Sir?" Janice said.

"Yes?"

"May we have one of the handguns back? You can take the bullets out of the magazine, but just havin' it to show, if need be, would help keep us safe out there."

"Melissa, grab one of the Glock 40s from the front seat of the Humvee and bring it to me, please."

Melissa left and was back in ten seconds with a Glock. I dropped the magazine and with my thumb ejected the bullets. I cleared the chamber and handed the gun and empty magazine to Janice. I then handed her the fourteen bullets I'd just removed. "Make sure you charge the thing before you try and fire it."

"Yes, sir. Thank you."

And they were off in a cloud of white and black smoke. I swished my hands back and forth in an attempt at clearing it away.

Payton was barking up a storm in the back seat of the ranch truck. "I bet she needs to pee," PJ said. "Jane, put her on a leash and let her do her thing."

"Once she's done, let's get going," I said. "Any humans need to pee before we head out?"

"Why not," Renee said. And sure enough, the power of suggestion prevailed—they all had to go.

Once they were finished, I keyed the comms, said, "Dawn and Renee, lead in the Humvee with Dawn driving. PJ, Jane, and Monica in the ranch truck with PJ driving. Kathy, in the looter's Chevy. Then the two Perdue trucks. And in last position will be me in the Cruiser. I feel I'm missing someone. Who?"

"That would be me," Melissa answered. "What, you can't keep track of us anymore?"

"Sorry, Lis. Must be my old age. Ride shotgun with Kathy in the Chevy."

There was movement in my jacket pocket and Journey stuck her head out and meowed. I tried to grab her, but she turned and dove back inside, her backside disappearing into the comfortable depths of the over-sized pocket.

WE WERE SOON BACK ON Highway 93 and headed north.

The comms chirped and PJ asked if she could stop at her dad's veterinary office. "It's right there on the right about a hundred yards up and behind that clump of pine trees."

"We'll give you five minutes," I said.

Which turned out to be five minutes more than necessary, for when the building came into view, we could see it was a burnt-out shell. A wooden power pole behind the building held the remains of a melted transformer.

"Sorry, PJ," Renee said.

"I am too," PJ said, her voice breaking. "No need to stop."

Dawn brought us up to forty-five. The highway was four lanes with a grass median. A new housing development was on the left and the Humane Society of Northwest Montana on the right. There were several people there, walking up to six dogs each.

"Kathy, how's the Chevy?" I asked.

"It's a rattle trap," she answered, her voice shaking. "The front tires are out of balance, and I can't get the transmission into fourth gear. If you could keep your speed at forty or less, that would really help."

Dawn had heard and slowed to forty.

"Is that better?" I asked.

"Much. Thank you."

The road started climbing, and we were soon driving through low-elevation clouds. It was much cooler at this elevation and snow still covered the open ground. The tree line was thick, and the smell of pine trees was a welcome change from the thick, eye-watering chimney smoke that hung in the air down in the lower valleys.

We crested the top of the hill, and the highway stretched out in front of us. The roadway quickly lost elevation, and on the right was the North Valley Hospital.

"The hospital on the right is where my sister Asta works," I said.

"It looks like a big-city hospital—large and modern," Melissa said.

"It serves a huge geographical area. It was built four or five years ago," I said.

"And there's a Marriot Suites Hotel," Renee pointed out, sounding surprised. "Nice looking place, too."

"Sound like you guys thought that Whitefish was some backwater wilderness outpost with no paved streets or indoor plumbing," I said. "The last ten years, the influx of out-of-staters and their checkbooks has changed all that."

"Guilty," Melissa said. "It looks nice and all, but it's still too rural for me."

"Starbucks up on the left," Renee pointed out over the comms. "And a Safeway grocery store next door. There are guards out front of the Safeway, Walgreens, and Exxon."

We crossed over the Whitefish River and entered the older, more established downtown Whitefish.

"Renee, make sure you follow 93. You'll be taking a sharp left onto East Second Street."

"Roger that," she answered. "We see it."

We crossed the Whitefish River again. The highway turned hilly, and we were driving through thick forests. Whitefish Lake Golf Club was on the right.

"You can't see it, but Whitefish Lake itself is on the other side of those trees to our right," I said. "And that golf course is where I broke eighty for the first time. It was a very important milestone in my life."

"Other than meeting me, you mean," Renee said, laughing.

"True that. Ever and forever, babe," I said.

"Oh, please," Kathy said. "You two sound like a Hallmark greeting card."

Five minutes later, we were nearing Skyles Lake Lane. I keyed the comms. "Renee, have Dawn slow to ten and let me pass. We're nearing the point where we turn and start climbing."

The convoy slowed and I took the lead.

"The first part of this road is very steep all the way to the top of the hill. Stay in first gear and keep your rpms high. You don't want to lose momentum and end up stopped on the hill—it would be very difficult to get going again. Kathy, we could switch vehicles at the bottom if you want, and I can drive the Chevy up the hill."

"Thanks, I've got it," she answered.

I wanted each vehicle to make their way up one at a time. That way, if one stopped on the hill, the following vehicles wouldn't have to backtrack down in reverse—not easy with a trailer behind you.

Three miles up, I turned right on Skyles and pulled far enough ahead to leave room for the following five vehicles. I keyed the comms and told them my plan for driving the hills.

This first hill was asphalt and appeared dry, so I didn't think traction would be a problem. But it was a very steep grade, and I worried that the engines wouldn't have enough oomph to get the vehicle and the trailer to the top. I started up the hill, kept the Cruiser in first gear and maxed the rpms all the way up the incline. The road was in good shape, and I never lost traction.

I crested the hill twenty seconds later and parked on level ground. There was plenty of room up there for all seven vehicles. I put the Cruiser's parking brake on, got out, and walked back to the edge. I looked at the waiting trucks below, keyed the comms, and told them to keep the transmissions in first the entire way up.

"Dawn, you're first up. Put it in low and leave it there."

"Roger that."

The big diesel roared with high rpms the entire way up, crested the hill, and parked next to the Cruiser.

It was Kathy's turn. "Go Kathy," I said.

The old Chevy lurched forward and started the steep climb. The rpms were high but halfway up the hill they started dropping and I could hear the engine missing.

"Jon, we're losing rpms," Melissa said. "Kathy doesn't think we'll make it." Kathy was less than one hundred feet from the top when the Chevy came to a stop.

"What do we do now?" Kathy asked.

"Put the parking brake on," I said.

"Done."

"Clutch in and put it in neutral and then put your foot back on the brake pedal."

"Now take your foot off the brake and see if the parking brake will hold you in place."

"Done and it does."

"Foot back on brake and rev the engine—see if that clears up the misfire."

I heard the old diesel miss like crazy then start to clear up. The engine was soon running smoothly.

"Kathy, it's a diesel and you should have plenty of hill climbing torque to bring you and the trailer to the top."

But rather than me telling her how to use a combination of parking brake, clutch, and accelerator pedal, I started walking down the hill.

"I'll drive you to the top. When I open your door, hop out fast. Okay?"

"Okay. And thank you."

I reached the driver's door, took hold of the door handle, said, "Ready?"

"Yep."

I opened the driver's door, and Kathy flew out of the seat. I grabbed hold of the steering wheel with my right hand. With my left I was able to take hold of her hand, stopping her from tumbling down the slope. She let go of my hand and took hold of the rear-door handle. I hopped in and the door slammed shut behind me. I left the parking brake on, revved the engine, put it in first gear, let the clutch out until I felt the tranny engage, then floored it at the same time I let the clutch out and released the parking brake. The rear tire spun, caught, and we flew up the hill. I parked next to the Humvee.

"Wouldn't want to do that again," Melissa said.

"Never again," Kathy said, taking her place back in the driver's seat.

"PJ, your turn."

PJ, then Becca and her father, had no problems getting to the top.

I got back in the Cruiser, said, "This road wasn't built with trailers in mind. We'll be hitting switchbacks, so please make sure you swing wide enough to keep your trailer's wheels safely on the roadway."

We passed the Skyles trailhead, and two miles further on, after climbing several switchbacks, the road turned into Two Bear Trail. All told, we'd just gained roughly twelve hundred feet in elevation.

After negotiating another switchback, I could see the ranch entrance ahead on the right. There was no sign hanging over the entrance or any indication as to what lay beyond. It was a very narrow road, lined on both sides by thick pine trees. It was well maintained, made of gravel and dirt, and it headed straight up a long gentle hill, eventually disappearing over the top.

"This is more like a trail than a road," Monica pointed out, as she turned onto the access road.

"This is a shortcut," I explained. "The commercial ranch entrance is twelve miles further up 93. My father had this built back in the late nineties. It's great when there's no snow, but unpassable in the dead of winter to anything other than a snowmobile."

"It's beautiful," Renee said. "It's like driving through a dream landscape. I keep expecting to see fairies flying across the road."

"I've gotta say, it's 'wow' beautiful," Kathy added.

"Once we get to the top of this hill, we'll be able to see the ranch laid out below us. I'll stop and point out the various ranch buildings. There's space for all of us up there so park abreast of each other."

We got to the top and stopped. The others pulled up in a line next to me.

Two men materialized out of the woods, one on our right and the other on the left. Both were in full camo gear and cradling black long guns. They had comms gear like ours but had headsets and personal boom mics. The one on the right held up his hand and waved hello.

"What the hell," Melissa said. "Where'd they come from?"

"That's Harold and Squeaky," I said, rolling down my window. "Evidently Dad has put these two up here to watch the road."

"Hey, Jon, been expectin' y'all," Squeaky said, in a deep southern accent. "Your dad saw y'all turn off of 93 and alerted us."

"Hi, Harold, Squeaky. Drone?" I asked.

"Remote wireless camera," Harold answered. "Got one at the north entrance, too. They're solar-powered with battery backup for cloudy days."

"Leave it to my father," I said. "Did he finally build those warming stations he's always promised you?"

"Yep, and they're nice and toasty like," Squeaky said. "The kitchen sends up a warm lunch for us so it's not bad duty. The cook usually has dinner ready by six thirty. Welcome back by the way. We'll see y'all later."

The two disappeared back into the wall of trees, and I turned my attention to the view that lay below us.

I exited the Cruiser and told the ladies to gather together. "I want to give you a quick visual tour."

I walked over to the Perdues and told them I was going to point out the various ranch buildings to the ladies and suggested they go ahead and head down. They both nodded and took off.

"Jeeze louise, Jon, there is absolutely nothing you could have said that would have prepared me for just how beautiful this place is!" Monica exclaimed, walking up and joining the group.

"That show on television, *Yellowstone* with Kevin Costner," Dawn said, "has nothing that comes close to the beauty that's before us here."

"I have to admit I was feeling a little apprehensive about the whole ranch thing," Melissa said, "but seeing this, I can see I shouldn't have worried."

"And it only gets better, Melissa. Right now, we're on the highest of the hills surrounding the upper ranch complex which encompasses a little over twenty-five acres—all of that on the high bench directly below us," I said. "The ranch house, the lodge, guest cabins, conference center and dining room are all located on this high bench, and it's that which provides the ranch house and each lodge room and guest cottage with unobstructed views out to the far horizon."

Melissa pointed to the furthest tree line out in the far distance. "How far away is that tree line?"

"Twelve miles, give or take a mile or so," I answered.

"Wow, looking out at this reminds me of the vistas we encountered on some of the highways in Nevada," Renee said.

"But instead of desert or scrub land, we're looking at pastures, meadows, and streams. Is all that part of the ranch?" Kathy asked, pointing to the far tree line.

"Yes. And another twenty miles to the west, thirty to the north, and ten to the east. We're standing on the southern boundary here. Plus, there's the National Forest and BLM land we lease. There are no straight boundary lines—it dips, bends, and bows."

We stood together and took in the view. From above, I watched Mr. Perdue and Becca pull into the ranch parking lot and park next to Asta's green '68 Ford Mustang GT. My mother and father emerged from the ranch house and greeted them. After hugs and cheek kisses, Mr. Perdue turned and pointed back up the hill to where we all stood. Mom waved, and I waved back.

"Is that your mother waving at us?" Renee asked, waving back. "It's pretty far down there, but even from here I can see she's beautiful."

"It is. And yes, she is. Beautiful, I mean. She was the 1975 Miss Montana runner-up," I said. "Dad snagged himself a good one."

"You make it sound like he caught her when he was out fishing," Monica said.

"Your father looks like he might have been a catch, too," Melissa said.

"The building to the far left is the ranch house." Going from left to right I pointed out the various buildings on the high bench. "Next is the conference center, the dining room and kitchen, the guest cabins, and on the far right is the guest lodge."

"Is that an infinity pool in front of the guest cabins?" Renee asked.

"Yes, it's built right on the edge of the slope leading down the hill to the other ranch buildings."

"I see steam rising from the water," Dawn said. "It must be heated."

"It is heated, and year-round. Dad installed geo-thermal heating a few years ago."

"Can we go for a swim later?" Renee asked.

"Sure, that sounds like a great idea."

"Wait, I don't think I have a bathing suit," Renee said. "Shit, all that stuff got left behind in the hotel room in Vegas."

"I don't have one either," Dawn said. "Hell, I don't have anything other than what the girls gathered together for me from my trailer."

"There's always skinny-dipping—communal style," Melissa said.

"Now that's a great idea, Melissa," I said. "And one I highly endorse. But there's a gift shop on the lodge's ground floor next to the main entrance. There must be suits in there you can have.

"The stream you see, it divides the bench in half and runs year-round. The ranch gets its water from an underground spring which is to our left and up the hill a hundred yards or so. The overflow from the spring accounts for the stream. It eventually flows into a small lake a few miles out to the east."

"The ranch house looks vaguely familiar," Monica said. "But I can't put my finger on it. It's the use of natural wood and stone that reminds me of another building I've seen."

"Is it the Ahwahnee Hotel in Yosemite?" I asked, after letting her think about it for a few seconds.

Monica's eyes lit up. "Yes."

"The original ranch house was destroyed by fire in 1930. Back then, it was located down on the flats where the horse barns are today. My great-grandfather had been to the Ahwahnee shortly after it was built and hired Gilbert Stanley, the Ahwahnee's architect, to draft something similar. Stanley simply downsized the plans for the Ahwahnee, and the result is what we're looking at. It was Mr. Stanley's idea to clear the trees from the upper bench and place the new home there. The trees that were cleared are the timbers that you see on the house."

"It also looks similar to Zion Lodge and Bryce Canyon Lodge," Kathy said.

"Good eye. Yep, all designed by Mr. Stanley. He also designed the Grand Canyon Lodge at the north rim."

"I like the grass on the roofs of the lodge and guest cottages," Jane said, kneeling down and petting behind Payton's ears.

"If you've ever been to Snowbird ski resort in Utah, you might have seen the Lodge at Snowbird. Dad took a picture of it when he attended a Cattleman's Association conference there and had a local architect here in Kalispell build its little brother down below. It's three stories of natural-colored concrete, wood timber, and floor-to-ceiling walls of glass. And again, all the timber was cut and milled from trees found on the ranch. It has sixteen one- and two-bedroom suites per floor. All the rooms look out over the valley below. The building is in the shape of a gentle V so that the hallways aren't long and tunnel-like. The elevator is located where the two wings connect.

"The conference center, dining room, and kitchen were designed by the same architect that designed the lodge, and were built at the same time."

"Why is it that I've never heard of this place?" Monica asked. "It's one of the most beautiful places I've ever seen."

"Abs has never advertised and doesn't believe in social media. It's always been strictly word of mouth. And quite frankly, repeat guests and our long-time corporate customers account for more than ninety percent of our guest services business."

"There's a man waving at us," Jane said, pointing down to the ranch house.

I glanced down, and there was my father waving both arms above his head. I waved back and his wave changed from a getting-my-attention wave to a come-here hand motion. Standing next to him was Susan. She was waving her good arm.

"We're being summoned, so real fast—the ranch commercial buildings are located down on the flats. The building on the far left is the hay barn. It's twenty thousand square feet and is one of four located on ranch property. To the right of that is the main paddock. Behind the hay barn and paddock is the horse stable which, in the winter, can accommodate forty horses. Connected to the stables via the short, covered breezeway, is the two-acre indoor horse ring. And to the right of the indoor ring is the outdoor ring. The large, tall building behind the rings is the cement-floored equipment barn which stores the ranch vehicles, farm equipment, and a full repair shop. It's also where Dad put his faraday room. And behind all that is the twenty-five-acre fenced horse pasture.

"The same stream that divides the high bench flows down the second hill and also divides the flats. The stream slows and widens to twenty feet once on the flats. The bridge you see spanning the stream can handle every piece of machinery the ranch has.

"To the right of the bridge and across the meadow is the original bunkhouse which we still use today... although it's been completely remodeled and modernized. Back in the day, before trucks and motorized farm equipment, the ranch employed dozens of ranch hands and the bunkhouse could house up to forty-five men. Now it houses a dozen, both men and women."

"What are the four large buildings behind the bunk-house and nestled next to the bottom of the hill?" Melissa asked.

"The first three are food storage buildings. They store all of Dad's emergency food supplies and are climate-controlled. The fourth is a seven-hundred-square-foot freezer."

"That's a lot of solar panels out there," PJ said. "Those weren't there that time I visited the ranch."

"Dad had those installed last year. I've never counted how many panels there are, but I do know it's five acres of solar which produces one megawatt, enough for one hundred homes. He's got a large battery bank as well."

"And they're working now? Even after the EMP?" Renee asked.

"My father is a firm believer in having the ranch's mechanical systems remain operational. Which means he always has spare electronic parts stored in the faraday room. Every electronic part, or even an entire electronic control system, has a spare he stores in the faraday room. That's why the drones, cameras, and comms are working. And I bet the solar farm is cranking away, too."

"Where are the runway and hangars?" Dawn asked.

"They're out past the solar farm and around the corner to the right. You can't see them from the upper bench. The shooting range and greenhouses are out there, too.

"Let's head on down," I said. "My parents are biting at the bit to meet you all, I'm sure."

There are two fairly sharp hairpin turns on the way down the hill. I swung wide and told the others to follow my lead.

"Let's not slide off the side of a hill this close to home."

We made it safely down and pulled into the upper bench's gravel parking area. My mother, father, Susan, Becca, and Mr. Perdue were there waiting as I exited the Cruiser. My mother crushed me in an embrace, while my father, a smile planted on his face, stood back and patiently waited his turn.

When people first met my father, he made quite an impression. Not only was he tall at six foot four, but at sixty-eight, he was still lean with a much younger man's physique. I got my blue eyes from both parents, but I definitely inherited his strong jawline. He had fashionably long, salt-and-pepper hair, and being from a Scandinavian bloodline, was fair-skinned. But his most prominent feature and what accounted for the unforgettable first impression, was the light purple scar that ran from just below his right eye, down past the corner of his mouth, ending on his chin. The scar came from a bear encounter when he was only fourteen. You might have thought that Dad got the short end of the stick in that fateful encounter, but if you walked into his office, you'd know it was the other way around, for that same bear now covered a good portion of the floor in front of the office fireplace.

He had on the long sheepskin jacket I gave him on his sixty-fifth birthday. On his head was his ever-present dark-gray Stetson. He also wore black operator pants with a well-used pair of black Tecova boots. His coat was open, and I saw he was carrying one of his Glocks in an outside-the-belt holster.

The ladies were standing behind me. Each had on their plate carriers and had their rifles attached to slings.

Dad stood there silently checking us out. "The group of you look like one of your Special Forces squads," my father said.

"That's the idea," I said. "People saw us, took in the Humvee, and just assumed we were military."

"Thank goodness you're home, Jon," my mother said, stepping back but holding my shoulders with both hands. "Your father kept telling me not to worry, but as your mother, it's my job to worry." She gave me another quick hug, said, "Hello, ladies. Welcome to the Double T Ranch, your new home away from home. Now, which one of you lovely ladies is Jon's Renee?"

"That would be me, Mrs. Kristen," Renee answered, raising her hand and stepping forward with Greta right beside her.

My mother and Renee hugged.

"Abigail told me you're beautiful, young lady, and you certainly are that, but I'm going to add the word gorgeous in there somewhere as well." She kissed both of Renee's cheeks European-style.

"That's very kind of you to say, Mrs. Kristen," Renee responded, turning beet-red at the compliment.

"Mrs. Kristen was my mother-in-law, please call me Andrea. That goes for all of you. Including you, young lady," she said, pointing to Jane.

Mom kneeled down and faced Greta. "And who might this be?"

Greta's tail thumped once. Greta then raised a paw and waited while my mother brought her hand up to shake.

"I think she likes you, Andrea. I've never seen her do that," Renee said. "Her name is Greta and she's a military working dog. Her handler was murdered down south, and we found her locked in a truck. Jon and I have adopted her. I hope it's okay that we brought her here."

"Oh gosh, yes. We're a ranch, Renee. We'll take in any animal that wanders by."

My father had waited long enough. He hugged me then moved on to Renee.

Becca had stood by, watching and listening. Evidently, she'd had enough of the family reunion, for she turned, crossed the pedestrian bridge spanning the creek, and disappeared through the lodge's ground-level main entrance.

I then made introductions. Both Mom and Dad hugged each of the ladies after their names were called.

After introducing PJ, Jane, and Payton, Dad said PJ looked familiar and asked if she was Doc Calhoun's daughter.

"You have a remarkable memory, Mr. Kristen. We met many years ago. I summer interned for my father at his veterinary practice down in Kalispell. Your vet, Dr. Woodbridge, asked my dad to offer a second opinion. I tagged along."

"PJ is a large animal specialist, Dad."

"Well, good. We happen to have lots of large animals," my father responded.

I kept Dawn for last.

"Mom, Dad, this is Dawn Tillman. We met up outside Arco, Idaho."

"Hello Mr. and Mrs. . . . ah, Andrea," Dawn said.

"Welcome, Dawn," Dad said. "You're one of my favorite actors." Turning, he addressed the group. "Our house is your house. And, please, everyone, call me Neil."

"We'll have plenty of time to get to know one another, but for now, let's get you situated in your cabins and rooms," my mother said.

My father took my arm and guided me away from the women.

"You look tired, son. Which is to be expected, considering what you've been through."

"You don't know the half of it."

"Well, there will be plenty of time to catch up. Why don't you help Renee get situated? Your mom is putting you two up in the Roosevelt cabin."

I looked up at the western horizon and saw that thick black clouds were headed our way. "It looks like rain or possibly snow headed toward us. We need to get our trailers into the equipment barn before either arrives. Wait until you see what we've brought you."

"I know what's under the cover on top of the Humvee. Abigail filled me in."

"That just the tip of the—"

The comms chirped and Abs's voice was clear and strong. "Jon, I've got you in sight. We'll be on the ground in two minutes," she said.

"Roger that. Meet us in the equipment barn. We're driving down now."

"That comms set-up you have is pretty nice," Dad said.

"It works great. Burt set us up. We each have comms, night vision, and Eotech red dot sights."

"Those rifles the women have are not civilian models. Burt again?"

"Yes. Burt made all of this possible. He set us up with camping gear, food, water, fuel, ammo. . . hell, even uniforms for the women."

"Speaking of Burt, three nights ago I had a ham radio conversation with Chris Casey. He says they missed you in Las Vegas by a couple of hours. They packed up all they could, locked the store, and were on the road later that day. They made the mistake of staying on Interstate 15 and ran into trouble on six separate occasions. Beth's brother, Dwight, was killed outside Cedar City, Utah. They're at their place in northern Utah, but they're having problems dealing with the tens of thousands of people leaving Salt Lake City. He says the Mormons have already formed a formidable fighting force and are attempting to take over most of the state. He says the church has sent scouting parties out in search of weapons and ammo. He's chased them off twice now, but feels the church hasn't given up on taking what they have. He's fairly certain they'll come back with a much larger force next time."

"Dwight was one of the good guys and will be missed," I said. "What are they planning on doing?"

"I offered them sanctuary here at the ranch. He said they may take us up on the offer. I haven't heard from him since that conversation, but it may be that they're on the road and can't communicate. Regardless, and just in case they do come, I've asked Mark Perdue to build a dormitory on top of the old cement equipment pad to the right of the bunkhouse."

"Rather than build a dormitory, why not negotiate a deal with the Missoula Airstream dealer for some of his trailers. They're set up for winter living and are actually pretty nice."

"That's a great idea. I know the owner of the dealership."

"Did Mr. Casey say how many members in his group?" I asked.

"Eleven."

"You have any concerns about supporting another eleven people?"

"Well, Chris says they have enough food to last them five years. Seven, if they cut back somewhat. But answer me this: when was the last time you were inside the three food storage buildings down below?"

"A couple months after they were built."

"I've been stocking up, son. I doubled down soon after Trump was sworn in as President, and I didn't stop stocking up after Biden replaced Trump. Then the Russian invasion of Ukraine started, and I tripled our purchases. We were receiving pallet-loads up to the day before the pulse hit. We could support triple our numbers and still have enough to last us fifteen to twenty years. I had the geo-thermal installed in the greenhouse earlier this year, and Terri, one of the newer ranch hands, has a green thumb. She's got all kinds of veggies growing. Then there's the cattle for meat, and pigs and chickens from the two contract farms. We've got our own chickens in commercial coops located next to the greenhouse. Fresh eggs, son, are the best."

"You were very smart to stock up like you did. PJ's father was a prepper, and we loaded up a fraction of the supplies he had stored. In fact, we need to go back and get the rest."

"Where is Doc Calhoun?"

"Dead. He was murdered by looters at his home. We ran into them as they were emptying his house."

"Sorry to hear that. I liked him. And the looters?"

"All dead, save two women I let go. It's bad out there, Dad. Killing, raping, hanging people—including children. We've seen it all."

"We've been lucky here. Edward has put together a potent fighting and quasi-police force. The area has had its share of looters, but he doesn't put up with them and hands out harsh punishment when they're caught. But enough of the doom and gloom. How'd the Land Cruiser run during its first long-distance journey?"

"Flawlessly."

"Did the faraday bag I gave you keep your electronics safe?"

"It did. And thank you for giving it to me. Dad, before we drive down to the equipment barn, I just want to be sure about something."

"What might that be?"

"My bringing the women with me. And then Susan, Dawn, PJ, and her daughter."

"We're happy to have them, son. Your Renee, especially. Your mother is tickled pink to have them all here. And PJ will be a most welcome addition at the ranch. Not sure if Abigail filled you in, but Doc Woodbridge passed away three days after the pulse hit. Asta thinks it's because of his dead pacemaker. So, PJ will be a very valuable addition here on the ranch."

"She has a trailer full of veterinary meds, equipment, and feed. She also has portable X-ray and ultrasound machines."

"The machines are actually working?"

"She claims they are."

"Now that's certainly a bonus."

"You still have that safe in your office?"

"Yep."

"I've got something that needs to be kept secure."

We both watched a bolt of lightning streak out of the clouds and hit the ground a mile or two out. The sound of thunder soon followed.

"That was close," my father said. "We best be moving those trailers. I'll drive one down."

Dad took out a small hand-held Motorola TALKABOUT and told whoever answered to open the equipment barn doors.

I keyed the comms, said, "A storm is moving in. We need to move the trailers down to the equipment barn. Everyone, grab their backpacks out of the vehicles and put them up on the ranch house front porch for now. Then, Melissa, you drive the Cruiser, PJ the ranch truck, Monica the Chevy, Dad Becca's truck, Mr. Perdue his truck, and I'll drive the Humvee. Let's move it!"

The women deposited their backpacks and personal gear on the ranch house front porch then hustled back to their assigned vehicle. I started the Humvee and waited for the others to line up behind me. Once they were ready, I drove left around the ranch house and headed down the hill. The road was steep and we traversed from one side of the hill to the other until we encountered the hillside's one switch-back. Then it was downhill from right to left until we were on the flats.

The equipment barn is out past the horse stables and riding rings. Roger, one of the permanent ranch hands, slid the door open for us, and the convoy drove through. The barn was sixty thousand square feet, with insulated metal walls, concrete floors and twenty-eight-foot-high ceilings. Sky-lights on the steeply sloped roofs provided plenty of illumination. It housed Dad's faraday room and the ranch armory and held all the ranch equipment—pickup trucks, ATVs, snowmobiles, and tools. It also housed the farm equipment, and sitting against the far back wall, were four giant, green-and-yellow John Deere machines: three tractors—one 8R Series and two 7R Series—and one L341 square hay baler.

"Pull up next to me and form a row. Leave keys in the ignition, please."

Once lined up and engines turned off, I unhitched the Cruiser's trailer and had Melissa drive them all back to the ranch house. Dad stayed with me in the barn.

"Those Deeres working?" I asked.

"Not right now, but we have duplicate spares for all their electronics—we'll get them running again come spring. Peter is working on getting the pickups, ATVs, and snowmobiles working first."

Peter Caine was the ranch's lead mechanic, and I could see the top half of his body hunched over the open engine compartment of one of the ranch's newer four-wheel-drive pickups. There were another six trucks lined up against the barn's right wall.

"Is Peter going to be able to get those trucks working again?" I asked.

"He's already got those six running," he answered, pointing to the row of trucks. "We tow them in from where they died in the pulse, but lucky for us, most were already back in the barn. Peter has another five to go. He'll then start working on the ATVs. He's got one of the smaller tractors running, and he uses that to tow the others back to the shop."

"I've got to hand it to you, Dad, you've done a hell of a job of being prepared for this. Having duplicate electronics for the equipment. . . I mean, who would even think of that?"

"Thanks, son. It was one of the more expensive preparations we did. We've already replaced all the electronic controls in the cabins and most of the lodge rooms. So, fridges, coffee makers, Sonos, HVAC and radiant floor thermostats, microwaves, washers and dryers, and hot water systems have been replaced. We also replaced the greenhouse electronics along with the solar controllers and its battery management system. We have a dozen laptops in the faraday room ready to go should we someday need them. The runway ARCAL system's guts have also been replaced and Abigail has tested it. It works."

ARCAL stood for aircraft radio control aerodrome lighting. This system allowed Abigail to turn on the airport approach lights, runway edge lights and taxiway via radio.

"It's incredible. I mean, the country is dark and falling apart, and here we are living pretty much as we did before the pulse hit."

"Well, there is one electronic item we decided not to resurrect."

"What's that?"

"The television sets," he answered with a hearty laugh which I joined. "Your mother does miss her nightly news with Lester Holt and Rachel Maddow. We did bring the big screen in the conference center back to life, though. Thought it might be nice to have the occasional movie night. We have all those Blu-ray discs, after all."

"That sounds like fun. But answer me this: what got you started on being so prepared?"

"Chris Casey. I've always listened to and followed his sound advice, and have had twenty years to get us to this point."

"I knew you were into preparedness, but your efforts never seemed that obvious."

"Keeping the ranch running profitably was always my primary emphasis. Then Abigail returned from Cornell and turned our ranch from a rustic dude ranch into a world-class lodge and dude ranch. Well, things just changed for the better from there. Better, in that we were making a bunch of money. With those profits, I was able to purchase our way to where I thought we should be in terms of being prepared."

"Well, you've done an incredible job in getting ready for a grid-down scenario. Let me show you something," I said, walking back to the Humvee's trailer.

"Show us what?" Eddy Taylor said, as he and Abs walked up to us.

I released the tarp over the trailer, leaned over, grabbed one of the M4s, and held it up for inspection.

"And there's thirty-nine more," I said, handing the rifle to an open-mouthed Eddy.

"Hello, my beauties," Eddy said. "These are military-issue. You have ammo for them?"

"Oh yeah. A little over thirty-three thousand rounds. And lots of magazines. And let's not forget about these." I held up one of the shotguns. "We have forty of these and 2,500 shells."

"Holy crap!" Eddy exclaimed. "Christmas has come early."

I jumped to the ground and lowered the trailer's ramps. I walked up the ramp and moved some cartons around which revealed the two wooden crates holding the .50 cals.

"Come on back here and see what else I've brought."

"You've got Kisses!" Abs shouted, jumping in place. She grabbed Eddy's arm and pointed to the cartons of Kisses.

"Well, yeah. That's one of our surprises. But it's these I wanted you to see," I said, pointing out the stenciling on the front of the .50-cal crates.

"Can we mount one in the back of the Beaver?" Abs asked.

"I've got two mounts: one tripod and the other a suspension harness meant for helicopter doors," I said.

"Or the cargo door of a Beaver," Abs shouted out.

"Tell me you have belted ammo for these two," Eddy said.

"I do. One hundred cans for a total of ten thousand rounds."

"Cool. I know ten thousand rounds seems like a lot, but in a battle or even a smaller skirmish, you're going to burn through several thousand rounds. We should make a real effort to secure more."

"What about your contact at the National Guard?" Dad asked Eddy.

"Yeah, I'll try and get ahold of him. In the days after the pulse, he was willing to supply us with all the ammo I asked for. To his mind, he says, we were a quasi-military force that was keeping the peace, which meant he and his men didn't have to play police. But now, I'm really having to plead for the things we need."

"I always taught my gunners to fire short bursts only," I said. "Not only conserves ammo, but accuracy tends to improve."

"Good advice from a ground grunt who has to lug his ammo on his back," Eddy said, laughing.

"Funny coming from someone that has others do the heavy lifting," I countered, walking up to him and almost touching chests. We did this comic routine pretty much every time we saw each other.

"Let's see. Me—lofty, very important, nationally known lieutenant colonel. You—lowly, though with some rank, master sergeant. By rights, you should be saluting me, soldier," he said, puffing his chest up comically.

"Okay, boys, enough with the bullshit chest-thumping," my dad said, with a chuckle.

"You're right, Mr. K. How much ammo do you have for the Minigun?" Eddy asked.

"Seventy cans, give or take a few," I answered. "We should consider mounting the Minigun in the Beaver."

"Absofuckinlutely!" Abs shouted. "Rain hell on a large group of vehicles or fighters. And the first group that gets to experience fire from above are those fuckers that shot my antenna off."

"First off, watch that mouth, Abigail," Dad said, pointing at her. "You can make your point without the use of four-letter words. I mean, what the fuck?"

And that's my dad.

"Sorry," she said, after controlling her laughter.

"Secondly, what group shot off what antenna?" my dad asked.

"The Beaver's antenna," Eddy answered. "We were fired on when we buzzed a convoy over in Idaho. I'm pretty sure they had a .50-cal mounted in the back of a pickup."

"Well," Dad said, "there's an easy way to stop that happening again—don't do it. If you feel the need to observe, do so from a higher altitude."

But we all knew Abs would continue doing what she'd been doing. . . loving father's advice aside.

"You've put together an impressive amount of firepower, son," my father said, walking over to the armory's heavy metal door. He reached into one of his cargo pants pockets and took out a very large jailer's keyring—there had to be seventy or eighty keys sliding along its metal ring. He held it up for display.

"These are the keys to the kingdom, people. If it's not in this pocket, it's in the bottom drawer of my office desk. Each key is numbered, and copies of the master number list are in the top drawer of the desk. With the exception of the lodge rooms and cabins, these keys open every lock on the property."

"I have keys to the hangar and gas tanks," Abs said. "You have copies of those on that ring too?"

"I do. Let's unload the weapons and ammo now and get them into the armory. This isn't something that should be left out—even here. The other stuff can wait till morning."

I keyed the comms, said, "Renee, we're unloading the trailers of weapons and ammunition. I'll be up in an hour."

"Sounds good. That'll give me a chance to get our stuff unpacked and put away, though we don't have much. By the way, this cabin is beautiful. The view from the living room and deck is breathtakingly gorgeous. I mean, the bathroom is nicer than the bathroom of most five-star luxury hotels I've stayed at."

"My room in the lodge is gorgeous, too," Kathy said. "Thank you, Jon, and your family, for having me here."

"Ditto that," Melissa said. "My room is mega-nice as well. And the view? Hello? I can't even begin to describe how beautiful it is. Can I help with the unloading?"

"Sure. Come on down. Take the Cruiser," I answered.

Using one key out of the dozens on the ring, my father unlocked the steel door and slid it open. He disappeared inside and came out a minute later pushing a pallet jack with a standard-size wooden pallet on it. "Let's start with the 5.56 NATO rounds," he said.

We started unloading the Humvee's trailer. Melissa showed up with Dawn halfway through, and both jumped right in with lending a helping hand.

Eddy introduced himself to Melissa and Dawn.

"You look familiar," Dawn said, after shaking his hand. "From television news maybe?"

"I do military commentary and I'm the go-to person on military matters for both Fox and MSNBC television news," he answered. "I've had quite a bit of airtime lately what with what's going on in Taiwan, the South China Sea, and Ukraine. And you look very familiar as well. Your name rings a bell, too."

"Hello? She's Dawn Tillman," Abs said, putting her palms up in question.

Which produced a blank stare from Eddy.

"Seriously?" Abs asked.

Eddy shrugged.

"All-American, Academy Award-winning actress?" Melissa added.

Eddy's face lit up in recognition, said, "That's right. You starred in *Ring of Fire*."

"I did. Yes," Dawn said.

"I'm embarrassed to say that I don't really watch movies and television much. But I did like that movie. You were great."

"Why thank you, kind sir," Dawn said, with an almost perfect, flirty-sounding southern accent. She then flipped her hair over her left shoulder.

Abs grabbed his arm and pulled him back to the trailer. "Stay on task, mister. I'm hungry and want to get this unloaded."

I detected some jealousy in Abs's voice. *Interesting. I wonder if there might be something between the two.*

With the added help, we soon finished loading the twenty wood crates. We followed Dad as he maneuvered the pallet jack back inside the armory.

The storm turned out to be bringing rain and hail. The sound of the hail hitting the barn's tin roof was deafening, making hearing each other all but impossible.

I hadn't been inside the armory in several years, and I was shocked to see it absolutely chock-full of most everything firearm related. Besides the usual ammo, rifles, handguns, and shotguns, Dad had plate carriers with various-sized armor plates, camo pants, shirts, jackets, and even helmets. He came to a stop next to a row of pallets loaded with carboard cartons. The cartons were labeled from the manufacturer: *Federal 5.56 NATO. 1,000 Rounds. Bulk.*

Dad watched us take it all in. "In case you're wondering how many rounds of 5.56 are here, we have seven pallets, each with thirty cartons of one thousand rounds each," my father said, cupping his hands around his mouth and yelling.

"Let's see," Abs said, forehead squinting in concentration.

"Two hundred and ten thousand rounds," Melissa yelled out in answer, having figured it out before I could begin to count.

The hail suddenly stopped. Now it was just rain falling on the tin roof.

"That's right, Melissa," my father answered. "I bought all the ammo you see from Chris Casey. He ordered it from Federal, and once he received it, he reshipped it here." He turned and inserted a key into a door directly opposite the pallets.

I'd seen the same door to the same freezer-like room at Burt's warehouse in Vegas.

"You have the same faraday room that the Caseys have in Las Vegas," I said.

"Chris and I flew to Arizona together and attended the auction at the decommissioned military base. I think we were the only ones who knew what they were, so snagged them for next to nothing. The expensive part was getting it from Yuma to Montana."

"Well done Mr. K.," Eddy said, sounding impressed.

"And in case you're wondering what all that 5.56 ammo is for. . ." he said, opening the door and flipping on the lights. Overhead lights came on and illuminated two dozen desert-brown, military-version Colt M4s standing up on wall-mounted racks. Fitted on each was an ACOG gunsight. Two dozen night-vision goggles were sitting on a shelf, the same model Burt had supplied us in Las Vegas. Sitting next to the night-vision goggles were the same number of comms systems identical to ours, but with the addition of boom mics and ear pieces. And surprise, surprise—there were eight thermal rifle scopes sitting on a shelf, the same model as the one Burt had given us.

"They working, Mr. Kristen?" Melissa asked, holding up one of the thermal scopes.

"They are. And please, call me Neil."

"These are from where?" I asked.

"Like I said, I ordered all of this from Chris. The ammo had to come from him. If I'd ordered this much ammo directly from another retailer or even a distributor, the ATF would have been on my ass asking questions before the ammo could be delivered."

"I take it you purchased this ammo before Biden was elected," Eddy said.

"The last pallet of forty S&W for the Glocks and pallet of shotgun shells arrived a month before the 2020 election," my dad answered. "Since then, it's been impossible to get any more of any caliber—even from the Caseys."

The comms chirped, and it was Renee asking when we'd be done. "Your mom is making a late lunch. She wants you up here in an hour."

I looked at Dad and he nodded his head.

"We'll be up in an hour or less," I said.

"Roger that. See you then," she said.

"Best not to keep Andrea waiting," my father said.

We hustled unloading the rest of the ammo and then hand-carried in the rifles and shotguns. We saved the two .50-cals for last. Finished, Dad locked up behind us.

I walked up into the trailer and carried out one of the mixed linen boxes we'd scored from the tractor trailer at the weigh station at Burns Junction. Melissa and Dawn each grabbed a Kisses carton and we loaded them all into the rear of the Cruiser.

My father and Eddy saw the Barrett at the same time. "You finally got your Barrett," Eddy said. "Merry Christmas, Jon."

"Saved our bacon outside Battle Mountain, Nevada," Melissa said. "Jon took out two trucks that were almost a mile out with that puppy."

"Really?" Eddy asked, sounding skeptical.

"Well, it was more like 1,500 yards by the time I got them stopped—my first two rounds missed, and it took the balance of the first mag and another full one to finally get the job done."

"He's being modest, people," Melissa said. "He had them both with frames sitting on the ground and on fire."

"Melissa, Eddy, Dawn, and Abs, in back please," I said, holding open the two rear doors. "Dad, ride shotgun."

"We can drive the ranch truck up," Abs said.

"Let's go together and save some gas," my father said.

"Will you teach me how to fire this?" Abs asked me, pointing to the Barrett.

"I can teach you," Eddy said.

"You ever fire one?" I asked him.

"No, but you can do it, so how hard can it be?"

"Oh boy, here we go," Dad said.

"Okay, we'll set you up at 1,500 yards and see how you do. And I would be happy to teach you, Abs. And you, too, Lt. Colonel Taylor."

I hopped in and started the engine. I was halfway out the barn door when I remembered the insulin and the bag of antibiotics that Doc Williams had put together for us. I brought us to a stop, said, "Sorry, I forgot something. I'll be right back."

I ran back to the Humvee and, after a quick search, found the two plastic totes. The bag full of antibiotics was there, too. I managed to carry the three back to the Cruiser's rear doors. Eddy took the totes, and I gave the bag to Abs.

"What's in those?" Abs asked, pointing to the two totes.

"Insulin," Melissa answered.

"Asta is going to be very happy to see these," Dad said. "I know they're facing a shortage of several meds, and insulin is one."

"And test strips, too," Abs added.

"Damn," I said. "We have test strips but I didn't think to grab them from the trailer. I'll do that tomorrow."

"And this one on my lap?" Abs asked.

"Antibiotics."

"Our sister is going to be very happy to see these."

SIXTEEN

Forty minutes after Renee's call we were parking in front of the ranch house. I decided to wait and tell my father about the gold bars after we'd eaten.

Asta came bounding down the rear porch steps and practically leaped into my arms. She wrapped her legs around my waist, and we whirled in a circle like we did when we were kids.

I set her down after five revolutions. She stepped back, looked me up and down, and came in for another hug.

"How are ya, brother?" she asked, looking at me in a more professional manner.

"I'm fine, Asta," I said, trying to stabilize the horizon. "A little dizzy from the ride, but no need for your professional services today."

"I'm just looking at you, big brother. I've missed your face. We've been worried about you."

"Well, we're here now and we're good."

I felt wiggling coming from my pocket, and Journey's head poked out. She looked at me then at Asta, meowed loudly, then extended her paws toward Asta in a pick-me-up-now motion. Asta lifted the kitten out of the pocket and held her out in front of her face.

"Well, aren't you the cute one," she said.

"Traitor," I said to Journey, scratching behind her ears. "Her name is Journey."

People said Asta was the spitting image of our mother. She was tall like the rest of us Kristens, had the Kristen blue eyes and blonde hair, but she was not lean. You could describe her as being a plus size which suited her well. She was strong, in both body and spirit. The name Asta came from an ancient Norse legend, and it meant: star-like, and love. She was a follower of Odin, a belief system which had its roots in Norse mythology. On her wrist was a small tattoo of Odin's horns: three interlocking drinking horns. Imagine a Viking fighting goddess, long blonde hair in a thick ponytail, holding high a giant sword . . . well, you'd be looking at Asta.

Lest you thought she was just another blonde beauty, she graduated top of her class at the University of Colorado Boulder, the same at Stanford Medical School and, breaking with tradition, was even asked if she'd like to do her residency at Stanford. She was a brilliant surgeon, could have picked any hospital in North America, but had made the decision to come home to Whitefish.

Asta, being the beautiful and successful woman she was, had had many suitors. Many men had tried their best to snag her, but my sister happened to like women. My parents were very open-minded when it came to romance and sex, allowing us to bring whomever we wanted home. "Better safe at home than in the back seat of a truck somewhere," they said. And so it had been for all three of us, ever since high school.

Asta was dressed in green surgical scrubs. Dark stains, which I took to be blood, were splattered across the front of her shirt.

"Is that Kris' blood?" I asked, pointing to her scrubs.

She glanced down. "Partly, yeah," she answered. "Looks worse than it is. Those larger cuts on her breasts are serious. They're infected, each and every one. The smaller cuts you closed with Steri-Strips are going to be okay—good job on that, by the way. The larger cuts will require weekly treatments by a wound surgeon. Lucky for her, I'm trained in wound recovery."

Abs and Eddy had climbed out of the back of the Cruiser, and each was carrying an insulin tote. Dawn carried the linen carton and Melissa the Kisses and antibiotics. They set those down behind the Cruiser's rear doors.

"Where do you want these?" Abs asked Asta.

"What are they?"

"Insulin."

"Really? Two full totes?" she asked, not sounding convinced. "Let me see."

Abs opened one of the tote's two plastic half-lids. Asta whistled. There were at least a hundred boxes with six vials in each.

"Do we need to refrigerate them?" I asked.

"Wow. That's a whole lot of insulin," Asta said. "No to the refrigeration. I mean, cooling them won't hurt, but it's not really necessary until after they've been opened. They will last longer if the unopened vials are stored in a cooler environment, but they can't be allowed to freeze, so we have to be careful. I can't take the totes with me to the hospital as our generators stopped running yesterday—they went silent after the natural gas stopped flowing. We're using portable gasoline generators to power the surgical suites, but there's not enough juice to keep the fridges going too."

"Let's put them in the conference-center kitchen's walk-in fridge," Abs suggested.

"That's a great idea," Asta said. "I can take some with me when I go to the hospital and dole them out as needed."

"How often are you going in?" I asked.

"I've been going in every day, but the remaining staff met yesterday, and now that the power is limited, we're going forward with two nurses, a surgeon, and one ER doc on site starting tomorrow. Which means two days a week for me. Supplies are limited without hope of replenishment, so who knows how long it will be before the hospital stops functioning altogether. What's in the red duffel?" Asta asked.

"Antibiotics," Abs answered.

"I was given those down in Battle Mountain by the town's hospital ER doc," I said. "I figured it would be a good idea to have a supply on hand here at the ranch."

"Good call, brother. On the second day of the blackout, we had a pair of armed looters come into the hospital. They overpowered the one guard who was on duty and ransacked the pharmacy. They mostly took heavy-duty drugs that would give a good buzz, but they couldn't have been total idiots as they also grabbed the antibiotics, too."

"Asta, I really want them to be for us," I said, concerned that she wanted to take them to the hospital.

"She's not finished with her story, son," Dad said. "Let her finish."

"Sorry, Asta," I said.

"No problem. One of the nurses recognized the looters as brothers who live two blocks over from her. That night, Eddy gathered together a few volunteers and early the next morning paid them a visit. The drugs were recovered, minus some of the heavier stuff they'd already used or sold. But all the antibiotics were recovered and returned to the hospital. That day, Eddy put four guards on hospital duty 24/7."

"And what did you do with the looters?" Melissa asked Eddy.

"We locked them up at the Whitefish jail," Eddy answered. "We then spread word we'd be punishing two looters and invited all who wished to see justice done to come witness the punishment being meted out for themselves. Two days later, we took the two prisoners to the county firing range. There were several hundred residents already waiting to see what would happen."

"Eddy, please hurry this up," Abs said. "I'm getting hangry."

"Will do, Abs. We zip-tied their hands behind their backs and walked the two looters out to the middle fifty-yard lane's dirt mound. We made them watch as an old excavator dug a hole ten feet deep by three feet wide behind them. Sheriff Whitaker then announced to the crowd that from this day forward what they were about to see would be the automatic sentence for those caught looting. He then turned and shot each looter in the forehead. They fell back into the pit. The smoke from the gunshots hadn't had a chance to clear before the excavator started filling in the hole."

"Brutal but necessary," Dad said.

"As intended, the news of that execution spread fast," Eddy said.

"Any more looting since?"

"Unfortunately, yes," Eddy answered. "If we catch them in the act, we now hold them until we have at least ten. We've gone through four sets of ten and one set of sixteen. That sixteen was two days ago. We announced that one in advance, and we had another several hundred residents show up. We haven't had any looting since."

"Well, you've also opened up several stores where you're handing out food and water to folks," Asta said. "That should be a huge relief to any wannabe looters."

"I admit we should have done that earlier," Eddy said.

"Were the looters locals or stranded out-of-towners?" I asked.

"A mixture of both," Abs answered.

"Anybody I know?"

They didn't answer me.

"Who?" I asked.

"Holly Jacobsen," Eddy said.

"Oh no."

Holly and I had dated for two years in high school, though I hadn't seen or spoken to her since I'd left for college.

"Holly and a man were caught looting a house. A house next door to Amos Mosgardner," Abs said.

Amos Mosgardner is the Whitefish sheriff.

"This happened before the stores were opened and food distribution was started," my father added.

"Amos caught them in the act," Eddy said. "Holly's two girls were with them in the house. The homeowners had been pistol-whipped and tied up."

"How old are the girls?" I asked.

"Eight and ten."

"The guy she was with is from Shelby. Holly said his car had died, down the street from her place, and he sort of moved into the spare bedroom."

"In exchange for protection," Abs said.

"The girls said it was the man's idea to break into the house, and was him that pistol-whipped the couple," Asta said. "And FYI—the couple will be fine."

Mom popped her head out the screen door and told us to get inside, that it was time sit down and eat.

"Were Holly and the girls—" I started to ask.

"I know what you're going to ask," Eddy said, before I could finish my question. "And no, they weren't. Abs and I pulled them out of the jail and drove them to Walmart. Set them up with food and supplies."

"Then drove them home," Abs said.

"The man?" I asked.

"In the second group of looters to be shot," my dad answered.

"We need to head in and eat," Asta said.

"You guys go ahead," I said, turning and heading back to the Cruiser. "I need to bring in the other two boxes."

I grabbed the boxes and carried them inside. I set them on the dining-room hutch where I was sure my mother would see them.

A few minutes later, we were seated around the huge twenty-two-person ranch-house dining-room table. I had grown up at that table, and sitting there now, with Renee, my family and friends, somehow made the world's horrendous problems disappear, even if only for a short while.

On one side of the table were Renee—with Greta at her feet minus her working vest—me, Dawn, Melissa, Monica, and Kathy. On the other: Kris, Abs, Eddy, PJ, Jane, Becca, Mr. Perdue, and a place for Asta. Dad sat at the head of the table, and my mother would be at the other. Asta and my mother were bringing out lunch: sliced ham and turkey for sandwiches, coleslaw, and potato salad. The aroma of fresh-baked bread filled the room.

My mother set the platter of sliced turkey and ham down in the center of the table. She turned and headed back into the kitchen and spotted the two boxes sitting on her dining-room hutch.

"What's this?" she asked no one in particular.

"Those are for you, Andrea," Renee said.

"What in the world. . .?" she said.

Mom spotted the Hershey Kisses logo on the side of the box, said, "I love Kisses." She tore open the top of the box, reached in, and held up an extra-large bag of red, green, and silver-wrapped Holiday Kisses. "Tonight's dessert, everyone!"

"Ah, while I admit to loving Kisses, do you by any chance have a slice of that Dutch apple crisp pie left, Mrs. K.?" Eddy asked. "I've been thinking about it all day, and while Kisses are wonderful, they simply can't compete with your pie."

"He really has been thinking about it all day, Mom," Abs said. "One track mind."

"Hey, it's the apocalypse, and freshly-baked Dutch apple crisp pies are in short supply," Eddy countered. "I'd head to a Marie Callender's if there was one."

Mom turned, said, "Edward, I made three. Give me a little credit. After all these years, I know what you like." Seeing no one making the first move on the food, she asked Melissa to start with the meat and send it clockwise. "Don't wait for me."

No one made a move to start the process as we were waiting for my mother to open the other box. She took a knife from her place setting and slit open the box of linens. She got the box opened and looked up at us in silence.

"Abigail, come take a look at what's in here," she finally said.

Abs screamed when she saw what we'd brought them. "We were going to bite the bullet and buy all new linens in the spring. It was going to be a huge expense, but we truly needed to replace them," Abs explained. "They're beautiful. And super high-end, too. Thank you."

"There's nothing wrong with the current linens," Dad said, ever the over-reasonable one.

"They're two years old, Dad," Abs said. "You can't have one of the highest-ranked lodges in North America with guests sleeping on two-year-old sheets."

"Whatever, Neil. It's moot now, anyway," my mother said.

"Very true, my love," Dad said.

"There's an entire pallet's worth out in the trailer, guys," I said. "Sheets, duvets, towels, bath rugs, shower curtains. . . you name it, it's there. You'll need linens for the dormitory you're building. Or the trailers. Use the current linens down there and the new ones for the house, lodge, and guest cabins."

"Great idea," Mom said.

"Where did you get a pallet of linens?" Eddy asked.

"Why don't we tell you about our journey while we eat," I said, by way of an answer.

"Good," my mother said, taking her place at the end of the table. "Dig in, please."

My mother was my best friend. It had always been that way. Before the pulse we had spoken two or three times a week and we never ran out of things to talk about.

At sixty-five, my mother was a vibrant, strikingly beautiful woman. She had thick, long, salt-and-pepper gray hair that was usually up in an intricate, gravity-defying combination of bun and ponytail. She was an inch taller than six feet and had blue eyes, a slender nose, and high cheekbones. She was a competitive swimmer in high school and college and had been an alternate in the 1976 Summer Olympics in Montreal, Canada. She still had the lean swimmer's physique.

With her beauty-pageant good looks and tall, stunning figure, she had moved to New York City after graduating college and within a few months became a model for the Ford Agency.

She had been born and raised in Kalispell, loved the high country and mountains, and had always found time to fly home every two to three months. She said her visits had been her way of recharging her soul.

Even though my parents had grown up a scant fifteen miles apart, my mother and father had never met until Chevrolet used our ranch to shoot a television commercial for its Blazer four-wheel-drive SUV.

My mother had played a mother who was caught in a snowstorm and the Blazer brought her and her two children home safely. They shot the commercial in an actual snowstorm and it was during a break in the shooting that she happened to glance out toward the far meadow where she saw a figure emerge from the falling snow like an apparition. Dad was a mile or two out, on horseback with a working dog running along on either side of his horse. He didn't veer off toward the stables, instead making his way directly toward the production crew. She had stood transfixed as he came closer, riding right up to where she was standing. He looked down at her with the most beautiful smile she'd ever seen, tipped his hat, and dismounted. He had towered over her by several inches, and considering her own height, that seldom happened. Then he said, "I've got to say, miss, other than my mother, I think I'm looking at the most beautiful woman that has ever stepped foot on our ranch."

He had stuck out his hand, said, "Welcome to the Kristen Double T Ranch. I'm Neil Kristen."

The snowstorm hadn't let up, and the crew ended up staying three days at the ranch, my father and mother spending every waking moment together.

That commercial was the last she ever made. They were married a month later at the ranch. Nine months after the wedding, though it could have been a month earlier, according to Asta who may have peeked at my birth certificate, I was born. Asta and Abs had followed.

Now, here we all were—home.

After putting four loaves of fresh-baked bread through a commercial-grade slicer, Asta handed the plate of still-warm bread to Melissa and took her place across from Renee.

My father clinked his water glass and held it up. "To both our new and old friends, welcome. Consider our home, yours. Andrea and I are so thankful that you're here with us. These are, and will be for who knows how long, terrible times. But we'll endure. Together. I'm sure of it."

"Here. Here," Mr. Perdue said, raising his glass. We all toasted to that.

"Thank you for taking us in," PJ said, hugging Jane sitting next to her.

"We're happy to have each and every one of you here with us," my mother said.

"One last thing before we dig into the sandwiches," my father said, setting his glass down and suddenly looking and sounding serious. "At ten tomorrow morning, in the conference-center dining room, we're going to have a mandatory all-hands meeting. This will also include the ranch hands— the only exceptions will be the four sentries we'll have posted at the two entrances. After the meeting, we'll be going to the shooting range to have some range time. Jon, you good to lead the session at the range?"

"You bet. I'll bring the Barrett and we can watch Eddy attempt to hit a target at 1,500 yards. That should bring some much-needed laughter and entertainment."

"Look forward to it, good buddy," Eddy replied.

Abs started passing bowls of coleslaw and potato salad down the table, said, "Let's eat and listen while Jon and the ladies fill us in on the road trip."

"And please don't filter any of the details," my mother said. "We want to hear everything."

It took two sandwiches, a refill on potato salad and coleslaw, and forty-five minutes to complete the narrative.

I STARTED WITH THE SECURETECH meeting in Las Vegas, the power outages in the hotel, the planes hitting the ground, the Feds taking our people back east, the promise we'd made to make our way back east, the three idiots in the parking garage, our time at Burt's place, sleeping that first night in the warehouse, and the drive out of Vegas.

"You promised to drive out east? Where to?" Eddy asked.

"Atlanta," Renee answered, evidently deciding not to share the secret Kentucky site with the table.

"What for?" Eddy asked.

"There's a project the Feds want completed, now more than ever, and Renee is the head of the software team," I answered.

"I'm pretty dialed in on projects the Feds have going on," Eddy said, "but I'm not familiar with any in Atlanta."

"You don't know everything the Feds do," Abs said.

"I guess—" he started to say.

"I also told Kris I'd get her back to Seattle. And promised Kathy I'd leave a note in her Seattle home for her husband, Bradley, to let him know her location."

"Where is he?" Abs asked.

"Europe," Kathy answered. "Barcelona, Spain."

"Shit, I'm sorry to hear that," my father said. "Do we know if any other countries were hit?"

"Beyond the list I mentioned before? No," I answered. "But who knows what could have happened since day one. Other countries feeling threatened and letting loose their own missiles as a preemptive measure would be a good guess."

"It's a bummer, but Bradley is a resourceful guy, and I know he'll find a way to get home," Kathy said.

"We also need to retrieve Dawn's sister in Vancouver Island, Canada. She's a student there," Renee said.

"Abigail, you can install the floats on the Beaver and take care of both the Seattle and Vancouver trips," my dad said.

"Easy, brother," Abs added. "A few hours flight which will take us over the Cascade Range. We can generally follow Interstate 90—the builders really followed the best route."

Renee picked up the story as I dug into a sandwich. Leaving nothing out, she told them about the A10 pilot, Brandon, and his expectant wife, Ruth, who had passed on the information about the pulse and its cause, the little boy we came across walking down the middle of the highway, killing his mother's two rapists, the roadblock in Alamo, and the first night camping out behind the hill in the desert.

"Burt set us up with every conceivable piece of camping equipment you can imagine," Monica said. "Not to mention enough Mountain House meals to feed us for six months."

"And our camos, too," Kris added.

"Oh, late that morning, Jon spotted an old Ford station wagon passing our location, which we found the next night," Renee said. "Sadly, it had been shot to hell, and the mother, father, and infant all dead from a gunshot to the head. Killed for a jerry can of fuel and water."

"They killed an infant?" my mother asked. "What the hell?"

"The more we traveled the worse it got. . . much worse, Andrea," Kathy said.

"That next night," Renee continued, "we came upon two women on horseback—Stacy and her mother Cathy—carrying a car seat each, holding an identical twin infant. They were headed to the sister's ranch and led us to a shortcut to Highway. . . ah. . . what highway was that, Jon?"

"Fifty," I answered between bites of one of the best turkey sandwiches I think I'd ever had.

"Yeah, 50, so we could avoid going through Ely, Nevada. While following the two riders, an older Harley trike came barreling down the road and had to stop to avoid hitting the Cruiser. Turns out the man driving the Harley was the one that killed the infant and its parents in the old station wagon. Melissa put him down, and we let his woman passenger go."

"After making her walk a half mile half-naked," Kris added, not in a kind voice.

"I won't even ask why you made her do that," Asta said.

"You had to have been there," Melissa said. "I was the one that made her strip and walk. At least we didn't shoot her."

The table fell silent.

"We decided to try driving in daylight, so we found a hill to camp behind that night, slept, and set out early the next morning," Kathy said, picking up where Melissa had stopped. Seeing no one stepping up to narrate further, Kathy continued. "Later that morning, we crested a high hill and we could see a large RV blocking both lanes ten miles ahead. We witnessed a young man executed and his female companion taken. We put together a plan, put down the killers—a mother and her son, and freed the woman. We also found a pile of bodies at the bottom of the embankment next to the RV.

"That engagement was my first," Ka thy said. "And my first killing."

"You did well, kiddo," I said. "It had to be done."

"Turns out the young woman was taken so that the mother could teach her son how to—excuse the wording here folks—fuck a woman," Monica said.

"Our timely arrival interrupted the impromptu lesson," Kathy said, between bites of her sandwich.

"Jesus Christ," Mr. Perdue said. "Unreal. I'm just so thankful we live where we do."

"I had no idea it was that bad out there," Becca said.

"Keep listening," Monica said. "It gets worse."

"After passing through Eureka, we came upon a mother walking her three young children home to their ranch just outside of town," Kris said, picking up the narrative. "They'd been walking from Austin to Eureka and had been out in the cold for a day and a half. We loaded them up, backtracked ten miles, and dropped them at their driveway. I think her name was Barbara Lopez."

Renee put together a third sandwich, saw me watching her, leaned in, whispered in my ear, "Eating for two here. Will you still love me when I'm fat?"

"Always and forever, hon. Which reminds me, I've got to ask Asta if she has any pregnancy tests."

Melissa put her drink down and picked up where Kris had left off.

"Heading north, we entered the old mining town of Austin, Nevada. We found it on fire and saved two school-teachers from being lynched."

"They were about to join three others who were already hung," Kris interjected. "Melissa and Jon killed three lynchers during the rescue."

"Then we headed north, and during a rest break, I was taken by surprise by two brothers intent on taking the Cruiser," I said. "Melissa here, displaying some incredible marksmanship, put one down from two hundred yards. Saved my sorry butt, for sure."

"During a search of the area we found Greta locked in a truck," Renee said. "Nearby were her handler and male companion—the woman strangled after having been raped and the man shot."

"You think the two men Melissa shot had killed the woman and man?" my mother asked.

"Pretty sure they did," Renee answered. "Later that day, as we searched for a hill to camp behind, we came across an old man in a walker waving us down."

"You know him, Dad," I said. "Sig Alderson."

"No kidding?" my dad asked. "You actually found Sig Alderson standing with a walker on the highway?"

"We did."

"Why was he out on the highway?" my mother asked. "And was he okay?"

"He was fine. He had managed to walk the quarter mile from his house to the highway, and he was hoping that someone would stop and help him with a few things on the ranch."

"His ranch foreman and hands happened to have been away when the pulse hit," Kathy explained, "and hadn't returned."

"I take it you helped him?" my mother asked.

"Oh yeah," I answered.

"Sig is the consummate gentleman," my father said. "And how is Molly?"

"She's doing great," Renee answered. "She's one tough cookie."

"That same day, Melissa and I fed the horses and got each and every one of the ranch's windmills operating again—they'd installed solar-powered pumps which had fried in the pulse. It was just a matter of releasing the blade brakes. Easy."

"Followed by a wonderful steak and potato dinner," Monica said. "Then enjoying a hot shower and soft bed in their new bunkhouse."

"The next day, we hooked up the ranch's horse trailer and with Sig acting as our guide, drove to Battle Mountain to retrieve Miguel and the other ranch hands," Kathy said, "along with their families."

"Our first stop was Miguel's house, and while waiting for him to load up, we heard gunfire coming from the hospital across the street," Melissa said. "Jon and I responded and found a deputy shot dead outside the front entrance and Susan here wounded and lying in her own blood in an interior coffee shop.

"We shot and killed the three killers. While a doctor attended to her wounds, we were able to gather the remaining three ranch hands and later swung back and picked her up."

"And thank you, Jon and Melissa, for saving my life," Susan stated, taking ahold of Melissa's hand and kissing it.

Continuing the story, Monica said, "On our way out of town, three pickups tried to stop us. The leading truck flipped over, and we later learned that three men died. The remaining two trucks were following us, and Jon, using the Barrett, shot and disabled them from like a mile out."

Perhaps because she knew what was coming next, Kris slid her chair back and stood. "Thank you for lunch, Andrea. I'm tired and need to rest." She turned and left the room. The table remained silent as we listened to her footsteps on the stairs and then heard her door open and close.

"One of the ranch hands, Lucas, was the ranch mechanic and was able to get an old pickup truck running again," Renee said.

"Which Kris promptly stole," Monica added.

"Really?" my mother asked.

"Oh yeah," Renee said. "Kris has not exactly been a team player during this odyssey."

"She's a thief and can't be trusted," Monica stated flatly, her voice strong and fists clenched tight. "She headed north toward Battle Mountain and was gone."

"And yet, she's here with you," my father said. "I guess you were able to catch her before she got far?"

"Not exactly," I answered. "But we'll get to that in a minute."

"Later that night, during dinner, three men staged a home invasion and held everyone at gun point," Renee said. "Jon and I were in the pantry and were able to escape undetected out the back door. You want to pick up the story, Jon?"

"Sure. With Renee's help, we were able to neutralize the situation."

"He means killing the three of them," Kathy explained.

"We then searched and found their vehicle close by," Melissa said. "It's the Humvee."

"We spent another night at the Alderson's and most of the next day getting ready to leave, which we did at about nine that night."

"You're leaving out the fact that, with Kris no longer with us, we decided to head to the ranch instead of Seattle," Renee said. "Though we did drive a route that would most likely follow Kris."

"The town of Battle Mountain asked us to tow a horse trailer with two horses up to Winnemucca," I said. "Which we did with the help of twin brothers, Tommy and Brent Carlisle."

"Those must be Charlie Carlisle's grandsons," Mom said.

"They are. We met Mr. Carlisle later that night."

"Jon, you're leaving out what happened at the rest stop," Renee said.

"I think we need to speed up the story somewhat," I said. "Maybe I should skip some things."

"I'm enjoying the story," Asta said, her chin resting on her hands. It's an incredible one."

"Take your time telling it. I want to hear it all," my father said, refilling his glass.

"Me, too," Eddy chimed in. "Pretty fascinating."

"Ditto," my mother said.

"Go for it, Jon," Abs said.

"I had no idea things had gotten so bad," Rebecca said again.

"Okay. I'll do my best," I said.

"Start up at the rest stop," Renee said.

"Okay. On the drive to Winnemucca, I saw unnatural-looking snow-covered lumps in a rest area's parking area. We stopped and found at least a dozen dead bodies, including one child. The killers were in one of the victim's old, but running, Dodge pickup with a slide-in camper on the back. We engaged and killed the three in the camper and one more out on the highway's center median. This man confirmed they had killed the folks we found in the parking lot."

"Man, the body count keeps going up," Eddy said.

"We kept running into assholes that had to be dealt with," Melissa stated emphatically. "Lots of 'em out there, Mr. Television Man."

"Whoa there, Annie Oakley," Eddy said, palms moving in a calm down motion. "I think you guys did an amazing job getting here. And in one piece. Job well done."

Melissa continued to stare Eddy down but then relaxed back in her chair. "Sorry," she said.

"Go ahead, Jon," my mother said.

"The Carlisle brothers took the camper, and we were at their grandfather's place an hour later. Mr. Carlisle was able to get ahold of Dad via shortwave radio."

"How are Charlie and Margaret?" my mother asked.

"Margaret Carlisle passed away four years ago," I said. "Mr. Carlisle is doing well."

"Poor Charlie," my mother said. "Those two were inseparable."

"He truly loved Margaret and spoke of her often," my father said.

"We hit the road shortly after the connection was lost with you. We crossed into Oregon an hour and a half later. Forty or fifty miles further on we almost had a head-on collision with an old Ford Bronco."

"It was dark and snowing like crazy," Renee explained. "While driving with running lights only, we touched the Hummer's front fender with the Bronco's drivers side mirror."

"Why only running lights?" Abs asked.

"To better see the top of the snowplow markers," Melissa answered. "There was deep snow on the roadway, and the only way we could stay in the middle was to navigate using the reflection off the top of the markers. Running lights worked best for the job. Plus, headlights attract attention."

"I've done the same a few times," Asta said.

"We stopped at Burns Junction and happened upon Kris," I said. "The truck she'd stolen from Sig had started bucking as it ran out fuel. She'd managed to park in a truck weigh station, only to have been dragged out of the truck the next morning by a stranded semi-truck driver. That truck driver put her in his rig, tied her up, raped and sodomized her, and cut her breasts each time she refused his demand for a blow job."

Horrified facial expressions coupled with stunned silence greeted this part of the story. I'd debated even telling it, as I thought it might be Kris' tale to tell, but her stealing the truck and taking off with it had changed our entire journey. In the end, I had decided her part had to be told.

"Which goes some way to explaining her attitude," Renee said, breaking the uncomfortable silence.

"We cleaned and patched up Kris as best we could," I said. "Clint, the truck driver, was handcuffed to the front bumper of his big rig and then, after a brief struggle and some nasty words, took a round to his knee. Kris then cut his penis in half and discarded it just out of his reach."

"Just punishment, in my book," my mother said.

"Rapists don't deserve anything less," Asta threw in.

"He got what he deserved," my dad said.

"As a group, we voted to allow Kris to rejoin us," Kathy said.

"I was the lone nay vote," Monica offered up. "Folks, under no circumstances should you trust her."

"Clint, bless his dead heart, was pulling a trailer load of the Holiday Hershey Kisses… forty-five thousand pounds of Kisses," Kathy said. We pulled twenty cartons off and then searched the remaining five trailers and came up with the linens and drugs."

Asta looked surprised, asked, "Drugs? As in plural?"

"Besides the insulin, we found an entire pallet of drugs bound for a new pharmacy opening in Henderson, Nevada," Renee answered. "Most of the names I didn't recognize. They're in locked plastic totes sitting in our trailer."

"We'll unload them tomorrow," I said, reaching in my pocket and pulling out the folded packing list and handing it over to Asta.

Asta skimmed through each page. "This is a pretty complete list of drugs and supplies you'd need to establish a full-fledged medical clinic. Just thinking out loud."

"I like your thinking, Asta." This from my father. "Jon, what do you think?"

"Fine by me."

"It's settled then," Asta said, giving two thumbs-up.

"We'd finished loading the totes into our trailer when Greta heard a vehicle approaching from the south. It was the Bronco that we'd touched a couple of hours earlier," I said. "Turns out the woman's husband and his parents had been killed by a group of men on her in-law's farm, and she and her son were driving back to her home in Burns. They, Emily Talbot and her son Peter, were being pursued by the killers. We set up a roadblock, stopped the convoy, and identified the two men that pulled the triggers. Another man was killed trying to thwart the roadblock. The two killers are no longer among the living. We let the other eighteen men go."

"Minus their weapons and vehicles, of course," Renee added. "Which Jon rendered useless—the vehicles I mean."

"One of the pickups was an old, but fully restored, Dodge Power Wagon. I couldn't bring myself to destroy it."

"You left it on the road?" Eddy asked, his voice filled with obvious disbelief.

"No, Eddy. I did not. I gave it to Emily Talbot's son. He drove it home."

"Nice gift, buddy."

"I didn't consider it a gift, rather, a reutilization of available resources."

"Boy oh boy. You can take the man out of the military but never the military out of the man," Dawn said, laughing.

"I'm sorry, but I've got to head to the radio shack soon for the afternoon check-in," my dad said, after looking at his watch. "I want to hear it all, but perhaps we'd get through it quicker with fewer interruptions. . . Edward."

"Sorry, Mr. K. I'll only open my mouth for Mrs. K.'s pie."

"Good boy," Abs said, patting Eddy on his head.

I waited for the laughter to die down before picking up where we'd left off.

"It was there at Burns Junction that we made the decision to head east and then north, rather than north and then east. We hit Rome, Oregon where we found a father and son who'd been shot and killed for propane bottles. Next up was the town of Jordan Valley. There we saw too many bodies to count in front of a motel and gas station.

"Then it was on to the junction of Highway 95 and 55 that we ran into a wall of truck drivers linking arms across the highway. They'd been caught in the parking lot of the truck plaza when the pulse hit. They've started a successful community of truck drivers and stranded skiers. They told us they'd heard helicopters, seen Abrams tanks roll through, and seen contrails from jets.

"Then we hit Shoshone, Idaho."

"Which is a place I'll never forget," Kathy said. "Hanging from every corner streetlight were the bodies of men, women, and children. I mean each and every streetlight. Each victim, and there had to have been fifteen or twenty of them, had their hands zip-tied behind them and had been strung up alive."

"Next to the town's Christmas decorations," Monica added. "Not so jolly."

"We extracted some revenge for those killed by killing nine of the local townsfolk who fired on us," Melissa said.

"Kathy was hit in the vest in that engagement," I said, which prompted her to hold up the bullet in question.

"Jon wussed out and let one of them go," Melissa said, a grin planted across her face.

"He'd been forced into the role by the corrupt sheriff," I explained. "He was a wounded ex-serviceman with multiple tours in the Middle East under his belt—just didn't feel right bringing further harm on him."

"It was nice of Jon," Renee said, affectionately rubbing my arm.

"That morning, we came upon the Craters of the Moon Visitor Center. We were getting tired, and the first rays of daylight were about to rise over the eastern mountains. We made the decision to spend the day there. While the ladies were getting the gift shop ready for some extended down-time, I took a walk around the center's grounds. I found a group camp area that was being used as a movie production staging area. What I came across was horrifying—a semi-trailer filled with sixty plus frozen bodies. They'd been herded in and executed."

The table once again fell silent.

"Christ almighty," my mother said. "Why?"

"From a witness, we learned that they'd been exterminated—the killer's words, not mine—because some of them were minorities: blacks, Asians, Mexicans, and Jews."

"I take it that it was Lassman and his group that killed them?" Abs asked.

"Yes," Dawn answered. "Of which I was the sole survivor thanks to Greta."

"Greta found Dawn and a male companion behind the campground's entry shack," Renee explained. "She had no discernable pulse but wrapped a finger around one of Jon's when he was examining her. We brought her up to the gift shop and over the next ten hours were able to warm her up."

"We placed her on her side and took turns sharing a sleeping bag with her, two of us at a time. . . naked, one in front and one behind," Monica said. "Jon placed heated water bottles under her arms and over her groin and a large, heated water filter over her chest. We changed the water bottles and filter every hour."

"And took her temperature," Renee added. "Dawn's temperature was close to eighty-six and her skin Smurf-blue when we found her. Nine hours later, we had her temperature up to just over ninety-six, and that's when we recognized her."

"You guys did everything right," Asta said. "Getting in the sleeping bag with her and placing hot water bottles where you did was exactly what I would have done. Good job."

317

"I burned the body trailer, put Dawn in the Humvee, and we left after sundown.

"We hit the town of Arco that evening and met up with an organized fighting force led by a woman and current Idaho National Guard member by the name of Sue Cleary," I said. "Ms. Cleary informed us of Lassman and his group and that it was Lassman that had murdered Dawn's colleagues."

"She also informed us of the existence of the Montana Protection Force," Melissa added.

"They lacked communication devices but had come up with an ingenious early warning system. They'd sent people to the top of eight mountains with road flares. When the spotter above Salmon saw Lassman and his fighters heading south, they'd light up flares."

"The Indians did the same thing with smoke signals," Abs said.

"A primitive but effective morse code," my father said.

Dawn picked up the narration. "After Arco, we hit the town of Mackay," she said. "We surprised another fighting force, also led by a woman—Colonel Melinda Hughes. While Jon was speaking with her, the mountain-top signal flares lit up. Jon organized an ambush and, using the Minigun destroyed eleven of Lassman's twelve vehicles."

"How many do you think were killed?" Abs asked.

"We didn't count, but I'd guess between eighty and a hundred," Melissa answered.

"The sole survivors were a young teenage girl and Lassman," Dawn said. "The girl had been kidnapped and used as a sex slave by Lassman and his male fighters. Jon and I killed Lassman."

"How did you both kill him?" my father asked.

"Jon put his hands over mine as I held the gun," Dawn answered. "But I pulled the trigger."

"Ah. . ."

"The rescued girl informed us that Lassman was holding a couple of dozen women and younger teen girls at a hotel in

Salmon and using them for nightly sex," Dawn said, continuing the story. "These hostages were being guarded by three women.

"We set off for Salmon ahead of the colonel's group. Entering the town, we came across eight bodies that had been lined up across Highway 93 and executed where they stood. They'd been left there, on the road, with hands tied behind their backs, and run over repeatedly. With the accumulated snow they appeared to be speed bumps."

"Lassman and his merry band of assholes were truly sick fucks," Susan said. "Sick fucks that no longer exist."

"At the hotel, Jon and I freed the women and girls and killed one of the guards," Melissa said, "We released the other two."

"One of the guards told us that Lassman stored his supplies, weapons, and ammo at a self-storage facility directly across from the hotel," I said. "That's where we found the fifties, rifles, and ammo.

"Once the colonel arrived, we took off. In Darby we stopped at a veterinary clinic in hopes of trading for some dog food for Greta. At the clinic, we met PJ and Jane."

"Shortly after the blackout, my ex-husband had bicycled by to check in," PJ said. "On his way out, he stole the clinic's old, but still working, pickup, which left Jane and I without a way to get to my dad's place outside Kalispell. We'd hoped that he would come back for us, so we loaded up the clinic's work trailer with the practice's medical supplies, food, and meds. We had about given up hope when Jon and the ladies showed up."

"PJ had only recently discovered that her ex was one of Lassman's senior lieutenants," Renee explained. "As such, she feared for her and Jane's safety, and rightly so, so we offered to tow their trailer to her father's home outside Kalispell. We hooked up their trailer—the large triple-axle enclosed cargo job behind Sig's ranch truck—and set off."

"In Hamilton, we ran into Abs's wannabe boyfriend, Ted Mitchell," I said, which earned me another middle finger from my little sister. "Just kidding, everyone."

"Abs flew in a few minutes later, landing on the highway," Melissa said.

"I passed on Colonel Hughes's request for a meet-up with Ted, Eddy, Sue Cleary, and herself in two weeks' time," I said. "She would like to establish a two-state fighting force to protect Idaho and Montana."

"That's a wonderful idea," Eddy said. "I'd want you with me, Jon."

"Sure," I said. "I'll hold your hand the entire time."

"That's cute, ground grunt," Eddy responded, with a quick laugh and wide grin.

"I'll fly you both down there," Abs said, stepping in before I could respond. "Where?"

"Mackay, I guess."

"We can work out the details later," Eddy said.

"I put Kris and Susan on the plane and sent them on ahead," I said. "We then hit Missoula. We stopped at a friend of PJ's, a fellow vet with a practice located on 93. While waiting for PJ to return, Mr. Perdue and Becca drove up and joined our caravan. I traded a few Mountain House meals for an old Honda XL trail bike from a motorcycle shop next door to the vet's building."

"What are you going to use it for?" Eddy asked. "Tool around the ranch?"

"I'm not sure. But I have an ultraquiet muffler that I need to install. It might be a good way to travel in more populated areas. I'll figure it out."

"On our way out of Missoula, we spotted an open Starbucks," Becca said, speaking up for the first time. "They'd been able to reopen and were serving up a choice of three items. That coffee will probably be the last Starbucks I'll have for who knows how long."

"It was good, wasn't it?" Renee said.

"Brought me back to the good times we had before the blackout," Melissa said. "Almost forgot about what was happening in our country and possibly the world."

"We took a lot for granted, didn't we?" Kathy added.

"And then reality bit us hard in the butt," Dawn said, "because as we were about to pass the Missoula Airport, we came face-to-face with a couple of hundred stranded passengers on the highway. And they were all, including a bunch of kids, running toward us asking for water and food. Jon was able to stop their advance by firing a full magazine over their heads."

"They were picked up and taken back to town," Eddy said. "Thank you."

"We then drove on to PJ's father's house," Monica said.

I could see my father fidgeting in his chair which I knew was his first sign of impatience. We needed to get the story up to date—and quickly. I glanced at my mother who, with a subtle finger-wave, motioned for me to hurry it along.

"We found four looters in PJ's father's golf course clubhouse," I said, resuming the story. "With Greta's help, I put down three men permanently and incapacitated a woman. We then discovered more looters emptying PJ's dad's house and his next-door neighbor's."

"My grandfather, his neighbor, and Grandad's dog were found murdered," Jane said, putting her hand on her mother's.

"Jon then silently took out four looters before being spotted by the remaining three," Melissa said. "He fired on two and killed them. A young woman managed to retreat into the neighbor's house, but Jon was able to talk her into giving up. Saved her life."

"We gave the two surviving looters one of their trucks back, a few supplies, and let them go," Renee said. "We took the remaining truck and two trailers, loaded some of PJ's dad's supplies, and headed out."

"And here we are," I said.

"That's quite the road trip you had, Jon," my mother said. "Thank you for telling us about it. Neil and I are relieved that you all made it to the ranch safe and sound. And I'm sorry to learn of Kris's ordeal."

"There's no accounting for stupidity," my father said. "And no place for dishonesty in the world we find ourselves in."

I was fairly certain he was referring to Kris. At least, that's how I interpreted his statement. And it was safe to say, the others had too, for an uncomfortable silence followed.

My father pushed his chair back, started picking up plates, said, "Why doesn't everyone head on back to your rooms and rest up. There's hot water for showers and working washers and dryers in the guest laundry room located on the lodge's first floor."

"Cabins have their own washers and dryers—no quarters or tokens required," my mother added.

We all laughed, and the tension in the room evaporated.

"It's getting late in the day, so we'll probably skip dinner tonight," my mother said. "There's lots of leftovers, so if anyone gets hungry later on, feel free to raid the fridge."

"We'll see everyone tomorrow morning at ten in the conference center's dining room," Dad said. "Enjoy your evening."

"We'll have breakfast ready at eight in the same place," my mother added.

"Ah. . . Mrs. K.," Eddy said, "About that piece of pie?"

SEVENTEEN

Renee and I pitched in and helped my mother clean up. After lunch, my father had headed to his radio shack out back, the women and Mr. Perdue to their rooms, Abs and Eddy back to the plane hangars, so it was just the three of us in the ranch-house kitchen. Greta was sitting by the dining-room doorway, watching us moving about the kitchen.

We were finishing up when my father walked through the kitchen's rear door. He hung his coat on a wall hook, and rubbing his hands together for some quick warmth, said, "Ah, I'm glad you're here—just the three I wanted to speak with." He stuck his head into the dining room, looked both ways, shut the door, came back into the kitchen, pulled out a stool from the kitchen island, and sat. A vestless Greta made her way over to my father, stood on her hind legs, and put her head on his lap. Dad gave her ear rubs which produced tail wags.

We'd been told by PJ to remove Greta's working vest when she wasn't working. She said working dogs such as Greta need lots of downtime not unlike humans. "Taking off the vest lets her know it's playtime," PJ had explained.

"What's up?" my mother asked. "Anything on the short-wave?"

"Nada. I was hoping to hear from Chris Casey, but the airwaves are quiet."

Mom rested her elbows on the granite island, said, "Didn't he say, if they decided to join us, that the journey could take several days?"

"That's true, babe. Listen, you two," he said, turning his attention to Renee and I, lowering his voice to a quiet whisper, "this isn't easy, especially after learning of her ordeal at the weigh station, but—"

I felt I knew what he was going to say, so I said it for him. "You don't want Kris here at the ranch."

He let out a deep breath and nodded his head.

"Jon made it clear to Kris that her living here was contingent on your approval," Renee said. "And after stealing the ranch truck and taking off with it, I'm sure she's half expecting you to deny the request."

"I'm sorry, but we can't have her here at the ranch," my dad explained. "We can't be having to watch her every move."

My mother walked around the island, stood behind my dad, and put her arms around his shoulders. "I agree with your father," she said, leaning in and planting a kiss on his cheek.

"Thank you for that, hon bunch," he said, affectionately patting her behind.

"I'll tell her," I said. "I promised to get her to Seattle, and I need to follow through on that. I'll sit down with Abs tomorrow and put together a plan to make that happen—maybe fly there as early as the day after tomorrow."

I tried to stifle a yawn but was unsuccessful. "It's been a long day, and I could really use a hot shower followed by landing in a soft bed."

"You ready to head to the cabin?" I asked Renee.

"You betcha."

I stood and helped Renee slide her stool back.

"One more thing before you two head to your cabin," my mother said. "It's about Edward and Abigail."

"Oh?" I asked, puzzled.

"It's good news," my mother said, seeing the look on my face.

"Abigail is pregnant," my father said, smiling. "Asta confirmed it with blood tests a few days before the pulse hit. It's Edward's."

"That's wonderful news. How far along is she?" Renee asked.

"Ten weeks," my father answered.

"We'd like to ask Edward and his parents to move up here to the ranch," my mother said. "Edward will be right here with Abigail, and Asta will be able to monitor his father more easily. We wanted to get your feedback before we talk to Abigail. I'm thinking we'll put Abigail and Edward in the Grand View cabin and Edward's parents in a room on the lodge's ground floor."

"I think it's a wonderful idea," I said. "And thank you for asking me."

"A Kristen grandchild. . . finally," my mother said.

"Make that two," Renee said, looking at me.

"Do you mean. . . you two?" my mother asked, her voice filled with excitement, eyes bright with expectation.

"I'm pretty sure," Renee answered. "We're hoping to confirm it with a pregnancy test."

"We weren't going to say anything until we'd done a test, but Renee knows her body and it's telling her it's happening," I said, wrapping my arm around her shoulders and bringing her in close.

"Hot damn, you two," my dad said, opening his arms wide for a group bear hug. "Congratulations. The two can grow up together. Asta brought home some tests from the hospital and they're here somewhere."

Seeing us in celebration, Greta danced around the kitchen, tail wagging a thousand wags a minute.

"I know where the tests are," my mother said. "I'll bring them by your cabin in an hour or so. Go on now. Enjoy a long, hot shower."

_____

OUR NEW HOME, THE ROOSEVELT cabin, was a fourteen-hundred-square-foot, glamorous, two-room rustic beauty.

There was a living room with a meadow-facing, folding Nano wall of floor-to-ceiling glass which led out to a large, light-gray Trex deck. Outside on the deck were two lounge chairs and four teak Adirondack chairs, each with ottomans. Between the Adirondack chairs and the deck's cable railing was a four-foot-long, twelve-inch-high stainless-steel propane-fed firepit to keep the feet warm. The lodge's infinity pool was down a set of stairs right off the deck.

On the right, looking back inside the living room, was a large wood-burning fireplace surrounded by river rocks found in the ranch's many streams and rivers. A thick, rough-hewn wood mantle spanned the width of the hearth. On each side of the knee-high, four-foot hearth, were recessed nooks, each holding forty or fifty pieces of pre-cut, kiln-dried firewood.

The room's twelve-foot ceiling was supported by six beams that matched the mantle. Light-oak-wood floors were covered by thick area rugs. A black leather U-shaped couch faced the fireplace for maximum warmth. A drop-from-the-ceiling seventy-five-inch television was currently in its hidden-from-view position. A top-of-the-line Sonos sound system fed music to each of the cabin's rooms. In the far-left corner were two high-back leather reading chairs which offered a cozy area in which to read and relax. Framed watercolors from local artists adorned the walls.

Located on the back wall of the living room was a kitchenette which had cupboards, sink, stove and microwave, dishwasher, and a Sub-Zero refrigerator. For coffee lovers, there was even a Miele built-in coffee maker. A Keurig was also there for quick, uncomplicated brews.

The bedroom was accessed through a doorway directly across from the cabin's front entrance. The bedroom shared the same folding-glass-wall system and view as the living room. It also shared the same deck. It too had a fireplace, identical in appearance to the living room's, but on a smaller scale. Wood beams spanned the room, large area rugs covered the light-wood floors, and the room featured the same concealed, drop-down television. A king-size bed sat atop a bedframe made of logs found on the ranch and faced the view. Nightstands on each side of the bed were made of wood milled on the ranch. A sitting area with two leather recliners and dual floor lamps was located next to the fireplace, providing a cozy area to read or watch television. My mother had given us two doggy beds and we'd placed one in front of each fireplace.

The bathroom had his and hers water closets, a shared eight-foot-long walk-in shower with two wall and rainforest heads, and a long vanity with two sinks. There was a stacked washer and dryer behind a sliding door next to the vanity. There was also a sliding-glass-wall system with a very large freestanding two-person bathtub sitting just inside the glass wall. You could soak in the tub while open to the air, admiring the view, or for privacy, you could flip a switch and the glass wall would close and turn opaque. And finally, my favorite feature: the entire bathroom floor, including the shower and bench seat, was warmed by an in-floor radiant-heat system.

We'd finished our shower—I'd shaved using one of Renee's razors—and were sitting on the couch enjoying a roaring fire while listening to an older track from Crosby, Stills & Nash on Sonos, when there was a knock at the door.

"Come on in," I yelled.

My mother opened the door, stuck her head in, said, "Hey there." She entered and sat on the left side of the sofa, handing Renee two pregnancy kits. Greta forced her snout between my mother's knees in search of ear rubs.

Renee thanked my mother, and I expected her to leave, but she continued to sit there smiling.

Renee figured it out first.

"You want me to use it now?" she asked, sounding surprised.

"Why not?" my mother asked, slapping her knees and performing an in-place happy-dance with her feet. "I'm excited!"

"I can tell," I said.

"Sorry, I can't help it," she said.

"Okay then," Renee said, standing and heading toward the bathroom, Greta hot on her heels. "Jon, you'll want to help, right? And neither of you will be too disappointed if it comes back negative. Okay?"

We both responded with the appropriate answer.

Renee and I headed for Renee's side of the bathroom. She handed me the kit, raised her robe, and sat on the toilet. I opened the box and removed the foil from the thermometer-shaped tester. I read the directions and went to the kitchen for a plastic pool glass. I handed the glass to Renee, said, "Pee, please."

Which she did. I took the glass and test kit out to the bathroom vanity and waited for Renee to finish up. I used the included eyedropper and sucked up a small amount of urine. Then I placed three drops in the space provided and, using my watch, started a three-minute timer.

"The test looks for the presence of hCG, a hormone that indicates pregnancy," I explained, glancing at my watch to make sure of the time remaining. "A solid vertical line will appear to the left side of the window which tells us the test is working. If after three minutes an identical line appears on the far right, you're pregnant. The test claims a ninety-nine percent accuracy rate."

A minute into the three, a solid line appeared on the left side. With thirty seconds to go, I wrapped my arms around Renee and hugged her tight. I looked at my watch and counted down from ten. At one, we both looked down and there was the solid right-hand line.

"We're having a baby, honey," I said, sporting the biggest smile I think I've ever had.

Tears were streaming down her cheeks. "I never thought I'd have children," she said. "Do you remember that day you asked if I'd be interested in getting together off-site—it was during that first Las Vegas year-end meeting?"

"I remember," I answered. "I'd finally built up my courage to ask you. I wasn't sure if I'd get a yes or a you're-fired."

"Hey, you two," my mother yelled out. "Are you?"

"And here we are ten years later. I am so fucking happy, Jon," she said, wrapping her arms around my neck and kissing me. "Even with all the bullshit happening around us."

"I'm the happiest guy in the world right now," I said. "Let's go share the news."

Renee grabbed the test, and I followed her back to the living room and my waiting mother.

"Well?"

"We're pregnant," Renee said, showing my mother the test.

"Whoopie! Way to go, you two," my mother shouted out. She hugged both of us. "Can I tell the others?"

"How about just Dad, Asta, Abs, and Eddy," I said, looking at Renee for her okay.

"Sure. We'll do another test in a few days, and if it still reads positive, we can tell the others," Renee said.

"I've been waiting for grandchildren for years and had about given up hope. And now—two of them," my mother said, tears free-falling down her cheeks.

"Maybe not," Renee said with a grin.

"Huh?" my mother said. "The test came back positive."

"Renee?" I asked, confused.

"My mother is a twin and my father's family includes twins," she said. "Which means. . ."

My mother stood up and shouted, "Twins! Maybe."

MY ECSTATIC MOTHER LEFT SHORTLY after the test results had been revealed. It was now dark out, but we were wide awake so decided to burn some energy in the pool. Wearing just our terry robes, we stepped off our deck, took four steps to the pool's edge, discarded the robes, and slipped naked into the warm water. The skies had cleared, and the stars appeared close enough to touch.

"My gosh, look at all those stars," Renee said.

"They're beautiful," I said. "With virtually no pollution being chugged into the atmosphere from cars and factories, the air is probably as clean as it's been since the early nineteen hundreds. Although, if China hasn't seen any retaliation from other countries with missiles and EMPs, then their pollution levels are likely still high. The jet stream brings us some of their—"

"Enough of the China talk," Renee said, as she floated into my arms. I cradled her close, and we kissed, which naturally led to other things. The pool lights were off, and we did our best to keep the noise down. Twenty minutes later, she was back floating in my arms when we heard a noise to our left. I turned us around to face the noise, and there was Dawn. She was wearing a white terry robe and standing on the pool's first step, water up past her ankles.

"I waited until you guys were done with. . . uh, you know, what you were doing," she said. "Can I join you? Uh. . . I mean, join you in the pool. Not, with you. Although. . ."

Dawn was uncharacteristically tongue-tied, and I was enjoying watching her fight through it.

"I know what you mean," Renee said. "Come on in."

"Thanks," Dawn said, taking her robe off and throwing it off to the side. She was naked, and her arms and breasts were covered with thousands of goose bumps from the cold air.

"It's beyond cold," Dawn said, entering the water and wading over to us.

"Being from Toronto, you're certainly no stranger to cold weather," I said. "I guess you've adapted to the Hollywood climate."

"Give me a break, bub. I've never stood naked and fully exposed to the cold like this," she said, a vapor cloud forming in front of her face after every word she said. "Look at the stars, you two. Unbelievable."

For several minutes, we stayed like that, treading water, heads tilted back, silent, stargazing. A shooting star, moving fast from east to west, made its way overhead then quickly disappeared behind the moonlit tree line out in the distance.

"Whoa! Did you see that?" Renee asked.

"I did. Maybe it—" I started to say.

Another shooting star suddenly appeared further north, moving south toward us, and burning out a split second before the eaves of our cabin's roof line would have obscured it. Then another. And another.

"Can you believe what we're seeing?" Renee asked.

"If I'm not mistaken, what we're watching is the Ursid meteor shower," Dawn said. "It's usually visible in mid- to late December."

"You know your meteor shower names?" I asked, surprised.

"In Vancouver, I have a telescope I bring out on my deck to stargaze. I also have an app on my iPhone that alerts me to upcoming meteor showers."

"That's very cool," Renee said. "I'm usually staring at a computer screen during the night. I'm gonna have to pay more attention to the environment down here on earth. And the sky, of course."

Over the next several minutes, there were another four sky-streakers.

"This shower is unusually visible—the norm is five to ten per hour. What we're seeing tonight is a rare treat."

"I'm lovin' it," Renee said.

"Did you know that shooting stars are actually dust grains trailing behind comets," Dawn explained. "In this case, it's Comet Tuttle."

"Thank you for the education, professor," Renee said.

"When we gather up your sister, we can bring your telescope back with us," I said. "How heavy is it?"

"Maybe twenty-five pounds. Not too heavy. I can easily carry it from my bedroom to the outside deck."

"Then we'll take it with us."

"Am I going with you to Seattle and Vancouver?" Dawn asked.

I debated if I should tell her that Kris would not be returning to the ranch.

Renee, still cradled in my arms, craned her head to the side, whispered, "Tell her."

"Yes, you're going with us. None of our group knows this yet, but Kris will not be coming back to the ranch. She'll fly to Seattle with us, but will not be returning."

"Oh."

"Jon's father made the decision."

There were another two shooting stars, both extinguishing a split second after appearing. Then nothing for several minutes.

"I'm ready to go back inside," Renee said, showing us the wrinkles on her hands and fingers. "I'm pruning up."

I carried Renee over to the steps and set her on the bottom one. She immediately climbed out and wrapped herself in her robe. She picked up my robe and held it open as I climbed out. I turned around, put both arms in the robe, and cinched it tight.

Dawn had watched us the entire time.

"Lookin' good, you two," she said.

"Thanks. You getting out?" Renee asked.

"I'm going to stay a while longer."

"Okay then. See you tomorrow morning," I said.

WE RINSED OFF IN THE shower and I started a fire in the bedroom fireplace while Renee combed her hair. Greta stepped into her doggy bed next to the hearth, circled three times, before finally settling down. It was a little after ten.

We crawled into bed soon after, and I fell asleep as soon as my head hit the pillow.

"Jon, wake up, babe," Renee said, gently pushing on my shoulder.

I came awake with a start. "Is everything okay?" Greta was at Renee's side but didn't appear to be overly concerned or on-guard.

Renee was wearing a robe. The fire was still going but looked about ready to die out. A quick glance at my watch read three thirty in the morning.

"There was a knock on the door. It's—" Renee started to say.

"Me," Dawn said, stepping from behind Renee and into view.

"She's afraid to be alone," Renee said.

"I can't sleep. Can I sleep in your cabin? At least for tonight?"

"It's okay with me," Renee said. "There are extra blankets and pillows in the closet. I can set her up on the couch in the living room. Is it okay with you?"

"Sure," I answered, shutting my eyes and turning away from them. "See you in the morning, Dawn."

DAY EIGHT

EXPECTING(S). FLIGHT TIME. SEATTLE. TOO MANY
STAIRS. VIVIAN. VICTORIA & VANCOUVER, CANADA.
AIRCRAFT CARRIER GERALD R. FORD.

EIGHTEEN

I heard knocking on our cabin door. I looked at my watch—eight thirty.

Renee was on her stomach and fast asleep.

I crept out of bed, donned my robe, shut the bedroom door, and padded toward the cabin's entrance door. Greta was right behind me and whined in desperation.

"Sorry, Greta," I said, opening the door. Eddy was right there, raising his hand to knock again.

Greta ran past us, down the outside steps, and disappeared behind some pine trees.

Eddy walked in, looked around, and asked where Renee was.

"Sleeping. What's up?" I asked, shutting the door behind him. I put a finger to my lips and pointed to Dawn sleeping on the couch.

I needed coffee—stat.

"Your dad told Abs and I that they told you and Renee about Abs being pregnant," he said, whispering but talking fast. "I want you to know that Abs and I were going to tell you today and that I'm sorry I didn't fill you in on Abs and I being in a relationship. I feel awful that you found out this way. I—"

"Eddy, slow down," I said, walking over to the kitchenette, inserting a full-roast morning-blend Keurig K-Cup and hitting the start button. "I'm good with you two being together and, more importantly, knowing that I'll be an uncle. I'm happy for you. And congratulations. Although, you need to know that you are now in for a lifetime of being bossed around like an underling. Abs will be wearing the pants in your family, good buddy."

"We're working on the relationship dynamics," he said, sounding more like an army policy pinhead than a father to be.

"This isn't the Army, good buddy," I said. "Check that. Maybe it is. With Abs being the Secretary of Defense."

"I'm ready for whatever comes my way."

"Well, that's good. Did my father relay our news?" I asked.

"He did mention the fact that Kris will not be joining us at the ranch."

"Not that."

"Earlier this morning, your mom asked me to ask my parents if they wanted to relocate to the ranch. If so, then she'll have a first-floor lodge room ready for them."

"Not that either. But I hope your parents take her up on the offer."

"Your dad did say that you and Abs are flying to Seattle and Vancouver tomorrow."

"Not that either, Eddy," Renee said, walking out of the bedroom and cinching the sash on her robe. She headed toward the kitchenette. "Coffee. I need coffee."

"Good morning, Miss Renee," Eddy said.

"Good morning, Eddy."

"Did I hear someone mention coffee?" Dawn said, standing up from the sofa and performing a full-body cat stretch. There was scratching at the front door. I opened it, and Greta ran in and made a beeline for Renee. I left the door open, hoping that Eddy would get the hint and leave.

He didn't.

Then he asked what the news was.

"We're pregnant as well," Renee said, opening the fridge and taking out a bottle of coffee creamer. "About ten weeks, same as you guys. Looks like our kids will be growing up together."

"Well, heck, good buddy. That's wonderful news," Eddy said, giving me a hug. "Congratulations."

"Thanks, Eddy."

"You're pregnant?" Dawn asked.

"We think so. Although we're not telling anyone until we get the results of a second test," Renee answered, pouring and then stirring in the creamer.

Dawn grabbed the cup from Renee and took a tentative sip. "Congratulations, that's very cool. My lips are sealed," she said, making the zipper motion across her lips. "And you can't be drinking coffee."

"What are you—" Renee started to say.

"It's true," Eddy said, interrupting Renee. "Asta told Abs that, as long as she's pregnant, she's not to drink coffee or booze."

"Well, she hasn't told me that, so give that mug back," Renee said, taking the steaming mug out of Dawn's hands.

"Oh, by the way, you're missing a great breakfast buffet, you three."

"We'll be there shortly," Dawn said. "Do us a favor and keep quiet about what you heard here this morning, Mr. Television Man. Please."

"I will, Ms. Movie Star Lady. I promise," Eddy said. He waved, turned, and left. I shut the door behind him.

"The news of what he heard will be known by everyone within the next five minutes," I said. "He's incapable of keeping a secret."

"He managed to keep his relationship with your sister secret, didn't he?" Renee said. "Not to mention having gotten her pregnant."

———————————————

THE LODGE'S EXECUTIVE CHEF, VANESSA Van Dorne, two senior members of her kitchen staff, Lauren Kelly and Michael Erskin, and a member of her waitstaff, Peggy Richards, had made the decision to remain at the ranch—all four were single with families on the East Coast. All four were year-round residents of the ranch and had rooms in the remodeled bunkhouse.

The four had put together a hearty breakfast buffet, and Michael was manning an omelette station. Pancakes and French toast were available and made to order.

After agreeing with Dawn that we should sit together at breakfast, Renee and I were first at the conference center's dining hall at nine fifteen. We loaded our plates and sat across from Abs and Eddy at a large circular table. The rest of our group were chowing down at the table in front of ours, Melissa and Susan holding hands. Kris was the only member of our group that was missing.

Abs reached across the table and took hold of Renee's hand, said, "We're very happy for you."

"And Jon and I for you, Abs."

Dawn made an entrance five minutes later. As expected, her arrival created a commotion.

The ranch hands, minus the four on guard duty, fussed over her. Dawn shook all offered hands and spoke briefly with each. Ten minutes later, she was able to grab a plate and sat across from us.

"I like wearing these camos—I don't have to stand in front of my closet for thirty minutes deciding what to wear," Dawn said. "It's a very easy decision when there's only one option."

I didn't see my parents or Asta and asked Abs where they were.

"There's Asta now," she answered, pointing to Asta as she entered the dining room.

Asta loaded up a plate and headed over to our table. "Good morning, group," she whispered. "I understand congratulations are in order, Renee. Mom shared the news with me earlier this morning. I'll be happy to monitor you and the baby throughout your pregnancy."

"Thank you. That would be great."

"Where's Mom and Dad?" I asked.

"Mom's back in the kitchen working with Vanessa on meal planning," Abs said. "And I saw Dad sitting on the ranch-house front porch," Asta said.

We ate and chatted for the next twenty minutes. At five to ten, Kris walked in, took a seat alone at the back of the room, a scowl planted on her face. My father strode in a minute later and walked up and tapped me on my shoulder. He gave me the follow-me finger-wave, and I followed him into the kitchen.

"I waited on the porch for Kris," he said. "When it was obvious she wasn't coming out of her room, I went up and told her she needed to attend the meeting, that it was mandatory. I don't give a rat's ass if she attends the meeting or not, but I wasn't about to leave her alone in the ranch house, let alone freely roaming the ranch while the rest of us are here."

"She doesn't appear to be a happy camper," I said, looking at her through the glass of the swinging kitchen door.

"That's a major understatement," he said. "I couldn't get a response from her after I said good morning and asked her how she was. I'm not leaving her alone in the ranch house or anywhere else, Jon. I don't trust her.

"Please tell her she's going with you tomorrow, or if Abs is good with the idea, maybe leave this afternoon. Perhaps the news will cheer her up. It's up to you when you tell her she's not coming back to the ranch."

"Sorry, Dad. I'll tell her she's going with us, either today or tomorrow," I said, turning and walking out of the kitchen.

I walked up to Kris and sat next to her. She didn't acknowledge me.

"I wanted to let you know that we're flying to Seattle tomorrow and that you're going with us. There's a chance we may leave this afternoon, but I need to work it out with Abs first. Get your stuff together, just in case we go today."

Kris turned her head, smiled, said, "Thank you."

"You're welcome. Why don't you grab something to eat before they start clearing it away? Then join us at our table."

"Okay," she said, standing and making her way to the buffet. She took a spoonful of scrambled eggs and a link sausage. And surprise, surprise, she sat down with us.

Dad and Mom appeared a few minutes later, Dad pushing a large, wheeled write-on-wipe-off board to the front of the dining room.

"Are your people here, Billy?" my father asked. Bill Eagan was our ranch foreman.

"Yes, sir, except the four on overwatch at the two entrances."

"Good. Vanessa, please come on out with your people."

Once Dad had a full audience, he began the meeting.

"Good morning, everyone. Thank you for attending this morning. We've been very fortunate in that we haven't had any incursions here at the ranch. Yes, we're away from the highway, and most wouldn't think to explore any of the access roads, but that will change as more folks make their way to the mountains from the population centers to our south. It's a matter of when, not if, and we need to protect what we have here."

He drew a large square on the board. He then put an N, S, W, and E on the appropriate compass points. He drew a line from north to south which touched the western boundary of the box. "This square represents the boundary of the ranch, this line here being Highway 93.

"We have 360,000 acres, which equates out to 571 square miles, which is way beyond our ability to patrol, let alone protect." He drew another square within the larger square. "This new square is 144 square miles, or twelve miles by twelve miles. This square we can patrol and protect. And this is how we're going to do it."

He put an X on each of the four corners and pointed to the two left-side, or west, Xs. "These two checkpoints already exist at each of the two entrances off Highway 93." He then pointed to the two right-side, or east, Xs. "And these two need to be built, or I should say finished, as we put the foundations and platforms in this fall. These wooden platforms are fourteen foot by fourteen foot and are ten feet off the ground, which should be high enough to remain above any snowdrifts. Metal stairs were fabricated by Roger and installed a few weeks ago. ATV tracks have been cut between the platforms and the ranch complex and from platform to platform. During the winter, snowmobiles will travel the tracks.

"The two new platforms are located on top of the highest elevated positions, each with three-sixty-degree unobstructed views. Think fire towers. Later today, we're going to be installing a thirteen-by-thirteen Snowtrekker Mega Crew canvas-sided tent on each platform. Each tent has a snowfly to shed snow, and a stove which, when fed firewood, will keep the interior toasty warm. We'll have cots in each, along with indoor porta potties which will be curtained off for privacy. We'll stock each with food, water, and other supplies. A solar system will run the radio, other electronics, and charge batteries. We'll be installing radio antennas connected to base-camp two-way radios. These antennas serve a dual purpose: for communication and extended drone control. It's the drones, folks, that will enable us to keep watch over this square."

He took a swig of coffee. "Each corner will be given two drones: one daytime and one nighttime. The daytime drone has a high-resolution camera and the nighttime, thermal imaging. The antennas will allow each drone to fly preprogrammed, repeatable flight patterns out six miles in each direction. With these drones, we can cover not only the smaller box but they'll cover a radius of six miles out into the larger box as well." Using a red marker, he drew a circle around each of the four Xs.

"These battery-operated drones are able to fly for thirty-four minutes at a speed of fifty-three miles per hour. At that speed, they'll be able to fly the entire preprogrammed route and bring themselves safely back to station. There will be a few extra minutes to allow the drones to hover in place should you want them to. Each platform will have extra sets of batteries. And needless to say, if you see something, say something. Any questions?"

"Eddy raised his hand, asked, "How well do these drones handle rough weather, such as snow, wind, or excessive cold?"

"They can fly in winds up to forty-four knots and temperatures down to minus twelve degrees. Snow will only obscure the daytime image.

"As far as manning these observation posts—the two posts on Highway 93 will change out every twelve hours, with shift changes at six each afternoon and morning. The two east-side platforms will each be manned by two people for three days. We have thirty folks at the ranch now. Of these, four—the kitchen personnel—will not participate in the day-to-day security functions.

"There's also a good chance that our family friends, the Caseys, will be joining us here at the ranch. They number eleven family members, nine of which are adults and able to work security. What this means is: each of you will be pulling one of these three-day shifts every month and several of the twelve-hour shifts. When you're not working security, you'll be helping Terri in the greenhouses and chicken coops, working with Billy on ranch operations, or on any of the many daily maintenance chores. Pick your partner for the platform duty carefully, as you'll be with them for twenty-four hours a day for three days. Any questions?"

Dawn raised her hand.

"Yes, Dawn."

"Will you be keeping the spa open?"

"Good question, but the answer is no," he answered, with a laugh.

"I want to sign up for the first three-day guard duty," Wilbur Filby, a ranch hand, said. "And I'd like Ms. Tillman as my partner."

There was more laughter and many calls of "you wish" and "good luck with that."

"Okay. Settle down. Andrea will now speak to you about the kitchen schedule."

Dad took a seat, and my mother now stood in front of the group. "First off, thank you, Vanessa and crew for the terrific buffet this morning."

The assembled group clapped in appreciation.

"I'm glad you all enjoyed it, because today's buffet will become a thing of the past—we don't have endless supplies to support such lavish layouts. But Vanessa and her team will be offering breakfast every morning and dinner each evening. Lunch will be on you to organize. The kitchen will put out fixings for sandwiches and sides, but you'll serve yourself. This new schedule starts tomorrow morning. That's it."

"Thanks, Andrea," my father said. "We're now going to make our way to the shooting range. Each of you, including the kitchen staff, will be issued a handgun, a 9-mill. Glock 17, along with a belt-mounted holster and a two-magazine holder. You'll be given lessons on its safe use. You'll wear this Glock at all times. The only acceptable time for you to not have the weapon on your person is when you're showering or sleeping."

"It's now ten forty-five. Let's take a forty-five-minute break and meet at the firing range at eleven thirty. See you there."

———————

"ABS, CAN I TALK TO you before you leave?" I asked. "Renee, I'll see you at the cabin in ten minutes or so, okay?"

"Sure, see you there," she answered, as she and Dawn left for the cabins.

It was soon just Abs and me.

"Do you think it would be possible to fly to Seattle and Vancouver later today?" I asked.

Abs thought about it for a minute before answering.

"I'm assuming we'll be doing water landings," she said. "Correct?"

"Yes. I don't see an alternative, for either Seattle or Vancouver."

"I'd need help changing the tundra tires for the amphibs, but that'll only take a couple of hours. I can ask Peter to help with that. Fueling, etc, another hour or so. So sure, we can leave this afternoon. What time are you thinking?"

"I'd like to arrive in Seattle a half hour after sunset, which I think would mean at six thirty. Are you comfortable with night water landings?"

"Yes, very, and are not an issue, though smooth water landings can be somewhat tricky. But I'm always careful, and use the power-on method during landings. And I never take anything for granted.

"As far as the timing goes—it's 380 miles from here to Seattle. To conserve fuel, we'll fly at 110 knots, so. . . it'll take us three and a half hours. Three o'clock is good for leaving. Who's all going to fly with us?"

"Me, Dawn, Kris, and Melissa. We're picking up Dawn's sister in Vancouver and leaving Kris in Seattle."

"Not Eddy?" she asked, sounding surprised.

"No. I've been in firefights with Melissa, and I know she can handle any situation that might arise. I don't know how Eddy would handle himself under fire."

"I get it. Dad told me about Kris. As you know, we can take six passengers and their gear. In this case, we'll be flying from Vancouver with four passengers without any gear, other than weapons, of course. We have ninety-five gallons of fuel in three tanks, plus tip tanks for another forty-six gallons, but we're going to have to pack extra fuel as cargo."

Abs closed her eyes, and I watched as her lips silently calculated fuel burn and distances. It never ceased to amaze me how quickly her mind worked.

"Fifty gallons will do it, leaving us with a buffer of a hundred miles or so," she said.

"Okay. Three o'clock it is. I'll get directions to Kathy's place so we can leave her letter there, and see you at the air-strip at three."

I walked down the hill and headed to the equipment barn, where I found the sliding door already open. I said good morning to Peter and Roger—Peter's helper for the day. They were working on a row of snowmobiles. I hopped in the Humvee, got it started, drove up the hill, and parked in front of the ranch house.

Dad was sitting on the ranch-house front porch. He was reclining in an Adirondack chair and swiping through an Apple iPad.

"Guard duty?" I asked, thinking he was watching for Kris.

"Partly, though I'm reviewing our stored food inventory."

"We in good shape?"

"Better than good, actually. Excellent would be more accurate. Vanessa says we have at least a year's worth of food stuffs in the conference center's kitchen pantry alone. We're very lucky to have her with us."

"Can you help me with something?" I asked. It was time to put Sig's gold in a safe place.

"Sure."

"Follow me then," I said, turning, walking down the steps, and heading toward the Humvee.

I opened the passenger door, released the bungee cords, and slid the first ammo can out from under the seat. "Grab one side of this, Dad."

Which he did. He lifted, said, "What the hell you have in here? Gold?"

"Yes."

"Yeah, sure."

"It really is—you guessed it, Dad. Four bars at twenty-eight pounds each."

We walked the ammo can through the ranch house, past my mother who was fiddling in the kitchen, and into his office off to the right of the rear-door mudroom.

We sat the can on his desk, and I opened the lid. Sunlight shining through the windows shone brightly off the bar's golden color.

"Holy smokes!" my father exclaimed, eyes wide. "You weren't kidding."

My mother, wiping her hands on a kitchen towel, came over and peered into the ammo can. "Is that what I think it is?" she asked.

"It is, and there's another just like it. Courtesy of Sig and Molly Alderson."

We brought the second can in, and I opened it for inspection.

"Why would Sig give you all these gold bars?" my mother asked.

"He said it was a thank you gift for bringing his foreman and hands back to the ranch, helping out on the ranch, and for handling the home invasion. Sig told me that each bar weighs twenty-eight pounds for an eight-bar total of 224 pounds, or 3,584 ounces. The last gold price before the pulse hit was $2,200 an ounce."

"That's a bunch," my mother said.

"I'd say $7,884,000 and change," my father said. "Give or take a few thousand."

"Sig has another three safes with dozens of cans identical to these two," I said. "He said, if we needed them for funding an army, to count on him for any amount we might need."

"Where in the world did Sig get all that gold," my mother asked.

"His grandfather founded the largest gold-producing mine in Nevada. His father sold the mine but only on the condition that future royalties be paid with actual gold."

"Now I know where Sig got his smarts," my dad said. "That amount of gold is now worth more than ever. . . priceless, really. It's too soon for a barter-based economy to have taken hold, but it will soon enough, and gold will be the. . . well, the gold standard—no pun intended. Mark my words. You just wait and see."

I looked at my watch and reminded them both that shooting class would be starting in ten minutes. Dad opened the safe and we put the two cans on the bottom shelf. I dug in my pockets and handed over my gold coins I'd purchased in Las Vegas.

"Where did these come from?" my father asked, putting the gold coins on top of the two ammo cans. He shut the safe door and spun the dial.

"The craps table," I answered. "I won big and exchanged cash for gold. Just like you've drummed into me, Dad."

"He does listen to me, Andrea. Can you believe it?"

I ran upstairs and brought Kris down. The four of us piled in the Humvee and drove down the hill to the shooting range.

Eddy was already there, handing out the Glocks, holsters, and belt-mounted extra magazine holders.

We broke into three groups and started by teaching them how to load magazines. Then how to break down the weapon for cleaning. And finally, actually firing off three full magazines each. They were then made to reload the now-empty magazines and given a box of fifty rounds to store in their rooms or cabins. We would teach them how to properly handle and fire the rifles in the next few days.

I made sure that Dawn was proficient with the Glock. I also taught her how to tear it down and clean it. I then gave her a private lesson on using the M4. After thirty minutes of firing and reloading magazines, she was good to go.

We were done with the classes at one o'clock. I gathered our group together and relayed the flight plans.

"Melissa, Dawn, and Kris, we're aiming for a three o'clock departure."

Renee asked why she wasn't included, and I explained that fuel conservation was of utmost importance and any extra weight cut down on time in the air.

"So, what you're saying is you think I'm too heavy to go along," Renee said, in all seriousness.

"No. That's. . . uh—" I started to answer.

Renee grinned, said, "Just fuckin' with ya."

"Got you good, Jon," Dawn said, laughing.

"It was a good one, Renee. And the last time I'm falling for it.

"Kathy, please write down your address and directions from the closest place that we can make a water landing," I said, handing her pen and paper. "Also, write a letter to Bradley telling him where we are and for him to make his way to the barricade outside Marion, Montana on Highway 2. Have him use my name, and they'll give him a ride to the ranch."

"You'll be landing on the water by Norseman's Restaurant on Lake Union. It's on the water and fifty feet to the left of the Ship Canal Bridge," she said. "You can tie up at their guest dock which I imagine will be vacant. Our house is right up the hill from the dock, not more than a three-minute walk. And please put the letter in the floor safe in the master closet underneath my shoes. I'll write the combination down for you. It's a manual dial, not electronic."

"Will do. Empty your backpack, and Melissa and I can gather some of your things for you."

"Cool. Underwear and thick hiking socks for sure, as many of those two things as you can cram in. My hiking shoes, which are sitting on top of the safe, are a priority. And hanging right above the safe is my dark-blue, puffy, down vest. Then in the bathroom, under the sink, is a big box of tampons and extra boxes of toothbrushes and toothpaste. If you can, and you're not pressed for time, there's a duffel bag in the hall closet. If you could, Melissa, just go through my drawers and closet and grab whatever you think I might want. Especially hiking and backpacking clothes."

"Get busy writing that letter," I said.

"I can stay with Abs in the plane and stand overwatch," Susan said. "Won't the plane be a sitting duck on the water as it waits for your return?"

"I considered that, Susan, but Abs will be bringing extra cans of fuel, and like Renee, your added weight would be too much."

"Okay. Thought I'd offer."

"Thank you for offering. It is a concern, and after Abs drops us off, I'm going to have her idle out and drop anchor a couple of hundred yards offshore. That should keep her and the Beaver safe. It'll be dark out there, and someone will be with Abs providing overwatch at all times.

"Melissa, after Kathy's, we'll be heading to my place, yours, and then Kris'. We'll then fly to Vancouver and then back to the ranch. Get geared up—camos, vests, rifle, Glock, night vision, and comms. Load up ten magazines for the rifles and another three for the Glocks. If necessary, we can reload in the Beaver during flight. Let's meet at the Cruiser at two thirty, and we'll drive down to the hangar.

"Kathy, make sure Dawn gets your vest, comms, rifle, and night vision. Renee, give me your vest, comms, and night vision. We'll need it for Dawn's sister."

"Thank you again, guys, for dropping the note off at my house," Kathy said.

"Not a problem," I said. "Let's go, folks."

———————

"MY FAMILY AND I AREN'T coming back to the ranch with you, are we?" Kris asked.

We'd emptied out of the Humvee in front of the ranch house, and Kris had taken hold of my arm and held me back.

I allowed myself to be stopped and told Renee I'd see her in the cabin. "Dawn, please go with Kathy and let her get you kitted out. Then come to my cabin."

"Will do."

"Well?" Kris asked.

"No, you're not," I answered, removing her hand from my arm. "I'm sorry, but my parents have made the hard decision."

"Well fuck," she said.

"You fucked yourself when you stole Sig's truck. And your shitty attitude here hasn't gone unnoticed. I promised to get you home, and I'm going to follow through on that promise. But I will not be delivering you to your doorstep and leaving you high and dry. I'm going to leave you with several pails of rice, beans, water, and a backpacking stove along with a bunch of fuel. I'm also going to leave you with two Glocks, multiple magazines and ammo. I'll ask Asta to give me enough meds to see you through your healing process."

"Fuck. Fuck. Fuck."

"Don't be pissed at anyone other than yourself, Kris. You'll wear your armor and night vision until you're safely back home. But we're taking both back with us."

"Okay. Okay. I'll gladly take anything you want to leave with me."

"Be at the Cruiser at two thirty and ready to leave."

"Roger that," she said, then turned, made her way up the steps, crossed the porch, and disappeared inside.

————————

FROM THE PARKING LOT, I had a good view through the front-door window of Kris walking up the stairs to the second floor and entering her room. The door shut behind her, and it was only then that I followed in her footsteps. Instead of going up the stairs, I headed to the kitchen where I found my mother and father sitting at the island eating a sandwich.

"I told Kris. She's upset, but I think she's madder at herself than at us. She's tricky, Dad, and should be watched until she climbs aboard the Beaver."

He nodded, reached into his vest pocket, and brought out the Motorola TALKABOUT. He brought it to his mouth, said, "Peter, please send Gloria to the ranch house."

"Will do, sir," came the reply.

"We'll keep an eye on her, Jon."

"Thanks. In case Abs didn't tell you, we're leaving for Seattle this afternoon at three."

"Abigail told us. Be careful, son," my mother said, sliding her stool back and giving me a hug and kiss on the cheek.

"He'll be fine, Drea."

I headed to our cabin, where I found Renee laying out my plate carrier, comms, night vision, and the thermal scope. She'd already loaded ten 5.56 magazines and five Glock mags with ammo.

I smiled and gave her a long hug and a kiss.

"Thanks for putting these out. Can you do me another huge favor?"

"Of course."

"Drive the Humvee down to the equipment barn and get five of the five-gallon buckets of rice, five black beans, five pinto beans, and five of PJ's dad's water cans out of our trailer. Also, one of the backpacking stoves and twelve of the Coleman propane cans. Then drive them to the plane and have Abs store them in the back with the extra gasoline cans. I'm pressed for time and that needs to get done."

"Is the food for Kris?"

"Yes. I couldn't leave her there without some supplies. Oh, you know those handguns and holsters we took from the looters at PJ's dad's house?"

"Yes, they're down on the front passenger floorboard of the Cruiser."

"Good. Grab two of the Glocks, two holsters, four boxes of fifty rounds of the .40-caliber, four extra mags for the Glocks, and put all of it in the Humvee."

"Those for Kris too?"

"Yes. Go now, okay, hon? Oh, and grab ten extra boxes of the .40-cal for us and a bulk can of 500 rounds of 5.56 from the trailer."

"Okay, see you at the plane."

"Thanks, Renee."

I slipped the plate carrier on and made the necessary adjustments then checked the Glock and stowed it in its vest-mounted holster. I took each mag and slammed my palm on the bottoms of each to make sure they were fully seated and filled the vest-mounted mag pockets with both 5.56 and .40-cal mags. Extras went into my pants cargo pockets.

I slipped the radio into its vest pouch and attached the mic to its shoulder clip. I put the rifle sling around my neck and attached the M4, the one on which I'd mounted the silencer. I attached the thermal to the rail and booted it up. A minute later, it beeped to let me know it was ready. It was fully charged and good to go for another fourteen hours. I powered it off.

I was grabbing some extra batteries for the NVs when Dawn and Melissa walked in. Both were fully outfitted and ready to go with rifles slung and Glocks in holsters. I went up to Dawn and spun her around, checking that everything was in place and adjusted properly. Then did the same with Melissa. I checked both sets of NVs and they were good. All weapons were safe, and each had the proper number of extra magazines.

They were carrying their camo jackets and boonie hats. I had them turn on their comms and did a check. Again, all good.

"Headlamps?"

They both reached into deep pockets and retrieved the lights.

"Okay. Let's go."

Kris was standing next to the Cruiser with Gloria.

"Thank you, Gloria," I said.

"No problem, Jon. Be safe."

We drove the Cruiser down to the hangars. Renee was handing the last white tub of rice to Abs who then stored it in the rear behind black cargo netting. Ten red, five-gallon, plastic gas cans were already in place.

It was two forty-five.

"I put the Glocks, magazines, and four boxes of ammo under the co-pilot's seat," Renee said. She handed me her plate carrier and NVs. She hugged me tight and, whispering in my ear, said she loved me. "Don't make me a widowed mother, mister. Come back to me."

I brought her in for a bear hug, said, "Love you, too. I'll be back. I'll have Melissa with me, so you know nothing's gonna happen to me."

Renee left my embrace then reached out and grabbed Melissa's vest with both hands, brought her in closer. "Don't let anything happen to him, Melissa." Then she whispered so only Melissa and I heard, "He's the father of our child."

Melissa looked from Renee to me then grinned. "Congrats, you two. Or should I say, you three. I'll bring him back safe and sound. Promise."

"Thank you," Renee said, retreating back to the Humvee.

"Go ahead and load up ladies," Abs said. "The bench seat in back holds three. Headphones are hanging above each seat."

"We okay on weight?" I asked.

"You four guys weigh eight hundred—I know that's high, but I always go higher. Extra gas is three hundred. The food, ammo, and weapons are probably another three hundred. Fourteen hundred total. We can carry up to two thousand.

"You remember how to help me get it started?"

"Yes."

"Then let's do this."

She climbed up into the pilot's seat, yelled, "Mags are off."

I spun the propeller and silently counted as each blade passed by. At six, I stopped and yelled, "Six."

"Step away," she yelled.

She primed the cylinders, engaged the starter, and counted out loud as five blades passed by, then switched on the magnetos. The other four cylinders caught, and white smoke engulfed the engine area. The wonderful deep sound of the nine-cylinder Pratt & Whitney radial engine turning over was music to the ears. Ka-thump, ka-thump, ka-thump.

The tundra tires had been removed, and Wipline amphibs attached. Much smaller wheels stuck out from the floats. Once airborne, they would be hydraulically retracted. In the water, water rudders would be lowered.

I took the chocks away and stowed them in the port storage locker. I reached up, took ahold of the hanging closure strap, pulled down, and closed the pilot-side Alaska lifting cargo door. I ran around the plane's tail, climbed into the co-pilot's seat, and shut the door. The interior immediately quieted down.

Abs turned the plane's comms system on, turned in her seat and, with her hand, pointed to the hanging headphones and then their ears. She strapped a small plastic tray onto her left thigh and then slipped a map under thin bungee cords.

"The engine has to warm up for ten to fifteen minutes," she announced in a muffled voice through the headphones. "Oil has to reach a temperature of 140 degrees." She then reached between us and pumped the flaps down to 35 degrees for takeoff.

"The western horizon appears clear," Abs said, pointing to the mountains out in the far distance. "We'll be flying low and slow so keep a lookout for those assholes that shot off my antenna." She leaned down and came up with binoculars.

Ten minutes later Abs was taxiing to the end of the runway. The wind sock was hanging loose with only an occasional flutter.

"It's a pretty calm day, so that's good," Abs said into the comms system. "But turbulence can rear its ugly head at any time, especially over the mountains, so make sure your seat belts are cinched tight.

"Here we go," she said. She goosed the throttle, and once the rpms were there, she applied more. We left the ground and slowly gained altitude. She retracted the wheels, and four blue lights appeared under the dash indicating wheels up. Abs was flying with her left hand while her right was busy with the boost and throttle knobs. She was also constantly adjusting the flaps via the pump lever to her right, and I knew she would finally settle them at seven degrees.

I watched the air speed indicator hover over eighty as we climbed. Five minutes later, we leveled off and the speed crept up to 110.

I scanned ahead with the binoculars and saw nothing of concern. We were flying low, and I did see the occasional person in a home's front yard or out on a highway. There being little to no wind, smoke from fireplaces reached up toward us.

With so few cars on the road and no coal-fed power plants running and factory pollution non-existent, the sky was as clear as I'd ever seen it.

"Can you believe how clear the sky is," Melissa said, voicing what I'd just been thinking.

"Take a few minutes and look at the stars tonight," Dawn said. "You won't get over how many there are and how close they seem. We saw a bunch of shooting stars last night and there will be more tonight."

We passed to the south of Coeur d'Alene. The lake was calm, and it was the first time that I'd seen it empty of boats and their trailing wakes. I glassed as far as I could see and didn't spot any large groups of people or moving vehicles.

We were flying due west and were soon over Spokane. I could see dozens of burnt-out buildings, some still smoldering, white smoke drifting skyward. Looted retail stores, parking lots littered with trash and shopping carts, were everywhere. Off our right wing, I could see the area I knew to be Riverfront Park. I glassed the area and spotted a large number of people running away from an armed group of pursuers. One of the pursuers took a knee and I watched as two of the runners fell to the ground in front of a looted Rite Aid pharmacy. The armed group reached the two fallen runners and backpacks were ripped off backs and boots and coats removed from the unmoving victims.

"What a cluster fuck," I said aloud.

"Why, what do you see?" Melissa asked.

"Nothing good," I answered. "I just saw a group of folks running down another group, two of the runners shot and their backpacks and clothing taken."

Several residential neighborhoods had barricaded off entrances and all were manned by folks armed with rifles. Several looked up as we flew overhead. I half expected for some to take potshots at us but none raised their rifles. In fact, one woman was waving at us.

"Dip your wings, Abs," I said.

She did, and I watched the woman wave with both hands while jumping in a circle.

I glassed further west and could see a number of folks on bikes, possessions tied to the bikes' frames every which way, their backpacks bulging.

People were getting out of Dodge.

"We're going to be following Highway 2 west all the way to Highway 97," Abs said, her finger tracing the route on her map. "We'll fly over Davenport and Coulee City, then continue west once Highway 2 turns south. From there, we'll aim for Leavenworth, and then it's a straight-line west to Seattle."

We flew on, and an hour later, we were over the mountains that ran north and south through the entire state of Washington.

"We may get some rough air ahead," Abs said, over the comms. "Mountains are not always small-plane friendly."

But the air was smooth, and it wasn't until the topography changed from mountains to hills that that all changed.

The sun was getting lower on the western horizon as we approached the small town of Carnation. We were flying along, pretty as you please, when the Beaver seemingly dropped out of the sky, dropping more, and more, then rocketing back up.

The women in back screamed. I managed to stay silent, but my stomach did a loopty loop.

Abs looked over at me with a huge grin, said, "That was fun, wasn't it?"

"Fuck that. Besides being scary as hell, I've really gotta pee," Dawn said. "Like soon. How much longer till we're on the ground. . . er. . . water?"

"Twenty-five minutes," Abs answered. "Can you hold it?"

"No way."

"See the netting on Jon's seat-back? Reach in there and use the unisex urinal. There's a small roll of toilet paper too."

Dawn reached in and withdrew the plastic urinal. It was shaped to fit a woman's body.

"Keep the plane steady, please," Dawn said.

"I'll do my best," Abs answered, looking at me. She was sporting a mischievous grin.

I shook my head and mouthed a silent, *Don't do it.*

Dawn undid her seatbelt, lifted her butt, and slid her camos and underwear down to her knees. She positioned the capture cup correctly and relieved herself. Forgetting others could hear, she uttered several aahs during the process. Finished, she screwed the top on, put the contraption on the floor, pulled up her clothes, and re-buckled her seat belt. "Anyone else want to use it before I put it away?" she asked.

No one did.

The sun set as we crossed over Redmond. "We're twenty minutes out, folks," Abs said. "Give me directions please."

There was still daylight left, and I could see the city of Bellevue south of our position. "Keep on this heading."

The top of the Space Needle was shining brightly in the sinking sun.

"See the Space Needle ahead?"

"Yes."

"Head for that and turn north, or right, before you'd hit it. Start losing altitude soon after your turn and head for that body of water directly north. That's Lake Union where we're going to land. The freeway that heads north along the lake's eastern shoreline is Interstate 5. That bridge is our target. We want to end up underneath it."

"Underneath? Really?" Abs asked.

"There's a restaurant right there called Norseman's Salmon House. Kathy says they have a dock that we can tie up at. If it's too exposed, we can unload at the dock, and you can then taxi underneath the bridge. It might be a better place to wait for us."

"Roger that. The bridge it is," Abs said. "We made good time, folks. Problem is, we've got another twenty or thirty minutes of daylight left. It's fading but still there. Good for landing, not so good for hiding."

Seattle hadn't fared well since the pulse. Dozens of fires were burning all over the city. Thousands of dead cars and trucks blocked roads and intersections. I could see people on the streets, most of them running, stopping behind buildings, then running again. Trash was flying everywhere. Stores had been looted, and there didn't appear to be any rhyme nor reason to the destruction—it was just. . . everywhere.

"It's much worse out there than I thought it would be," Melissa said, glancing out of the bubble window toward the ground.

"Melissa, get ready. You're going with me. Make sure you take Kathy's backpack. Dawn, you're staying and will provide cover for Abs and Kris." I reached into my backpack and took out Renee's NVs and comms. I powered them on and held them up for Abs to see.

Abs nodded but was too busy with flaps and throttle to pay much attention. "I've turned them on, Abs. Simply put them on when it gets dark."

"Okay. Thanks."

"Let's do a comms check. Testing, testing," I said.

"All good," Melissa reported.

"Me too," Dawn said.

We were over water now, and Abs flew over the landing area looking down and checking the water for submerged logs or other floating objects. She doubled back the way we'd come, then hung a sharp U-turn, and we were once again headed for the bridge.

"We're headed into the wind which is a good thing," Abs announced. "The water has some ripples on it which is another good thing—glassy conditions can be dangerous. And we have four blue lights."

"Four blue lights?" Dawn asked.

"Means the wheels are up," I answered. "Terrible things happen when you land on water with the wheels hanging down from the floats."

Abs pumped the flaps down, and I watched the flaps lower even more. She put the Beaver into a pitch attitude, the nose held high and in a wing-level attitude. The floats' rear-ends touched water, and we quickly slowed. Abs had brought us within a hundred feet of the bridge.

"There's the dock," I said, pointing to the restaurant. "Bring us in on my side and I'll tie us up." The engine was basically idling, and we were making two knots at best. I opened the door, grabbed my rifle, and stepped down onto the starboard pontoon. I took hold of the docking lines and when Abs touched the dock I jumped onto the concrete pier and tied us to a cleat. I opened the rear passenger door and helped Melissa to the dock.

"What do you say, Abs. Stay or get under the bridge?"

A shot rang out, and bits and pieces of concrete exploded fifteen feet ahead of us and then another ten feet to our right as the shooter adjusted for the angle of fire.

"It came from up on the bridge," Melissa said, calmly bringing her rifle up and scanning the pedestrian railing for shooters. Evidently spotting someone, she fired off several controlled bursts. Pieces of the bridge railing exploded, and a body fell the hundred and fifty feet to the water, landing two hundred feet to the Beaver's left.

I kneeled, brought my rifle up, and searched the bridge for further targets. It was clear.

"Under the bridge," Abs said. "Untie us, please."

I untied the line and threw it back on the pontoon. I pushed it off, and the Beaver drifted away, turned, and taxied toward the bridge.

I keyed the comms, said, "Her house is very close; we shouldn't be more than fifteen minutes tops. Dawn, keep an eye out, please."

"We'll be here," Abs answered. "Give me a five-minute warning, and I can meet you at the dock. That way we won't have to wait for you."

"Roger that. Five-minute heads-up."

"I'm watching, Jon," Dawn said. "And why would that idiot fire on us?"

Kris spoke for the first time since this morning. "Because he could."

"But what was he hoping to accomplish by firing on us?" Dawn asked.

"It's called a target of opportunity," I said. "The Beaver was there and was a target. No other explanation."

"I guess," Dawn said.

During the flight, I'd studied and memorized Kathy's written directions.

"There's the flight of stairs. Follow behind me and watch our six."

The bridge had carried tens of thousands of cars across the lake every day, and this area would have been super noisy. Now it was quiet, eerily so, with only an occasional gunshot in the distance.

We climbed the steep flight of stairs and came out at Northlake Way and Fourth Avenue NE. We turned left, passed an empty lot and came to Kathy's building.

"Hers is the top-floor corner unit on this side. She says it overlooks the water," I said. "Her unit is 3G. We enter around the corner through the outside garden gate."

We rounded the corner to find a family of four standing in our way. The father and mother were studying one of those free tourist maps hotel lobbies are crammed with. They took one look at us in our battle gear and ran the other way, the parents practically dragging their kids behind them.

"Is it something we said?" Melissa asked, watching the four run up the hill.

We were at the gate. I dug in my shirt pocket and took out one of the keys Kathy had given me. Melissa watched our six as I unlocked the gate and stepped through. We quietly closed the gate behind us and approached the building's owner entrance.

The area between the gate and building was lush and heavily landscaped with green grass and forest ferns.

The same key opened the heavy, metal security door, and we entered a small, tile-floored lobby. A wall of mailboxes was on the left and an elevator straight ahead. A door to the right was labeled *Stairs*. We entered and climbed three flights of cement steps to the top, exiting into a carpeted hallway. We turned right toward the building's front, and there was Kathy's door.

The building, at least this floor anyway, was in pristine condition, and looked as if commercial cleaners had cleaned it that morning.

"We're at Kathy's door and ready to enter," I said into the comms.

"I hear you," Abs responded. "We're idling out here and all's well. Although we have quite a few lookie-loos watching us from the decks of their houseboats."

"We'll make this fast," I said.

I took the second key and inserted it. Melissa took hold of the back of my vest, and we walked into Kathy's condo. We entered a short hallway which led to a spacious living room and dining room. Floor-to-ceiling glass walls faced the water, and I could see the Beaver waiting under the bridge, propeller spinning. I turned the corner toward the kitchen and reared back as a wooden baseball bat whizzed by and broke the drywall next to my head. I swung the rifle to my side and rushed the guy before he could swing again. He was big, my height and weight, and I put some extra oomph into the tackle. We crashed to the kitchen floor with me on top of him. My weight had knocked the breath out of him, and he pushed me off, trying to get some air into his lungs. I brought the Glock out and was aiming for his chest when he waved his hand back and forth in front of me. He then pointed to himself.

"Jon?" he managed to squeak out in question.

I stood and backed off, but still kept the Glock on him.

"Bradley?"

"Yes."

He was getting air into his lungs and his color was returning. I offered my hand and helped him stand.

Melissa had her rifle up and aimed at his head. Before she did something rash, I put my hand on the barrel and pushed it down. "Please check the hallway and then shut the door."

"Roger that."

"You're supposed to be in Europe. How'd you get back?" I asked.

Melissa returned and quietly shut the door.

"The negotiations with the Spanish government went smoothly and both parties signed the contract a full day earlier than planned. One of Amazon's cargo jets was leaving early the next morning, and we were able to hitch a ride all the way back to Seattle. I didn't call Kathy because I wanted to surprise her.

"You're Melissa," Bradley said, pointing his finger at her. "Melissa from the office."

Melissa extended her hand, said, "Yes, we met soon after I started. Nice to see you."

Melissa and Bradley shook hands.

"How is Kathy? Please tell me she's okay."

"She's doing well. After Las Vegas, we made our way to my family's ranch in Montana. We're here to leave a letter for you and grab some of her things." I dug in my jacket pocket, came out with the letter, and handed it to him. "Read it later. We've got to get moving."

"Wait, how did you get here? And what happened to the power?"

I pointed out the window to the Beaver, said, "We'll explain once we're airborne. That's assuming you're wanting to come with us to Montana so you can be with your wife."

"You bet."

"Then start packing a backpack or duffel. You've got ten minutes. Melissa, start loading Kathy's stuff."

They both set out and began packing up. It was now dark, and Melissa donned her headlamp. Bradley did the same.

"Abs, we've got an extra passenger for you—Kathy's husband Bradley. We're going to need a few extra minutes."

"Roger that," Abs said.

"We have a couple of rowboats approaching," Dawn said.

"Armed?"

"I don't think so. I have the NVs on."

"They're probably looking for information. Tell them to stay twenty feet away from the plane then answer any questions they may have."

"Okay."

"Can I help load?" I asked Melissa and Bradley.

"No. Thank you, I'm almost done," Bradley answered.

"I'm done," Melissa answered, stepping into the living room with a full backpack and duffel bag.

Bradley was finished a minute later. He strode into the kitchen with two pillows under his arm. He dropped his duffel and backpack and stuffed both pillows into the duffel. He saw me watching, said, "Kath loves these pillows. She's had them since she was a kid."

He now sported a desert-brown handgun in a belt-mounted holster. He grabbed another backpack and was filling it with his backpacking stove, hiking pots and pans, freeze-dried meals, and fuel.

"Leave all that. We've got that and tons more at the ranch."

"Oh, okay, but give me thirty seconds to bring my neighbor over here … she could really use all this."

"Okay, but please hurry."

He opened the front door, turned right, and sprinted down the hallway. He knocked on his neighbor's door which opened ten seconds later. He took hold of the woman's hand and led her to his condo.

His neighbor was an early forties-something Asian woman with long, jet-black hair tied in a ponytail. She was tall, thin, and very elegant looking.

"Jon, Melissa, this is Kaitlin Chan. She's the—"

"News anchor for KOMO-TV," I said, finishing for him. "I watched you at eleven every night."

We shook hands.

"Kaitlin, I'm leaving with them, and I'm not taking any supplies with me. So, please, take all the freeze-dried meals, water, stove and fuel. . . hell, anything you want. There are enough freeze-dried meals to last you two or three months if you ration. There are several large sacks of rice in the pantry as well. And take this," he said, reaching into his backpack and coming out with a black semi-auto Glock. He reached in again and brought out two extra magazines, a box of shells, and a brown leather inside-the-waist holster. "And here's the key to the condo."

"You know how to use the gun?" Melissa asked.

"I do," she answered, stepping forward and hugging Bradley. "Thank you."

"Can you tell me what's happening with the power?" she asked, addressing the question to Melissa and me.

"Nuclear explosions over Colorado and Ohio created an electromagnetic pulse," Melissa answered. "The missiles were sent by North Korea, but China is suspected of supplying the knowhow and missiles. The power could be out for a decade or longer."

"We have to go. Now," I said. "Abs, we're on our way."

"Roger that. Taxiing to the dock."

"That's your plane?" she asked.

"Yes."

Melissa threw the duffel's strap over her shoulder and stuffed the backpack on top of the duffel.

"You get her down vest?" I asked.

"Yep, in here," she said, putting her hand on the duffel bag.

"Goodbye, Ms. Chan," I said. "Best of luck to you."

Out of the corner of my eye, I saw movement on the bridge. Six or seven men were running from the direction of Seattle, each armed with a rifle or handgun. They were running, then stopping and looking over the railing, then running again. They had to be searching for the Beaver.

"Abs, stay put. Shooters on the bridge. They're west of your location but will be over you in less than sixty seconds."

"Roger that. Headed back under the bridge."

I watched the Beaver turn and head back underneath the bridge.

"What do we do?" Melissa asked. "And I count seven of them."

"We wait and see what they do. If they keep on heading east, passing over the Beaver toward land, we let them go. If they stop directly over the Beaver and look as if they're getting ready to fire, we fire. Bradley, open the balcony slider. Now, please."

I booted up the thermal and then walked out onto the small wooden deck. There was a metal railing that ran the length of the deck. I scooted a grill out of the way, rested the barrel on the railing and watched the thermal's screen as it booted up. The light was fading, but it was cold, and the thermal would work just fine in picking out the warm bodies.

"Melissa, come out next to me. Set your rifle for three-round bursts. If they stop, I'll take the four on the left and you the other three."

"You got it," she answered, settling in to my right.

The seven men continued to run, stop, and check over the side.

"I can hear the Beaver's engine from here," Melissa said. "Those men can't help but hear it."

"Let's see if it's the Beaver they're after."

It was. They came to a stop directly over the idling Beaver. They craned as far out as possible and fired down toward the plane. I could see the shots hit the water, but the angle wasn't enough to get near the plane.

"We're being fired on, Jon," Abs calmly reported.

"We see, Abs. Stay well under the roadway. They can't get a bead on you that far back. We'll take care of this."

"Thank you, brother."

"Yeah, thank you," Dawn said. "Quickly, please."

Bradley and his neighbor were standing behind us, and I had them take cover inside the condo. "Get in the kitchen and take cover behind the cabinets."

The thermal was fully booted, and I set the crosshairs on the shooters. The screen said the targets were 260 yards out. The roadway of the bridge was at the same elevation as us on the deck.

"Safeties off, Lis. We need to get all seven," I said. "We can't have any of them left to fire on us as we take off. Can you see them?"

"I see them. Can I fire?"

"Yes. Aim a little high to account for a slight drop."

Melissa opened fire at the same time as the crosshairs on the thermal started to pulse. I fired on full auto and watched as the initial rounds hit low. I adjusted, and my four shooters were hit, two falling over the railing to the water below, the remaining two collapsing onto the pedestrian walkway. I dropped the magazine, rammed in a new one. Two of Melissa's shooters were down but the third was taking cover behind a metal pillar. I selected semi-auto and put rounds into the heads of my two downed shooters on the bridge.

"I've got one shooter hiding behind a pillar," Melissa said.

"Hold your fire but keep your sights on him."

"Roger that."

"Change your magazine out. I've got him."

The man suddenly stood, dropped his rifle, and held his hands up.

"What shall we—" Melissa started to ask.

I sent one round out, hitting the man dead-center chest.

"We can't have anyone on that bridge, Melissa."

"You don't have to explain anything to me, Jon. I get it."

"Abs, situation is resolved."

"Good, approaching dock."

"Bradley, let's go."

"Ms. Chan, I suggest you and your neighbors get up on the bridge, gather those weapons and check pockets and backpacks for extra ammunition. Take the firearm Bradley gave you."

"Good idea. We'll do it."

"Goodbye again. Good luck to you."

With Melissa and Bradley trailing behind, I led the way down the corridor and into the stairwell. We hustled down the stairs and exited into the lobby. There were several people in the small area, and they started peppering us with questions.

"Talk to Kaitlin," Bradley answered, as we left the lobby for the yard's entry gate. Melissa and I booted up our NVs. We exited the gate, turned left at the sidewalk, made another left onto Northlake Way, and sprinted toward the stairs. I could see the Beaver down below as it made its way to the dock.

I could also see quite a crowd gathered at the top of the stairway. There was at least a dozen, but none appeared armed. However, they were purposely trying to block the path to the stairway. They were smoking and sharing several doobies, the air thick with the sweet scent of burning marijuana.

"Can you believe these assholes," Melissa said. "Didn't they hear the gunfire? There has to be more in those joints than just plain old pot."

I stopped and told them to step away from the stairs and to let us pass. None responded to my verbal command.

"What's happened to the power, dude?" one asked, holding out a joint to us to share in. He had long hair and was slurring his words. He reminded me of the surfer from the movie *Fast Times at Ridgemont High*.

"It's out," Melissa answered. "For the next ten years. Nuclear explosions over Colorado and Ohio created an EMP. Now step the fuck aside, or I'll fuckin' blow your stoner head off."

"Fuck you, bitch," one of the women said. She had a shaved head with only a thin strip of hair sticking up, running from her forehead to the top of her neck in back—a punk mohawk. Several bright silver rings hung from her nose, and her eyebrows were weighed down by a dozen more. "Talk to us like that, and I'll—"

"You'll what?" Melissa asked, raising her Glock.

"I'll kick your ass," she answered, running toward Melissa. Melissa aimed and fired off one round.

The woman screamed, shouted, "You shot my ear off, cunt."

Melissa then shot the same woman in her left foot. She fell to the ground, screaming. The rest of the crowd ran up the hill, leaving the woman to fend for herself.

"I hate that word," Melissa shouted out after them, watching the crowd run up the hill. "Fucking assholes."

Bradley was staring open-mouthed at the woman on the ground. He bent down as if he was going to help her. I grabbed his arm and dragged him down the stairs. "You'll soon learn that, for Melissa, that was a remarkably restrained response. Let's go, you two."

We ran down the stairs and then across Norseman's parking lot to the dock. The Beaver floated in, ten seconds later.

"Bradley, get on the floor behind the bench seat and hold on," I said. Melissa threw the backpack and duffel in after him then climbed in and onto the bench seat. I pushed us off the dock, stepping onto the pontoon. I closed the passenger door behind Melissa, climbing up into the cockpit and closing the door behind me.

We taxied out to the center of the lake. Twenty seconds later, we were airborne.

NINETEEN

Turn back toward the Space Needle and keep going south past it. We're going to land in front of the Seattle Aquarium and tie up at their dock."

"I love these night-vision goggles," Abs said, as she adjusted the Beaver's boost and throttle.

From this altitude we could see all the fires burning. There was no section of Seattle proper that had been spared.

"Turn west, Abs. Then thirty seconds later, turn south and start descending."

Abs turned, cut the throttle and lowered the flaps. I spotted the outline of the aquarium and Abs performed a flyby, checking the surface for objects or anchored boats.

"Wind is blowing from the north and the water looks calm," she said. "I'm going to turn around, then again, and land into the wind."

We were soon taxiing toward the aquarium's dock. Several large vessels were tied up, but they were docked bow-in which left the far dock clear for us to use. It was a good spot to tie up as the large ships blocked anyone from seeing us out here on the end of the finger pier.

"Melissa and I are going to my place and then hers. We'll hustle, but this could take an hour or so. Bradley, please stay put and help Dawn with overwatch. Abs, I think you'll be safe here, but you might want to consider leaving the engine on in case you need to move away quickly. Dawn, come on out here and stand overwatch from the dock. If anyone but Melissa and I come walking down this dock, tell them to turn around or they'll be shot. Can you shoot someone if they refuse your command?"

"Absolutely," she said.

"Okay then. Melissa, let's go."

With me leading the way, we ran down the length of the dock, passed the aquarium itself, crossed Alaskan Way, and came up to the Pike Street Hill Climb.

The sound of gunshots was constant.

"It sounds like a warzone," Melissa said.

"Very similar, except there aren't bullets whizzing by our heads," I said. "Yet."

"Don't tell me we have to climb these?" Melissa grumbled, looking up the stairs which appeared to reach up into the sky.

"Yes. Come on, you bike to work every day. You're supposed to be in shape," I said, laughing.

"Lead the way, old man," she said, pushing me toward the stairs.

We made it to the top, both of us breathing hard. We crossed Western Avenue and hit the second set of stairs.

At the top, Melissa asked for a sixty-second break. I nodded and tried to relax. There were people out, but it was dark and no one had noticed us. The air up here was filled with the smell of burning, but not the nice smell you'd get from a campfire—more of a mixture of burnt wood, wire, and who-knows-what else.

Melissa said she was good to go, and we ran up Pike Street, crossed First Avenue, then turned left on Second Avenue, and dodging startled walkers, crossed Pine Street to my building.

"This is it," I said.

"Please tell me you're on a lower floor."

"Nope, top of the building. Twenty-second floor."

"Fuck, Jon. Really?"

There was a gunshot, followed by quick four or five return rounds. It wasn't close, but out of an abundance of caution, I pulled Melissa toward the building's wall. People ran by us, escaping the firefight.

"Come on, the entrance is around the corner on Pine Street."

We sprinted the fifty yards to the double, glass entrance doors. With Melissa covering our six, I dug out my key and opened the heavy door. We slipped into the lobby and closed the door, locking it behind us.

"You better be a resident of this building," a male voice said. It had come from behind an overturned desk. "You have a key which is why I didn't shoot your ass."

"I'm a resident. Jon Kristen from the twenty-second floor. The water-facing penthouse."

Four figures emerged from behind the desk, one I recognized—Stu Ney, the building's homeowners' association's president and a retired financial advisor. The other three—two men and a woman—I didn't know. Each was armed with a shotgun.

"Oh, hey, Jon. Good to see you," Stu said. "We're guarding the entrance."

"I can see that. Have you been having problems?"

"Four days after the blackout, a couple of dopers followed Mrs. Markowitz of 3B into the building. They took her food and liquor but didn't hurt her. Since then, we've had several assholes try and get through the door there. We now man this door 24/7. Three eight-hour shifts per day."

"How's Mrs. Markowitz?"

"She's doing okay. The building's remaining residents chipped in food for her," Stu answered. "But she's pretty depressed."

"She misses her liquor more than her food," the woman said, which produced some mild chuckling.

"How is it your electronics are working?" Stu asked. "Ours crapped out when the blackout happened."

"They were protected in faraday rooms and bags," Melissa answered.

"Listen, Stu, we've gotta get a move on," I said. "We're running late."

"You late for a flight?" the woman asked, sarcasm plain to hear.

"This is Vivian Tomassen. She's a pilot for Alaska Airlines," Stu said, as if that would explain the question.

"We are," Melissa said. "It's tied up at the end of one of the piers."

"No shit?" Stu asked.

"It's a Beaver," I said. "Restored a few years ago to original specs, so other than some FAA required comms, it has no electronics that could get fried."

"I learned to fly in a Beaver," the woman said. "My father's, out of Fairbanks."

The woman was in her mid-thirties, five-five or -six, with shoulder-length brown hair. She wore glasses with thick, black frames, held in place by a fabric leash. She was lean, but not muscled-up. Looked like a runner, not an iron-pumper.

We should have been passing the eleventh floor by now.

"Listen, guys, I have quite a bit of food and water in my place. You're welcome to it. But I'm going up now to get some of my stuff and then relocking it. Follow me if you want it."

I opened the stairway door and started climbing, Melissa behind me and two of the four—Vivian and Stu—following her. I'd taken the NVs off and donned the headlamp.

On our way up, Melissa filled them in on what had happened to the power. They didn't seem surprised by the news.

"I suspected as much," Vivian said, "though I always figured it would be the Russians or Iranians that would have the balls to do it."

"Things are bad here in Seattle," Stu said. "There's only a handful of folks still living in the building."

"Where'd they go?" Melissa asked.

"Some have cabins up in the Cascades or over on one of the islands out there in the Sound. Most of them took off on foot or bicycle after hunkering down here for three or four days."

"The ferries aren't running. How would they get across the water?" I asked.

"Don't think they'd thought that part out," Vivian answered. "Though had it been me, I'd have stolen a kayak, sailboat—whatever was handy."

"There's gunfire all the time. We've seen people kill other people for the backpacks they're wearing," the woman said. "The stores have all been looted, offices in skyscrapers ransacked for water and food. The worst thing you can do is trust anyone anymore."

"Even your friends," Stu said, a hint of sadness in his voice.

"I witnessed a young woman gang-raped right outside the building's entrance," Vivian said.

"Why didn't you stop it?" Melissa asked.

"There were ten men surrounding her. All armed," Vivian replied. "I was alone down there with a shotgun with two shells in it. After they left, I brought her in. She's living with another woman in the building now. She's a university student from Iowa."

"I'm afraid the building will catch fire," Stu said, laboring to keep up with us. "Too many candles and propane space heaters being used."

"How do you cook meals or boil water?" I asked. We were passing the nineteenth floor.

"Camping stoves. Myself and five others may have made a quick trip to the REI store down the street the day of the blackout," Stu said rather sheepishly.

"Well, good," Melissa said. "You gotta do what you gotta do to survive."

We came to the top floor, and I opened the stairway door to my floor. There were only four units on the top floor, each occupying a corner. My unit was on the other side of the building facing the Sound. I unlocked my door and stepped in. It was exactly as I had left it.

"Looks good, Jon," Stu said.

"Much too high up for any stoner-looter to climb," Melissa said, taking in the condo.

I walked over to the window and keyed the comms. "Abs? Dawn? You read?"

"I read you," Dawn said.

"We're in my place and will be heading to Melissa's in five minutes."

"Roger that. All's quiet here," Abs said. "Although we can hear almost constant gunfire."

I took out the headlamp, opened the sliding door to the deck, and stepped out.

"Just for kicks, look up on the hill and tell me if you can see this," I said, turning the headlamp on and off a few times."

"Affirmative, we see it."

"Talk to you in a few," I said, stepping back inside.

"Quite the place you have here," Melissa said. "My place is so small you could fit the whole thing into your kitchen."

"I bought at the right time. Plus, the developer was the grateful father of a wounded soldier I carried on my back three miles to our FOB."

"FOB?" Stu asked.

"It means forward operating base," Vivian answered. "I was an A10 pilot in the Air Force and flew a bunch of sorties supporting you guys. You SF or regular Army?"

"Special Forces."

"We met another hog pilot outside Vegas," Melissa said. "He's the one that provided the details of the attack."

I opened the hall closet and came out with an old ratty duffel bag. It was the bag I'd had when I left the service and held duplicate camos, T-shirts, socks, underwear, and another pair of boots.

"The pantry is off the kitchen. My parents visited a couple months ago and stocked it with survival food and gear. There are bags of rice, beans, water, camp stoves and fuel. Help yourselves. There's Trader Joe's canvas shopping bags you can use to carry it downstairs. When Melissa and I leave, I'm locking the door behind me so move everything you want out to the corridor."

"Melissa, watch the door and corridor, please."

"Roger that."

The condo was three bedrooms, four baths, plus office, and was just under thirty-five hundred square feet. My bedroom and guest room were furnished only with a bed, nightstand, and lamp. In the living room, there was a leather sofa, one end table with a lamp, and a coffee table. That was it—no dining-room table, chairs, stools sitting in front of the twelve-foot granite island. The only thing hanging on a wall was the seventy-five-inch Sony television in the living room. The wood floors had never seen an area rug or carpet.

During the day, the floor-to-ceiling windows, and wrap-around decks, provided an incredible view of Elliott Bay, Puget Sound, and Bainbridge Island.

Like Kathy, I had a favorite pillow that I'd had since high school. I stuffed it in the duffel along with more underwear, socks, T-shirts, jeans, sneakers, and hiking shorts. I walked down the hall to the office.

My office's only furniture was a gun safe. I was in the process of opening the safe when Vivian walked in, said, "I can see you never hired an interior decorator."

"One of my sisters offered to help me buy furniture and whatnot. But I bought the place after getting out of the service and I'd gotten used to spartan living conditions. I saw no reason to change."

"Hey, makes sense to me," she said.

She stood beside the safe watching me. She appeared antsy, like a shy person that didn't know what to say in a sudden one-on-one conversation with a stranger.

"Something on your mind, Vivian?"

I got the safe opened and took four handguns off the top shelf and threw them in the backpack. Next were a dozen loaded magazines, holsters, and six boxes of ammo. I had twenty one-hundred-dollar bills, a Remington 870 shotgun, and a dozen boxes of shells still in the safe which I left. I closed the door, spun the dial, and stood.

"Spit it out, Vivian. I'm sorry, but we're pressed for time."

"I have access to a Beaver. Like yours, it's fully restored and fitted with the original controls and instruments. The owner, a man down on sixteen, a fellow Alaskan Airlines pilot, was on a flight to London to visit his parents when the pulse hit. I know because I took him to the airport. His plane would have been somewhere over the Midwest when the pulse hit—he'll never be back. I have the Beaver's keys. It's sitting in a hangar, fueled up, and ready to go."

"And you're telling me this why?"

"I can take the Beaver, but I need some place to go. You must have that someplace."

"Ah. Got it. Hold on a sec. Melissa, turn down the volume on your comms, please."

"Done," she responded.

"Shut the door, Vivian. I don't want Stu to hear this."

As soon as she had the door closed, I keyed the comms, said, "Abs?"

"Yes?"

"I have a woman here who is an ex-hog pilot and claims to have access to a fully restored Beaver."

"Where is it?"

"It's at Vintage Air in Sidney, BC," Vivian answered.

Abs had heard the answer. "That's the same outfit that refurbished ours. It's right on the way to Vancouver. Does she know for a fact that it runs?"

"I don't know for sure, but it has no computer systems other than newer comms. It should start right up," Vivian said. "It's a '62 non-turbo model, bubble windows, cargo door, and has amphibs which are on the plane now. Thirty-five-inch bush tires are supposed to be in the cargo area. It's fully gassed. I was to have picked it up for the owner the day after the blackout hit. I have the paperwork authorizing release of the plane to me."

"She needs a place to live," I said. "You want to have another plane and pilot at the ranch?"

"Sure. I can't think of a reason not to. Heck yes. I think it's a great idea."

"Okay then. We'll have another passenger. Can you handle all of us?"

"Easy."

"Listen, Vivian. We live on a ranch outside Whitefish, Montana. We have a five-thousand-foot runway and two large hangars on-property, all built to handle larger private jets up to Gulfstream Sixes.

"We flew in from Montana this afternoon. We have two more stops: one right around the corner near Ballard and the second at Vancouver, Canada. You can follow us, there will be a moon later, so it won't be difficult. You have experience landing on water?"

"Oh gosh, yes. Lots," she said. "Along with my Airline Transport Pilot rating, I also have a seaplane ATP."

"Good. Then go down to your place and pack a backpack or duffel. And limit it to what you can carry. Melissa and I are going to her place a couple of blocks away, and we'll stop by the front entrance on our way back. Be there and be ready. We won't wait for you to show up. We don't want a stampede, so don't tell anyone you're leaving."

"Roger that, Master Sergeant."

We joined Stu and Melissa at the front door. Stu had all the food and supplies in the corridor. It was a lot of stuff.

"This will last several months," Stu said. "Thank you, Jon."

I closed the door and locked the three deadbolts. It was a thick, heavy, metal security door set in a steel frame—you'd need to detonate a strip of C4 to get it open. Vivian grabbed two of the loaded Trader Joe bags and helped bring them down to Stu's place on seventeen. She placed them in his corridor and then turned and hightailed it down the stairs using a pair of headlamps I'd given her.

"Good luck to you, Stu. Stay strong and safe," I said, shaking his hand and shoulder-bumping.

"Let's hustle to your place, Melissa."

We hustled down seventeen flights of stairs to the lobby, the duffel bag heavy and awkward. The same two men were still pulling guard duty. I put the duffel in a corner and told the two men I expected to find it untouched when we returned. I kept the backpack on. I opened the door and relocked it once we were outside.

"My place is three blocks down on Pine between Fifth and Sixth Avenues. It's on the other side of the street."

We took off running, Melissa leading the way. We had our NVs on, and we dodged and weaved our way around trashcans and discarded shopping carts. There were people out, but they were running like us, and for the most part, we were able to avoid them. We crossed Fifth Avenue then crossed to the other side of the street. Melissa stopped in front of a burnt-out building.

"It's gone. I lived two floors up from the Old Navy Store. It's just gone."

"Sorry, Melissa," I said, adjusting the backpack and scanning our six and sides.

"Shit. I really wanted to grab some of my stuff."

"There's a Nordstrom's across the street. The doors are open. Let's take a look inside and see if there's anything left. With our NVs, we should be able to navigate our way to the women's department. We can spare twenty minutes. Gives Vivian a chance to collect her stuff."

"Okay, thanks."

With glass crunching under our boots, we entered, walked up two flights using dead escalators and found the women's department. With the exception of broken and overturned displays of high-end purses, we found the entire floor untouched. While I stood overwatch, Melissa was able to grab yoga pants, underwear, bras, socks, sweaters, shorts, wool scarves, hats, and a bunch of other stuff. Stuffing everything into her backpack, we retreated back the way we had come. We stepped out of the broken door, and I spotted a large group of older teens coming toward us.

"I told you I saw them two with backpacks on," one of them said.

"Let's get 'em," another said.

"One kid on the left is armed," Melissa said. "The others have crowbars and baseball bats."

"We don't have time for this," I said, raising my rifle and firing a short burst over their heads. Even with the silencer, it still sounded lethal. All but one of the teens took off. The kid with the handgun stood there.

"Put the weapon on the ground," I said, advancing toward him. "And leave." But instead of listening to me, he raised the gun in a two-handed grip. Before he had the weapon leveled, Melissa fired a single round, hitting him in the chest.

"Fucking idiot," she said, picking up the gun and running back up Pine toward my place. "Renee never would have forgiven me if I'd let that idiot shoot you."

I followed her until we came to the entrance to my building. Vivian was there, unlocked the door and stepped out. I stepped in, grabbed my duffel, thanked the two men watching it, stepped out, and relocked it. She waved to the two men inside and followed us as we made our way back to the Beaver.

I stopped at the top of the stairs, keyed the comms, said, "Abs, we're at the top of the stairs. Coming down now."

"We're ready for you."

I turned to Vivian. "You have the keys to the Beaver?"

"Oh shit, I knew I forgot something," she said, frowning.

"You're shitting me, right?"

"Yes, I'm shitting you."

"I like her, Jon," Melissa said, high-fiving Vivian.

"Really funny, you two."

We made our way down the stairs, crossed Alaskan Way, and were stepping aboard the Beaver two minutes later. Vivian took Bradley's hand, and he pulled her up and into the cargo area. I pushed us off the dock and we were airborne sixty seconds later.

TWENTY

Fly north on the east side of the Space Needle, then turn northwest. We're landing in Shilshole Bay outside the marina there."

We flew over the Ballard Locks, and I had Abs start her approach. "Follow the shoreline until we see the marina."

Abs leveled off at one hundred feet, and the marina appeared on our port side.

"There's a long finger pier with empty docks on the end," Abs said. "Should be fine."

She did her standard fly-over, checking for obstacles, and we were taxiing toward the finger pier soon after. I reached down and pocketed the two Glocks, magazines, and extra boxes of ammo. I climbed down, stood on the pontoon, and jumped to the wooden dock. I fiddled with the floats until I had the Beaver pointed away from shore. I tied each float to a cleat.

"Kris, Melissa, let's hustle. Bradley, please unload those tubs onto the dock. If you have time, bring them further down the dock and put them next to the marina office."

"Dawn, you're on overwatch again."

Bradley turned on his headlamp, and Dawn was bathed in light.

"You could be the twin of that actress, Dawn Tillman," Vivian said. "You even have the same first name."

"Maybe she is. Are you?" Bradley asked, lifting two buckets of beans from the Beaver to the dock.

"I am," Dawn said, shielding her eyes from the bright headlamp.

"Yeah, sure you are," Bradley said, "and I'm the pope."

Abs turned in her seat, shouted back, "She is, dummy. Now get those pails off my plane and onto the dock. Quickly, please."

"Evan has a mountain bike with a child trailer he tows the kids around in," Kris said. "He can probably take six tubs at a time in it. He'll need to make three or four trips, but it's no problem for him."

"Let's get a move on," I said.

Kris turned and thanked Abs for the ride. She then hugged Dawn.

"Kris, take off the vest and NVs and hand them to Vivian," I said.

Once Kris had made the handoff, we started running down the wooden dock, Melissa leading the way. It wasn't nearly as stable as the aquarium's dock and the thing wobbled something fierce with every step.

We had rounded one finger and were headed toward the central dock when we saw our path was blocked by a dozen or more sleeping sea lions. I'd seen this same thing at Pier Thirty-Nine in San Francisco.

"What are we gonna do?" Melissa asked.

"One thing we're not going to do is shoot them," I said, addressing Melissa. "We'd never be able to move them off the dock."

Kris got within ten feet of the group and started yelling and stomping her feet on the dock's wooden slats. The herd woke, raised their snouts, and spotting her, silently slid into the water.

Kris had started running past where they'd been sleeping when the dock suddenly dipped down to the right. She instinctively shifted her body weight to the left but was too late. She slipped and fell into the water feet first. I was instantly there.

I reached down and grabbed her by her jacket collar, lifting her out of the water and onto the dock. I'd done it so quickly her head hadn't had a chance to get wet.

"How far to your house?" I asked a shaken Kris.

"If we climb the hill, it can't be more than a quarter mile. If you want to stay on city streets, then we have to go to the right down Seaview Avenue, turn left at Northwest Sixty-First Street, climb the hill using city streets, then backtrack on Thirty-Fourth Avenue Northwest all the way to Northwest Seventy-Fifth Street. Staying on city streets will add two miles or more."

"How steep is the hillside?" Melissa asked.

"It's steep, but there's a dirt trail that the locals use as a shortcut."

"Hillside it is," I said.

I gave Kris one of my spare headlamps, and she led the way.

We crossed Seaview Avenue and a paved walking path that sported a white outline of a bike with a pedaling stick figure. We plunged through thick underbrush and trees and began climbing a very steep slope. The dirt path was narrow and worn, traversing the hillside via a series of switchbacks.

Three minutes later, we emerged on top of the bluff. Had it been during the day, we'd have had a great view of the marina and the Beaver tied to the furthest finger pier. Kris turned left and walked between two large well-established, upscale houses. She then started to run down Thirty-Fourth Street.

We were alone out on the streets. The homes all appeared intact and untouched by fire or looters. Unlike Seattle, it was quiet here, and the only sounds were our boots hitting the ground as we ran along the tree-lined streets. We were about to cross Seventy-Third Street, two streets shy of Kris's house on Seventy-Fifth, when I saw movement in the NVs.

"Stop. Kris, turn off the headlamp."

The three of us stopped shy of Seventy-Third Street. The street ahead took a gentle curve to the right, but this far back, we were out of the line of sight of Seventy-Fourth Street.

"You two stay here. I'm going to check it out."

I hugged the retaining wall next to the right-side sidewalk and slowly inched my way forward. I rounded the gentle corner and could now see a barricade ahead. The barricade was made of cars and trucks that had been rolled into place, effectively blocking the road and both sidewalks. The NVs picked up four men, one of whom was holding what looked to be a rifle. I backtracked and reported what I'd seen.

"We used the same approach in Afghanistan," I said. "You start with one square block and slowly work your way out until you've secured the entire town or village. Someone here knows what they're doing. We could try and go around it, but I bet they've barricaded other streets and have created a boxed-shaped safety zone."

"It's got to be manned by my neighbors," Kris said. "I'll go ahead and speak with them. My house is two blocks up this street at Seventy-Fifth. We're right across from Sunset Hill Park."

"Works for me. Take cover behind something before you call out," I said. "We'll cover you."

Kris hugged the same retaining wall but got herself closer, standing behind an abandoned Toyota Corolla.

"Hello there. My name is Kris Edwards. I'm a resident here and live directly across from Sunset Hill Park. My friends and I need to pass through."

A man walked out from behind the barricade, said, "Krissy, is it really you?"

"Evan?"

"Yes, baby. I can't believe it," he shouted, as he sprinted toward his wife.

Kris ran to Evan, and like in the movies, they collided in each other's arms.

Melissa and I hung back and let Kris reunite with her husband.

Kris untangled herself from her husband. Both were crying, but Kris waved us forward, said, "Evan, this is Jon and Melissa."

"They're your co-workers at Securetech, right?"

"Yes. We've had quite the journey from Las Vegas. And I'll tell you all about it later. But I want to see my babies first. Are they okay?"

"Yes, we're all doing fine. Your parents have proven to be angels in this hell we find ourselves in. Your mother watches over the children while your father and I help man the barricades. Tonight, your father is stationed at the barricade on Seventy-Seventh Street."

"How is the food situation?" Kris asked.

"We ran out a few days after the blackout, but Mrs. Granger's pacemaker stopped working and we were with her when she passed. Before she died, she told us to check her basement. Turns out she was a devout Mormon and had accumulated quite the emergency supply pantry—we have a good year's worth of food. She saved us, Krissy. The neighborhood group decided not to combine resources, so we now have all of her supplies at our place."

"God bless Mrs. Granger," Kris said. "Can these other men spare you for a couple of hours? Jon has left us with several months' worth of food down on the marina docks. I thought you might use the children's bike trailer to bring it up."

"They're in five-gallon tubs which weigh roughly twenty-five pounds each," I said. "It will take several trips to bring them up."

"How'd you get here?" Evan asked. "And do you know what's happened to the power and our electronics?"

"We flew in," Kris answered. "The plane has pontoon thingies and we landed on the water. We tied up on the furthest dock at the marina. As to the power outage: two nuclear missiles detonated—one over Colorado and the other over Ohio."

"We thought we heard a plane. You're soaking wet, Krissy. Did you swim in to shore?" he asked.

"I fell off the dock."

"Poor baby. We'll get you into some dry clothes."

It was time for Melissa and me to leave. I took out the two Glocks, magazines, holsters, boxes of ammo, and remaining antibiotics.

"These are for you," I said, handing the lot over to Evan. "You're going to need these. Kris knows how to use and care for them. Kris, here are your meds. Make sure you take them."

"Thank you, Jon. Any firearm is now priceless," Evan said. "The four of us here share an old shotgun. I'm usually armed with a nine iron. And why are you taking meds, Krissy?"

"We need to go," I said. "I'm sorry the ranch didn't work out, Kris, but it seems as if things are in good shape here."

Kris took off the headlamps and made to hand them over to me.

"Keep them. You'll need one to see your way to the marina, Evan. The pails should be next to the marina office. Best hustle down there soon. You don't want to have those pails sitting there unguarded for long."

Kris hugged Melissa and then me.

"Thank you for bringing me safely home. I'm sorry I was such an asshole. And for taking the Alderson's truck. You may not know it, but I've paid attention to everything you've taught us, and I know I can put it to good use."

Evan shook my hand, said, "Thank you for bringing her home to us. The children have really missed their mother."

"Good luck to you," I said, turned, and with Melissa beside me, started running back the way we'd come.

We were soon at the bluff top. I keyed the mic, said, "Abs, we're working our way down the hill. We should be there in less than five."

"Roger that. Starting engine."

We'd crossed Seaview when I heard the Beaver's engine start. We passed the marina's office, and there were the pails neatly stacked up against the wall.

"Melissa, grab a pail of rice and beans, and if you can, carry them back to the Beaver," I said, grabbing a pail of rice and a five-gallon water jug. There was plenty left.

I keyed the comms, said, "Dawn, please send Bradley to the marina office and have him haul a bucket of rice and a bucket of black beans back to the plane."

"You figure Kris and Evan already have enough supplies?" Melissa asked.

"You read my mind. And we might run into someone that could really use it."

We hustled down the dock, staying as best we could to the middle of the rickety, wood, floating obstacle course. The sea lions hadn't returned, although I heard a couple of honks from another pier. Bradley ran past us in the opposite direction.

The engine was idling as we came up on the Beaver. I opened the cargo door and placed the pails in back. Vivian climbed over the bench seat-back and arranged the buckets as I set them in the cargo door. Melissa climbed in and belted into the bench seat next to Dawn. Bradley showed up a minute later carrying the two buckets. He climbed into the cargo area and stowed the pails as I handed them up. I shut the cargo door, stepped aboard the port pontoon, untied the two lines from the dock and climbed into the co-pilot's seat.

"We'll taxi and bring up the oil temp," Abs said. "Once airborne, we've got a forty-five-minute flight to Vintage Air. I've been to their facility several times, and we can land in the water or on their runway."

"Do you know where the plane's located, Vivian?" I asked. "On the tarmac or in a hangar?"

"I know at one point it was on a tarmac parking area waiting for me to pick up. But I bet they moved it into a hangar for safe keeping after the blackout."

"A working airplane is now one very valuable piece of machinery," Abs said. "And if it's still at their facility, it's not going to be as simple as us walking in and flying it out. If I was Vintage Air, I'd have guards there 24/7. I mean, your working plane, Vivian, is likely just one of many."

"I do have the key and a Vintage Air Authorization to Release form filled out and signed by the owner."

"Let's hope Vintage Air will still release it," I said. "Abs, land on the runway."

"Roger that," Abs said as she accelerated and pulled the yoke to her stomach. We were soon airborne, and I watched Abs work the flaps, throttle, and boost knobs. According to the altimeter, Abs had leveled off at twenty-five hundred feet. We were cruising at 110.

"What's our fuel situation?" Vivian asked

"Tip tanks are empty. We transferred twenty-five gallons back at the marina. I kept the empties in the hope that we might fill them up at Vintage Air. Regardless, we should have enough gas to get us home, but I always like to have more on board just in case."

It was now a few minutes after nine o'clock. I shut my eyes and tried to catnap, hoping the Beaver's sound and vibrations would lull me into sleep mode.

TWENTY-ONE

Vintage Air is ten miles ahead," Abs announced. "Starting descent."

I looked at my watch—I'd managed to nap for thirty minutes.

Abs had stuck a small penlight in her mouth and was aiming it at the map strapped to her thigh.

"I'm going to do a flyby to check for objects on the runway and the sock for wind direction," Abs said, pumping the flaps down.

We were soon leveled off at three hundred feet. Abs released the wheels, and I heard the reassuring clunk as they locked into place. I watched as four red lights appeared below the dash signifying wheels down.

"There's the tower off the starboard wing," Abs said, as we flew over the airstrip. "Runway is clear. Wind out of the north at five knots or so. Coming around."

"That's a huge airport, Abs. Don't know why I thought it was a small private strip."

"They share the runway with Victoria International Airport. But we're not talking JFK here, brother. The pulse hit at around five in the morning. This place would have been locked up and empty when things turned dark."

Abs was in a steep bank when the landing strip lit up. There were six bright lights, three on each side of the runway and spaced at least three hundred feet apart. They weren't the real runway lights but would certainly work for position reference.

"Well, that answers the question of whether anyone's home," Vivian said.

"I don't know if their comms are working, but let's try our old one," Abs said. She powered up the Beaver's original radio, took hold of the microphone, said, "Vintage Air, this is Kristen Ranch Beaver out of White Fish, Montana, bound for Vancouver. Permission to land?"

"Permission granted, Beaver," came a reply.

And a long minute later, "Welcome back, Ms. Kristen," a woman said. "Wind is four knots out of the north. Turn left on the first taxiway and head for the maintenance hangar. I've put a blue blinker in front of the sliding doors."

"Blue blinker in sight. Lolly, is that you?" Abs asked

"Affirmative, Abigail."

"See ya in a couple," Abs said.

"Roger that, Beaver."

"Lolly is Vintage Air's customer care representative," Abs explained. "She handles all of Vintage's resto's and guided our project from start to finish."

Abs had brought us around and was now lining up for the runway. She reduced throttle, floated us along and over the threshold stripes, touching down on the four rear wheels, then gently bringing the spindly-looking bow wheels onto the runway. She'd landed smooth as silk on the second centerline stripe.

"Nicely done," Vivian said, from the back seat.

The runway lights were extinguished.

Abs turned left at the first taxiway and made her way over to the maintenance hangar. A figure holding two flashlights walked out of a door and indicated an area to the left of the giant sliding doors.

Abs followed the instructions.

"Park facing the runway, Abs," I said, "and leave the engine running. Vivian, climb down and join me on the tarmac. Please bring your key and paperwork. Melissa and Dawn, provide a close-in overwatch."

I climbed to the ground, released the thermal from my rifle, and scanned twice through 360 degrees. All I saw was the woman standing by the hangar's office door. I took off the NVs, powered them down, took out one of Burt's headlamps, powered it up, and slipped it on. I climbed up and placed the thermal on the co-pilot's seat.

Once Vivian was on the ground, we walked together toward the person holding the flashlights. The flashlights lit us up. Whoever was holding the light, turned and ran back inside the hangar office.

"I think we might have scared them with the battle gear and weapons," I said into the comms.

"I'm Jon Kristen, Abigail's brother," I yelled out. "Lolly, hold up, please."

The figure opened the door, shone the light on the both of us, then on the Beaver, settling on Abs in the pilot's seat.

"Sorry, Mr. Kristen," a woman said. "There's only two of us here watching over the entire complex. You're the first to show up since the blackout."

I stopped a few feet from the woman. "Thank you for turning on the runway lights. It helped."

"Heidi rigged those up using a truck battery. Glad it worked for you. You can tell Abigail to turn the engine off. We are not a threat."

I took everything in and decided to trust her.

"Abs, shut down then join us."

"Roger that."

"You're Lolly?" Vivian asked.

"Yes."

"I'm Vivian Tomassen, Lolly. I'm Walter Sorensen's friend and fellow pilot at Alaskan Airlines. I'm here to pick up Walter's Beaver. I have the key and release forms."

"I recognize your name, Ms. Tomassen. The plane is ready for you inside. Heidi and I pushed it in the day after the blackout."

"Hi, Lolly!" Abs shouted from across the tarmac as she placed the chocks under the rear wheels. Abs then ran up to us, hugged Lolly, and thanked her for the landing lights.

"It's good to see you guys," Lolly said. "You're the first folks we've seen since the blackout. Oh, here's Heidi now."

A woman in stained mechanic's overalls and a dark-brown down jacket joined us.

"Hi there," Heidi said, waving hello. "Welcome to Vintage Air. Can you tell us what happened to the power and our electronics?"

I spent the next few minutes filling them in on what we knew.

"Shit," Heidi said. "They finally did it."

"If by 'they', you mean North Korea, along with China's help, then yeah, they really did it."

"Why are you two alone?" Vivian asked the two women.

"We've heard a bunch of gunfire to our south and east," Lolly said. "We think some folks might be blocking other folks from entering Sidney and Victoria. We both live in Sidney but didn't want to leave the facility unguarded."

"Not with all the planes inside," Heidi said, pointing over her shoulder.

"How'd you happen to be here so early in the morning when the pulse hit?" Abs asked.

"It snowed the night before, so we decided to stay here in the employee lounge. We woke up to the blackout and waited for other employees to show up, but no one has," Heidi said.

"Do you by any chance happen to have any food or water you can spare?" Lolly asked. "We've gone through all the snacks and most of the bottled water in the cafeteria."

"And don't feel safe searching outside the compound," Heidi added.

"We do. Do you have a way to heat water?"

"We have a propane stove and burners in the cafeteria kitchen."

"Follow me, and we'll get you fixed up," I said.

We walked back to the Beaver, and I had Bradley hand down the pails.

"Glad you had us grab those from the marina," Melissa said.

"You still have that pistol you picked up from the street across from your house?" I asked.

"Yes."

"What caliber?"

"Forty. It's an old Ruger. You want to give it to them?" she asked.

"Yes. And a box of shells, too."

Melissa turned to gather the ammo.

"Has anyone ever told you that you look a lot like Dawn Tillman?" Lolly asked Dawn.

"All the time," Dawn said. "And I do look like her, because I am her."

"No shit?" Heidi asked. "How'd you end up here of all places."

"Long sad story. Too long to tell it here. Sorry."

"Oh, okay," Heidi said.

The rest of us grabbed a pail and carried them back to the office.

"Cool. Thank you so much. This will last us a couple of months. Good thing I like rice, huh, Lolly," Heidi said.

Melissa walked in and held out the Ruger.

Both women held up their hands, said, "Whoa, thanks, but no thanks."

Canadians are permitted to own handguns, but license requirements are so cumbersome that few do. And from the time they're children, Canadians are taught the evil dangers of firearms, especially handguns.

"Listen to me, you two," Melissa said in a stern voice, "you're going to be confronted by bad people. Maybe not anytime soon, but they'll eventually be here. Trust me, as women, you're going to want to have this."

I could see that Heidi was leaning toward taking the weapon.

Abs said, "If you'd seen what these folks have seen you would take it, no question. So please take it."

"How does it work?" Lolly asked.

"Melissa, give them a quick lesson," I said. "Maybe even fire off a few rounds."

"You bet."

"Ladies, how do we open the hangar doors?" Vivian asked.

"Normally, you'd just press a button and they'd slide open, but without power, you now have to manually pull down on the chains." Lolly pointed us toward the hangar door, said, "Go through that door. The chains are hanging off the ceiling; they slide through eyelets secured to the building's side walls."

"We're taking Walter's plane. Did you try and start it?" Vivian asked.

"No. Neither of us would know how to maneuver it if we did start it. So, we just pushed it into the hangar."

"Well, fingers crossed then," Vivian said, walking toward the door leading to the hangar.

"Would it be possible to get some gas?" Abs asked the two women.

"Sure," Lolly said. "Once the hangar doors are open, you can push the fuel cart out to your plane. It's a manual pump so there shouldn't be any issues."

"One last question: you have any extra Beaver antennas?"

Heidi went to get Abs an antenna.

Lolly guided us to the chains. I took the left-side chains, and Abs and Vivian the right. Lolly released the door brakes and we pulled for all we were worth. The doors slowly slid apart. It took us ten minutes to get them opened far enough for the Beaver's wing tips to slip through.

Vivian climbed into the Beaver to check the systems.

"Yay, we have battery power and instrument lights," she said, looking down at us from the pilot's seat.

This Beaver's bright-yellow wings and gleaming, dark-green fuselage were beautiful, even in the headlamps' harsh light.

"It looks as if it had just come off the assembly line sixty-one years ago," Abs said.

"It should," Lolly said. "Mr. Sorensen told us to refurbish or rebuild it from the wheels up. And I mean everything—inside and out. And we did. Took us over two years to do it, but here it is. And the only non-original thing on it is your FAA's mandated modern radio and transponder. But we left the old radio in after making sure it worked. It also has a rebuilt engine. And you should know that Mr. Sorensen paid us to do the initial engine break-in for him. It now has a tad more than fifteen hours of flight time on the engine. The oil has been changed and everything that could be adjusted has been. You're good to go."

"What are we waiting for?" Abs said. "Let's get her outside and started up."

I removed the chocks and stowed them in the smaller aft storage compartment. We each took hold of a landing strut and pushed. For such a big-assed plane it didn't take much effort.

"Jon, I'll help Vivian with the startup if you'll get the fuel cart to our plane and start fueling," Abs said. "Start with the tip tanks as they're empty. The cart has built-in telescoping stairs you can use."

I walked back inside and picked up the cart's tongue that would normally be hooked up to an aircraft tractor. I must have looked like an ox pulling a wagon as I dragged the loaded fuel cart out onto the tarmac and over to our Beaver. I enlisted Dawn in the effort, grabbed the nozzle, and climbed the steps until I reached the top of the starboard wing. I opened the cap, stuck the nozzle in and told Dawn to start pumping the lever like you would an old-fashioned water pump.

"This isn't easy," she said, as she pumped away.

"Exercise will do you good. Work the arms."

From atop the cart's stairs, I watched as Abs stood in front of the other Beaver awaiting instructions from Vivian. Ten seconds later, I heard Vivian yell out, "Magnetos are off. Spin 'em."

Like I'd done at the ranch, Abs spun the propellers and counted off the spins. She then stepped back, and a few seconds later Vivian turned the props, and the engine fired up. The Beaver was surrounded by white smoke and then settled into that wonderful sound of a radial engine idling.

The tip tank was full, so I told Dawn to stop pumping. I secured the cap, climbed down, and pulled the cart over to the port wing. The Beaver had three main tanks, and the caps were located to the right of the pilot's door. I opened the far-left tank and stuck the nozzle in the tank's filler neck.

"Okay, start pumping," I told Dawn.

Dawn looked at me, then waved Bradley over and had him take over pumping duty. Dawn grinned and flipped me the bird as she resumed her place on overwatch.

I smiled back, said, "During the meeting this morning, which ranch hand put his name in for a three-day stay with you in a border tent? Remember him? Well, guess what?"

Dawn stared at me with impossibly large eyes and a frown planted on her face which I took to mean *you wouldn't dare. . . would you?* She started to say something then remained silent, seemingly at a loss for words.

"Yeah," I said. "I'm responsible for setting watches. Payback's a bitch, isn't it?"

Which earned me another finger. . . minus the smile.

I heard gunfire behind us, and there was Melissa standing behind Heidi. Melissa's arms were wrapped around her student, and she was demonstrating how to grip the weapon. They fired off another round at an old barrel with soda cans perched on top as targets. Melissa stepped back, and Heidi fired two more rounds on her own. Melissa then repeated the same procedure with Lolly.

The soda cans remained untouched on top of the barrel. But it was dark, with only a faint moon and Melissa's headlamp for illumination.

Ten minutes later, I had finished fueling our Beaver, including the port tip tank, and over the comms asked Vivian if she needed any.

"Gauges read full. But thanks."

"Don't forget to fill the empty fuel cans in the cargo area," Abs said, as she climbed into our Beaver's pilot seat.

I had forgotten. Bradley pulled them out, I filled them, and he secured them back in the cargo area as each was filled.

Finished with the fueling, Bradley and I pulled the cart back into the hangar. We closed the sliding doors, exited the office onto the tarmac, and headed toward our Beaver.

Lolly, Heidi, and Melissa were headed there too, and we converged next to our Beaver's pilot door. Abs climbed down and hugged each of the two Vintage Air employees.

"Thank you for the gas, ladies," Abs said. "And for the antenna."

"You're most welcome. And a huge thank you for the food and protection," Heidi said, holding up the handgun.

"Can't forget the shooting lessons, Melissa," Lolly said, as she hugged Melissa. "It's nowhere near as scary as I thought it would be."

"Bradley, why don't you go with Vivian," I shouted. "No sense in her flying alone."

Bradley nodded, hung a quick U-turn, and headed back toward Vivian.

"Let's turn off the headlamps and transition to NVs, ladies," I said.

"You ready to turn her over?" I asked Abs.

"Yep. Mags are off. Safe to spin 'em."

I spun them, then she spun them with the starter, and a few seconds later, she had the engine warming up.

I hugged Lolly and Heidi and thanked them for their help. Dawn was next with the hugs and wished them well.

Melissa and Dawn climbed into the rear and settled onto the bench seat. They buckled in and donned headphones. I shut the port rear passenger door behind them, removed the chocks, ran around the Beaver's tail, and climbed up into the co-pilot seat. I put the headphones on and asked for a check.

"Good," Melissa said.

"Hear you," Dawn responded.

Abs gave me a thumbs-up.

"Vivian, I'm going to call you Beaver Two," Abs said. "We're headed to Vancouver. Dawn, where in Vancouver?"

"Kitsilano Beach. It's west of downtown Vancouver and directly north of the airport."

Abs raised her NVs, turned her penlight on, and studied the map on her thigh.

"Got it," Abs said. "Is there an actual beach? Like with sand or pebbles?"

"Yes. It's a sand beach. No rocks like so many other beaches in the area."

Abs relayed the destination to Vivian.

"I've flown dozens of times from here to Vancouver. Hop, skip and a jump in an Airbus."

"Fifty miles give or take a few," Abs said. "Thirty minutes. We'll stay low and go slow. Let's avoid having folks taking potshots at us, so nav lights off."

"You're in Canada now, and folks here are much too polite to be shooting at an airplane, don't cha know?" Vivian said in a passable Canadian accent. "But I'll turn them off."

"I need another five minutes to get my oil warm," Abs said.

"Then let's burn the fuel by taxiing to the runway," Vivian said. "Wind is still out of the north."

"Spoken like a jet jockey," Abs said, laughing. "These things sip gas at idle. Will taxi to the south end of the runway."

We left the runway at five after ten. The moon was rising in the east and was welcome company to our right.

TWENTY-TWO

Four blue lights lit up. "Wheels are up," I said.

"Four blues," Vivian repeated. "In position below and behind your starboard wing. It's good to be in the air."

"Leveling off at twelve hundred feet," Abs said.

"Twelve hundred," Vivian repeated.

"Vancouver International is below," Vivian announced twenty minutes later.

"Starting descent—three, two, one, now," Abs said, the Beaver bleeding altitude.

"Dawn, you and I will retrieve your sister. Melissa, stay with the Beavers and stand overwatch."

"Vivian, level off at seven hundred," Abs said. "I'm going down to two hundred and checking out the landing area. Stay up here so I don't run into you."

"Don't like flying in formation?" Vivian asked, chuckling.

"Never done it before. And it is night, after all."

"Sorry, I spent twelve years flying in close formation and have to remind myself that not every pilot has had US Military training."

We flew north over the beach itself which gave Abs a perfect view of our likely landing area out the pilot-side window.

"I see a few mooring balls close in to shore, but they're far enough apart for us to slip through without a problem. The shoreline itself is level with the water which means we can pull in and turn ourselves around and face the ocean or whatever it is out there."

"It's called the Burrard Inlet," Dawn said.

"Thanks. . . the Burrard Inlet. We're good. Winds are coming from the north again," Abs said, beginning a steep bank to starboard to bring us back around.

Which left Dawn on the starboard side looking down toward the ground at a forty-five-degree angle.

"There's the sand volleyball courts. My house should be. . . I can see my house!" Dawn shouted out. "It's right below us."

"Nice," Melissa said. "Beachfront property."

"It's quiet out here. And private, which is what we wanted."

Abs leveled out and then brought us down lower. "Beaver Two, headed south and will turn north and land. Turning north now. One hundred feet and descending."

"Roger that, Beaver One. Will circle back south and wait for your instructions. Over."

"Blue lights are on, Abs," I said.

"Thank you," she said, left hand on the wheel and right hand busy with the usual knobs and flaps pump.

I felt the pontoons touch water. We skipped along, finally settling down into the water. The surface was somewhat choppy, and we rocked and rolled not unlike a boat would. We taxied toward the beach where the surface appeared calmer. Even without the NVs, and using the moon for illumination, I could see the mooring balls ahead to starboard and port.

"Jon, I'm going to head directly for the water's edge and beach. At the last moment I'm going to turn us north and parallel the beach. I want you and Dawn to step out on your pontoon, grab the starboard aft tie-down line and then jump to the sand. Let the plane's wing pass you by and then grab hold of the starboard-side horizontal stabilizer. I'm going to turn the engine off, and you two hold on tight. When you feel slack, go ahead and move your hands to the tail and then to the port side horizontal. Dawn, you then pull on the tie-down line. She should slowly point out to sea. Then pull us back as hard as you can and ground the rear of the pontoon onto the sand. Melissa and I will then take hold of both aft tie-down lines and hold her in place."

"Hundreds of people probably heard us flying overhead. Many will come out to investigate," I said.

"They heard us fly overhead, not land. I'm pointing out to sea and can start the engine and move us far enough out to be safe."

"Okay," I said, opening my door. "Dawn, you ready?"

"Ready," she answered, opening her door and climbing down to the pontoon. She shut her door, slung her rifle to her side, and hung on.

I joined her on the pontoon. Abs turned the Beaver north at the last second and we were as close to sand as you'd ever want to get.

"Jumping," I said. Abs shut down the engine and the Beaver instantly slowed. The wing passed. Dawn grabbed the aft line, and I took hold of the horizontal stabilizer, then the tail, and then the port horizontal stabilizer. The plane was now facing out to sea. The pilot's door opened, and Abs climbed down to the pontoon, grabbed ahold of the aft tie-down line, and jumped to the sand.

"I usually do that alone when I land on a lake and I'm by myself," Abs said. "It's much easier with helpers."

Melissa took hold of the line from Dawn.

"We're good here as long as the wind doesn't come up," Abs said. "Go, you two. Keep us updated, please."

"LET'S GO, DAWN. YOU LEAD and I'll be right behind you. When you stop, I'll put my hand on your vest so you know I'm right there with you."

I heard Vivian splash down.

"We're holding her on the beach, Beaver Two," Abs said over the comms. "Come on in to calmer water but don't beach."

"I have an anchor and a hundred feet of line. I'll come in to calmer water, throw the anchor, and shut down the engine. We'll be out fifty feet from you."

"Understood," Abs said.

Dawn was fast-walking across the sand. We cut through sand volleyball courts, nets down for the winter, but the fabric court outlines, for some reason, still in place. Basketball courts were to our left and then a residential street.

"Hold up here," I said. "Let's take a knee and wait a couple of minutes to make sure no one comes out to check on the engine noise."

"Okay, sure," Dawn said. "There's my place right there." She was pointing directly across the street to a corner house. It looked big—maybe two to three times the size of other lots—and was surrounded by a ten-foot-high hedge. From this vantage point, there didn't appear to be any entrances through the hedge. I could see a house behind the hedge, but only the top floor of windows, a deck, and roof. There were four chimneys, two on each end.

"How do you get in?"

"Around the corner on Whyte Avenue is a gate and a bit further on is a motorized gate for the driveway. The hedge is a good four feet deep and both gates are recessed into the hedge."

"I take it you have a gardener who takes care of that hedge."

"Yes. He's the best around. I'm away more than I'm here, so there's no way I could take care of it. And my little sister has never touched a live plant in the garden."

"It doesn't appear that we've attracted any undue attention, so let's go."

I keyed the comms, said, "Approaching the house now. Are things quiet on the water?"

"Very," Abs reported.

We crossed Arbutus Street and came to the hedge. We turned right on the sidewalk, turned left at the corner, and a hundred feet of hedge later came to an opening. A wooden gate with an ornate, heavy-duty lock was in front of us. I could see a surveillance camera looking down from the top of the gate support and an intercom with a speaker button to our right at chest-level. Dawn took a key from her pocket and opened the gate. We stepped through and secured the gate behind us.

The house behind the hedge was a surprise, for in a neighborhood of century-old, stately houses, Dawn's couldn't have been more different. I was staring at an ultra-modern, glass-walled, mid-century beauty.

"I wasn't sure what I was expecting to see behind the hedge, but this wasn't it," I said.

"You saw the other houses and thought you'd be walking into a Tudor-style monstrosity, right?"

"Yes."

"I love everything about it. Well, maybe not everything. Even with radiant heat throughout, the heating bill is astronomical."

"Well, all that glass gives you a great view of the hedge," I said.

"That's true, but with the hedge I don't have to worry about curtains and nosy neighbors."

"Let's get your sister and head on home."

"Good idea," she said, taking another key out of her jacket pocket and holding it up. "The key to the glass house."

She unlocked the door, and we stepped inside.

"Cassie, honey, it's Dawn," she shouted out, her voice echoing in the huge space. A metal staircase led upstairs, and Dawn started climbing.

I grabbed the back of her vest, said, "Let's clear the ground floor first. Then we'll start working our way up."

"She's not here, Jon. I don't feel her presence."

I took her elbow and told her to follow me. We walked the entire first floor, passing through the kitchen, family room, study, and formal dining and living rooms.

"Nothing is out of place or any different," she said. "The kitchen is clean and neat. Wait, let me check something." She turned and made her way back to the kitchen. She pushed in on a panel, and a door popped open. Her headlamp lit up a walk-in pantry.

"She's been home. All the Mac and Cheese is gone. She loves Kraft Mac and Cheese, and I always have a couple of dozen boxes in here."

"You have a basement?"

"No."

"Let's check upstairs," I said.

We climbed the stairs to the second floor. There was a home movie theater, a television room and two guest bedrooms, both with their own bathrooms. But no Cassie.

On the third floor was Dawn's bedroom and Cassie's. Dawn's room was neat and organized while Cassie's was a total disaster.

"Can you tell if anything is missing. Like maybe she grabbed some clothes and went to a friend's house."

"Look at this room. I can't tell."

I had an idea. "If she left you a note, where would she have put it?" I asked.

She thought for a minute, then turned and ran into her bedroom. And there it was: an envelope taped to the eyepiece of her telescope.

With tears flowing down her cheeks, she tore open the envelope.

"She's at her friend Victoria's house. It's around the corner on Maple Street."

"Let's go."

"Shall I pack—" she started to say.

"No. First let's get her, then we'll come back."

We double-timed it down the stairs, opened the front door, shut it but didn't lock it behind us, then through the outer garden gate to the sidewalk.

"Which way?"

"Left. Then another left onto Maple. They're two doors down from the traffic circle."

"Let me lead. Stay behind me and watch our six. When I stop, you stop and grab hold of my vest so I know you're there."

We stayed on the sidewalk and fast-walked down Whyte toward the traffic circle. We rounded the corner onto Maple Street.

What a difference one block made, for Maple Street and its homes were a quarter the size of their neighbors a block west—no yards, fences, hedges, or driveways here. These were low rent, unkempt fixer-uppers that hadn't seen a paintbrush or hammer in years. Both curbs were crammed with dead, five- to ten-year-old cars.

"It's the house across the street," Dawn said, pointing to an older home with a brick façade. It might have been a nice home at one time, but it had been divided into two and was now a townhouse—an entrance door and steps on each end. The steps leading to the left-hand door were lopsided and the second riser from the ground was missing. The house had no front yard, and the steps landed on the public sidewalk. There was a space between the two sets of stairs, but it was bare dirt with an overgrown juniper to the right of the left-hand stairs. The porch had had a railing at one time, but now only the bottom support was there, along with a few vertical spindles sticking up at odd angles. The porch was a good six feet above the ground, and you'd hurt yourself if you were to fall off.

"Which door? Right or left?"

"Left."

"Let's cross. Quiet now."

We'd just stepped off the curb behind an old Honda Accord when the left side-entrance door opened a crack, light spilling out into the street. I stopped, put my hand over Dawn's mouth and backstepped her behind the Accord. She wiggled and tried to free my hand from her mouth. The door opened further and then shut again. It was as if someone had been leaving but had changed their mind. Their indecision had allowed me to see inside the house.

"Quiet down," I whispered in her ear. "And quit fighting me. I saw two women tied to chairs with duct tape over their mouths and three men standing in front of them. The men are Asian."

She calmed down and I took my hand off her mouth.

"What?" she hissed.

"Just what I said. A woman with reddish blonde hair and the other with black hair."

"Cassie has reddish blonde hair. And Victoria has black hair. Victoria is Asian. And there are no men living in that house—there's only Victoria and her grandmother."

"Stay right here and don't move. I'm going to get closer. Turn your comms volume all the way down. You'll stay here and stay down?"

"Yes," she whispered.

I looked her in the eye as if doubting her.

She saw the look, said, "I promise."

I nodded, then ran across the street directly toward the front steps and flattened myself behind the juniper. The door opened and a man half stepped out, turned and stuck his head back inside, said in heavily accented English, "We'll be back in one hour. I want the Asian girl, and Li will take the white one. Don't trade them to anyone else, Quon. You hear me, bro?"

I couldn't hear the response from inside, but my man responded with, "I know. Twenty sacks of rice, twenty black bean and twenty pinto."

Another man inside the house said something.

"Yes, and seven, five-gallon jugs of water," my man said.

The porch man still had his head in the door, and I took the opportunity to run back to Dawn.

Crouching next to Dawn, I whispered, "Someone is trading the girls for food. Two of the men are leaving to get the food and will be back in an hour."

"Trading, as in selling?"

"Yes."

"What are we going to do?"

"You are going to stay right here. I'll take care of the two men that are—"

The door opened and two men stepped out onto the porch, the door closing behind them. The men stepped off the porch and made their way down the steps, both carefully avoiding the missing riser. They turned left and, staying on the sidewalk, headed toward the traffic circle. Both were Asian, one tall and skinny, the other short and overweight.

"Stay here." I stepped out, ran across the street and onto the sidewalk, released the safety on the M-4, and raised the rifle, the silencer still attached. I ran toward them and, when I was fifteen feet behind the two, whistled softly. Both stopped and turned. I double tapped the tall one, both rounds hitting his chest, then moving the rifle to my side, I ran straight toward the remaining man. The shot was very quiet, and I doubted if Dawn had heard it.

He raised his hands and said, "Don't—"

Before he finished his sentence, I placed both my hands on his chest and shoved hard. He fell back and tripped, falling on his ass. I flipped him over and sat on his back, his left cheek pressed hard on the concrete sidewalk. With my left hand, I held both of his behind his back. I took the Glock and put it against his right temple."

"How many men are in the house?" I asked.

He said something in Chinese.

"English."

"Two."

"Weapons?"

"No. Not that I saw."

"Where in the house?"

"In the living room."

"With the two girls?"

"Yes."

"You were buying them? And don't lie to me."

"Yes."

"There is an old woman in the house. Where is she?"

"Dead. Quon killed her and put her in the basement."

"Quon is the seller?"

"Yes."

"How did Quon learn of the three women in the home?"

"The granny traded for rice from a neighbor two doors down. That rice seller told Quon. The neighbor is in the house now, watching the two women with Quon."

"What is your first name?"

"Jimmy."

I holstered the Glock and took out the Ontario. I released his hands. I raised his chin with my left hand and using my right, slit his throat from left to right. He was clawing at his throat and making sucking noises, though not nearly loud enough to cause alarm. I wiped the blood from the knife on his shirt cuff and left him there on the sidewalk. I ran back to Dawn.

"Two men are inside. They were selling the women," I said, catching my breath.

"The other two who came out?"

"They're suffering from a bad case of buyer's remorse."

Dawn gave me blank stare.

"One dead and the other almost there."

"Oh, of course. What now?"

"We're going to knock on the door, or more specifically, you are."

"And?" she asked.

"You're going to knock and then step to the left and back," I said, putting my left hand on her shoulder. "And then I'm going to shoot both men and take Cassie with us. Simple, really."

"Simple?"

"Sometimes simple is best. They'll be annoyed at hearing the knock, but thinking it's the two buyers wanting to ask another question, they'll open the door. I'll kick the door fully open and shoot both of them. Always let surprise work for you. Simple."

"What about Victoria and her grandmother Li Mei?"

"One of the dead men said that Quon killed the grandmother and put her in the basement."

"Oh my God," she said, covering her face with both her hands. "Killing people. Selling people. Fuck, Jon. It's just unbelievable."

"It is, but we need to take care of this problem, now." I keyed the comms. "Abs?"

"Go ahead, Jon."

"Dawn's home was empty. We're at another house down the street. Dawn's sister and her friend are being held and in the process of being sold. The buyers have been dealt with, and we're about to deal with the sellers. We'll then go back to Dawn's house so they can pack some things."

"How long?"

"Thirty minutes."

"Okay. We're good here."

I clicked an acknowledgment.

"Let's get this done," I said.

"Sling your rifle to the side and take out your Glock. One of the risers is missing so be careful climbing the stairs."

We crossed the street, climbed the steps, and stood in front of the door. I took a step back, raised the M-4, took off the NVs and placed them on the porch. Ready, I told Dawn to knock. Dawn knocked, stepped to the left and then back.

I heard heavy footsteps from inside approaching the door and then stop.

"Ho?" a voice from inside asked.

"Jimmy," I whispered.

I heard the chain being undone and then the deadbolt released.

"What do you want now, Jimmy?" a man asked, the door opening a couple of inches, a face peering out from behind the door.

I slammed my boot into the door, and it flew inward, knocking the man behind it onto his back against a wooden entry table.

410

A hissing Coleman lantern teetered on the entry table, casting weird patterns of light all around the room. This was an older man, with gray, unkempt hair and unshaven gray stubble on his face. I sent two rounds into his head and then pivoted to my right to deal with the second man. I reached out and steadied the lantern.

This guy was young, no more than twenty, and short, maybe five-four or -five, most of him sinewy muscle. I guessed his weight at maybe one twenty, max. He was dressed in what looked to be black yoga pants and a form-fitting black shirt of some kind—his choice of clothes struck me as what a wannabe ninja might wear. He was unarmed. He was standing in front of the two women, making it too difficult to shoot him without risking hitting them. The women were watching the events unfolding with wild, terrified eyes.

I couldn't fire, and he knew it. He smiled, and without taking his eyes off me, reached down and removed his shoes. He was now slowly coming at me in some form of martial arts routine of moving hands and legs. I slung the rifle to my side and charged him.

A close-in hand-to-hand combat instructor had once told me that a good way of dealing with a situation like this was to rush the guy, crowd him, and use your weight and bulk to your advantage. I ran straight at him. We had been ten feet apart, and I ran for all I was worth—all six foot four and 230 pounds headed right for him. He seemed surprised at this, for he stopped and stepped to his right, putting his weight on his back foot which I knew was a prelude to some form of roundhouse kick. But all that practice, with insufficient real-life experience, hadn't prepared him for the confines of a small room with a pissed-off mass of human being running full tilt toward him.

I was too fast and already too close. I put my right hand around his neck, lifted him off the ground, and squeezed with everything I had. He panicked; all those years of practice seemingly forgotten in this real-life moment. He tried to pry my hand away with both of his, but his hands were puny and fingers small—he couldn't even get his fingers around one of mine.

411

I planted my feet, threw him higher, and spun him around so that he was now facing away from me. I had released him in order to accomplish the spin, and now I put my hand around his neck from behind. I put my left leg in front of him, let go, and pushed. He released his hands in an attempt to keep himself from face-planting on the floor. I took my left forearm and put it under his chin and, with my right, twisted his head the other way, snapping his neck. He fell to the floor, a limp pile of arms and legs, directly in front of Cassie's friend, his dead eyes open and staring at the ceiling.

Both women were hopping in their chairs, trying to distance themselves from the carnage.

"Is there anyone else in the house?" I asked them.

The Asian woman shook her head.

Dawn stepped into the room, and both women stopped their thrashing about. I took hold of the duct tape across Cassie's mouth. "Sorry, this is the best way to remove it," I said, ripping it off in one quick pull. I did the same to her friend. I took the Ontario and cut the duct tape binding their hands and ankles to the chairs.

Dawn and Cassie hugged, Cassie crying and Dawn hugging her as tight and close as she could. Victoria, ripping duct tape remnants off her hands, ran from room to room calling out for her grandmother.

Cassie was average height and weight with reddish blonde hair. Watching the two sisters, I could see that they shared some DNA but that perhaps they only had one parent in common. Their noses, eyes, and brows appeared the same, but the mouth and chins were much different—Dawn's lean and sculpted, Cassie's full and rounded. Shared DNA aside, both Tillman sisters were quite beautiful.

"Dawn, watch the front, please. We don't want to be surprised."

I opened all the doors until I found the one leading to the basement. I took a headlamp from a cargo pocket and aimed the light down below. A woman's body was crumpled on the basement floor below. I took the stairs two at a time and checked the woman for a pulse and found none. She was cold to the touch, legs and arms in unnatural positions. I hustled back up the stairs and shut the door behind me.

Dawn was at the front door. I caught her eye, pointed down the stairs, and shook my head.

"Victoria, honey, come here, please," Dawn said, opening her arms and waiting for her.

Victoria walked past me and melted into Dawn's embrace, crying, chest heaving with sobs.

"Honey, your gran is down in the basement. Those men killed her. I'm so sorry. But there is no time for grieving. Do you have somewhere you can go?"

"My auntie Jingjing and my cousins, Changying and Daiyu," she answered, between heaving sobs. "They have a house three miles from here. I can run there in the morning. Oh, Gran."

"Pardon my manners. Cassie, Victoria, this is Jon. We flew here on a float plane which is waiting for us at the beach next to the volleyball courts. Cassie, we have to go back to our house and pack. We're flying to Jon's family ranch in Montana."

Cassie shook her head and pointed to the dead younger man. "His brother is the one that set this up. We are not the first women he's taken and sold. Can we stop him from taking more women? He lives two doors down. Most of the neighbors are older Asians and can't offer any resistance."

"We should really go," I said, looking at Dawn.

"It would truly help the entire neighborhood," Cassie said, pleading. "Not only by doing away with a dangerous person, but I bet his house is full of stolen food that the folks here in the neighborhood could really use."

"Jon?" Dawn asked.

"Two doors down?" I asked.

"Two," Cassie said again.

"How many are in the house?"

"Just one lives there. This one's older brother, Peng," Victoria said. "But I can't guarantee he's alone."

"Dawn, you stay here and provide overwatch."

413

"Will do."

"Victoria, walk with me and point me at the right house."

I walked with Victoria behind me. We hit the sidewalk and turned right, away from the traffic circle.

"This one," she said, pointing to a single-story ranch-style American house, ugly as shit, with stained, moss-covered stucco and useless window shutters hanging askew and rotten.

"You're sure this is his house?"

"One hundred percent sure," she answered. "Without a doubt. One hundred percent sure."

"Go back to your house."

She turned to leave, stopped, turned, and hugged me. "Thank you. I forgot to say thank you."

"You're welcome. Go back to your house now."

I watched her run down the sidewalk to her place. There was light escaping between two drawn curtains which was very careless on his part. I walked up the stairs onto a dark-green Astroturf-covered wooden porch. The door was a cheap Home Depot hollow unpainted replacement door. It's one redeeming feature was a spy hole three-quarters of the way up. I knocked on the door, said, "Peng? Peng, it's Quon."

I set the fire selector to full auto, took two steps back, raised the rifle, and watched the spy hole. When it went from light to dark, I fired a sustained burst into the door, from head height to stomach. The spy hole lit up. I tried the door: locked. I took a step back and kicked it in. It swung in, bounced back and then slowly swung fully open. Peng was face-up on the floor, his head a mess, his nose and mouth hit multiple times. I dropped the magazine, stowed it in a cargo pocket, and slammed in a fresh one.

His living room and dining room were filled with canvas bags of rice, beans, and five-gallon water containers. Down the hallway and in the two bedrooms—rice and more rice. Enough to feed hundreds for months, maybe even a couple of years.

I did a quick search of the home and found no one else inside. He'd been sitting in an old floral-print armchair with threadbare arms when I'd knocked—a cigarette was still burning in an ashtray next to a burning candle, both sitting on an end table next to the chair. I put the cig out and stepped outside.

Even with the suppressor, the neighbors must have heard the shots, for several were standing in the street watching me as I stepped off the porch and walked back toward Victoria's house.

I turned to the neighbor's, brought my rifle up, pointed the business end in their direction, and told them not to go in the house. I called out for Victoria, and she, Dawn, and Cassie stepped off her grandmother's porch and onto the sidewalk. I met them halfway.

"He's dead. You were right, Cassie, there's a bunch of food and supplies in there—enough to feed you and your neighbors for months. But before you invite the neighborhood in for a food giveaway, get a message to your aunt and have her come over and share in the supplies."

She turned to the crowd of onlookers and said something in Chinese. Two men, both in their early twenties, sprinted off down the street, turned a corner and disappeared from view.

"They went to high school with me and know where my auntie lives. They'll bring her and my cousins back. They'll also store our share of the food in their house while we figure out how to get the food to my aunt's place."

"Good plan," I said. "Now pick four men from the crowd and ask them to stand guard until your aunt gets here. Do you know these people?"

"Yes. Most of them."

"Do it now," I said. "While I'm here."

We watched her stride over to the crowd. She pointed to four men, turned, and walked them to the house with the food. The four men entered the home and came out thirty seconds later carrying the dead kidnapper. They carried him behind the house and reappeared a minute later without the body.

I took Victoria's arm and stood with her in front of the four men. "Translate, please. There is enough food and water in this house to feed you and your neighbors for months. You four will guard this home with your lives. Do not let anyone enter this house until Victoria here gives the okay."

Victoria translated my message. I watched the four men nod in understanding.

"Two men guard the rear and two the front. No one enters the house until Victoria gives the okay. I will be down the street and if I find out that you've not done what I say, I will come back and kill you and your family."

Victoria looked at me with questioning eyes but translated the message after an initial hesitation.

The men nodded again. One of them saying something to Victoria.

"He says to tell you that they will guard this bounty with their lives."

I nodded. "We need to go," I said. "No more delay. Especially now that people are gathering. Have you filled the women in on what caused the blackout, Dawn?"

"I did."

"Share with them what you know, Victoria," I said. "They should be aware."

"I will. What do I do with the dead bodies?"

"Have some of the men help you take them out. There are two more down on the sidewalk a few doors down—the two men that were buying you and Cassie. Gather them together and burn the bodies in the street."

"Gasoline works best," Dawn said.

"Okay."

"Say your goodbyes, you two," I told the two women, as I retrieved my NVs from the front porch.

The two friends hugged. Both had tears free-flowing. They parted but then started with another hugathon.

Dawn let it go on for a full minute before finally stepping in and separating the two friends.

TWENTY-THREE

A minute later, Dawn and Cassie were walking hand in hand down the sidewalk toward their glass house. They came to their outside gate and turned into the hedge tunnel. I followed them inside the house.

"Pack a couple of backpacks with your stuff, Cassie," I said. "You too, Dawn. If you have duffel bags, pack one of those as well. Most important are underwear, socks, T-shirts, bras, hoodies, vests, hats, and jeans. You're not going to need makeup or any of that stuff, but tampons, toothbrushes, toothpaste, shampoo, sunglasses, and any prescription drugs should be packed. You get the picture. You have fifteen minutes. Cassie, take my headlamp."

"I have backpacks," Cassie said, taking the headlamp and putting it on, "but not sure about duffel bags."

"We have the ski bags," Dawn said. "They're up in the storage room."

They both ran upstairs.

I stayed downstairs waiting.

"Abs?"

"Yep," came the quick reply.

"We have Dawn's sister. We're at their house, and they're packing some of their things. I've given them fifteen minutes. We should be with you in twenty."

"Roger that. We'll start the engines."

"Did you hear that, Vivian?" Abs asked.

"Affirmative. Starting engine."

"How's it going?" I yelled up the staircase.

"Almost done," Cassie answered.

"Me too," Dawn shouted down.

And then I remembered what I'd told Dawn last night in the pool—that I'd take the telescope back to the ranch.

I donned the extra headlamp and ran up the two flights of stairs, turned left, and hustled down the hall to Dawn's bedroom. I saw Dawn in her bathroom, shoving stuff from her drawers into an opened backpack.

The telescope was sitting on a tripod. I lifted the telescope itself and it came off the tripod. Thirty or thirty-five pounds. It wasn't a sleek, long scope, but looked more like a small, black beer keg with all kinds of dials and doodads on it. I set the telescope on the bed and folded the tripod legs.

Dawn came out of the bathroom, saw me with the tripod, said, "Thank you, thank you! You remembered. I have a travel case for the telescope under the bed."

She dropped to her knees next to the bed, reached underneath, and slid out a padded case with shoulder straps. "Let me put it in. It takes some practice and the optics inside the barrel are insanely fragile."

"I'll be careful," I said, watching her place the delicate instrument in the case.

She zipped it closed, put the strap over my left shoulder, and handed me the tripod. Which left my right hand free for the rifle. We made our way to the top of the stairs and waited for Cassie. Dawn had two backpacks and a duffel. I helped her put one backpack on, took the duffel, and walked down the stairs to the ground floor.

Cassie and Dawn soon joined me. Cassie had one backpack and a rolling duffel bag with wheels and a collapsible handle.

"All windows and doors locked?" I asked.

"I don't know," Dawn said. "Does it really matter?"

"Well, I think it does. I locked everything when I left for Victoria's place," Cassie said. "We should lock the front door and gate behind us for sure. I mean, we might be back someday, right?"

"I hope so, Cass," Dawn said, locking the front door and then the sidewalk gate behind us.

"Let's get a move on, you two," I said over my shoulder, already headed across the street toward the beach.

We were walking past the volleyball courts, and I could see Melissa up ahead watching us approach. Cassie was having a hard time pulling the duffel through the sand. I took hold of the duffel's bottom and we buddy-carried it past Melissa.

The Beaver's engine was warming up, and I could see Abs in the pilot's seat.

"Put your stuff down and get in the plane," I told them, and watched as Dawn stepped onto the port pontoon, opened the passenger door, and climbed into the cabin with Cassie right behind her. I made three trips loading their backpacks and duffel bags, the third trip solely being for the telescope—wedging it between the backpacks and duffel bags. I took Dawn's rifle and placed it in the back next to mine.

I glanced out toward Vivian and watched as Bradley retrieved the anchor and line, stowed it in the cargo area, climbed up into the co-pilot's seat, shutting the door behind him. Vivian increased engine rpms and slowly made her way west past the mooring buoys.

I keyed the comms and told Melissa it was time to load up. She stepped onto the pontoon, handed me her rifle, and climbed up onto the bench seat next to Cassie. All three were putting on headsets and securing seatbelts.

I put my headphones on, settled back into the seat, and watched Abs go through her preflight checks. It was now eleven o'clock.

Vivian was airborne first. She climbed to three thousand and circled, waiting for us.

We were soon with her. Abs climbed to five thousand and headed southeast.

Abs's voice came over the headphones. "We've got a three-and-a-half- to four-hour flight ahead of us. We'll be flying over the Cascade Range. Some of the mountains get up to just shy of nine thousand feet, so to be safe, I'm going to take us up to ten thousand.

"Beaver Two, climbing to ten thousand," Abs said. "Turning nav lights on."

"Roger that. We're flying straight across the Cascades then?" Vivian asked.

"Affirmative. Save some fuel going direct to Bonners Ferry, Idaho then on to Kalispell. Let's up the speed to one thirty."

"Roger that, one thirty. Where is Bonners Ferry?" Vivian asked.

"Directly north of Coeur d'Alene, Idaho."

"Roger that."

"Does this plane have a heater?" Melissa asked. "My feet are freezing."

"It sure does," Abs said.

Abs had had Vintage Air install a winter exhaust system underneath the fuselage. With clever systems of plates and levers, the system could heat the cabin within a couple of minutes. The cabin was soon heated and after fiddling with the settings, Abs had it about perfect.

"Thank you," Melissa said.

"You're welcome. And welcome, everyone, to Kristen Airlines, where no request is unreasonable."

"It's so dark out. How can you tell if you're flying level and not headed to the ground?" Cassie asked.

"That's a really good question," Abs said, taking out her penlight, switching to red-lens, and shining it on the instrument panel. "This one here is the attitude indicator which shows the aircraft orientation relative to the actual horizon. I watch this one like a hawk. Next to it is the altimeter which tells me our altitude. This one is the airspeed indicator. And this one is the compass. Keep watching these four gauges and you're good."

"Thank you for the lesson," Cassie said. "Will you teach me to fly? I promise to be a good student.

"I'd be happy to."

"Cool."

The flight was smooth with an occasional bump here and there. I was able to catnap.

I FELT MY LEFT SHOULDER being nudged. I opened my eyes and checked my watch. One fifteen.

"Hello, brother," Abs said. "Have a good nap?"

I felt pretty good. "I did. What's up?"

"I need to pee. Please take the controls. Will one of you pass me the pee jar?"

Melissa handed up the jar.

"Where are we?" I asked, taking the controls.

"Over Colville, Washington, on a course for Sandpoint, Idaho. We've got another hour to go."

Abs was still peeing when the plane was lit up by a super bright light.

"What the fuck?" Vivian screamed over the radio.

"Good mornin' to the two slow pokes at ten thousand," a male voice said over the radio and into our headphones. "And no, the light is not from an alien spacecraft."

Abs quickly finished, put the cap on and handed the jar back to Melissa. She pulled up her pants and buckled back in.

"Taking control, Jon."

"Where y'all headed?" the voice asked.

"Who are you?" Abs asked, not at all kindly. The bright light went out.

"Look to your left and fifty feet above," the voice said a few seconds later.

"Is that an F-35?" Vivian asked.

"You'd be correct, ma'am. And the light was from my landing lights. Sorry about that, but I needed to see what I was dealin' with. You two are the first aircraft, civilian or military, we've seen since the pulse hit."

"Who's we?" Abs asked.

"Aircraft Carrier *Gerald R. Ford*, ma'am."

"You're a long way from an ocean, pilot," Vivian said.

"They saw you soon after you took off from Vancouver. Told me to give chase and follow on this bearing. I picked you up on radar a hundred miles back.

"This is the first time I've flown since the blackout. Scary too, as we weren't sure all the electronics would work. But so far, so good."

"How's your fuel, pilot?" Vivian asked. "By the way, I'm Vivian, and I fly for Alaskan Airlines. Also, an ex-hog pilot with two-hundred-plus missions to my name."

"Hello, Vivian. I've got enough fuel for another three minutes of conversation before I need to get on home to Mama. Air Force, huh? Well, I guess someone's gotta fly their planes."

"That's funny, pilot. But I like flying low and slow, and blowin' up shit, up close and personal like. You Navy pukes get nervous when you see something three hundred miles away on a radar screen."

"That's not even close to being correct, Vivian. I don't pee my flight suit until they're two hundred miles out."

"We're all on the same side, you two," Abs said, chuckling. "Last we knew, pilot, the North Koreans sent four missiles to us, two of which exploded over Colorado and Ohio. Missiles were also sent to Moscow, London, Brussels, Paris, Rome, and Tel Aviv. That's all we know. Can you add to that?"

"Well, that was the opening salvo, ladies. Moscow's thinkin' is along the same lines as us in believin' China was behind the initial salvo. Moscow then sent four missiles to China and spanked their butts. Israel then said, *what the hell, let's get in on the fun* and sent a few to their long-time BFFs in Saudi Arabia, Iran, and Syria. Pakistan decided the time was right to rid themselves of India. Then, of course, India detonated one over Pakistan. We were told that several targets in South America were hit, too. Venezuela was one for sure.

"It is, however, important to note that restraint was exhibited by all, as the missiles, and I mean every single one, exploded high in the atmosphere. Which, of course, set off a multitude of EMPs that put most of the world out of action. As of this morning, the only places we know of, for sure, that haven't been affected are New Zealand, parts of Australia, Iceland, and Greenland.

"There certainly could have been more and probably were," he said. "Belgium, Germany, France, the UK, Italy, and South Africa all have nuclear weapons."

"What's our status in Washington D.C.? And our military?" Abs asked.

"We were in contact with the Pentagon for the first two days, then the comms went silent. We haven't heard a peep from anyone, anywhere, since then. We've been sittin' out at sea waitin' to see what will happen. Captain says, if we don't hear somethin' soon, he's sendin' a couple of escort ships south around South America and up the east coast to check on things."

"Why not through the Panama Canal?"

"Don't know if it's operational," he answered. "That journey would take quite a bit of gas only to find it closed for business. And even if it was operational, it could be clogged with dead ships. They'd have to then head south and backtrack around the tip of South America.

"Are the Chinese going to attack us?" Abs asked.

"No idea, ma'am. We were in the South China Sea, keepin' an eye out for Taiwan, when the world went dark. We hung out there for a couple of days and saw nothin' amiss. Captain then headed us east toward home. We haven't seen anyone since. Intel people think the missiles from Moscow might have put the kibosh on any plans China might have had to overpower the US."

"What about our submarines?" Vivian asked. "They shouldn't have been hit by a pulse. I mean, they're under the sea

423

and should have escaped without any damage to their electronics."

"We haven't heard from them, but comms for subs are handled via land-based antenna arrays and satellites. I expect one will pop up off our beam someday soon and scare the shit out of everyone. But nothin' yet. For now, I'd better find out what y'all are doin'."

"We're from Whitefish, Montana. Flew to Seattle and then Vancouver yesterday afternoon to pick up family members. Vivian picked up her plane from a place near Victoria, Canada and needed a place to call home, so she's tagging along.

"Listen, pilot, our ranch has a six-thousand-foot runway that can handle birds up to the size of Gulfstream six hundreds, so your planes would land easy like. We even have two hangars that could fit a dozen or so. If you ever find yourself in the area, look directly west of Whitefish, Montana. We're the place with the long runway. Can't miss it. Drop in and say hi."

"Well, that's mighty nice of y'all. Might take you up on that if we find ourselves flyin' back east. What's your name, ma'am?"

"Abigail Kristen. And yours?"

"Richard Blackledge, ma'am. Call sign is Hillbilly. I've got all kinds of lights and buzzers goin' off in here which means I need to turn around pronto—no gas stations up here anymore."

"It's been nice chatting with you, Richard. Perhaps we'll meet up some day."

"I hope so. See ya, Vivian,"

"See ya, Hillbilly."

I watched as his nav lights disappeared from view.

"Well, now that was interesting," Vivian said.

"The Chinese are now in the same boat we are," Dawn said. "Serves 'em right."

"There is that," Melissa said, "but what concerns me is the fact that Washington D.C. and the Pentagon have gone silent. That can't be a good thing."

"Maybe they're moving locations," Cassie said. "I mean, if you were the Pentagon or White House, would you stay in a building that you knew had a bullseye on the roof?"

"You've got a point there," I said, thinking that Cassie might be smarter than the average bear.

"Your sister tells us you're a college student," Melissa said. "What's your major?"

"Forestry management. I've got three-quarters left on my PhD program at UBC—sorry, that's the University of British Columbia, Vancouver."

"A PhD. A doctorate in forestry management," Abs said. "Wow, I'm seriously impressed."

"What is forestry management?" Melissa asked.

"It's all about the health and sustainability of the world's forests. It's. . ."

I settled back in my seat and tried to sleep. I kept thinking about the Chinese, the Russians, those folks who shot the antenna off the Beaver, and the Mormons that the Caseys had said were a problem.

———

I WAS DREAMING THAT I was holding off a squad of screaming Chinese trying to overrun the ranch, when I heard a voice say, "I hate to interrupt your dream but it's time to wake up."

I opened my eyes and checked the time: two thirty.

"That's right, sleepyhead, we're on final approach to the ranch," Melissa said.

"That wasn't a dream," I said; "it was a nightmare."

"Four red lights," Abs said, which meant the wheels were down.

Abs clicked the transmit button on her yoke five times in rapid succession, and I watched the runway lights come on.

"Dad replaced the lights?" I asked.

"Not the lights, but the control box and receiver," Abs answered.

"Now that's a sight to behold," Vivian said.

I keyed my mic, said, "Renee, you there Renee?"

"Right here, babe."

"We'll be on the ground in two minutes. Come pick us up?"

"Already here. Along with Eddy, and your mom and dad. Your father says to taxi right inside the larger hangar. The doors are open."

I looked over at Abs who said, "I heard."

"Please tell him to leave the runway lights on," I said. "There's a second plane behind us."

Abs set us down gently on the runway and taxied right into the hangar.

"Vivian, did you see where I went?"

"Affirmative, into the hangar."

Abs spun us around, so the Beaver was facing the door. She shut the engine down, and the sudden quiet was overwhelming. I opened the co-pilot's door and stepped down to the pontoon and then to the hangar floor. I was stiff from sitting, and I tried to work out the kinks, then I grabbed the chocks and placed them. Renee came running up, jumped into my arms, and wrapped her legs around me. We were still hugging when my father, mother, and Eddy walked into the hangar and stepped to the side as the gleaming yellow-and-green Beaver taxied through the door, hung right, then executed a perfect one-eighty. Vivian shut it down.

Vivian and Bradley climbed down, and after placing the chocks, made their way over to the assembled group. I introduced Cassie, Bradley, and Vivian to my parents, Eddy, and Renee.

Renee went up to Melissa and hugged her tight, said, "Thank you for bringing him home safe and sound."

"No problema. Only had to step in once to save his sorry ass," she said.

"It may be a sorry ass, but it's mine," Renee said, hugging Melissa again.

"Andrea, what room is Kathy in?" Renee asked. "We have a husband here who very much wants to surprise his wife."

"Two zero eight. Second floor, end unit on the left."

"Bradley, come with me," Renee said, taking ahold of his elbow and guiding him toward the parked Land Cruiser. "I'll be right back, Jon."

"Let me get our backpacks and duffels out of the cargo hold first," Bradley said, opening the cargo door of our Beaver. Renee took a backpack and duffel from him, and they headed toward the Cruiser.

"That's gonna be one happy reunion," Melissa said, watching the Cruiser head out.

"That's a beautiful plane you have there, Vivian," my father said. "Did Vintage do the restoration?"

"They did. It was finished a few days before the blackout. The plane is actually owned by a fellow Alaskan Airlines pilot who asked me to pick it up and fly it back to Sea-Tac for him. Unfortunately, he was somewhere over the Midwest when the pulse hit and will not be coming home. He was a colleague, but also a good friend."

"I'm sorry for your loss," my mother said. "I guess we'll have to learn how to deal with loss on a larger scale from here on. On a more positive note, Cassie and Vivian, welcome to our ranch. Please consider this your new home. Cassie, your sister is in the Aspen cabin which is a two-bedroom unit. I know sisters can sometimes want some space, so each of you have your own bedroom. Vivian, we'll get you set up in the lodge."

"Thank you, ma'am," Cassie said.

"Call me Andrea, please. And this here," she said, pointing to my father, "is Neil. We're pretty informal here."

"Thank you, Andrea and Neil, for allowing me to live at your ranch. Please tell me what I can do to earn my keep. Anything you need done, I'll do it without question."

"Well, thank you for that, young lady. But first, would anyone be interested in an early-morning meal?" my mother asked. "We'll eat in the ranch house."

Nine hands were raised, counting the two I'd put up. "The extra is for Renee," I said.

Vivian retrieved her backpack and duffel from our Beaver. She handed Dawn and Cassie their backpacks and duffel bags and Melissa her backpack. I climbed up into the cargo area and carefully carried the telescope down to the ground.

There was a ranch truck sitting outside the hangar office. "That ranch truck working, Dad?" I asked.

"Yep. And keys are in it."

I went back for the tripod and then walked both telescope and tripod over to the ranch truck, placing both on the rear seat.

"Grab the other door, son, and let's get it locked up," my father said, turning off the hangar lights and grabbing the left-hand sliding door. We pushed the doors closed, meeting in the middle. Dad gathered a wrist-thick chain, looped it through the handles, and secured the chain ends with one of the largest locks I'd ever seen. Renee pulled up in front of the hangar a few minutes later, and my mother, Abs, Eddy, Dawn, Vivian, and Cassie piled in.

Renee rolled her window down, waved, said, "See you at the ranch house."

"How did it go with Kris?" my father asked as we walked over to the truck.

"Pretty well, actually. Her husband was there and turns out they have quite a bit of food. The neighbors have banded together for mutual protection. I left them with a couple of handguns and a box of ammo. I think they're going to be okay."

"Good to hear."

———

IT WAS NOW THREE THIRTY in the morning, and we'd finished a hearty breakfast of scrambled eggs, bacon, hashbrowns, and toast.

We'd reviewed the events of the previous day with our fellow diners.

"They were actually selling women?" my mother asked.

Melissa pushed her plate forward and her chair back, said, "Before our journey had begun and we were still at the hotel in

Vegas, Jon had warned us that women would become a commodity to be used, traded, or sold. I have to admit that at the time I didn't believe him. But I became a believer that first morning when we came upon the rape in progress right on the highway. Since then, we've seen it time after time—women have become targets of opportunity."

"What I'll always remember from those days of being tied to that chair and bid on by disgusting men, is the utter feeling of helplessness—that my free will had been forever taken from me," Cassie said.

"Then Jon kicked that door in, shot the one man, broke the neck of the Bruce Lee wannabe, and gave me a second chance. I will never again allow myself to be put in that situation. . . to feel that terrible sense of helplessness."

The dining room fell silent until Melissa spoke up.

"You want to be a real-life Wonder Woman? Well, you're at the right place. You'll need to learn to shoot, both pistol and rifle—Jon here is a firearms expert. He'll be happy to train you. Right, Jon?"

"Any time," I said. "There's a shooting range close to the hangars. Shooting is a skill that will allow you to be on a level playing field with men. Learn it, hone it, allow it to serve you."

"Amen to that," Abs said.

All of us at the table were buzzed, and we talked into the wee hours of the morning.

It felt good to be at the table with family and friends. I scooted my chair back, stretched my legs out, and put my right arm on Renee's chair back and my left on Abs's.

I watched my father telling stories about my mother and he when they had first met, and my mother smiling and playfully hitting his arm when he said things that probably should have remained only between them.

I watched Dawn telling stories of some funny and amazing things that had happened to her during her years as an actor.

I watched Cassie go from watching to engaging as she spoke of the forests, trees, and the animals that made them their home. "Man has truly messed up the fragile balance between the forest and its inhabitants, what with overcrowding and climate change. But now, given that the next ten years will be a decade of recovery, maybe the balance can be restored."

I watched it all. Content for the first time in a long time.

Then my pocket started vibrating, followed by a low-volume alarm, not unlike one of those old-fashioned nightstand alarm clocks—a clanging tone.

Renee looked at me, put her left hand in my cargo pants pocket and withdrew the little gizmo that Wilma Patterson had given us in Las Vegas.

Pre-order your copy of the last book in the series

DARK HIGHWAY HOME
BOOK THREE – REBOOT

Releasing January, 2025.

Printed in Great Britain
by Amazon